D0615277

MR. EMMANUEL

MR. EMMANUEL

A NOVEL BY

LOUIS GOLDING

New York

THE LITERARY GUILD OF AMERICA, INC.

1939

CL

PRINTED IN THE UNITED STATES OF AMERICA

MR. EMMANUEL

FOR

JIM WATERMAN WISE

BECAUSE OF A CABLE

FROM MID-ATLANTIC

1

I

MR. EMMANUEL turned the angle of Blenheim Road at Mrs. Poyser's shop and walked down Magnolia Street to his house at number thirteen. It had been a hot day. His feet dragged a little. The point of his small white beard was a little blurred. His head swung uncertainly on his neck, like a toy balloon tugging at its string.

He had had a big day at his desk; and though there were times when he still looked quite young, he looked all his years this evening: sixty and more, he preferred not to remember exactly how many more. A woman making a belated purchase at Mrs. Poyser's called out good-evening to him, and he called back again, but he was not aware who it was. He was very tired.

Arrived at the door of his house, he fumbled in his back-pocket for his key. As he stood there swaying a moment or two on the bottom doorstep, a chalk-mark on one of the panels of the door caught his eye. It had not been there when he left the house that morning, so far as he remembered, and he straightened his pince-nez to get a clearer sight of it. It was a swastika.

A lump rose in Mr. Emmanuel's throat, and he had some difficulty in swallowing it. It must be those new people, he said to himself, who had come to live opposite at number ten. It was said of them they were blackshirts. What harm have I done them they should make a swastika on my front door? There was a funny taste in the back of his mouth, like he had eaten something bitter.

He had the key in his hand by now, but it took some time before he could fit it into the keyhole. His hand was unsteady, and he had to blink hard to get a tear out of his eye.

It is because I'm so tired, he thought. It is going to be hard work the next few days. What I need is a nice glass of strong tea with lemon.

He had by now closed the front door behind him. He was in the lobby. As he shuffled forward over the door-mat, his foot kicked a letter a few inches before him. He stooped and lifted it, and stuffed it away in his breast-pocket. He had had enough letters over at the Board of Guardians all day long.

A glass of strong tea with lemon, he said to himself again. Then what after that? He was not a particular one for food, but she always saw to it there was something tasty after these big days in the office. Perhaps there would be bean-soup and a nice brown leg of chicken, and then after that a baked *lockshen* pudding with raisins.

He was at the kitchen door by now, at the end of the lobby. He turned the handle, and the silence and emptiness came up towards him like a white sheet flapping. The room was empty. She was dead. He woke up to it as if he were waking from a night's dreaming, not a day's work. Slatta was dead. She had been buried a month ago. They had been married a long time, more than forty years. It is not easy to get it into your head that your wife or husband is really dead when you've been married such a long time. He walked across the kitchen to the table under the window. It was spread with a cloth, and there was a loaf of bread under a napkin with a knife beside it. There was also some cold something-or-other on a plate, with another plate over it. At the corner of the table was a glass with three lumps of sugar already in it, and a thick slice of lemon. It had a spoon, too, so that the glass should not crack when you poured the hot water into it. All you had to do was go into the scullery and boil the kettle on the gas-stove.

She was a nice little woman, that Ada Hummel from number three. She had a key, and came in every day and tidied things up, and left him something to eat. It had to be cold, of course, for she had her own house to look after and her boy, Leo, and her little parlour-shop. Yes, she was a nice little woman, like all those Bermans—she had been Ada Berman once. But it was not like Slatta.

He went and sat down at his place under the cupboard, at the head of the table. But he did not feel like eating now. It was too much trouble even to go over into the scullery and boil the kettle for the tea. He just sat and closed his eyes and thought. They were sad thoughts. He was lonely and tired. A swastika on my front door. But they do not look like low-lives, those people who have come to live at number ten opposite. Why should they hate me? Why should they hate Ada Hummel? How can it be such a world with so much hatred in it?

Once I saw such pretty pictures, like on a postcard. It should be Love everywhere. Love on both sides of the street. Love on both sides of the sea. All races and peoples going hand in hand together along the road of Universal Love and the crowds on both sides of the road throwing flowers at them. Throwing flowers. Like it was at the

Magnolia Street Party. Five years ago. It is like five hundred. It is not Love now in Magnolia Street. It is a swastika on my front door. It is not flowers now for throwing . . .

No, it is not flowers. His mind swivelled violently and toppled over into sleep. It could not bear to conjure up a picture of the things the crowds were throwing now, from the gun-emplacements, from the bombers roaring across the sky.

He had not been asleep for long, perhaps half an hour, for it was hardly any darker when he was awakened by the sound of a stick knocking at the back-yard door. Once—twice, the stick went, then once—twice again. Yes, yes. That was his friend, Mr. Silver, from Oleander Street. His back door faced Mr. Emmanuel's back door across a narrow entry. Funny he should still knock like that, once—twice, then again once—twice. Like it was when he was an anarchist, and all the anarchists came to his house, a long time ago, before the Magnolia Street Party. Before the War. A long time ago.

Mr. Emmanuel got up from his chair and stretched out his long legs. He descended the one step into the scullery and unbolted the scullery door. Then he went out into the yard to let Mr. Silver in.

Mr. Silver used to be an anarchist, but he wasn't an anarchist any more. He had made big profits out of rain-proofs in the War, and had become a very rich man. But he was not a rich man any more, either. He was just a working-man from Oleander Street. He had been coming in like this to join Mr. Emmanuel in a glass of tea, and a cigarette . . . nearly every evening since . . . since . . .

Well, it is not the worst thing to be dead, Mr. Emmanuel thought, shaking his head. To be dead—is that a disgrace? But to be like that woman . . . Mr. Emmanuel put his hand up to his heart. It was a sharp pain there, like a nail.

She was not only Mr. Silver's disgrace. She was Mr. Emmanuel's, too. She was everybody's disgrace. For all Doomington. The whole Jewish people.

If she had been dead when she had been born, it would have been a better thing. He hated himself for thinking a thought like that. But is it my fault? he asked himself miserably.

He pulled back the bar along its rusty socket, and opened the door. Yes, it was Mr. Silver. Who else could it be knocking once—twice, then once—twice again? He was not looking a young man any more, either, even though he still wouldn't grow a beard. It was a lot of grey hair now among the black, in his big, bushy moustache, in his eyebrows also.

"Good evening, Mr. Silver!" Mr. Emmanuel exclaimed, swaying towards his friend from the height where his pince-nez were. "You come again? I am so glad. Come in, please. I was just making myself a glass of tea. You will join me, yes?"

"Well, Mr. Emmanuel, if the tea is there, shall I say no?"

Mr. Emmanuel thrust the bar back along its socket again. Then he turned. The small old man followed the tall old man into the scullery.

"One moment, please!" said Mr. Emmanuel. "I shall boil the kettle!"

"I will get another glass. I know where they are kept," said Mr. Silver. He took a glass down from a shelf fringed with scalloped paper. The paper was getting a bit frayed and dingy. Mrs. Emmanuel would have put different paper by now, mused Mr. Silver. Such a wife she was, everything clean like snow.

"Go in and sit down, please," urged Mr. Emmanuel. "I will look after it."

But he was not displeased when Mr. Silver, making a sound like tscha-tscha, showed he insisted on giving a hand. It was a friendly noise, the fingers making the cutlery rattle in the box, the spoon tinkling into the glass.

"Like two boys making a camp," murmured Mr. Emmanuel, with a wan smile.

"Lemon, please. Where is some lemon?" requested Mr. Silver, very busy and practical.

The lemon was produced. The tea was measured into the pot. The boiling water was poured out.

"Come, now! Let us go in!"

Mr. Emmanuel led the way into the kitchen, and set the pot down on the table.

"Sit down, please!" he requested. "You know your chair, Mr. Silver." Mr. Silver knew his chair. Both men sat down.

"What?" cried Mr. Silver. "You have not eaten yet?" He noticed the untouched meal, the loaf under a napkin, the dish of food under a plate.

Mr. Emmanuel shrugged his shoulders.

"Please! You should not worry! I am not hungry tonight!"

"It is very wrong of you!" said Mr. Silver quite hotly. "You must eat! Did you ever hear from such a thing!" He lifted the reversed plate. "Such beautiful fried fish!" He brought his nose closer to it. "A halibut steak, yes? You must eat at once!"

"Perhaps later. I cannot eat now," begged Mr. Emmanuel. "It has been so hot in the office, like an oven. And then when I came in—" He stopped suddenly. No. Not to Mr. Silver, of all people. It was not to Mr. Silver he could talk about a swastika chalked up on a door. It is worse for him, a thousand times over than for me, he said to himself.

"Yes?" inquired Mr. Silver. "When you came in?" Mr. Emmanuel thought he detected the faintest note of apprehension in Mr. Silver's voice.

"When I came in I was so tired, I fell asleep in that chair. You can see how hungry I was."

"You look tired. It is a shame. You need a holiday."

"Am I not going to get a holiday?" Mr. Emmanuel reminded him. "A long one!"

"Tscha-tscha!" muttered Mr. Silver. He felt rather foolish. Of course. Mr. Emmanuel's days as clerk to the Jewish Board of Guardians were numbered.

"How much longer?" he asked softly. "It is only ten more days, isn't it?"

"What day is it today? Wednesday? Yes, ten more days," said Mr. Emmanuel. "I have been there a long time, no? It is time now for a younger man. There is more work than there used to be."

"Yes," Mr. Silver sighed. "These German refugees coming into Doomington." His head bowed swiftly towards his glass. A tear formed in his eye, sudden and smart. There was one who had stayed behind in Germany. Better for her——

"You think I will be lazy when I am no more with the Board of Guardians?" the voice of Mr. Emmanuel broke briskly into his thoughts. (Now he is comforting me I should not think, mused Mr. Emmanuel. Now I am comforting him *he* should not think. Oi! Oi! It is funny! It is like a game!)

Mr. Silver raised his head.

"If you should be lazy for a change, it will do you no harm."

"I will have meetings," continued Mr. Emmanuel, disregarding the remark. "I will have committees. Some more tea, yes? What am I thinking of? I have some of your own wife's cake that she baked for me. Perhaps you did not know," he said, wagging his finger with a pale effort at mischief.

"No cake, thank you, I am full," said Mr. Silver. He was silent for a moment or two, then, resting his weight on the palms of his hands, he leaned forward across the table. "Listen now, Mr. Emmanuel. I want you should listen. It is enough now with all these meetings and committees. You are going to Palestine, yes? You have made up your mind? What is there you should stay for here in Magnolia Street?"

"You're right," said Mr. Emmanuel quietly. "What is there I should stay for here in Magnolia Street? I got a letter from my son Moisheh, this morning. By aeroplane it came!" He paused. Even in this moment of sad reflection it seemed to him a little odd his son Moisheh should be sending him letters by aeroplane. By horse and cart, yes, but by aeroplane? "Such a nice letter it was, God bless him! It must have taken him a whole day he should write it. My son Moisheh was never a professor."

"No," agreed Mr. Silver shortly.

"He says now . . . now he will not take it no shall be an answer. It breaks his heart his mother will not come, too. But that is all the more, he says, for why his father must go quick."

"And is he not right perhaps? A son you have there, and a daughter-in-law, and four grandchildren, God bless them! It will be like a new life for you!"

"A new life!" protested Mr. Emmanuel, a shade of bitterness in his voice. "An old man sitting on a bench against a wall! A new life, he calls it!"

"What do you mean talking like that!" Mr. Silver protested. "You will not be able to tell them to love each other, over there in Palestine? Believe me, those Arabs and those Jews, they have more need of love than the two sides of Magnolia Street. You will have plenty of work over there, everybody should love each other."

"I know," said Mr. Emmanuel quietly. "I know. And even in the colony itself, my Moisheh tells me, it is not all like honey and butter. Now it is a Left Wing, now it is a Right Wing—there is plenty of explosions in the colony as well. I know all that. But I am not so young like I once was. I am a bit old to begin again. You see, Mr. Silver . . . for me this Magnolia Street, though it was so little, yet it was at the same time so big. I always felt—if Love should win here, it should win in the whole world. But what has happened?" He got up from his chair, and strode up and down the room a few times, his pince-nez trembling in his hand. He saw the thing outlined in the air before him more clearly than he had seen it chalked up on the front door, the malevolent and melancholy swastika.

He sat down again on his chair under the cupboard. His shoulders drooped. His head came forward three or four inches.

"Yes," he said heavily. "I will go to my son in Ain Charod, in Palestine."

Mr. Silver remained silent for a minute or two. Then he spoke again, almost in a whisper.

"You should not think I am wanting to get rid of you. Such old friends like we are. How many years is it? Thirty? More even. Oi, better not think of it. Listen, Mr. Emmanuel. When do you think you will go?"

"Three months, four months," said Mr. Emmanuel, without raising his eyes.

"For why so long?" pleaded Mr. Silver. "Each day it will be to you like a week."

"I have a policy. It is for payment in October. There will be money for tickets, there will be money for presents here, money for presents there. That is why I wait. For the policy."

"Please, Mr. Emmanuel, you should not be offended. I am not a rich man any more, thank God, but if you will let me, I think I can fix it. That you should have the money in advance, I mean. What? What do you say?"

But Mr. Emmanuel was not saying anything. He sat with his chin on his chest, his beard ruffled up on his shirt-front.

"Are you asleep, Mr. Emmanuel?" asked Mr. Silver, a little fearfully. "Are you offended?"

Mr. Emmanuel lifted his head from his chest. There was a smile of great sweetness on his face. He rose.

"You are like a brother to me, Mr. Silver," he said. "So you should know me by now. For somebody else I will borrow from a strange man in the street, he will not know what day it is. For myself, I will not borrow from my own brother. I will stay in Magnolia Street till they pay the policy. Then I go. Have a cigarette, Mr. Silver."

Mr. Silver had a cigarette. He knew when it was any

use talking to Mr. Emmanuel and when it wasn't. The two old friends sat talking of this or that for half an hour or so. Then at last Mr. Silver rose.

"I must go," he said. "You are tired. You should go to sleep. And before you go to sleep, you should eat. It is a shame your son Moisheh should have an invalid to look after when you go to Palestine. If I should have a son, I should not give him such aggravation," he added, a little sorrowfully. Mr. Silver had had five daughters, one after another. He had never managed to bring off a son.

"Perhaps I will eat," Mr. Emmanuel conceded. He too rose to his feet. "What, you must go so early? Well, good night, Mr. Silver. It was nice you should come in."

"Good night, Mr. Emmanuel. Not to trouble, please."

"I will just come and wriggle the door after you."

They shook hands on the steps that led down into the entry between the two rows of houses. There was something sorrowful and ceremonial in that handshake. It was almost as if Mr. Emmanuel had one foot already on the gangplank of the steamer that was to take him a long way from the street he loved well.

Mr. Emmanuel bolted his back door. Five seconds later he heard Mr. Silver bolt his back door. Then he turned back into his dark kitchen.

II

He sat down to his meal again, but he did not feel like eating. He lit the gas and reached for a book, but he did not feel like reading, either. He felt curiously ghost-like, as if already he did not properly belong to Magnolia

Street any more. He felt himself fluttering in a dim to-and-fro between the Doomington roof-tops and the shivery eucalyptuses of the Palestine plantations.

"Milk!" muttered Mr. Emmanuel. "With milk he started! With milk he finishes! Till a hundred and twenty years!" he added hurriedly.

He was thinking of Moisheh, his eldest son, who had been bothering him a long time now to come over and settle in Palestine. Horses had been Moisheh's passion, milk his livelihood, from his earliest days. He had been born, so to speak, in a milk-cart. He had started life as an unofficial milk-boy, was promoted in course of time to official milk-boy, and by the time the Great War happened he had become a fully fledged milk-man. "Hup! Hup! Hup!" he shouted behind his horse, proud as any Roman charioteer in the well of his chariot. Then the War came and he became a gunner.

He bombarded Gaza, cleared the way to Ramle and Ludd, and cried: "Hup! Hup!" mightily, while he and General Allenby entered Jerusalem. The War over, he came back to Doomington, made a Jewess out of the Gentile lady with whom he had lived out of wedlock, married her, and took her back to Palestine. They were accepted on the roster of Ain Charod, a colony in the Valley of Esdraelon.

There was a coloured photo of Moisheh on the mantelpiece, beside the clock—white smock embroidered round the collar with forget-me-nots, shorts, sandals. His face was brick-red. In the time of the gathering in of the sheaves he went up behind his team from the fields against Gideon's brook, cracking his whip and crying: "'Hup! Hup!" till the whole valley rang all the way to the hills of Gilboa.

Latterly he had been in the dairy. The cows were his friends, the calves his playmates. It turned out he was just as good with children, too. They all called him *Sar-Hachalav,* these days, Prince of the Milk, for he had put himself in charge of all the processes relating to the supply and distribution of milk in the colony, with special reference to the children, who must have all the milk they needed, whoever else went without. That was the news contained in the letter Mr. Emmanuel had received by air mail that morning. Mr. Emmanuel smiled wistfully. Hup! Hup! The milk-cart clattering down Magnolia Street, the hooves striking sparks from the cobbles. Hup! Hup! The milk splashing into snow-white pails in a cool cow-shed by Gideon's brook!

That letter. Where did I put that letter? Mr. Emmanuel asked himself. For Moisheh it was a long letter. I didn't have time this morning to read it properly. He put his hand into his breast-pocket. Yes. It is here. Not one letter. Two letters. He brought them out. Where did this one come from? I remember. Of course. What a head I have got! It was the letter he had picked up on the door-mat when he had entered the house that evening. From who is it? Do I know this writing? He adjusted his pince-nez. Perhaps he had seen it before, perhaps not, he was not sure. The postmark? He screwed his eyes up. Ringwood. The name was vaguely familiar.

What? *Ringwood?* In the South somewhere, in a forest, isn't it? That is where Rose lives. Rose Berman! What foolishness I am talking! Rose Cooper!

She has heard of my sadness. Her sister Ada has told her, Ada Hummel. Oi, how nice of her she should write! A heart like gold! Like her mother had, peace be upon her!

He slit open the envelope, removed the letter, and read as follows:

Shipscar,
Ringwood,
23 July 1935.

My dear Mr. Emmanuel,

I have been away and have only just read Ada's letter. I won't try and tell you how sorry I am. She was *such* a darling, always so kind and fussy and gentle, and always so proud of you all. It is years and years since I have seen any of you, yet she remains as real and close to me as if I had left Magnolia Street only yesterday. I remember how she used to bring in little delicacies for my mother, when she was not up to form. . . . She was very good at stuffed chicken-neck, wasn't she? and Mother used to make an absolute pig of herself. It can't be much fun for you now, dear Mr. Emmanuel, over there in Magnolia Street. There are not many people left over from the old days, are there?

Ada tells me you are soon going to retire from your position at the Board of Guardians. You'll feel a bit lost without that, won't you, after all these years? But she says you've been thinking of going over to Palestine to join your eldest son there. How exciting! How I envy you! That will be a bit of a wrench, too, leaving the old street. It always meant so much to you in a funny sort of way. (It did to me, too. John, for example.)

Ada has the idea you won't be able to get away for a few months. Is that true? Because if it is, I have a proposition to make to you.

The long and the short of it is, I need your help. I have a party of German refugee boys staying with me. It's all been arranged through one of the refugee committees in London. They wrote round asking for people who'd put the boys up during their holidays—they're all at school, you see. I thought I could put up two or three for a few weeks, but actually I've acquired five.

I adore having them, but they're rather a handful. John left about a fortnight ago. I don't expect him for four or five weeks, though that's very good really, he's on a short run now, you see. I don't know what he'll say when he comes back. Of course he'll be as good as gold, but he doesn't like a lot of leggy boys about the place. He has enough of them on board, I suppose.

Some of the boys are full Jews, some are Jewish on one side only. Like our own children, when you come to think of it. All this Aryan business—did you ever hear such wicked nonsense? I can't tell you how sensitive these boys are, in their various ways. Like most uprooted things. It all needs tact, and patience, and understanding. And a knowledge of the German language is useful, too.

Could you help me out, *dear* Mr. Emmanuel? You have all those qualities. It is not easy for me to say it, but I never knew anybody with more. With John away, my own children need a bit of looking after, I can tell you. Excepting, of course, for Dick, the youngest, I hardly ever get a sight of him. He's the private property of Mary. You remember Mary, John's sister. She sends you her sympathy and her best wishes.

How would it fit into your time to come over to Shipscar for a few weeks? Perhaps they'd let you off a week or two earlier? It would be grand if you could give me a hand. And we could talk about Magnolia Street, too. How we'd talk! I'd want you to stay on till John comes back, of course. As long as you like. There's any amount of room here, you know. The place expands, like an opera-hat.

Have I been dreadfully selfish, rattling away like this? You know how I feel about your sorrow. I can't write about it. I don't know if I'll be able to talk about it, either, when we meet. I know if John were here, he'd send you his deepest sympathy.

Please, can I hear from you soon?

Ever yours with love,

ROSE COOPER.

Mr. Emmanuel put the letter down on the table. He felt a little muzzy, as if he had had a drop too much wine.

There was a knock and twitch in his knee-cap, as if his legs already wanted to be up and away.

He got up.

I must go over and tell Mr. Silver, he muttered. I must go over at once. So they think I am finished, eh? Rose Berman does not think I am finished. Poor little boys. No mother, no father, no home. He had got to the door of the scullery by now. Then suddenly he remembered. No, I cannot go to Mr. Silver. They are little German boys. Poor Mr. Silver! Such a year upon that daughter of his!

He was back in the kitchen again. He went up to the cupboard over his chair and took out a writing-pad and a bottle of ink. No. I will make blobs, he decided. I will go out first for a little walk, my hand should get steady. He was in the lobby now, with his black trilby hat on and his walking-stick in his hand. He lit the hall gas, for the place was not quite so empty to come back to with the hall gas burning. He closed the door behind him, descended the three steps into the street, and turned right towards Aubrey Street, then right again. He walked a hundred yards towards the brick-croft, then turned back sharply.

A picture of Rose Berman formed itself suddenly in his mind. (Rose Berman! he protested. How long is it she's married, and always Rose Berman!) He saw Rose standing in a casement, looking forlornly into the night, one hand uplifted, holding a curtain back, the other held drooping across her forehead. There was a glint of tears in her eyes. The image was after the pattern of a pre-Raphaelite painting he paid his respects to from time to time in the Doomington Art Gallery, Hero watching vainly for the hapless Leander, whom you see dashed to pieces on the rocks below. He was not quite clear in his mind for the moment which of them corresponded to Leander, himself or Rose's husband, but Rose-Hero was at once clear and urgent.

I will go back at once and write, he murmured, I should catch the last post.

He let himself in again, sat down to the table, and wrote as follows:

13 Magnolia Street,
Longton,
Doomington,
24 July 1935.

My dear Rose,

How glad and happy I was to hear from you. It was so kind you should write like that about my poor Slatta, peace be upon her. She did not ail for a long time, either, only three or four months, but Dr. Shulman said if she had lived, it would have been always pain. Like King David said in the Bible from his son, I say for her: I shall go to her; but she shall not return to me. She often talked about you like you were her own daughter, even when all the women were so angry they were like savages you should marry a Christian. But everything is different now since Hitler. Who cares now so much any more? Those poor boys you have with you, for instance, what harm have they done? But if I start writing, it will be for all night, and I want to catch the last post, it is ten o'clock, and it is now ten minutes to. Of course I would love to come and give you a help with those poor boys. It will be a holiday, as well. Mr. Silver, you remember Mr. Silver, he was saying tonight I needed a holiday. Only to see you it would be a holiday, and your children, and your husband. And also Miss Cooper. Thank her for sending me her kind wishes. I do not forget how she came into our house that night we heard our poor David was killed at the front. Please, my thanks and best regards to her. Meeting you, and Miss Cooper, and perhaps John, will be like a Magnolia Street Party. I finish from the Board in ten days. My visit to you will be something to look forward to. I will be with you, please God, before the end of the month. Thank you very much.

I am,

Your sincere friend,

ISAAC EMMANUEL.

Mr. Emmanuel blotted the sheet, addressed the envelope, stamped it, stuck it down. The nearest pillar-box was on the opposite side of Blenheim Road, by the clock where the trams clocked in. In five minutes he was there and back again.

I feel hungry, he said to himself. It would be a shame I should not eat the nice halibut steak Ada fried for me.

It was cooler now. He made a good meal, smoked a cigarette, then he went to bed. He got off to sleep at once. It was several months since he had slept so soundly.

III

Magnolia Street is a small street in the Longton district of Doomington, in the North of England. It is one of several streets called after the names of flowering shrubs that run parallel to each other right and left across the central thoroughfare of Blenheim Road. It is mainly Jews who live in the streets south of Magnolia Street, though some Gentiles live there. The converse holds of the streets north of it. Magnolia Street itself is different from these others because Jews and Gentiles live there in equal numbers, the Jews in the odd-numbered houses on the south side, the Gentiles in the even-numbered houses on the north.

That has been the situation for several decades, and

there was a time when it would have been as unthinkable for a Jewish family to live on the Gentile pavement as for a Gentile family to live on the Jewish pavement. The two sides of the street virtually did not exist for each other, except when certain major public occasions, like the Great War, or certain dramatic private occasions, like a wedding or a death, reminded the folk they were made of pretty much the same stuff, spirit and mind and flesh. There had even been one or two marriages between people from the opposite sides of the street, but on the whole these had not much affected the general situation, though they had caused a good deal of chatter at the time they happened.

Now, in 1935, there were one or two Jewish families on the Gentile pavement, and vice versa, though on the whole the street remained as it had been, out of a sort of inertia. The taboo that had once existed did not prevail. Certainly the landlord of the property, who had once been very stringent about the admission of Jews to the Gentile side, had forgone all his scruples. You could not pick and choose your tenants these days, with the Building Societies competing to provide the humblest workman with his own house on easy terms, houses with gardens on the fresh edges of the city, electric light, indoor sanitation, hot and cold water.

It is in the front room of number thirteen, on the Jewish pavement of Magnolia Street, that Mr. Isaac Emmanuel is now sleeping, the time being one a.m. He is on his own side of the street. Who is this young man who, as the clock strikes, turns the corner of Aubrey Street into Magnolia Street, walks on for a minute or so, then stops at the door of Mr. Emmanuel's house? Is he on his own side of the street? To judge from his appearance, as the light falls on him from the lamp-post a few yards away, he is not. He has a tousle of fair hair, his eyes are blue or grey, he has a short snub nose and a deeply cleft chin. He looks like some manual worker, a mechanic or a driver, perhaps, who does a bit of boxing now and again.

Something has attracted his attention, a chalk-mark on Mr. Emmanuel's door. He goes closer. Yes, he confirms it. It is a swastika. "The bastards!" the young man mutters under his breath. He takes out his handkerchief, spits on it, and rubs the chalk-mark out. Then he walks on a few yards, crosses the roadway, and lets himself into one of the houses on the Gentile pavement. He disappears from this tale. The annals of Magnolia Street have no record of his name.

2

I

ROSE COOPER, whose letter Mr. Emmanuel had read up in Doomington with so much pleasure, had been Rose Cooper for a long time, though Mr. Emmanuel found it hard to think of her as anything but Rose Berman. The Magnolia Street people were all like that. They tended to think of those who had gone from among them as they once had been, rather than as they were now. Rose was one of two sisters who had lived with their mother at number three. The mother had died during the War; the other sister, who still lived at number three and had a home-made sweets shop there, was the Ada Hummel who had been tending Mr. Emmanuel since his bereavement. Rose was one of those Magnolia Street folk—they had been few—who had married on the opposite side of the street.

The young man's name was John Cooper; his family, which was of gentler origin than most of their neighbours, lived at number six. He was in the merchant-service when he and Rose first became aware of each other; when they got married, late in the War, he was in command of a mine-sweeper in the Channel; and now, in 1935, he was the captain of a fruit cargo boat in the Blue Funnel Line plying between the Cape and

Southampton. They lived in a house called Shipscar, some miles from Ringwood, in the New Forest. It had been hardly more than a cottage when they had gone to live there after their marriage, but it had become quite a house as the years had gone by, what with the various buildings-on and outhouses which John delighted to contrive during his periods of leave.

They had three daughters, and one son. The daughters were called one after Rose's mother, one after John's mother, and one just Ailsa, because they thought it a pleasant name. The son was called Dick, and it was exactly because the son was called Dick that another member of the Cooper family lived in that neighbourhood, in a cottage called Wain Cottage, three miles from Shipscar, on the edge of a heathery common. This was the boy's aunt, Mary, the elder of John's two sisters. John had had a brother, too, also called Dick, a golden-haired blue-eyed boy, a rough youngster despite his good looks. This boy had been greatly loved on both sides of Magnolia Street, whilst his sister, Mary Cooper, had had no existence apart from him. He had been, as it were, the breath in her lungs and the light in her eyes. He went to the War and survived it, but two years later somebody swiped him on the head in a football match, and in an hour or so the boy whom the embattled forces did not destroy—bombs and machine-gun bullets and shrapnel-shells—was dead. For years it seemed that for the most part Mary Cooper was dead too. She spent the greater part of the day sitting at the window of the ground-floor sitting-room. She became almost as much part of the inanimate furniture of Magnolia Street as the doorsteps and lamp-posts.

And then at last, in 1930, when John and Rose had a

boy baby the infant succeeded where everything else had failed. Mary Cooper was induced to go to Shipscar, not on the plea that Rose needed her, but because the baby would be called Dick if she went, and anything, even Ebenezer, even Jeroboam, if she did not. Dick the Second wove the spell that had been anticipated. Mary Cooper did not return to Magnolia Street. The sale of the house provided her with almost as much money as was needed to buy Wain Cottage. Before the crash in her father's fortunes which had sent him and his family hurtling into Magnolia Street, she had lived in the country with an aunt and a number of dogs. She now lived in the country again with a number of dogs and a nephew, or at least the greater part of a nephew. He was allowed to sleep at Shipscar and his mother would often see him during the day for as much as an hour or two at a stretch.

The long Magnolia Street years had gone, like the mist on a mirror. She was happy enough. She had this second Dick, and the family, and dogs, and an acre or two of rough garden with a stream in it. But there were times when ghosts came up from the crystal depths of the mirror. Sometimes it was a youthful ghost, with a flicker of yellow hair and blue eyes; and when this apparition shook and swung in the depths, she would seize Dick in her arms and press him so close to her bosom that she hurt and frightened him. But mostly she was sensible. She did not spoil him, or her brother John would have put his foot down soon and hard.

Now and again other ghosts from that in-between time came up and smiled, or mouthed a word or two, and disappeared. The most amiable of these was that tall Mr. Emmanuel, with the little pointed beard, and the pince-nez, and the head that swung to and fro. She sometimes hoped they might see each other again, but that did not seem likely; it was a long way from Ringwood in the New Forest to Magnolia Street in Doomington.

II

It was the second afternoon after the dispatch by Mr. Emmanuel of his letter to Rose. Mary Cooper was at work on her lawn. The grass had grown skimpy where sun and rain had been kept from it by the clusters of aubrietia that hung over the low brick rim of the herbaceous border. The dogs had burned away a few patches here and there. And her nephew Dick had done some damage in an attempt to dig up Captain Kidd's hidden treasure from the corner near the vine-trellis.

This afternoon the dogs were safely out of harm's way, scampering about in the paddock behind the cottage—all except Tessa, the black spaniel bitch, who, lying with her nose between her paws, looked up and adored. Young Dick was building houses and things in the glass portico. The aubrietia had been thinned out. Mary Cooper was free to get on with it. She was loosening the bare patches with a fork, and raking in a thin scattering of wood ashes. She looked a little witch-like, with that rake, the drooping bonnet, the stern grey eyes, the spellbound animal following her least movement. But Dick Cooper did not seem perturbed. Having built up a big, big house, he knocked it down again and got to work on a big, big ship.

A car hooted and slowed down as it turned from the road into the lane. The dogs in the paddock barked. Tessa inflated her cheek-flaps, but said nothing.

"There's Mum!" called out Dick. "P'waps she's got ice-cweam!"

"You're to have no ice-cream in the morning!" his aunt said. She looked rather less like a witch than like Tessa as she turned to him. "Your stomach will be like an iceberg!" The car braked. The engine was switched off. "Get up, please! Come and say good-morning to Mammy!" One door, then other doors, were opened and slammed to. There was a thud of feet tumbling out into the roadway. It sounded like a platoon of soldiers discharging out of a transport-wagon.

"She's brought them all with her! The whole lot!" murmured Mary Cooper. She dropped her rake, hurriedly crossed the lawn, and ran over to the wicket-gate. It occurred to her that a mob of growing boys and girls tramping over the lawn would be no better for it than a valance of aubrietia, three dogs, and a digger for secret treasure. Her sister-in-law, Rose Cooper, was being helped out of the car by a broad-shouldered dark young man in green plus-fours. She was looking very bright and fresh in a suit of brown tweeds, her brown eyes twinkling, a blue silk motoring-scarf tied round her clustering dark hair and under her dimpled chin.

In the lane was a gang of young people, four more lads, two girls. They had clearly all come along in the same conveyance, though it was not easy to see how it had been done. The girls were Rose Cooper's daughters, but they might almost have been her sisters. It was hard to believe she was not more than three or four years the junior of the grey-haired spinster who came up a little forbiddingly from round the hedge of flowering shrubs, the languishing spaniel at her heels.

"Good morning, Rose!" Mary Cooper called out. "Good morning, all of you!"

"Good morning, Mary! Good morning, Aunt!" came

from the females, in breezy English voices. "Gut morning, Miss Cooper! *Guten Tag, Fräulein!*" came from the males in a more exotic accent. There was a click of heels as five lads came smartly to attention in the German manner, and bent forward stiffly from the waist.

"Yes," said Rose. "A bit like a musical comedy, isn't it? Can I come in and see the lodger, please?"

"Hello, Mum!" a child's voice called. A child's nose thrust itself through the slats of the gate. "Any ice-cweam?"

"What's that you're holding behind your back?" the aunt asked the mother sternly.

"We found there was one over!" exclaimed Rose guiltily. "I thought Dick might as well have it!"

Mary Cooper folded her arms and set her jaw.

"I won't hear of it!"

"Be a sport!" cried the two girls.

"I'm just patching up the lawn! There's wood ash all over the place. What do you want them to do, Rose?"

There was a tug at Mary's apron. She felt a small smooth cheek nuzzle against the back of her hand.

"Please, Auntie Mawy!" the small boy wheedled.

"I won't hear of it!" said Aunt Mary, with less conviction.

Rose came forward to the gate, bent over towards her son, and kissed him. Then, a little diffidently, she passed across a small carton.

"She says just this time, and never again!"

"Thank you, Mum!" the small boy said placidly. He turned his back, and for the time being took no further interest in the proceedings.

"I want to see you for a minute," said Rose nervously.

"All right, come in. What do you want the others to do?"

"Can they go round into the paddock, please, Mary?"

"The other way. Round by the hedge."

"All right, Aunt, we'll take them!" the elder of the two girls called out. "We'll see they don't chew up the apple trees!"

"Blease!" said the broad-shouldered boy in green plus-fours. "We bromise! There shall be no damage! It is very kind!" The youth had a sense of responsibility.

"Very well, Bieber. It is Bieber, isn't it?" said Mary, and smiled at him. A smile made a lot of difference to her face. "I rely on you!" The boy clicked his heels again, like a sergeant-major. "Where's Sarah?" Sarah was the eldest daughter.

"She's gone out riding!" explained Rose. "These young men are a little too young for her! Can this one come in with us? He and Dick seem to like each other."

She put her hand on the shoulder of the smallest and youngest of the lads. He seemed not quite fifteen. He had unruly chestnut-coloured hair and green eyes with brown specks swimming in them. He had a full sensitive mouth, a full chin, and a rather waxy complexion, bloomed over with the summer sun. The boy's eyes were not happy.

"You're Bruno, aren't you? Of course, he can come in!"

The boy opened the gate and let Rose through. The gesture was a little courtly, almost stilted.

"Inside?" asked Mary. "Dick!" she called out to her nephew. "Here's Bruno! He'll give you a pick-a-back. Not on the lawn, Bruno! Round the hut there, in the deep grass!"

"Pick-a-back?" asked the German boy.

"Like this! Like this!" The English boy showed excitedly. The two boys being safely disposed of, the two women passed through the portico into the little sitting-room on the left.

"You've heard?" said Mary. "Please sit down!"

"I won't sit down. Yes, I've heard!" exclaimed Rose, bubbling. She snapped her bag open. "He swallowed the bait, hook, line, and sinker. He sent me the loveliest letter." She rummaged about among a sheaf of bills and things. "Where *is* that letter? Oh, here it is! Listen, Mary! Don't you think it's lovely?" She read it out, with both tears and laughter in her voice. "Isn't he a pet, Mary!"

Mary had sat down. She was sitting on the edge of an easy chair, her body arched forward, her hands on her knees. Her eyes stared straight before her, as if there were no vision in them. She said nothing. The silence became disconcerting.

"Mary!" Rose called out sharply. "What are you thinking of?" Then, after a further silence, again she called out: "Mary!"

The eyelids flickered. The pose became less rigid. "I'm sorry!" she brought out.

Rose was over at her side. She lifted one of her hands and chafed it between both her own.

"My poor dear!" she breathed. "Will nothing ever make it up to you? It's such a long time ago!"

"It seemed like yesterday, as you stood there reading. Forgive me, Rose! And you are so generous!"

"My dear!" said Rose. "I really couldn't manage Dick on top of all these others! No room for a sardine!"

Mary smiled faintly.

"Why do you smile, Mary?"

"Where are you going to find room for Mr. Emmanuel?"

"We'll manage somehow," returned Rose. "Look here, Mary. I'm rather unhappy. It's not going to . . . is it going to upset you? I mean . . . bring things up again?"

"I have my darling," said Mary. There was a note of savagery in her voice. "And besides, I like the old man. He's . . . he's a gentleman. It will be good to see him again."

"He *is* a pet, isn't he!" Rose exclaimed happily. "I suppose he'll want more looking after than all the boys put together."

"I think you're wrong," said Mary quietly. "You underrate Mr. Emmanuel. Tell me"—she changed the subject brusquely—"of course that boy hasn't heard from his mother yet?"

"Bruno? No. He hasn't. Poor kid!" Rose sighed. "I don't know what to do with him."

"There isn't anything you can do with him. Not till he's heard from her. I don't think he will."

"You can't tell, Mary, you can't tell . . . these days in Germany. Anything might have happened. But if she'd been dead—" She broke off.

"Yes," said Mary sombrely. "You'd have thought he'd have heard if she'd been dead. Do the other boys still treat him so badly?"

"Not Bieber, of course. Not Klaus. You know what boys are. It's just thoughtlessness. I've tried . . . Hello!" she interrupted. "Is that you, darling? Yes, Dickie, Mummy's coming!" The child's hand was straining up to the latch. It was just too high for him. She went up to the door, opened it, and caught the child up in her arms. "Aren't you playing any more? Where's Bruno?"

"Won't play!" Dick pouted.

Rose strode swiftly out into the glass portico. Mary followed. Through the panes on their right hand they looked out on the patch of rough grass where they had left Bruno and Dick playing together. The German boy was sitting in the roots of a walnut tree, his hands clasped round his knees. He stared straight in front of him. Large tears were coursing down his cheeks.

"Let's leave him!" bade Mary, with the authority of a specialist in grief. "There's nothing we can do." They turned back into the sitting-room. Both women sat down in easy chairs. It was in Mary's lap the small boy ensconced himself, his arms round her neck. "I think it's a good thing you've asked Mr. Emmanuel to come," she said in measured tones. "I have a feeling he'll be more helpful than you think."

"I'm sure," said Rose. There was no conviction in her voice. "He'll be coming early in August. I'm going to pick him up in Salisbury. Would you like to come to the station to meet him?"

"Of course I would."

"Me too," requested Dick, fearful of missing anything.

"You too," murmured Mary.

Tessa lifted her head and blew inquiringly.

"You too," said Rose. "I think I ought to go out to that young man," she went on rather miserably. "And you'll want to be getting back to your lawn."

"Yes," Mary said with decision. "I hope they've not let the dogs out of the paddock. I think Dick's falling asleep. I'll wait here for five minutes. Good-bye, Rose."

"Good-bye, Mary."

Rose closed the door behind her and went over to the forlorn boy under the walnut tree.

III

The train that brought Mr. Emmanuel to Bruno arrived at Salisbury, ten days later, at four-thirty in the afternoon. There were two women awaiting his arrival on the platform; he recognized them at once, though the train was still travelling quite rapidly as it passed them. He thrust his head out of the window and waved to them energetically. "Rose!" he cried out. "Miss Cooper!" The movement of the air put his little white beard awry. His pince-nez swung out dangerously. Beard or no beard, he looked like an excited schoolboy; and it had been a long journey, from Doomington round by Euston and Waterloo.

The train drew up. The nice soldier with whom he had maintained an animated conversation all the way from Andover lifted his suitcase from the rack. It was very big and heavy.

"God should bless you!" said Mr. Emmanuel. "You shouldn't have to go to any wars!"

A porter came up. The soldier handed the suitcase down. Mr. Emmanuel came bustling down from the carriage.

"Bit on the 'eavy side," said the porter jocularly. Mr. Emmanuel's smile was infectious. "Any dead bodies?" The porter upended the suitcase to get the balance better adjusted. A long, low wail issued from its bowels. "God a'mighty!" exclaimed the porter, almost letting the suitcase fall. He looked up quickly into Mr. Emmanuel's face. Strange things had been left in station cloakrooms. But suspicion and that face were not kinsmen. "Some gadgets for the kids, eh?" hazarded the porter, smiling broadly.

The two women had come up by now, Rose preceding, both hands outstretched.

"Rose!"

"Mr. Emmanuel!"

He took both her hands, then stooped towards her, and kissed her first on the right cheek, then the left.

"Not one day older!" he pronounced. "Not one day older! And this is Miss Cooper! Oi, Miss Cooper, how nice it is you should come to meet me! One from each side of Magnolia Street, eh?"

("He is never far from Magnolia Street," each of the women thought. "He carries Magnolia Street about with him!")

"I am so glad to see you, Mr. Emmanuel! Welcome!"

He looked from Miss Cooper to Rose, then back again. "Like yesterday!" he was burbling. "Like yesterday!"

"Where to, madam?" the porter asked Rose. The old gentleman was clearly not capable of giving a coherent reply.

"There's a car outside! Come!" cried Rose, seizing Mr. Emmanuel's elbow. "You'll be wanting a cup of tea!"

"But those boys!" he exclaimed. He looked up and down the platform. After all, delightful as it was to meet two ladies from Magnolia Street, it was to give a hand with those poor refugee boys that he had been summoned from Doomington. "Where are those boys?"

"Oh, there's time enough for them!" said Rose breezily. They were at the ticket-barrier by now. "You'll have all you want of the boys! That's our car, porter, over there! We'll have to strap it on at the back, I think."

Mr. Emmanuel stopped. His jaw fell.

"What!" he exclaimed. "It cannot be such a thing! Two little boys like that!"

There were two boys in the back of the car. One, very young, was standing up. The other sat in the corner, a black spaniel on his knee, his face pressed against the window.

"No, no!" laughed Rose. "The little one's Dick, my son and heir!"

"Oh, Dick! Your son! Of course! What a beautiful boy!" (I will not, a voice within him insisted peremptorily. I will not remember! It was once another Dick Cooper! If the tall one sees I remember, it will be like a stab inside her. Perhaps, please God, she has forgotten. Who knows?) "Just like his father, God bless him!" he exclaimed. And indeed he was, the same grey eyes, the same square chin with the cleft in it.

"This is Uncle Emmanuel, Dickie. Say how do you do."

"How do you do?" asked Dick. He lifted his hand and projected it across the window-rim. "I'm vewy glad to meet you." The only son of the family, with a father away for a good deal of the year, he could play the host quite neatly when occasion required.

"And that one?" asked Mr. Emmanuel. He could not see the boy clearly, for his pince-nez was lop-sided, and the inside of the car was overshadowed by a van on the other side. But the boy was foreign. He gathered that from the cut of his clothes, and from the mode of his greeting. He was making efforts at an outlandish salutation, much constricted by the shape of the car. He was, of course, a German boy, one of Rose's young refugee guests.

"He is one . . . he is from your party, yes?" Mr. Emmanuel brought out the words with difficulty; pity and anger were like birds' wings beating in his throat. The boy's face as a face underwent further obliteration. It had no quality, fair or dark, sympathetic or displeasing. It was the face of a boy who, because vast powers had willed it, vast as the sea and cruel as a wildcat, had been uprooted from his own place, and sent forth to be among strangers, a boy who should be at this moment beside his mother, among his friends, in the streets or the green fields where he had been reared.

"Yes, that's one of our boys," said Rose breezily. "His name is Bruno. We thought the run would do him good. Be quiet, Tessa! Will you get in the other side, please, Mary?"

"I hope you are well, Bruno, yes?" Mr. Emmanuel said, extending his arm through the window. "Can you play mouth-organs? I have brought three mouth-organs." Apparently Mr. Emmanuel did not intend to mark time in the execution of the duties that had been assigned to him.

"Mouth-organ?" the boy asked a little blankly. He thought for a moment or two. "Oh, *Mundharmonika!* Yes!" he admitted. "I do not play so very badly!" There was quite an edge of brightness to his voice.

"A bull's eye first time, Mr. Emmanuel!" exclaimed Rose. "Well, I think we ought to get along. The bag all right, porter? Thank you. Will you get in beside me, Mr. Emmanuel? That's right. Are you all right, there, Mary? How about a nice cup of tea?"

They had tea in a teashop in Salisbury. As they sat down, Rose breathed a word of condolence in Mr. Emmanuel's ear. He muttered a word of thanks, but the subject of his bereavement was not touched on again, not here and now, in the presence of two children. Rose poured tea; Bruno passed it round. There was so much to ask, so much to say, they found it quite impossible to decide who should begin first, and at what point. They had not, in fact, met for about eighteen years, and had hardly written to each other, except at the conventional times of greeting. Yet they had remained friendly, very much aware of each other. During most of that period John Cooper's sister Mary had lived in Magnolia Street. Rose's sister Ada lived there still. There had been other contacts, direct and indirect, from time to time.

Yes, there was much to ask, much to say. Divining the difficulty, Mary decreed that the tea-party be devoted chiefly to tea. Certain major facts, none the less, emerged. It was established that the three Cooper girls were as presentable, in their various ways, as their small brother Dick; they had carried off the other four German boys for a long tramp through the Forest, taking picnic lunch with them; Rose's sister Ada, up in Magnolia Street, was very well; so were her two children—Annie, the married one, and Leo, who had passed his first medical examinations. The conversation then turned to plans for the immediate future. It was stated that no excursion for the German boys had been arranged for the next day. Everything had, of course, been held up pending Mr. Emmanuel's arrival.

"And what do you think we should do tomorrow, Bruno?" asked Mr. Emmanuel, turning guiltily to the small boy beside him. He and Rose had been so busy rattling away about this and that, he had quite forgotten the boy's existence all this time. (A fine one! he reproached himself. I am asked here I should be nice to the refugee boys, and I forget them like there isn't any Hitler any more.)

The boy bent his head and speculated.

"If I am having a *Mundharmonika,* I like to go out into the trees and play," said Bruno.

"Into the trees and play?" repeated Mr. Emmanuel, in a rising tone. The picture etched itself upon his mind, a boy going out all by himself among trees to play a mouth-organ. This must be a sad boy, a lonely boy, his quick sensibility told him. Why should he want to go out, all by himself, so young a boy? He adjusted his pince-nez and took a furtive glance at the boy's face. No, it was not a happy face. Why that droop about the corners of the mouth? There was pain in those eyes. A boy with a mouth-organ . . .

"Like my David!" he exclaimed suddenly. A memory of another lad had arisen that superseded the sharp imagination of this one, his own lad, hardly older than Bruno, who had died in the Great War. "He too played mouth-organs. He would sometimes go out to Sefton Park and play by himself all afternoon. He could play lovely." He stopped. He could not remember his David, in the presence of Mary Cooper, without remembering also another youth, her brother, who had died about that time, not during the War, but shortly after. He looked up from under his eyelids, and saw Mary's head had fallen forward, her eyes tightly shut. "Forgive me," he breathed. "I should not bring it up again about the old time."

There was silence among the grown-ups for some moments. Then Mary Cooper spoke. Her voice was cool and grave. Her eyes were open again. They were fixed on Bruno.

"He is not at all unlike your David, as I remember him. He was a dear child."

It was only Mr. Emmanuel who seemed to be aware of Bruno's embarrassment, the faint flush spreading across the cheeks. If Mary Cooper was aware of it, she would not allow it to perturb her; there would be always something detached about her, something not quite human, in all things not pertaining to the dead or the living Dick.

"You are right maybe," he said hurriedly. Then he changed the subject. He asked for news of Mary's sister Enid. He gave news of his own son Max, the painter, away in Mexico somewhere. He talked in rapid succession of certain Magnolia Street personalities who had impressed themselves on all their memories.

But however busy his tongue was, his heart was with the small refugee boy, humped over the blue and white tea-plate. And when the lad raised his head and turned his eyes for one swift moment upon him, he knew it was a sign of gratitude for his understanding, a forlorn gaze of friendship from a boy with nothing to give to an old man with hardly more.

Perhaps he is like my David, the thought was running in his head. Maybe. But should I have liked it if my David when he was fifteen should have to go to a foreign country away from everybody? From his mother, from his father, from his brothers, from his friends? This little one is missing his mother something terrible. I know it. I know it. . . .

"I beg your pardon, Rose? Another cup of tea? No, thank you, please. Such a nice place! All real oak, eh? It's wonderful. Isn't it a wonderful place, Bruno?"

He placed his hand fleetingly on Bruno's shoulder as

he rose. But he felt the boy would not miss the significance of the gesture. It meant, translated into words: "Whether you are like my boy or not like him, does that matter? But we shall be friends. Yes, Bruno?"

IV

Mr. Emmanuel had never been to Salisbury before, and it was impossible not to take him to see the Cathedral before they left the city. He was so moved and overawed that he seemed to think it an irreverence even to breathe. It was only when he got out into the Close again that he dared trust himself to speak.

"It is not like men built it," he murmured. "It is like angels."

Bruno was by his side. Bruno had not left his side since the party had descended from the car.

"I am not thinking there are any angels," said Bruno.

Mr. Emmanuel looked swiftly at the boy, then away again.

"I have lived a long time now," he said. He seemed to be addressing no one in particular. "I, too, have thought often there are no angels. I think now they are a long way away, very far. I think they have never been further away from the world than they are now. But I think they are there still."

Dick was ahead between his mother and aunt, chattering away volubly. The two others kept a few yards behind them, as they moved back to the car. Mr. Emmanuel did not remember the moment at which Bruno's hand had sought his, but by the time they reached the car they were walking hand in hand. Rose held the door open for Mr. Emmanuel to get in front beside her.

"I have one or two things to talk over with you, Rose," said Mary. "Do you mind if I go in front? Do you mind, Mr. Emmanuel?"

"Perhaps Bruno and I have a lot to say to each other. Why should I mind?"

"Come, Dick," bade Mary. Dick went in front. Tessa remained behind, scarfed up in her ears. They soon left the old city behind them. On the west the yellow humps of the Wiltshire downland heaved like a shoal of great whales. On the east the Avon coursed through bright meadows fringed by pollard willows. The water slid in the weirs like moving floes.

For some time, fifteen minutes or more, the boy behind remained quite silent, as his habit was. Mr. Emmanuel remained silent too, though his habit was the reverse.

Be quiet, you, Isaac! he bade himself. The boy wants he should talk to you. It will make him feel better in the heart when he talks. It is beautiful all this country, is it? Well, let it be beautiful! Don't get so excited!

They passed the village of Downton. Breamore lay ahead of them. Rose turned her head.

"That's Breamore," she pointed out. "Are you all right, Mr. Emmanuel? All right, Bruno?"

The boy's thoughts were far off. He made no sign of hearing. Mr. Emmanuel raised his head and made a gesture. Hush, dear Rose. It's all right. Not to worry.

A herd of cows held them up at Fordingbridge, where the river widens and the ranked loosestrife withdraws as before an attack. Some distance further, a great field of barley, bleached flaxen-yellow for harvest, came up and blew, as it were, against the car windows, on the left hand where Bruno sat.

"It is like that. Yes, it is like that." The boy was talking, as if he spoke out of a dream. Mr. Emmanuel said nothing.

"She is very beautiful," murmured Bruno.

"Your mother?" whispered Mr. Emmanuel. But he knew the boy meant his mother.

"She is so *beautiful,*" the boy insisted, as if someone were arguing with him. "Her hair is silver and yellow, like that . . . barley. It is barley, yes?" He turned to Mr. Emmanuel. Mr. Emmanuel nodded, though he was not sure. "Her voice is so quiet, like very early in the morning, when birds are sleepy and they are singing. Is that foolish, please?" Mr. Emmanuel shook his head, to show he did not think it foolish.

"We have a box, when you open it, it is making music," the boy continued. He seemed suddenly to have found his tongue. "It is rose-wood, I think. It is painted on it, with ladies and gentlemen dancing. She sings very low, like that box."

Rose nudged Mary significantly.

"You see?" she said. She was not more specific than that, lest she frighten the boy's shy spirit back into its lair. She had not heard him utter so many consecutive sentences since his arrival. What she meant was: "You see, Mary? Didn't I say Mr. Emmanuel would work wonders if we got him down here? Wasn't it clever of me?"

"I see," Mary admitted dryly.

"It was in Haus Anna, that box," Bruno was saying. "Haus Anna, that was our bungalow, you know. It was in the Spreewald, near Lübbenau. It is not any more," the boy added sadly. "It is not any more."

The boy relapsed into silence again. The wheels hissed on the road like water sprayed on leaves. The road, following the pattern laid down for it by the gait of those prehistoric caravans of pack-horses whose track it was, swung in steady regular curves.

"Do you see?" cried Rose, lifting her head from the wheel and pointing to the high land on the east, fringed by a ribbon of darkness. "That's the Forest, of course! We're more than half-way."

They continued in silence for another five or ten minutes, then the boy turned suddenly to Mr. Emmanuel.

"Please, will you tell me?" he begged. His mouth was constricted with pain. "Why is she not writing? It is a long time. It is a very long time. Since March. It was eleventh March, Monday." He counted the months on his fingers. "March, April, May, June, July. That is too long. Why does she not write?"

Mr. Emmanuel put his arm round the boy's shoulder and brought him close to his chest.

"How much longer, Rose?" he called out.

"Not much. Ten minutes."

"Only ten minutes and we shall be in," he murmured in the boy's ear. "Let be now. I want later we shall talk and talk. For hours we shall talk, up in the Forest there. And then we shall write to this one and to that one."

The boy nodded. Mr. Emmanuel cast about energetically in his mind for a new subject.

"You are at school here in England, Bruno, yes? Where is it? Do you like English puddings?"

"Haslemere," answered Bruno. "Greystones." He said

nothing after that for some seconds. Then, "No," he added, "I do not like English puddings."

"No," Mr. Emmanuel temporized. "Some English puddings are not nice."

There was silence for several more minutes. Then the car turned left-handed and proceeded for some half-mile over the belt of farm-land that separates the road from the high ground of the Forest. Farm-land petered out into heath-land, with gorse and clumps of oaks. Then the car lurched suddenly from the by-road into a lane. There was a swish and scratch of leaves and twigs against the near-side windows.

Rose turned and smiled.

"Yes," she said, "it gets quite thick here. We'll be home in a few minutes."

A few minutes later they drew up within a few yards of a gate standing obliquely from the road on the left hand. A wooden plaque nailed over the top bar stated this was Shipscar. Ahead and behind the car, on each side of the lane, the trees marched. Above the gate on the left the trees climbed on rising ground.

"We're here!" Rose exclaimed. "Welcome!"

"It is like in a magic lantern!" gasped Mr. Emmanuel, some painted square of green and pink prettiness swimming up inconsequently from the dim Edwardian past.

"Hello! Here they are!" cried Rose. "They heard us coming!"

There was the sound of feet crunching along gravel, scampering through trees. In a moment the place was full of young people hallooing and saluting. "My daughters!" said Rose vaguely. "The boys!" One of the boys unlatched the gate. "Hello, Mary! Hello, Ailsa! Hello, Klaus!" There was a quick patter of greetings.

"Come on now, out of the way, everybody!" Rose backed the car a few yards, then swung round into the drive.

It was all too quick for Mr. Emmanuel, there were so many faces. His head bobbed to and fro.

"Like a magic lantern!" he repeated helplessly.

The car continued for about fifty yards, with the wood still about them, then the drive turned the base of the hill and the ground opened out. The house was on a sort of levelled platform, close up against the hill-slope. On one side extended a space of lawn with gay borders round two edges. Below was an irregular terracing of rock-garden, built up over the drive. On the right of the drive was a meadow of coarse grass. Further away were kitchen-gardens and chicken-runs. At odd places, slap up under the hill, in the centre of the meadow, in a clearing beyond the rim of the wood, were certain supplementary constructions, a caravan, a tent, a hut or two. It was all a little bewildering, and gay, and hot, and dry, poppies in the rough grass, sweet peas, carnations, canterbury bells in the borders, swallows over the chimneys, bicycles against walls, magazines, chickens, ragwort, butterflies.

Rose heeled round towards the garage and turned the bonnet of the car towards the gate again. Then she got out, followed at once by Bruno, who held the door open for Mr. Emmanuel.

"Polite little boy, isn't he?" smiled Rose. "What about you, Mary? Won't you come in?"

"He's asleep," breathed Mary. "I won't disturb him. I'll take him back at once, if you don't mind."

"Very well, Mary." Rose turned to her guest. "I'll see you to your room, Mr. Emmanuel, then I'll run Mary back. You see, she's looking after Dick for me while the house is a bit full. Get one of the boys to help you with

Mr. Emmanuel's bag, please, Bruno. This way." She was very brisk and efficient.

Mary Cooper held out her hand.

"Till tomorrow, Mr. Emmanuel. We have a lot to say to each other. I'm so glad to see you in these parts. Good-bye."

"Yes, please," said Mr. Emmanuel, shaking her hand vigorously. "Thank you. Good-bye. Pleased to meet you." He was rather flustered, and more staccato than was usual with him. He followed Rose round to the front of the house, where she stood framed in the arched brick doorway, trellised over with tea-roses.

"Welcome to Shipscar," she smiled at him. "I want you to have a rest before supper." She went before him across a small hall and up a polished oak staircase. "Up here, please. The bathroom is straight opposite." She led him along the landing and threw open the door of his room. "The boys will be here with your bag in a moment. They'll help you unpack. Do you think it'll be all right?"

"All right?" he repeated. "Like the Lord Mayor's parlour in the Town Hall and she asks if it's all right! Good-bye, Rose. Till later on." He entered the room as she turned and left him. It was perhaps not so imposing as the Lord Mayor's parlour, but it was pleasant enough, with a flowered blue carpet, a blue glazed chintz curtain, a blue-grey eiderdown on the bed, an easy chair in the bay window, a bookcase. There were flowers on the bookcase, on the mantelpiece, on the bedside table. Mr. Emmanuel closed the door behind him, then stationed himself in the centre of the carpet. He looked round, and sighed deeply.

"She's just like her old mother, peace be upon her,

everything neat and tidy and beautiful." The thought of another Magnolia Street matron, dead more recently than Rose's mother, presented itself to him. He felt guilty and ashamed she had been out of his mind so long. "How she would have loved this room, my Slatta! What sort of a curtains are these?" The sheen on the glazed chintz had caught his eye. "You should be able to wash them with a sponge, yes? How nice it would have been for our parlour window! What a lot of trouble it would have saved her!"

He blew his nose hard. It did not matter to her any more now, trouble or no trouble.

There was the sound of a heavy load being bumped up the stairs and along the landing. Then a knock at the door.

"Yes, come in, please!"

It was Bruno and another youth, with the bag between them. The door opened.

"Klaus Bieber!" exclaimed the other youth, and dropped the bag, nearly bringing his companion to the ground with the smartness of the movement. He stood to attention with both arms outstretched along the seams of his green plus-fours.

"Come in, please!" begged Mr. Emmanuel, a little embarrassed. He was not used to being treated like a sergeant-major.

"We shall help to unpack," specified Klaus. "Mrs. Cooper asks it." The boys brought the bag in and began to unstrap it.

"Please, that will be all right," implored Mr. Emmanuel, his hands fluttering before him. "I will unpack." He did not want to take the edge off his surprises, his darling secrets. He wanted to bring them out in his own time and at his own pace, to a succession of incredulous and joyous exclamations from a pack of shining-eyed boys.

"Mrs. Cooper asks," repeated Klaus heavily. The lad had the shoulders of a young bullock. There was no dislodging shoulders like those.

The suitcase was open now. On top was a layer of clothes. "In the dressing-table, Bruno!" ordered Klaus, lifting out the shirts, the underclothes, with Teutonic care. Bruno as carefully bestowed them in the drawers. Then, beneath a layer of thick brown paper, came the secrets, the gadgets, the treasury of boys' delights. Out they came, one and all, the games with counters, with dice, with balls, with pegs. Out came the tricks, the rings you have to put together, the rings you have to put apart, the handcuffs you have to get into and out of, the magic string. Out came the jokes, the side-splitting jokes, the glass of brown ale that doesn't pour, the mouse ready to jump, the rubber roll of bread, the fly on the lump of sugar. Out came the musical instruments, the jews' harp, the tin flute, the three mouth-organs, the cylinders that, when you reverse them, moo like cows or bleat like lambs. Out came the two bulky objects to which the weightiness of the bag was chiefly due—one, the board with a narrow wooden cylinder attached to it; you try to drop rope quoits over the cylinder from some distance away; two, the unfolding wooden contraption attached to a tennis-ball by a long piece of elastic; if you cannot play tennis, that is how you can teach yourself; if you can, you play anyway.

There was also a solitaire board.

Out they came, one and all, with, from Klaus, not a single observation, not a change of expression. They might have been lumps of firewood or telephone books. Bruno was visibly interested, perhaps even excited, but he uttered no word, either; the sobriety of the older lad checked his tongue. Methodically, carefully, the two boys packed the stuff away at the base of a deep cupboard let into the wall.

"Thank you, thank you," sighed Mr. Emmanuel. He had a sudden helpless feeling that he stood more in need of sympathy than the bullock-shouldered boy. "Such very kind boys—" he began.

"Please," requested Klaus. There was to be no nonsense of excessive thanking for the mere efficient doing of a thing enjoined by one's hospitality-giver. "Come, Bruno." He went off towards the door, followed by the younger boy.

"No, please. You shall stay, Bruno." Mr. Emmanuel insisted tremulously. "I have something I had promised him," he explained. Klaus shrugged his shoulders, disclaiming responsibility. At the door he turned, clicked his heels and bowed, turned again, and went out. The door clicked like an echo.

"You shall have your mouth-organ," said Mr. Emmanuel. "Your *Mundharmonika.*" He went over to the cupboard and brought it out. "Here it is, Bruno." Bruno removed it from its case.

"So beautiful," Bruno murmured. "I have never seen more beautiful." He was a polite little boy.

Mr. Emmanuel sat down in the chair near the window. "Come," he said, patting the side of the bed. "Will you play me a little tune, yes?"

Bruno sat down.

"What shall I play?" he asked. "I cannot play American."

"Play from your own country," murmured Mr. Emmanuel, "when it was happy."

The boy held the instrument to his mouth and blew out a few notes.

"*'Drei Lilien,'*" he breathed. "I shall play *'Drei Lilien.'*" He played the little air, so gay, so unbearably sad. Then he played another melody and another, the boys' songs, the soldiers' songs, of his lost country.

"That was *'Die geliebte Pimpanulla,'*" said Bruno. "Did you like?"

"I liked it very much," Mr. Emmanuel answered, and turned his head slowly away. "Play again!" he bade. The boy played a more poignant tune, *"Morgenrot."*

Enough, it is enough! Mr. Emmanuel's tormented heart insisted. It is like my little boy David playing, all alone in Sefton Park, when it was a holiday. Or in the trenches, on the evening before the day he died.

"It is a nice mouth-organ, yes?" he said aloud. "It has a nice tone, I think."

"Very nice."

"Bruno!"

"Yes, Mr. Emmanuel?"

"I want you should talk to me."

"I want also."

"About your mother, Bruno."

"Yes, Mr. Emmanuel."

"I want it should not be in your inside all the time. Are you comfortable, Bruno?"

"Yes, Mr. Emmanuel."

"Talk to me."

So the boy talked to him, in the summer dusk of the New Forest, in the blue-grey room at Shipscar, with the moony flowers of clematis poking round the window, and the bats faintly twittering. This is what he said.

"She is Aryan, you see," murmured Bruno. "My father was not Aryan. I did not know. I think my father did not know. I think perhaps he has forgotten. I was baptize, because my mother said it is nice for little German boys and girls should be baptize, but we had not religion in our family. I think my father's father and mother were non-Aryan peoples, but they were baptize. We did not think of Aryan or non-Aryan or baptize or anything."

Aryan, non-Aryan, Aryan . . . the words dinned lamentably in Mr. Emmanuel's ears. It was as if the child, marooned in some outpost of civilization, had picked up a few syllables of the gibberish of a jungle tribe, insensately repeated on tom-toms, as the dance contracted in narrowing circles upon the doomed garrison.

"My father was a painter," Bruno went on, "and my mother sings, and it was, oh, it was so happy. And we had many friends, and they come to our flat, and also come to Haus Anna, in Lübbenau. And one day my father is coming home and is telling something to my mother and she cries. And days and nights she cries and Father is not working, and I find out at last he cannot sell paintings or show in exhibitions, and that is because he is non-Aryan. It is becoming not nice for me also in my school. For it is written a letter I am of non-Aryan father, and one or two teachers and one or two boys are always nice but many are bad, very bad. And I must sit on other form with non-Aryan boys and I am unhappy. And some people come to our house, not the same people, for many friends are not longer friends now. I think Socialist and Catholic people, because they are very unhappy, and some non-Aryans. And my mother is frightened, but she is so nice, so kind, and we sell our motor car and our big radio-gramophone and we have food for friends. Then there is not much food and some friends are not coming because there is not much food, and some because of concentration camp. And my mother is much frightened because of concentration camp and also am I.

"But really my father is not saying anything bad, he is only unhappy. But one day come the S.A. men and he is not there and they stay many hours and he is not coming, for some friends have seen the S.A. men and are telling him and he does not come again and I never see him. But I think he has written to the Committee in London, and also friends have written to the Committee, so last summer I come to London and I go to school in the country near Haslemere. And I am not wanting I shall leave my mother, and my mother is not wanting I shall go, and we are crying. But they are not giving permit she shall come, and she is staying in Berlin, and is writing me many letters. Oh, such beautiful letters.

"Then also I am receiving letters from my father in Switzerland; in September and October I am receiving letters. He tells me I shall not write to my mother I am receiving letters from him, and where from he is sending them, only I shall say Busi is well. For his name is Norbert, but she sometimes is calling him Busi, and she shall know. And he writes he shall go quietly to Berlin and he shall take my mother to Switzerland, and then I can go in holidays and see them in Switzerland, and perhaps next year he will get permit and come to England with my mother, and he shall be painting and she shall be singing and it will be again happy. And November there is no letter from my father and the Committee is writing me and saying he has died of pneumonia. And I do not believe it shall be pneumonia. I think they are shooting him when he tries to go quietly to Berlin, and I am frightened I should ask my mother, and perhaps she does not know and she will be so unhappy. And she writes me beautiful, beautiful letters, not always every day like sometimes. Sometimes a whole week she is not writing. And then again she is writing each day. Perhaps S.A. men are watching her; do you think so?"

The boy looked up. Mr. Emmanuel inclined his head. The tale continued.

"And then I am becoming ill after going in a stream in a cross-country run. And I have rheumatic fever. And I think I shall die if my mother is not sending me letters each day, though myself I am not writing, for I cannot hold the pencil. But the matron, she is writing for me, and sometimes I am putting a cross on the letter and then I have a relapse and am not putting a cross. And they read letters to me from my mother and I am not hearing them, but I am like seeing her and smelling her near my bed. So I am getting better and they are always reading me letters.

"And one day I understand all of a sudden it is not a new letter, but an old letter they are reading. Why shall they read an old letter and pretend it is arriving today? Why? I am not saying anything. But the day after tomorrow is another letter and they are reading it, because it is for medicine. And then I say—where is the envelope? What is the date? And nurse is going red and goes to matron and matron is so kind and at last she is telling me my mother is away perhaps on holiday, or perhaps she is hurting her hand. Soon she will write, certainly she will soon write. But she tells me no letter has been coming from my mother for two weeks. On eleventh March was the last letter from my mother. But I must be good, and not unhappy, matron says, and also Mr. Forsyte, the headmaster. I must get strong again. A letter will soon certainly come. Perhaps the next letter from my mother will say she is coming to England, to Greystones, to see me.

"So I am good and take all my food and medicine. Because I *know* my mother shall be writing soon. It *must* be. But March and April is going by, and June also. The London Committee is also writing to our apartment in Berlin, in the Motzstrasse, but it is no reply. And it is July, end of July. It is not one word from my mother. Oh, please, please, why is she not writing?"

Mr. Emmanuel was quite silent for half a minute. Then he took his handkerchief out of his pocket and wiped the tears from the boy's eyes.

"Hush, hush, Bruno," he said at length. "We shall find out. We shall write, to this one and to that one, and we shall find out. But you must not be so unhappy now. We shall play games and we shall have music and we shall walk in the Forest. And then there will be news." He got up from his chair and went and opened the cupboard where the gadgets had been stored. "Let me see now," he murmured, tugging at his beard. "Let me see." He surveyed in his mind, for it was too indistinct to see them, the chasers away of grief, the joy-bringers. The puzzles, it seemed to him, were a little finicky. The glass of ale, the mouse, were perhaps too hilarious. He remembered the solitaire board. "Do you play solitaire?" he asked hopefully.

"With cards?" asked Bruno.

"No, no!" He rummaged down in the cupboard and brought up the solitaire board in its case. "Look!" he said delightedly, and set it down on the bed. "You see? With alleys, like we call them. You put them out in these holes. But this one is empty, in the middle. You see? You jump over this way, you jump over that way, you take away what you jump over. You see? Then you jump, and you jump, and you jump, and take away, and take away, and take away. And you must leave it only one left, in the middle here. You see?"

"I see," said Bruno.

"Well, I try and you try. And the one who leaves fewest, he wins. It is not easy to leave only one—oh, no! We will put them out again, yes? That's right, Bruno. You start!"

Bruno started. He did not do badly. He left four. Mr. Emmanuel went after him. He left, to his chagrin, seven. He insisted on having another try, and did not do much better—six. He was quite convinced he would get the knack of it again if he tried a third time. He was engaged on his third effort when Rose knocked at the door. Getting no reply, she opened it. She saw the two heads bent close over the solitaire board, the grey-haired old man's, the chestnut-haired boy's. She stood for some moments and gazed down on them, without saying a word.

"Come along, you boys, now!" at last she called to them. "It's time for supper!" She turned away and mopped her eye.

V

With all these young people about, supper was rather a sketchy affair at Shipscar. Tonight it consisted chiefly of a huge tureen of chicken stew. You took a plate over to the tureen and helped yourself, or one of the boys helped you; they were very polite, if, on the whole, a little awkward. Sarah, the eldest Cooper girl, was out; she had cycled over to a house where the young men were older, and conversation was a little more fluent. Ailsa, the youngest girl, went to bed directly after supper. It had been a long day for a child of eleven. It was Mary, the middle girl, who had taken in hand the job of being assistant hostess. Seeing her mother and Mr. Emmanuel engaged in deep conversation, she set to work. She got Bruno and little Heinrich Levi, a dark little boy about the same age, down to a game of draughts. Another youth buried his nose immediately in a pocket game of chess he was playing with himself. The other three were apparently more men of the world. She got them to turn back the rugs, switched on some dance music, and went on to do a few solemn turns in and out of the furniture, herself and the youth Klaus Bieber, then herself and the fifth youth, a lanky tow-haired lad with a very aquiline nose.

"It is not very gay," murmured Rose to Mr. Emmanuel. "I know. But what can you do? Their minds are not with us. They're thinking of their mothers and their school-friends. One or two of them had girls already."

"Please, will you tell me about them? They cannot hear, I think, no?"

It was not likely they could hear. There was not only the dance music and the shuffling feet. The tow-haired lad was very talkative. There was also a shrill running commentary in German from Bruno's partner in the game of draughts.

"The one with Bruno is Heinrich Levi," Rose explained. "His people were very rich. They had a department store in Hamburg. They've got very little left now. They're still in Hamburg."

"He is on two sides Jewish, I think?"

"Yes. He and the big one, Klaus, are the only ones Jewish on both sides."

"That Klaus is so German," marvelled Mr. Emmanuel, "like Bismarck."

"But not so German as the tall one, dancing with Mary now, Siegfried Jacobson. You never met anything so German."

"With a nose like that?" Mr. Emmanuel was quite puzzled. "He is blond, yes—but a nose like that!"

"I think one grandfather was Jewish. He loathes him for it. I think he'd turn the old man's body out of its coffin and spit on it if he got the chance."

Mr. Emmanuel sighed. "Not a nice boy!"

Rose preferred not to commit herself.

"I wouldn't like to say that. But he treats poor Bruno rather badly—he and the little one playing draughts, Heinrich. That's why I keep Bruno with me as much as I can."

"I see." Mr. Emmanuel's eyes darkened. He was quiet for a little time, studying first the one boy, then the other. Then he continued. "And that nice-looking one? The quiet boy, playing chess?"

"That's Hugo, Hugo Baum. He's a Catholic. He goes to a Catholic school. He talks about becoming a priest. When he's not got the chess-board before him, he's reading some saint's life. A very religious boy."

"I see. A very religious boy, eh?" He suddenly felt a bit dizzy. He did not quite know where he was for a moment or two. It occurred to him rather frighteningly it was a long way from Magnolia Street, from the synagogue at the corner, from the Board of Guardians in the Begley Hill Road. He put his hand into his coat-pocket to take out a handkerchief and found it cluttered with the tricks and gadgets he had stuffed there the last moment before coming downstairs. The thought presented itself to him that for a young man who spends all his spare time reading the lives of saints, a synthetic ink-spot and a glass of ale that will not pour out might not be very absorbing pastimes.

He looked from that young man to Siegfried Jacobson, the tall blond quarter-Jew dancing with Mary; from Jacobson he looked to Bieber, then to the two boys playing draughts. They were German, not English. He understood the minds of English boys, whether Gentile or Jewish, almost equally well, for he had had many years of schooling on both pavements of Magnolia Street. These boys were alien. Even the two of them who were fully Jewish were not Jewish in the sense familiar to him, the warm vocal hand-clapping manner of Eastern Europe. They were all boys from the rich bourgeoisie, a higher social status than his own.

He felt helpless, useless, something of an interloper. Then it chanced his eyes travelled to the two youngsters bent over the draught-board. He saw that the dark little boy, Heinrich, was not studying the game at all. His mouth was a few inches from Bruno's face. He had suspended the high cricket-like chirp he had been emitting since the game began. He was whispering something, his eyes twinkling with fun and wickedness. The boy was was perhaps fourteen and a half years old, younger, if anything, than Bruno. Yet he looked at that moment like a bad old man of sixty.

"Es ist nicht wahr," he saw Bruno's lips shape. "It's not true! It's not true!" He did not raise his eyes from the board.

"Aber bestimmt!" the other insisted. "It's quite certain!"

"I take one, two," Bruno said, his king making two moves.

Heinrich dropped his eyes to the board, a happy smile on his face. The cricket-like chirp began again.

Mr. Emmanuel turned to Rose and took her hand and pressed it between his own.

"I am happy," he murmured, "you should let me come among these boys. Perhaps an old man can help too."

"But of course," said Rose. "They'll love you. It'll be marvellous for them. Tomorrow you must bring out some of those things you brought with you. But I want you to go to bed very soon now, Mr. Emmanuel. You've had a very long and tiring day."

"I have some things in my pocket here," said Mr. Emmanuel. "I shall show some now, yes?"

She was quite firm.

"Tomorrow," she said. "What use will you be unless you have a good night's rest?"

"Perhaps you're right," he admitted. He lingered five minutes, ten minutes. Rose went on contentedly with her crochet. The dance music went round and round. Klaus revolved with Mary like a performing bear. Hugo was rapt at his game. Heinrich and Bruno set out the draught pieces again. Mr. Emmanuel rose.

"Good night, everybody," he said. He felt a little lonely.

"Good night, Mr. Emmanuel," a polite chorus returned.

"Come now," said Rose. "I'll see you've got everything you want for the night. I'll be down in a minute, my dears."

"Please, thank you," muttered Mr. Emmanuel.

VI

Perhaps Mr. Emmanuel should not have discharged all at once all the bolts from his locker. If he had spread them out over the next few days, games in the morning or after lunch, jokes and tricks in the evening, they might have scored a more signal success. Or perhaps the mind of the German boy is not attuned to that sort of frivolity. The fact remains that his Pandora's box fell flat. Mr. Emmanuel, assisted by their hostess and the housemaid, laid the various objects down on the lawn after breakfast next morning, and the youths, on being summoned, came up respectfully enough.

When Mrs. Cooper explained that Mr. Emmanuel had brought them for their special delectation, they expressed their gratitude. They examined the exhibits with a seriousness more appropriate to geological specimens than to aids to more joyful living. They threw the rope quoits and struck at the anchored tennis-ball seriously, and with immediate efficiency. They mastered the tricks within a minute or two, and were entirely unamused by the jokes. In less than an hour Hugo Baum was back at his saint's life again, at the further end of the lawn; little Heinrich had torn the synthetic fly from its lump of sugar and removed the cork from the base of the glass of beer-coloured water; Klaus Bieber was on his stomach again, with his eye on the focusing-lens of his camera;

Siegfried Jacobson was expounding the glories of his Leader and the Third Reich to young Mary Cooper, and Bruno Rosenheim was away in the wood somewhere, making music on the mouth-organ. Sweet and sad the melody filtered down between the trunks of the oak-trees:

Es war einmal ein treuer Husar
Der liebt sein Mädchen ein ganzes Jahr,
Ein ganzes Jahr und noch viel mehr,
Die Liebe nimmt kein Ende mehr.

"I do not think they like my little playthings," murmured Mr. Emmanuel to Rose. They were sitting side by side in wicker chairs on the southward-facing veranda that ran along the sitting-room windows. His eyes were smarting a little. He felt unhappy, and a little humiliated.

"Poor boys," she breathed. "They're neither in Germany nor England. They're floundering in the North Sea! Hello!" she exclaimed suddenly. "Here's Bert!" She jumped out of her chair, ran over to the edge of the veranda, and picked up a spade that was lying as if left there for some definite purpose. She then walked several yards further into the grassy edge of the woodland, and turned up the soil for the space of several inches. Then she sat down again.

"Bert!" exclaimed Mr. Emmanuel, very puzzled, almost alarmed. "I see no Bert!" Really, living in the country had the most extraordinary effect on people, even sensible town-bred people like Rose.

"That's Bert!" Rose explained. She pointed to a leggy cock thrush that was reconnoitring the ground ten or twenty yards away. "Just be quiet one moment, will you? He doesn't know you yet." Mr. Emmanuel remained dumb. After a minute or two the thrush came over to the place where the soil had been turned up. He bent his head and a second or two later raised it again, with a fat worm wriggling in his beak. "There you are, see!" cried Rose triumphantly.

"Yes, I see," murmured Mr. Emmanuel.

"What were you saying?"

"I wasn't saying anything, was I?"

"You were going to say something."

Mr. Emmanuel thought. "You're quite right. I was, Rose!"

"Yes?"

"You said something last night. About that blond boy with the big nose."

"Siegfried Jacobson. Yes?"

"And the other one, the very Jewish-looking one, Heinrich. You said they treat Bruno badly. You said that's why you keep him with you as much as you can."

"That's perfectly true."

"I saw Heinrich saying something to Bruno last night while they were playing draughts. It made Bruno a big pain. What was he saying?"

"I'll tell you. It's all very sad."

"I want to know, please."

"They're both tragic boys, Heinrich and Siegfried, just as much as Bruno. That's why it's so difficult. One has to be equally kind to them all. First the little one, Heinrich. His father was a rich man in Hamburg, but it seems he paid out a lot of money to the friends of one of the wrong parties. They called for him one night and dragged him out of bed. They beat him up and sent him back more dead than alive. But they hadn't finished with him. Six months later they got at him again. He was carried off to a concentration camp and was shot while trying to escape. That's what they called it. Are you listening?"

Mr. Emmanuel's hand covered his eyes. His head had fallen forward. It seemed almost as if he had fallen asleep.

"I am listening," he said, in a voice that seemed to come from a long way off.

"They sent back his ashes in an urn with a bill for expenses. That happened last year."

"And the boy?"

"The boy knew all about it. It's made a devil of him. He may have been a bit of a devil to begin with."

"But what"—Mr. Emmanuel had not removed his hand from his eyes—"what has he got against Bruno?"

"That's how he gets his own back. He's suffered. He wants someone else to suffer."

"What does he do?"

"He talks to him about his mother. He says she's alive. Oh, yes, he's sure she's alive. The same sort of thing happened to his father as is now happening to Bruno's mother. They didn't hear from him, either, for months. They were beating him up, too, with rubber truncheons and pieces of lead piping. That's why *he* couldn't write. You see?"

"I see. Poor little fellow! Both of them poor little fellows. Heinrich! Bruno! It is like a knife in my heart here! How do you know all this, Rose? Does Bruno tell you?"

"No. Bruno has said nothing. I got a few details from the people in London, but I hear about it from Klaus chiefly. There have been several fights between Klaus and Siegfried, I gather. All this is a bit of a responsibility, you know."

"What's wrong with that one? His father is also in a concentration camp?"

"No. I think his people are fairly all right. It's something else with him. He's a Nazi. He'd have given his right arm if they'd have let him join the Hitler Youth Movement. I think for a long time he genuinely knew nothing about the Jewish grandfather. It had been kept a deadly secret. All his family were fierce anti-Semites. But his nose and his name prevented him from getting anywhere. And now that he knows about it, the drop of Jewish blood in his veins is like a poison."

"So he also gets his own back from Bruno. In the same way like the other boy?"

"In the same way. I don't know what to do. Klaus has been very helpful, you know. He's a nice lad, even if he's a bit pompous and Prussian. So's Hugo, whenever he comes down to earth. I've sometimes thought I ought to ask the people in London to take Siegfried and Heinrich back. Or if not them, Bruno. But where would they go to? Some drab boarding house in West Hampstead or Brondesbury. They're happy enough here, I think, as happy as they can be."

"Do not send them back," murmured Mr. Emmanuel.

"I wouldn't dream of it when it came to the point," said Rose.

"I will see they are not together. I will be with Bruno. I think it will not hurt him in the heart so much when he talks about his mother and his home, and this thing, and that thing. I will go now for a walk in the trees. Perhaps by accident I will meet him."

VII

By the time a couple of days had passed, Mr. Emmanuel realized that, so far as the four other German boys were concerned, he hardly existed. He was to them nothing more than a guest of Mrs. Cooper's, like themselves—which, in a sense, was true. Klaus Bieber was hoping to go into a film studio, and most of his time was devoted to his camera and his lenses and his exposure-meter. It was not at all easy to break down the reserve of Hugo Baum, and Mr. Emmanuel was not encouraged to. The boy had inner resources which kept him secure. Siegfried Jacobson, the Nazi enthusiast, embarrassed him. The youth was too well bred to be actually rude to a fellow-guest, but it was evident he did not set any store by the good opinions of a slightly shabby Jew from a working-class street somewhere in the northern wilds.

There were moments when Mr. Emmanuel felt that this was much the most tragic case among these boys. The others knew of their exclusion, and with varying degrees of bitterness accepted it. Somehow, in the course of time, if they lived long enough, they would come to terms with their fate. Siegfried Jacobson never would. Excluded from the world that had won his blazing devotion, he loathed the world he was relegated to. He was young, but it did not seem any life could be long enough to resolve his dreadful dilemma.

Mr. Emmanuel persisted longer with Heinrich Levi than with any of these. It was impossible not to be intensely sorry for the boy, and Heinrich actually seemed friendily disposed. He felt it might do some good if he made a party of three out of it now and again, himself and Bruno and Heinrich. Perhaps that might help to purge some of the mischief out of Heinrich's system. It was Rose herself who requested him a day or two later not to go out of his way to have any dealings with Heinrich. As she spoke, her face burned and her eyes sparkled angrily. He guessed that the boy had been fooling him in some odious way. He sighed, and shrugged his shoulders, and left it at that.

During the rest of the time the German boys were at Shipscar, Mr. Emmanuel and Bruno were never far from each other. They sat by each other at meal times and kept side by side in the picnic excursions to heath and forest. Above all when letters were handed out, Mr. Emmanuel saw to it he was close at hand—letters for Jacobson, Bieber, Levi, Baum, letters for Rose, letters for himself, no letters for Bruno Rosenheim.

"You must have patience," Mr. Emmanuel murmured. "If not tomorrow, then the day after. Be a brave boy, Bruno."

Bruno turned away his hurt and puzzled eyes.

"Yes, tomorrow!" he whispered. "Perhaps tomorrow."

On the days when Mary Cooper senior did not bring her nephew to present his compliments to his mother, Bruno and Mr. Emmanuel often went over to Wain Cottage—it was not too much for the old man if he walked one way and got a lift the other. And while the two boys occupied themselves on the lawn with dogs and bricks under the watchful eye of the elders, the elders talked, or carefully did not talk, about old times in Magnolia Street, faces long gone, and troubles long blown over.

Bruno was not unhappy there at Wain Cottage, with Dick and the dogs and the old people, and macaroons for tea, and potato pikelets. He was taken out of himself.

But Mr. Emmanuel did not need long to realize that Bruno was furthest from unhappiness when he was most taken back into himself, into the life he had known before his world broke into fragments about his head.

So he let the boy talk, as they went walking on the common, with the warm wind tugging the clumps of heather; or wandered down the paths of the forest, with the plumed bracken on either hand splashed over with gold and the butterflies heeling over between sunlight and shadow. It was chiefly of Haus Anna the boy talked, the bungalow in Lübbenau, summer holidays in Lübbenau, though the family had lived for most of the year in an apartment in the Motzstrasse, in West Berlin. The boy left him with an extraordinarily vivid impression of the place, as vivid as if he had himself spent summer upon summer there.

The red-tiled roof projected a great many feet beyond the walls. The tiles ran up to each other prettily, like little waves on a beach. The bungalow was surrounded on all sides by a deep edge of flat red tiles. There was a portico in front; on both sides you stepped straight out through latticed French windows. On the left there were two forms with a table between them, all of which were fixtures. They would usually eat there, when they did not take their meals in the punt with them. On that same side there was a row of pear trees, and when the petals fell they got into your hair and you looked like the Christmas Man. At the back the ground went down to one of the channels of the Spree—there were hundreds and hundreds in those parts.

They had a punt moored under a weeping willow. You steered it with a thing that was not a pole and not an oar. They would be in the punt sometimes all day, in and out of the water, or sunning themselves in clear spaces. They had a stove with them, and they would cook dinner on the bank, and Father would fry steaks and Mother would make omelets; she made omelets like feathers, better than anyone in all the world; and there would be several sorts of cake—he was always a great one for pastry—*Käsekuchen* and *Streuselkuchen* and *Nusstorte*. But often he would spend the whole day on land instead, at Fritschke's mill, or at one of the farms, for the farmers were such friendly people. He loved going into the barns and stables, and talking to the horses and cows and brushing the flies from their faces. Or he would help bring in the hay, and he would be so thirsty, and Father would send drinks out to the haymakers, beer for them and for him a glass of *süsser Most,* sweet cider. And in the night-time Mother would sing at the little standing-up piano—they had a big one in the Motzstrasse—and the lamplight falling on her hair as she sang made her so beautiful he would be frightened, for fear she was not after all human, and one moment she would be there and the moment after there no longer.

But old Jo was there. He was always there. There was a good deal in Bruno's memories regarding Jo; he figured second only to Frau Rosenheim herself. He was a valorous white rabbit, a Kosciuszko among rabbits, a Don John of Austria. A seasoned traveller, too, the way he travelled about from Berlin to Lübbenau, and back again to Berlin. In the Motzstrasse they used to keep his hutch on a balcony they had at the back of the apartment, overlooking the interior courtyard. But nothing would prevent him from walking into the sitting-room, large as life, whenever he felt like a little company. You could always tell, however, when holiday-time got round, for

Jo would get restless and start drubbing with his hind legs on the floor as if it were a drum. On the journey between Berlin and Lübbenau he would settle down snug in his hutch like a king in his coach. He preferred Lübbenau, of course; the rest of the year was just intervals between Lübbenau. So it was for Bruno, too, in a manner of speaking. He used to dig deep holes for himself, this Jo, in the roots of the trees and alongside the fences. But you wouldn't expect a poor rabbit not to try to make himself comfortable, would you?

Oh, a great fellow this Jo was; one ear up he had and one ear down, and a tiny plumed puff of a tail, and he had black eyebrows and big white whiskers and round, brown eyes with blue-grey pupils. His hind legs were like sledge-hammers—you should see him careering upstairs—and claws that turned round and grew backwards, so you had to cut them with Father's razor-blades; even so he could dig up a hole in the garden like a sand-pit. He was as good as gold, really, but he could not be trusted with carrots, though he liked anything crisp, he would eat greenstuff all day, and he was very naughty with sweet pea shoots and shoots of young raspberry.

A local dog attached himself to them once at Haus Anna; his name was Fips; and it was grand to see how Jo would chase poor Fips round and round, and if Fips stopped to put up a fight, Jo would be round with his teeth in his hind legs quick as a flash. He could not abide cats, either; he would chase them off and they would run for their lives, except for the cat from the next garden; they were great friends, and it was pretty to see them drinking together from the same bowl. Then he would wash himself, as if he were just another cat, turning his head to lick the back of his neck; or, lifting his paw to his mouth, sometimes his leg stuck up straight behind his ear like a gun. Oh, but prettiest of all was to see my mother with a leaf of lettuce between a thumb and two fingers, and Jo nibbling closer and closer till he got down to Mamma's finger-nails, and he would stop then, as if he must not hurt her.

I hope he is well, Mr. Emmanuel. I hope they are looking after him at Lübbenau, whoever has our bungalow now. No one can wish to do him harm.

No one *could* do him harm, Bruno. Is he not like a little lion? Have you got your *Mundharmonika* with you? Play me again that Pim-pam-pam. What? It is not Pim-pam-pam? How do you say it? Pim-pam . . . No, I cannot. Play it for me again, Bruno.

So they walked through the English forest, by brakes of harebell and foxglove and tall hemp agrimony, the old man and the small boy, to the wild and silly and magic melody:

Die geliebte Pimpanulla
Schreit einmal Hula! Hula!
Und flugs ist sie im Walde
Und hakt den Schnabel ein.
Hula! Hula! Hula!
Sie hakt den Schnabel ein.

"Pim-pam . . . pim-pam . . ." Mr. Emmanuel tried again. "No, I cannot say it. It cracks my teeth."

Now and again Mr. Emmanuel talked too; not for the reason that he was by nature a loquacious person, but because he thought it wise not to let the boy relapse into the moodiness that sometimes befell him, even within a few moments of a flare of gaiety. Mr. Emmanuel's life had been Doomington, the Board of Guardians, the two pavements of Magnolia Street. But it was not of these things that he talked. He knew they would be to Bruno without meaning and without colour, like a foreign language spoken by dull people. Finding his gaze blocked as he looked into the past, he let his eyes rest on the future and, seeing Palestine there, talked of Palestine. He was making the journey, not because Zion was a mainspring of his heart, but because he seemed to have come to a dead end in Doomington, and one of his two surviving sons was out in Palestine and had called him over. He had read a good deal about the country, both the new towns there and the new colonies, but he had rather a hazy idea of it all. The pictures he painted for Bruno's edification were incorrect, but they were enthusiastic, and for two reasons: he could not talk for long about anything without getting enthusiastic about it, and there was no hope of cozening Bruno out of his unhappiness with anything but bright colours and gay images.

The whole of Palestine in Mr. Emmanuel's account, from Lebanon to Sinai, was one Vale of Sharon; orange groves massed their bronze lamps over all the uplands of Judea and Galilee; in the Vale of Esdraelon chickens laid eggs as prodigally as cows gave milk; picturesque Arabs in flying head-dresses performed equestrian feats worthy of Hagenbeck's in the environs of their villages; Dizingoff's Tel Aviv was a city of enchantment like Harun al Rashid's Baghdad. The result of all that was that he began to discover in himself a certain excitement with respect to his migration to Palestine that he had not been conscious of before.

"And when you are grown up a bit," he added, "maybe

you also will come over to Palestine, Bruno, on a visit. And you will stay in my son's colony; Ain Charod, they call it. My son has a quarter of a house there, with his wife and his children, God bless them, and it will be his father there also, and what a welcome it will be for you, Bruno, oi, what a welcome! And perhaps you would like to milk the cows there, yes? My son will let you. He is the *Sar-Hachalav* there, the big one for the milk. Perhaps even there will be a rabbit like Jo. Do you think there are no rabbits in Palestine?"

The boy sighed.

"There is only one Jo," he murmured. "I wonder where Jo is now. I hope they are not forgetting to cut his claws when they are growing backward."

Mr. Emmanuel studied the boy through narrowed eyes. Nothing meant anything to him, he saw, nothing that was not his mother or was not Germany. They were, in fact, the same thing. He might as well have talked of Doomington or China as of Palestine. He might as well have read out a tale from a story-book.

"Perhaps tomorrow," he said to himself, "Rose will be getting another letter from the Committee in London. There may be something we can tell him he should have a little comfort. Please God!"

Mr. Emmanuel had wasted no time in fulfilling the promise he had made to Bruno within a couple of hours after their first meeting. The very next day he addressed a letter to the Committee in London that had in hand the affairs of the German refugee boys in London. The letter, endorsed by Rose, and stating the official position he had till lately occupied in communal affairs in Doomington, asked for all the information they had it in their power to give in the matter of Frau Rosenheim, the mother of the boy Bruno.

The reply was frank and friendly. The Secretary stated that her Committee was happy to note Mr. Emmanuel's interest in Bruno. They regretted they could give no information at all respecting the present whereabouts of Frau Rosenheim. The last letter dispatched by her to either themselves or her son had been dated March 11. Since then they had written to her repeatedly at her address in the Motzstrasse in Berlin, but there had been no reply of any sort. A disturbing element in the situation was the fact that not one of their letters had been returned. Aware of the extreme unhappiness of young Bruno, they had addressed an inquiry to the offices of the Jewish Community in Berlin, though this would in any case have been done as a matter of routine.

After a long delay, a reply had been received to the effect that inquiries had been made in Berlin along the lines indicated, and it was regretted that no information whatsoever could be supplied. The tone of the letter, as well as its contents, was very discouraging. The Committee had not thought it wise to conduct any further researches into the matter. However, if fresh facts from any source should come to light, they would be pleased to communicate with Mrs. Cooper, who had taken so warm an interest in these unfortunate boys. Doubtless Mrs. Cooper would keep Mr. Emmanuel informed. Doubtless, too, she had let him know all that was known about Bruno's father, regarding whom only one fact was certain—that he was dead. Since October of the previous year, it was desired to add, the Committee had undertaken complete responsibility for Bruno's welfare. The Secretary begged to remain his sincerely.

No further letter from the Committee on the subject of Frau Rosenheim came to either Rose or Mr. Emmanuel during his stay at Shipscar. The idea occurred to him more than once that it might be of some use to address to the Community offices in Berlin a more urgent and personal letter than perhaps had so far been sent them. But he dismissed it. It seemed hardly wise or decent to go over the heads of the Committee in that fashion. There was nothing to be done or said, nothing to tell Bruno, that might be a crumb of comfort for him. So a fortnight went by, at Shipscar and Wain Cottage, in heath and forest, with mouth-organ and solitaire board. The boy did not lack courage, the old man did not lack tenderness. They had value for each other.

Then, on the morning of Monday, the nineteenth of August, two communications reached Rose. One was a wire from her husband John, announcing that his ship had arrived at Southampton. Would Rose and the girls go down and pick him up that evening at five o'clock at the company's offices?

The second was a note from the Refugee Committee. It stated that they had been able to arrange to send the greater part of the boys under their care to several holiday camps throughout the southern counties. They wished to express their profound gratitude to Mrs. Cooper for having given such generous hospitality over so long a period to no less than five boys. They had received from all of them glowing accounts of the marvellous time they had had. None the less, the Committee had felt it to be a real imposition, and they were pleased to be able to transfer the burden of hospitality elsewhere.

One camp, on the south coast near Eastbourne, had

volunteered to take on three boys for the remainder of their holidays. This was run by Father Wedlake, a parish priest from Poplar. Another camp, run by a Colonel Gillespie near Margate, would take on the two remaining boys. If Mrs. Cooper would be so kind as to divide up the group in the way she thought would be happiest for the boys, the Committee would be most grateful. There followed various details regarding equipment, times of trains, and renewed assurances of gratitude.

Out on the veranda Rose and Mr. Emmanuel discussed the two communications. The young people were scattered up and about the place. Bruno was not far off, his nose in a picture-book.

"I think he's two days ahead of time," said Rose. She was talking of John, her husband. "Of course, there's not much fruit to bring back from South Africa this time of year."

"It will be such a pleasure to see him!" said Mr. Emmanuel. "Such a pleasure! We will talk about old times! I wonder if he remembers. He should have given away once a gold watch—"

"A gold watch?" asked Rose vaguely.

"Let be! Let be!" Mr. Emmanuel dismissed the matter. "It is good I shall see him before I go back to Doomington!"

"Before you go back to Doomington? But you mustn't talk of going *back* yet! You've only just come!"

"You don't remember why I came, Rose? Now that the boys are going away, what for should I stay? You have had enough already with visitors!" There was a certain sadness in his voice. He was aware that his being there had made exactly no difference to most of those boys.

Had he, after all, let Rose Cooper down? There was, however, Bruno. Yes, certainly, there was Bruno.

"But boys or no boys—" she began. Then she stopped. She did not want him to suspect the degree to which the boys had been a pretext. "John would be furious," she continued, "if you ran off merely because he came home."

"They will be happy in those camps, yes?" His mind was off on the tack of the boys. "The other boys will not make a fun of them because they do not talk like we do?"

"You mustn't worry, dear Mr. Emmanuel. The Committee will have made quite sure they'll be properly looked after. I hate losing them, but we've got to think of it from the boys' point of view, haven't we? It'll be much more exciting for them, with games and sea-bathing and that sort of thing."

"You're right, Rose."

"We have to divide them up, Mr. Emmanuel. Three and two. How would you do it?"

"Where Bruno is, neither Jacobson nor Levi," said Mr. Emmanuel sombrely.

"Yes, I agree with you. Then it's Klaus, Hugo, and Bruno at Roman's Bight, the two others at Margate. Oh, but look! You know what Siegfried is. How will that be for little Heinrich?"

"He can give as good like he gets," returned Mr. Emmanuel shortly.

"You know," said Rose, "it's a good thing the letter came today, the same time as John's wire."

"Why do you say that?"

"Of course I never asked John about putting up these boys. There wasn't a chance, was there? Not that he'd have objected for one moment, the darling."

"Why do you say it is a good thing?"

"I don't know. I'm probably doing him an injustice. But the fact is—he has such a completely *masculine* time on board . . . you know what I mean? If it was five little refugee *girls* now. No. That's not fair!" She turned eastward and north towards Southampton, as if she were apologizing to John somewhere across there in the docks or the shipping offices.

"Of course, my dear," Mr. Emmanuel protested gently. "I understand. It will be nice for him when he comes back he should be alone with his wife and his daughters! Who would not, with such a wife and such daughters!"

"And such a son!" she reproved him.

"And such a son!" he corrected himself. "You should forgive me. I forgot!"

"You're not the only one who forgets!" she said a little tartly. Mr. Emmanuel looked up. "I'm sorry!" Rose was muttering. Her cheeks were as red as beetroot. "I don't know what's the matter with me today! The things I'm saying!"

Mr. Emmanuel regarded her with fond eyes.

"Underneath you're a bit excited, Rose. Isn't it only natural? Isn't he coming back today?"

"Oh, how right you are!" she exclaimed impulsively. "He's only been away for six weeks and it feels like six years! I'm an old woman with four children——"

"Tscha! Tscha!"

"—and each time he comes back I'm as excited as I used to be, oh, hundreds of years ago, when I was a little girl in Doomington!"

"God bless you!" murmured Mr. Emmanuel. He fumbled in his breast-pocket for his handkerchief. There was a mist over his eyes, and in that mist he saw the blurred lineaments of a picture; he saw a hearth in a Magnolia Street kitchen, but no fire burned in it; he saw a table laid for one, and strange hands had laid it; he saw a spectacle-case on a sewing-machine, but no hands extracted those spectacles from their case any more.

"Oh, it was so funny!" Rose was saying. "Do you know, when he came back from sea, we used to hide in a café miles away on the other side of Doomington, in case anybody from Magnolia Street should see us!"

"Yes, yes. I think it was a talk once! How they used to chatter, those women! They have other things to talk about nowadays!"

"They don't have to go till Wednesday," said Rose. "Those boys, I mean!" The anecdotal mood had passed. She was suddenly practical again. "We'll have to get another car for the luggage. Major Townley might give us a hand. He's such a darling! Or we can send it on in advance by the carrier. Mr. Emmanuel! What are you looking so depressed about?"

"Depressed? Such nonsense!"

"Of course! What an old gasbag I am! You'll miss little Bruno frightfully, won't you? How stupid of me!"

"I was not thinking of myself. Have I not a lot of preparations to make? Is it round the corner, Palestine? I was thinking of Bruno. He is a little boy; you can hurt him so easy like you hurt a small kitten. He will be happy, you think, in a camp? A lot of boys playing jokes in tents and running about like lions and tigers?"

Rose looked concerned.

"You're right. He's a delicate little chap. I wonder whether it wouldn't be too much for him?" She stopped and pursed her lips. Then an idea struck her. "Why on earth shouldn't he stay out his holidays here? Why on earth shouldn't he? I'll fix it up with John today. Then I'll write to the Committee. What do you think of that, Mr. Emmanuel?" She did not give him time for a reply. "Oh, good Lord!" she exclaimed, rising from her chair. "I'll have to go and get that boy's bed out of his den! Then I must run over and pick Dick up. I don't know what John would say if he knew he was at Mary's all this time! You go and play with Bruno, Mr. Emmanuel!" she requested, and disappeared into the house.

Mr. Emmanuel sat there a little glumly, his neck tugging on its tendons.

"I know what he will say about Bruno," he muttered, "that strong man. A boy should learn to stand on his own legs. A boy should go into the world, he should knock off the rough corners. Perhaps also he is right. Who knows?"

VIII

The door seemed to open of itself as in the smack of a wind from the sea.

"Here's Daddy!" cried Dick Cooper excitedly, appearing in the doorway. Then he disappeared. Then John Cooper appeared there, flanked by the four women, Rose, Sarah, Mary, Ailsa, all clinging to him as if they grew on his clothes. He was very blunt, broad-shouldered, sea-scarred—altogether rather frightening. So were his eyebrows, so was the hand-grip, so was everything about him but the voice, which was quite subdued and even.

"Glad to see you again, Mr. Emmanuel, after all these years!"

"How are you, Captain Cooper? Such a pleasure!"

quavered Mr. Emmanuel. His hand dropped limply to his side. Did that Goliath of a man once stretch himself out in a Magnolia Street bedroom? It was not possible.

"Where are those boys now?" asked John. "Come on! Let's have a look at 'em!"

"They're up and around," said Rose. "I'll call them!"

They were summoned and looked over. There was something a little perfunctory about the inspection, as if it were a parade of deck-hands. But again the voice belied the manner. The voice was thoroughly warm and hospitable, though not many words were wasted.

"Hope you've been comfortable, boys! Sorry I'm going to see so little of you! Perhaps I'll see a bit more of you another holiday!"

The short phrases, the air of authority, brought out all the Prussian in his guests. The answering salutation was like a movement in a drill-hall.

John Cooper's eyebrows lifted, and declined at once.

"See you soon, boys! Must go and have a wash! Don't go, Mr. Emmanuel! We'll have a drink when I come down!"

The inference was, if Mr. Emmanuel was not to go, the others might. They hung about uncertainly for a moment or two, then they went, Klaus shepherding them.

John Cooper left the room, carrying his load of women. Mr. Emmanuel sat down, feeling a little weak at the knees.

"He will have to go, my little Bruno," he murmured. "Of course he will have to go."

It was all hands on deck for dinner that evening. John liked a good lay-out when he got back. His sister Mary came in for dinner too, accompanied by the deplorable

Tessa. It would really have been a little difficult if the boys themselves had not given a hand. Everything went well, excepting for the sweet—it was a sort of pineapple pudding with whipped cream.

"Good God!" the captain exploded. "Pineapple again! The whole ship's been stinking with pineapples!"

The pudding was quickly spirited out of the way. A great lump of Stilton was put into its place.

"That's fine!" approved the captain. He cut off a large wedge with his knife. "Here, you!" he exclaimed, handing it to the boy who happened to be nearest to him. "Take this! It beats all that German junk!"

The boy happened to be Siegfried Jacobson. It might as well have been Klaus or Heinrich or Hugo or Bruno. It was clear to Mr. Emmanuel that the five boys were just as indistinguishable to John as five Chinese coolies. But it happened to be Siegfried Jacobson. The youth blushed to the ears.

"Perhaps it is not a bad thing," mused Mr. Emmanuel, "the boys are going. There might be troubles!"

The boys went to bed earlier that evening than usual. It was Klaus, tactful if ponderous, who seemed to be ushering them away, though all of them might have been feeling that the minds of the Cooper women were not quite with them for the time being. Everything was set as for a family party. Sarah, the eldest girl, seemed to be the silliest of the Cooper women in regard to her father. She sat on a tuffet, with her mouth slightly open, and just stared at him. She had perhaps inherited more than her sisters, if it was not too early to judge, her father's devouring interest in the opposite sex. This being the first night after his father's homecoming, Dick was still up, though it was hours after his bed-time. The elder Mary Cooper was staying the night in this astonishingly elastic house, which seemed to offer more room the more demands for room were made upon it.

Mr. Emmanuel was at least as delicate and tactful a person as Klaus Bieber. He thought he ought, perhaps, to have a headache.

"Excuse me, Rose," he murmured. "Will it be rude if I go soon to bed? It feels a bit like one of my headaches is coming."

"Oh, Mr. Emmanuel," exclaimed Rose, very concerned. "What a shame! We're too noisy for you! Isn't it a shame, John! Mr. Emmanuel's got a headache coming on! He thinks he ought to go to bed! We *were* looking forward to a good old pow-wow!"

"I'm sorry, Mr. Emmanuel! Tough luck! It *is* a bit noisy, isn't it, after the desert silence of Doomington! I wanted to ask you all sorts of questions. What's happened to that juicy wench? You remember? Came back from America some years ago, up to the neck in diamonds? Well, never mind, that'll keep!"

"It will be time yet for nice long talks!" Mr. Emmanuel murmured.

"But look! Just before you go! I wanted to have a word with you about that kid!"

"Which one, please?"

"The poor little devil who's in such a state about his mother. Rose was telling me. Which one was it? I didn't get them straight."

"Bruno!" the girls said. "The one with the nice complexion and wavy hair."

"He was sitting between me and Miss Cooper," Mr. Emmanuel explained.

"Oh, yes, I think I remember. Rose has told me how nicely you've been looking after him. Good work!"

Mr. Emmanuel shrugged his shoulders.

"A poor little orphan! Who should help it?"

"There was some idea about keeping him back after the others leave?" John continued. "That's so, isn't it?"

Mr. Emmanuel looked nervously from John to Rose and back again.

"We thought maybe—" he began again.

"Wouldn't do!" said John. "Don't think I want to get rid of the kid! Not for one moment!" He was obviously entirely genuine about that. "But it wouldn't do! Oughtn't to make exceptions. Cigarette? Might help to clear your head! You don't mind my pipe?"

"Please!"

"Anybody else? No? All right! Invited to camp, eh? Fellow called Father what, Rose? Oh, yes, Wedlake! Good fellows, these priests! Knew the hell of a fine fellow in Tampico. Once, when a whole boat-load of our fellows got jugged . . ." Then he stopped and changed the subject hurriedly. It did not seem quite the right type of family anecdote. "Camp, you said. It'll do the kid a world of good! Take him out of himself! Knock the rough corners off him!" He sucked the draught down his pipe-stem. "A kid should learn to stand on his own legs! Shouldn't he, Mary?" He turned with a certain grimness to his sister.

"Of course!" she replied, without expression.

"Well, then!" John concluded. Clearly the matter was to be regarded as settled. "Sorry about that headache! Take a blow on deck, won't you, before turning in?"

"Good night, all!" Mr. Emmanuel said meekly.

"I'm going to see you're all right," said Rose.

"Good night, Mr. Emmanuel! Good night! Good night!" the chorus followed him.

IX

The acquiescence with which the German boys heard that they were to move on to a holiday camp in a couple of days was a little distressing to Mr. Emmanuel. They all made the polite remarks which more or less well-bred boys might be expected to make in such circumstances. What a pity it was! They were enjoying themselves so much in Shipscar! How much they hoped they might be allowed to come again some time! Yet it was obvious they knew that whatever they felt was quite irrelevant. They had got into the habit of being forwarded from one place to another like parcels, with just a change of labels.

As for Bruno, he seemed quite unperturbed, though it was clear to him, as to the others, that the boys with whom they were going to spend the next fortnight were going to be a tough lot on the whole. Both Rose and Mr. Emmanuel felt a bit silly about the anxiety they had expressed to each other. Bruno might be, in fact he was, a sensitive lad, but the idea of roughing it with a lot of hard-boiled youngsters from the London slums did not make him turn a hair.

On the contrary, as those two days went by, it seemed to Mr. Emmanuel that the boy was attaining a sort of serenity he had not hitherto shown. He did not fail to ask each morning whether the dreamt-of letter from Germany had arrived, but he asked almost mechanically, with almost no pain in his face or voice.

Perhaps it is possible, after all, mused Mr. Emmanuel,

you are a bit foolish, Isaac Emmanuel. You are an old man, no? How shall you expect to understand the way the mind from a little boy works? He is glad to get away from those two boys, Siegfried and Heinrich; that is only natural. Perhaps he is also glad to get away from an old man and a lot of women? Well, what a good thing it is, thank God! Are you a little bit disappointed, just a little bit, Isaac, that he should be glad like that? I am ashamed of you, Isaac. You have a son, a painter. Years go by and you don't get one word from him. Yet it hurts you a strange boy should forget you in half an hour like you were an old newspaper. What? He should not look so much like your little David, peace be upon him? Do not make a fool with yourself, Isaac Emmanuel. It would be the same thing he should look like Little Red Riding Hood. You see? Captain Cooper was right. Already it is taking him out from himself. Thank God, you should say. He will play games, it will be sing-songs round a camp-fire, it is near the sea, he will go bathing in it. . . .

Apparently it was somewhat along the same lines that Bruno's mind was working too.

"So it is near the sea, Mr. Emmanuel, where it shall be our camp? Oh, that will be so nice! We were not often going to the sea, my mother and my father and I. We were going to Lübbenau. But one year some friends took our bungalow and we were going to Föhr. You are not knowing Föhr, Mr. Emmanuel? No, you are never travelling to Germany, I am forgetting. Oh, it is in Föhr so nice. It is an island in the North Sea, and it is white sands like snow, and it is some pine trees. Is Roman's Bight being like Föhr? We had *Strandkörbe* in Föhr. Do you know what a *Strandkorb* is? It is a big beach basket to sit down, and it is like a roof coming overhead. And I am swimming in the sea, and I am coming out again, and my father is drying me and mother is wrapping me round in a dressing-gown towel and we are sitting together in the *Strandkorb* and she is sitting with arms around me and it is being so happy. . . ." The boy's eyes clouded over with a reminiscent haze. His voice was more plaintive than it had been, when he spoke again.

"Do you think there are *Strandkörbe* in Roman's Bight?"

Mr. Emmanuel raised his hands.

"In Blackpool and Southport it is not so. I only know Blackpool and Southport. But who knows? Perhaps it is another fashion in seaside places by Eastbourne?"

But Bruno paid no attention to the reply.

"And perhaps they will let me play my *Mundharmonika* by the camp-fire? Do you think so, Mr. Emmanuel?"

"I am sure they will ask you to play your *Mundharmonika*. I am sure Father Wedlake is a very nice gentleman, otherwise the Committee would not send you to him, and Klaus also, and Hugo. You must play for them '*Die geliebte Pimpanulla*'! You see, I have got it right this time!"

"Certainly I will. It is a good song for the camp-fire. *Hula! Hula!* It will be like in the Spreewald, all the boys singing together, and the echo is coming back through the pine trees!"

"I wish," murmured Mr. Emmanuel, "I should be there to hear you!"

"Oh, yes! Please! Please!" cried Bruno enthusiastically, seizing Mr. Emmanuel's hand. "You must try to come to camp one day! Will you not please try to come?"

Mr. Emmanuel blushed with pleasure.

"I—I don't know," he protested. "I am busy. You think it is like going to Liverpool, going to Palestine?"

"It will be so glad for Klaus," urged Bruno earnestly. "Also for Hugo."

"Perhaps—who knows?" Mr. Emmanuel temporized. "I have in any case to go back through London. Perhaps for one day I might go. In Palestine it will be a long way away."

"Perhaps I am going to see you also in Palestine. Perhaps—who knows?" the boy said, echoing the old man's phrase.

X

The original idea had been that Mr. Emmanuel should stay at Shipscar till a day or two after the boys were safely off the premises. Perhaps even a day or two longer. Then he would have to go back to Doomington, to see to the various important affairs that awaited his attention before he turned his mind to the preparations for the Palestine journey. What these important affairs were was not quite plain, and of course Rose did not question him. She realized he was the sort of person who would be quite lost if he did not himself believe, and have others believe, that he was the centre of important affairs.

Now that the boys were leaving a fortnight earlier than had been intended, it was arranged that, as a concession to these important affairs, he should curtail his visit by a week or so. That would give the opportunity for the payment of ample and uninterrupted tribute to old times. It would also mean that the sailor would have his family all to himself during the following week, before he went to sea again.

The boys left with expressions of deep gratitude. There was even a little excitement in their demeanour.

"Good-bye, Bruno," said Mr. Emmanuel, as he walked along the station platform at Salisbury, with Bruno's hand tightly holding his. "Perhaps you will write me once, if I cannot get down to Roman's Bight?" He wanted to try to suggest once more to the boy that if ever anything should arise that he might do, in the matter of his mother and her whereabouts, he would do it. Yet what could he do? he asked himself. What had official agencies been able to do? And as for the boy himself, somehow, for some mysterious reason, the pain was dulled in him. Wasn't it better to let things rest so?

"No, please, Mr. Emmanuel," insisted Bruno urgently. "When you are going back through London, you shall come to camp also. Please, is that *frech?*" he asked plaintively. "Is that impertinent?"

"No," said Mr. Emmanuel, and looked away sharply.

"In here, please, porter!" Rose pointed out. "In you get, boys!"

The porter unleashed the three suitcases from his straps and lifted them onto the rack. One was considerably heavier than the others. This was Bruno's. It contained a good many of the objects that had made Mr. Emmanuel's suitcase so heavy on his original journey to Salisbury.

"Bit 'eavy, this one!" the porter exclaimed jovially. "Bit of a dead body, eh?" It seemed to be the same porter who had, a fortnight ago, made the same jovial remark regarding Mr. Emmanuel's suitcase. Once again, as the suitcase was upended, the mechanism in a hidden cylinder turned over, and a plaintive mooing filled the air.

"You don't catch me again on that lark!" he said, and laughed uproariously. Everybody else laughed, including the solemn Klaus. As the train went out, the three boys were still smiling.

"Thank you, thank you, Mrs. Cooper!" they called.

"I am seeing you soon, please, Mr. Emmanuel!" cried Bruno.

It was a happy leave-taking.

3

I

FOR the next day or two, Mr. Emmanuel was rather disconsolate, and Rose saw it. She put herself out to be, if possible, even more charming to him than before, for she knew the disappearance of Bruno had left a certain gap, she knew how important to him was the sense of virtuous employment.

The lads had come and gone. So, on one or two occasions, a handful of the girls' friends had come and gone. It was that sort of household. The master of the house had come back, and he had hardly more than caught sight of these German boys. He was pleased to think his wife had put herself out for them. And that was about all there was to it.

The name of Bruno came up rather more often than the others. Everyone had liked him and been sorry for him. Rose, too, had noticed that he had been easier in his mind the last day or two.

"He's getting over it," she said. "He's got to shake down sooner or later."

Mr. Emmanuel wanted to think so too.

"You can't live," he said, "and have such a lot of pain like that boy. Either you've got to die or the pain's got to die. Well, please God, with Bruno let it be the pain."

Only Mary Cooper remained cold and silent. She seemed to believe the dictum was unsound. It was possible for a human being to live, and a pain to live within it, for long long years.

However, after that first day or two, there was no doubt Mr. Emmanuel was happy, or as happy as he could be, so soon after his wife's death. The three girls were pleasant youngsters to be with. In a more reserved way so was the elder Mary, who was up at Shipscar every day now that Dick was back in his own home. But it was, surprisingly, John himself who gave Mr. Emmanuel most pleasure. He was a little moody now and again; sometimes he was downright rude, except to Mr. Emmanuel. It is very strange, thought the old man, he does not make me a fright any more. Of an evening, after the youngsters had gone to bed, they would sit out on the veranda and talk of Magnolia Street. John Cooper would puff away at his pipe, and dig up reminiscences, and ask questions, as if he had been waiting for years for this opportunity to question somebody, anybody, about the dim little street where he had once lived for a few years.

But it did not deceive Mr. Emmanuel, who was a shrewd person in some ways. It was true that in that small street John Cooper had met the girl he was to marry, and his young brother had died. Yet Mr. Emmanuel felt that the street and the people who had lived in it mattered to John hardly more than the dockside cafés of some port which a ship of his had once touched at and he no more called at now. When John, by a feat of memory, recalled the Derrickses, who lived at this number, the Seipels, who lived at that number, the Poysers, the Tawnies, it was an act of grace towards his guest. Mr. Emmanuel's eye kindled with pleasure. It is good, he thought, when a strong man with a neck like a bull can be also such a nice gentleman.

The boys did not let much time go by before they wrote letters from camp, expressing their thanks and saying what a fine time they were having. They wrote on Thursday from both Margate and Roman's Bight, and the letters arrived in a bunch on Saturday morning. The letters were addressed to Mrs. Cooper, though Mr. Emmanuel had one all to himself from Bruno. It was a trivial note, but it gave Mr. Emmanuel a lot of pleasure. He well knew how easy it is for people much older than Bruno to receive more substantial kindnesses and to forget all about them the moment any distance at all separates giver and taker. Yes, he was happy the boy had remembered him.

It was not until Wednesday morning that they received word again. Rose and John and Mr. Emmanuel were sitting out on the veranda, smoking an after-breakfast cigarette. They did not feel very active. They wanted to sit about and talk. It was Mr. Emmanuel's last day at Shipscar. Mary junior appeared with the morning letters and handed them to her mother.

"Here are the letters, Mummy!" said Mary.

"Thank you, darling!" murmured Rose, without turning her head. "Put them on the table, will you?"

Mary put them down and went off. Her bicycle wanted some attention. It was sitting on the lawn on its saddle with its intestines streaming from it.

"I don't know what's happened to him," said Rose. She was sitting forward on her canvas chair, staring out on the grass side between the tree-trunks. "There still hasn't been any rain. He should have been here by now." She was talking of Bert, the cock thrush. He was several minutes late already for his morning worm. "Ah, there he is!" she cried. She ran over for the spade and dug up a few inches of earth. Then she sat down again. Bert waited a minute or two, then half fluttered, half goosestepped to his plot of loose earth. He found his worm and flew off into the undergrowth.

"Not even a thank you!" reproved Rose.

"I like it here!" said John briefly. It was likeable. The wood-pigeons cooed from high up among the trees. Over in the clear spaces of sky the swallows and martins formed and re-formed their arrowy phalanxes. In the borders the flowers pressed their plaques of colour cheek by jowl like slabs of mosaic. A robin sang out from a laurel, brief and shrill.

"Oh, yes, the letters!" said Rose, as if letters on a morning like this were rather a nuisance. She lifted them from the table, and glanced over the envelopes. "Tradesman; tradesman; Major Pilkins, I think; catalogue; one for Sarah. Oh, here's one from one of the boys. Postmark, Roman's Bight." She turned her head and addressed Mr. Emmanuel. "I suppose it's Bruno. You see, it's addressed to both of us. 'Mrs. Cooper and Mr. Emmanuel.' " She handed the letter over to him. "One stamp, poor boy. He must be getting short of funds."

Mr. Emmanuel held the letter for a moment or two, then handed it back again.

"Please," he said. "It's your name first. You open it."

She smiled.

"Very well," she said, and opened it. "I'll read it aloud. He's got such funny little ways of expressing himself." She began reading:

"Dear Mrs. Cooper and dear Mr. Emmanuel,

"Please. I so wish you shall not be angry with me. You have been so very kind to me and I do not wish you shall have unhappiness from me."

Rose stopped, and looked away from the letter. There were doubt and trouble in her eyes.

"What on earth's the boy getting at?" she asked. Mr. Emmanuel was sitting bolt upright in his chair. She resumed the letter:

"It is today my birthday. I was saying to myself all week, all day and all night, for my birthday she is writing. Never before she has forgotten my birthday. If she is not writing, I know she is dead. But she is not writing. It gives no letter."

Rose stopped again. Her face was constricted with pain.

"I can't go on!" she said. Without turning her head, she thrust her arm behind her towards John, where he sat behind the low garden table. "Take it!" she begged.

John took it from her and read it. As he read, Mr. Emmanuel remained rigid in his chair, looking neither to right nor to left. Then John handed the letter to him.

"Read it!" he requested.

As Mr. Emmanuel reached his hand forward for the letter, his rigidity went out of him. The head started swinging disastrously to and fro on the neck. His hand shivered so that he could hardly hold the sheet of paper. He read as follows:

But she is not writing. It gives no letter. She is dead. I have lost my mother. I have lost also my country and my companions. They are not wanting me any more. I have nothing in all the world. Why, please, shall I want to live? You shall not be angry, please. You will understand I am sitting writing this in my tent, and I shall finish it and I shall put it in the post office for the camp and you shall get it in one day or two days. But I shall be dead then. Tonight I shall slip underneath out of the tent, when all the boys and men are sleeping, and I shall go out over the hill of stones and I shall go into the sea and I shall be also dead like my mother, and it may be perhaps I shall afterwards see her, but I do not know. I am not thinking so. I am so sorry for making trouble for you and for Father Wedlake and for the men here. You have all been so kind to us German boys. Good-bye, and I am sending you love and kisses.

BRUNO ROSENHEIM.

The sheet of paper fluttered to the ground from between Mr. Emmanuel's fingers. For several seconds no one said a word. Then at last Rose spoke, her hand sealing her eyes, her voice hardly raised above a whisper.

"What does he say? You must tell me!"

John got up with such decision from his chair that it fell backward.

"I'm going off to Roman's Bight in a few minutes. It's a long way. There's no need for you to come, Mr. Emmanuel."

"I shall come," said Mr. Emmanuel.

"What has happened to that boy?" cried Rose. "What has he done to himself?"

"It looks bad," said John. He strode over to the edge of the veranda and called to Mary. "Where's Sarah? How soon will your bicycle be ready? I want one of you to go off at once to your aunt and tell her to come and spend the day with your mother!" He returned to the others. Both had risen from their chairs. Rose had picked up the note and was reading it.

"That woman ought to get put onto the telephone!" John muttered.

"I think," said Mr. Emmanuel in a low voice, "perhaps we should telephone the Committee in London. If there is any news, perhaps they will have it!"

"We shouldn't have let him go!" cried Rose bitterly. "It was cruel! A poor broken-hearted little boy!"

John opened his mouth to speak and closed it again. It was Mr. Emmanuel who spoke. He went over to her and put his arm round her shoulder and patted it.

"He was much happier that last day or two. How should anybody know, Rose? How should anybody know it was his birthday coming, and he was so sure on that day the letter must come? Be good, Rose!"

"I'll go over and telephone those people in London!" said John. "What's the number?"

"It's on their notepaper! There's a letter lying on my desk!" She made a movement as if to enter the house.

"I'll find it! Come, Rose! Be a sport!" He made her sit down again.

He entered the sitting-room through the French windows. They heard him go over to her desk. After a moment or two he had found the number he was looking for. He strode out into the hall, lifted the telephone receiver and asked for long distance. He gave the number. The line, apparently, was engaged. They heard him shift impatiently from one foot to the other. Two or three minutes later he was through to somebody.

"No! I don't want Telegrams! I want Trunks! What? A telegram for Mrs. Cooper? Yes? I'll take it down! One moment! Yes?" There was a pause while he took it down. "Yes. I'll repeat it. *Come at once if possible Bruno Rosenheim ill. Wedlake.* Thank you! Not necessary! No copy!" He replaced the receiver, and was recalled at once by the ringing of the telephone bell. "What? Trunks?" He hesitated a moment. "No! Not now! Cut it out!"

He came out onto the veranda again.

Rose was mopping her eyes. Mr. Emmanuel stood beside her, comforting her.

"Did you hear?" he asked.

She nodded.

"Thank God!" murmured Mr. Emmanuel. "He's at least alive!"

"It doesn't seem so bad after all!" said John.

"Yet bad enough!" said Mr. Emmanuel.

"Yes," agreed John, "bad enough! Queer little cuss! The wire was for you, Rose. What do you want to do?"

"I'm going over, of course! Will you get the car out, while I talk to Smithers and get some things on? You're coming, Mr. Emmanuel?"

"I go for my hat and coat. He's at least alive!" he went off muttering. "Thank God! Thank God!"

Mary junior was standing in the offing, looking white and apprehensive. Evidently something serious had happened.

"What is it, Mummy?" she asked. "Is it anything awful?"

"Little Bruno's ill," Rose answered. "We're going to see what's wrong."

"You're going, too, Mummy? What about Aunt Mary? Do you still want me to fetch her?"

Rose turned inquiringly to John.

"No! We'll find out how things are first! We don't want Dick in on this!"

"Of course!" Rose murmured. "Mary, find Ailsa for me while I get my things on! I want her to promise to be good! You'll look after things for me, won't you? Where *is* Sarah! Oh, *what* a girl!" She turned to hurry away, when Mary called out to her once again.

"When will you be back, Mummy?"

It was her father who answered, half-way over to the garage.

"Very late! Nobody's to stay up!"

"We may bring Bruno back with us," her mother called out from inside the house. "If he's well enough!"

II

A long drive lay before them, well over a hundred miles—to Ringwood, to Southampton, to Chichester, to Brighton, to Eastbourne, and Roman's Bight a few miles further. John drove; Rose sat beside him; Mr. Emmanuel sat in the back of the car.

They had sent a wire to Roman's Bight before leaving. There was nothing to do but get there. Nobody did much talking; John was not loquacious by nature; Mr. Emmanuel, who was, did not feel talkative now. Now and again, in brief snatches, Rose broke the silence.

"I'm sorry, John!" she said.

"What for?"

"I've got you into all this! Perhaps I shouldn't——"

"Don't be a fool!" said John. A minute or two later, as if he felt his tongue had been a bit rough, he added: "Who else has the kid got?"

Mr. Emmanuel thought he heard a sniff. He saw Rose lift her handkerchief to her eyes. There was silence for a good many miles after that.

They had passed Southampton, they were well on the way to Chichester, when Rose spoke again. She spoke in a low voice, as if she preferred Mr. Emmanuel not to hear what she was saying.

"John!"

"Yes?"

"Have you realized?"

"Realized what?"

"Little Bruno!"

"Well?"

"It might have been our Dickie!"

"How do you mean?"

"Don't you see? He's only half Aryan, too!"

John was silent for a full minute. Then he whistled, a low long whistle.

"Of course!" he said at length. *"The cowsons!"* he added grimly. *"The bastards!"*

"It is a strange thing!" mused Mr. Emmanuel. "It has only just come into their brains! I was thinking the same thing, the very same thing, the moment I saw them together, those two children, Dick and Bruno, outside the station at Salisbury!"

They had lunch at Worthing, where the back of the journey was broken. Then came Brighton and, an hour after that, Eastbourne. Roman's Bight was beyond Pevensey. The last stage of the journey was along a shingly track bordered on the right hand by a stone dike, on the left by low-lying marshes slashed with channels and ditches. A row of bungalows ran for some distance along the west of the dike, then it ceased abruptly. Some quarter of a mile further a martello tower commanded the beach. In the open marshland between, flanked on the inland side by a stream and, further, by the railway-line, some forty or fifty bell-tents extended along three lines of a square. Beyond the line nearest the sea the camp's more permanent buildings spread out—a few small wooden huts, a large marquee, a large wooden hut, kitchens, store-tents, and the rest. A number of boys, a hundred or two, perhaps more, were engaged as players or spectators in a variety of games on the camp-site. Others were coming away from the field or trailing back towards it. A group, in shorts or bathing costumes, with towels over their arms, were scrabbling up the slope of the dike towards the sea.

John let down the window of the car.

"Father Wedlake's camp?" he asked, of a small boy who seemed as if he might know.

"Yep!" the small boy said.

A gate led into the field at an oblique angle. John reversed and drove through, turned again, and made for a fairly level neck of ground between the troughs. A number of boys came running up from roundabout, interested not so much in the car's occupants as in its mascot and gears and dashboard. They opened the car's doors politely. John stepped out, Rose and Mr. Emmanuel following.

"Where shall we find Father Wedlake, please?"

" 'E's watchin' the cricket!" the small boys shrilled. "Shall we bring 'im?"

"We'll go along!"

But the word had already gone forward to the cricket-watchers that a strange car had arrived in the camp. A figure detached itself from the recumbent huddle stretched along the boundary of the cricket pitch. It was attired in a copious purple sweater, a pair of grey shorts, a pair of outlandish sandals. The head was bald. The dark eyes were shrewd and kind. He came up and took Rose's hand.

"Mrs. Cooper, I take it? He's all right."

"Thank God. Where is he? Oh, forgive me. This is my husband. This is our friend, Mr. Emmanuel."

Father Wedlake's eyes twinkled.

"The great Mr. Emmanuel? I've heard a lot about him this last week. How are you, Captain Cooper?"

"How are you, Father?"

"Pleased to meet you, Father."

"You've had a long drive. I'd like you to come and sit down in my hut for a minute or two."

"Is he in the camp, Father?"

"We thought it better to put him in one of those bungalows there. It's owned by friends of ours, the Gibsons."

The priest led them along the field, beyond the hut and the marquee and a small chapel, then stopped at a trailer, with its rear flap let down as a sort of ramp. There were a bed and a chest of drawers along one side, a desk and a small washstand on the other. Above the bed was a ledge, on which a small crucifix stood, flanked by vases of flowers. There were folding chairs below the desk and the bed.

"Not much room," said Father Wedlake. "Would you sit on the bed, Captain Cooper? A drink? You, Mrs. Cooper? A cup of tea? I could have one made at once."

"Later, please. After we've seen Bruno. What happened, Father Wedlake?"

"Go away!" exclaimed the priest, dismissing a handful of interested boys who had gathered in front of the trailer. "I don't want anybody to know," he explained. "Nobody does know, except my colleague, Winterton. He's the one who fished him out. And the people at the bungalow, of course. Everybody else just thinks he's got a bad cold."

Rose clasped her hands.

"Poor little Bruno!" she murmured. "I can't tell you how guilty I feel, Father. I should never have let him go."

The priest was standing in the rear end of the trailer, the ledge with the crucifix beside his head.

"No," he said earnestly. "You have nothing to reproach yourself with. The same thing would have happened at your house, or anywhere else he might have been. And there mightn't have been anyone at hand, either. He was miserable all day, several of us noticed that, but who on earth could have expected that the boy . . . ?" He stopped and shook his head sadly. "Poor little fellow!" he sighed.

Rose opened her bag and brought out the letter that had been received that morning at Shipscar.

"I'd like you to read this, please."

Father Wedlake read the letter and handed it back to her. He was deeply moved.

"The Lord help us!" He crossed himself. "Poor, poor little chap! I got the main outlines of the situation from the Committee people, of course. I learned more from Klaus Bieber. A good boy that. And about this—this birthday—I learned from Bruno himself. Today, I mean. I didn't want him to worry himself; but he insisted. He was very apologetic. I thought it a good thing to let him get it off his chest."

"It's all right, Rose!" muttered her husband. "The kid's all right now!" She was showing signs of breaking down.

"I know you'll be wanting to see the boy," continued Father Wedlake. "I don't want to keep you talking here. But I thought you'd better know the lie of the land. I sent the wire off first thing this morning, after he'd gone off to sleep. At first he was rather unhappy about it. It's not that he doesn't want to see you, of course. He's talked about you most enthusiastically. Particularly you, Mr. Emmanuel."

"I am happy," murmured Mr. Emmanuel.

"He's been wonderful with the boy!" Rose insisted.

"But he's feeling very guilty," Father Wedlake resumed. "I have a feeling that if you went to see him first, Mr. Emmanuel, it would be easier for him. That's why I thought I'd have this word with you first."

"No, please," protested Mr. Emmanuel, embarrassed. "I was only a guest staying by Mrs. Cooper."

"Of course!" cried Rose. "You must go over to him at once! I know you're the one person he wants to see!"

Mr. Emmanuel opened his mouth to protest again, but John thrust in a word and settled the matter.

"We'll wait for you!" he said.

"We'll go along at once, shall we?" asked Father Wedlake. The others got up and preceded him out into the camp field. "Do you see those bungalows beyond the martello tower? It's the third one along. Thank Heavens the Gibsons have an extra room. We've had a town doctor in, of course, as well as the camp doctor. There's nothing much wrong with him today. Just a bit of a cold. This marquee is the officers' mess and the big hut is the boys' dining-room. But I'll show you round the camp later if you're interested. Do you see that man in the group with the medicine-ball? I'd like you to meet him later, too. That's Winterton. Yes, the fellow who pulled the boy out."

They were at the gate now. Father Wedlake held them up for a moment. "I think I'd like you to understand how it happened. Winterton had turned in, but he couldn't sleep. He had a bit of a headache, and he thought a breath of sea-air would help. He got up, I should say about half an hour before Bruno stole out of his tent, and went over to the beach. He propped himself up on this side of the groyne and took out a cigarette. Bruno's tent is further along the line, so he came down towards the beach well over on the further side of the groyne. Winterton says he heard the sound of someone coming down to the beach, but there wasn't anything to worry about in that. Our grown-ups come down to bathe at odd times, and it isn't our private beach, either. But it wasn't till Bruno had swum well out this way that Winterton realized that the person, whoever it was, had actually gone into the water. Even then he didn't know it was a boy. It was a milky sort of night, and Winterton doesn't see very well. He only realized that something was wrong when he saw the swimmer start beating about and go under. He kicked his shoes off and flung off into the water. The boy struggled a bit and then passed out. He had him landed in a couple of minutes. That's how it was," concluded Father Wedlake.

They had by now reached the third bungalow beyond the tower. "I think I might just go in and let him know, Mr. Emmanuel," he said. The door was unlocked. He went straight through.

"We'll go and sit on the beach," John stated. "Give us a shout when you want us."

"Do tell him," Rose insisted, "nobody's cross. Everybody's terribly, terribly happy it's all right. You'll tell him that."

"Yes," said Mr. Emmanuel, swallowing hard. "I'll tell him."

He was alone for a moment or two before Father Wedlake came to him again.

You should be ashamed of yourself, Isaac, Mr. Emmanuel reproached himself. An old grown-up man like you, you should want to start crying! Phui! He swallowed again, shook his head hard, and was all right.

Father Wedlake came to the door and beckoned him in.

"He's immensely happy you're here," he whispered. "Don't let him get excited, will you? That's the room. The Gibsons are out. I'll go and join Mrs. Cooper," he added, and went off.

Mr. Emmanuel knocked.

"Please come in," Bruno's voice called.

Mr. Emmanuel entered. The room was darkened by sun-blinds. He closed the door behind him with immense care.

"Please," Bruno said. "I am not dying. I am all right. I am a naughty boy. Are you very angry, Mr. Emmanuel?"

Mr. Emmanuel stepped over to the bedside. The boy reached his hand forward and Mr. Emmanuel took it in both of his. He still held it as he sat down in a chair by the bed.

"I am not angry," he murmured. "You are not naughty. I am only very, very happy you are today all right."

"You are coming such a long way, Mr. Emmanuel. You are so kind. And Mrs. Cooper. She is also so kind. And Captain Cooper. Where are they, please?"

"They are over on the beach. Father Wedlake said I should see you the first one."

"I am happy. Mrs. Cooper is so kind, but she is a bit

like a strange lady. You are not like a stranger. If you are being angry, I am not so much frightened."

"No one is angry, my Bruno. We are so, so sorry you have such unhappiness."

"I was not last night unhappy. Slipping out of the tent it was like playing Indians with the farmer's sons in Lübbenau. At night, with a big moon, in and out of the big things of corn—how are you calling them? It was a big moon also last night. I was crawling through the wire fence and then I was crawling flat on my stomach no one shall see me. My feet made a big noise with the stones, and I was being much frightened someone shall hear me."

"Bruno! Bruno!" begged Mr. Emmanuel. The tears brimmed in his eyes. "Father Wedlake said I should not let you get excited!"

"Please, Mr. Emmanuel. It is nothing! I am not excited! Look! I am here! Everything is being all right! Please, shall I talk and it is not feeling so heavy here?"

"Talk, Bruno!"

"It was so warm and happy and the night warm and I am wearing fat pyjamas and I am not being cold and frightened. Only it is cold for one minute when I go into the water and it is not deep. But when it is deep it is not cold. And I want I shall swim and swim, and then I shall be tired and if I want I shall turn back, it is too far and my pyjamas are too heavy. And I am swimming, but I am not swimming very far, because my pyjamas are very heavy. But I am not unhappy. I am swimming east, and I am saying inside myself I am swimming to the North Sea and over there is Germany. And my head is a bit going round and I am saying perhaps my mother is also somewhere in the sea and she is swimming to me, and we shall be swimming together like in that summer in Föhr. And it is all like rolling fishes like barrels—how do you say them?—and they are all silver, and I am hearing the rose-wood box, painted on it with ladies and gentlemen dancing, and it is making music. And it is high up over me, the water, and it is under me, and then it is the man—he is coming up from everywhere and I am not happy. And I think I am a little fighting, I think he is not a very good man. . . ."

"Bruno!" cried Mr. Emmanuel. "No! Bruno! No!" He put his fingers over the boy's lips. "You must forget last night! It is over! You are with us again! You are young! It is much to do in this world!"

"They do not want I shall do it," said Bruno. "My father is non-Aryan."

"What is to be done with this boy?" Mr. Emmanuel asked himself desperately. "He has not come back out of that water. He is a lot over there yet." His head drooped upon his chest.

"Mr. Emmanuel!"

"Yes?" He did not raise his head.

"I am being again naughty. You will not like me any more."

Mr. Emmanuel rose from the chair and placed his hands upon the boy's shoulders.

"I like you, Bruno, like my little son who died in the War." He stood looking down into his face, his eyes, accustomed to the semi-darkness, seeing quite clearly now. The living boy had never before so much resembled the dead boy.

"I am not deserving you shall like me," whispered

Bruno. "I shall be good. I shall take nasty medicine."

"That is fine, Bruno." He sat down again. "You shall take your medicine and you will be strong. And we will be pleased with you, the Committee in London, and Father Wedlake, and Mrs. Cooper, and Captain Cooper, and Miss Cooper, and the three girls, and Dick, and also me." It sounded an impressive list.

"There are nice men here in the camp also, and nice boys. Klaus also is nice. Also Hugo."

Mr. Emmanuel's heart beat a little more happily. It seemed as if the boy, like a boat at its mooring on the turning of the tide, were swinging round slowly. He was enumerating his friends. He was taking stock of such assets as he had to face Time with.

"Is Captain Cooper here also?" asked Bruno.

"Yes," said Mr. Emmanuel eagerly. "He is with Mrs. Cooper. Did not Father Wedlake say? They are both together over there on the beach. They are waiting I should call them and they will come to see you and tell you all about how it has been in Shipscar all this week, and Mary's bicycle is punctured, and that bird that comes for worms, they dig up the ground for him, did you ever see such a thing? They all want you shall come again quickly, little Dick as well, as much as anybody. Perhaps today, perhaps tomorrow, when it is not red your nose any more."

"Please not to ask Captain Cooper," begged Bruno. "He will think me a very bad boy, not a sport. Mrs. Cooper, yes. She is so kind, so nice."

"Let it be only Mrs. Cooper. Shall I go now, Bruno?" It seemed to Mr. Emmanuel he had kept the boy talking far too long already.

"Please, one second, Mr. Emmanuel."

Mr. Emmanuel rose from his chair and went over to the door.

"One minute, two minutes, not more, Bruno." His hand turned the door-handle.

"Mr. Emmanuel?"

"Yes?"

"It is not right I shall not tell you."

"Tell me what, Bruno?"

The boy was silent a moment or two. He was smiling. There was no sadness in his smile, only a little mischief.

"Next time," said Bruno softly, "it shall be done properly. No one shall stop me."

Mr. Emmanuel did not turn round, did not move. His hand stayed on the door-handle. His heart seemed cold and spent, like a stone. A minute passed so, perhaps more. Then Bruno spoke again.

"I know you shall not forgive me. It is not my fault. It is finished. Please. Can I see Mrs. Cooper? She will not see me if you tell her. Please not."

Mr. Emmanuel swung round. It was a swift gesture for an old man. The blood was pulsing in his veins. Behind his temples a hammer beat loud and clear as upon an anvil.

"Bruno!" he cried. "I know you are not making a fool of me! I know you mean what you are saying! I cannot blame you! It is a bad world, a wicked world, it should treat like this a little boy! I want you to listen to me!" He came over to the bedside and once again placed his hands on the boy's shoulders, but this time there was such pressure in them that they hurt. "Are you listening, Bruno?"

"Yes, Mr. Emmanuel!" the boy whispered.

"I want you to make me a promise! What promise?

I shall tell you! You are only a boy. You are very unhappy. You think too quickly a bad thing. Perhaps your mother is dead, yes. You do not know. Nobody knows. Perhaps your mother is alive. Perhaps she cannot write you. Perhaps it is bad for her she should write, perhaps it is bad for you.

"Well, I make you first a promise! I am going to Germany to find out. I will go everywhere. I will ask everybody. I will find out! And you, Bruno, you! This is the promise you shall make me! You shall be a good boy until I come back from Germany and tell you what it is with your mother! You know what I mean? *You shall be a good boy!*"

The boy's head lay on one side, the eyes closed. The tears were rolling steadily down his cheeks. He spoke, but his words were almost soundless.

"I shall be a good boy, Mr. Emmanuel!"

Mr. Emmanuel took his handkerchief from his pocket and wiped Bruno's eyes, and mopped his own forehead, and wiped Bruno's eyes again.

"Come now!" he said. "Come!" He pulled the sheet taut across the bed. He lifted Bruno's head and straightened the pillow. "I go now for Mrs. Cooper! She shall stay only one minute! Then you must sleep! Will you sleep, Bruno?"

"I will sleep!" the boy murmured.

Mr. Emmanuel crept out of the room and closed the door softly behind him. He made his way to the group by the beach, over the pebble dike. They looked up and stared aghast when he spoke to them, as if he had seen a ghost.

"Come, Mrs. Cooper!" he whispered, against the slap and thud of the sea, as if Bruno would hear if he spoke louder. "He wants he should see you, Mrs. Cooper. But I think he will be asleep when we go in."

He was, in fact, asleep.

III

Later that day the doctor saw Bruno again. After a brief consultation, Father Wedlake came over to them.

"The doctor has a feeling," he reported, "it would be a good thing if Bruno left the seaside as soon as he's fit to travel. In fact, tomorrow. He's not certain the sea hasn't a morbid effect on him."

"Please, no!" Mr. Emmanuel heard himself objecting sharply. "The sea has nothing to do with it. In the middle of the desert it would be the same thing."

"I incline to agree with you," Father Wedlake admitted.

"In any case that's what we've come for," said Rose. "To take him back to Shipscar, the moment it's all right."

"It's immensely kind of you, Mrs. Cooper. I'll admit that was in my mind. I got on the telephone to London, and told them that was my idea. They were greatly relieved. Somebody would have come down today, but they're short-handed. They have a new contingent of boys today, coming in at Liverpool Street."

"We're only too happy," Rose murmured.

"Do you realize," exclaimed John, as if he were asking himself to play with the idea that black was white, "do you realize that it might have been *our* kid?" He went red and spluttered with fury.

"Or almost anybody's!" breathed Father Wedlake.

"So we'll take him off some time tomorrow," said Rose. "Hadn't we better send a wire home, John?"

"Why shall I not wait and bring him, Rose?" asked Mr. Emmanuel. "Is it necessary you shall have all this trouble?"

Rose and John wouldn't hear of it. The wire was sent. Rooms were fixed up in Pevensey, and the three visitors spent the evening in the camp. It was pleasant to see Klaus and Hugo again. There was a camp concert in the big dining-hut, and the Shipscar party, all but Mr. Emmanuel, sat perched together on a narrow bench in the back as if they had known each other for years.

The concert was well advanced by the time Mr. Emmanuel appeared again. As he opened the door, so terrific a volume of noise issued from the assembled company, it was almost like holding a door open against a hurricane. A small moon-faced man was strutting up and down the platform, his thumb in the arm-holes of his waistcoat, a bowler-hat stuck over on one side of his head. *Any old iron,* he sang, and the company sang with him:

Any old iron,
Any, any, any old iron.
You look sweet,
You look a treat,
You look dapper from your napper to your feet.

There were a few inches vacant in a form behind the Shipscar party. Mr. Emmanuel sat down and touched Rose on the shoulder. She turned.

"How is he?" shrilled Rose, making a trumpet out of her hands.

Mr. Emmanuel could not hope to outshout that tumult. He gestured with both hands and rolled his eyes roofwards. He's fine, that meant.

Rose turned again. The small moon-faced man was clanking the comic watch-chain strung across his waistcoat.

Dressed in style,
Dressed in style,
Brand-new tile,
Your old man's old green tie on.

Mr. Emmanuel's heart leapt within him like a lamb in a meadow.

"I know that song! I know that song! My boys used to sing it once, in Doomington! Yes, yes, a long time ago!"

His voice added itself to the tumult, no more perceptibly than a rivulet adding itself to the sea.

I wouldn't give you twopence
For your old watch-chain.
Old iron! Old iron!

IV

Next day, Thursday, was the day on which Mr. Emmanuel had arranged to be in a train heading for Doomington. It turned out that he was in a motor car heading for Ringwood. Well, that was nobody's fault. The important affairs in Doomington would have to wait a few days. John was due to return to Southampton on Monday. He was not destined, this leave anyhow, to have a few days all to himself, in the bosom of his family. That was nobody's fault, either. Or perhaps it was Bruno's. Bruno himself breathed a word or two vaguely along those lines, but he was suppressed at once, gently but firmly. The boy was, so far as anyone could see, quite well in three or four days. His immersion seemed to have left no ill effects. It was taken for granted that he was to stay out the summer holidays at Shipscar.

It was not until three evenings after the return from Roman's Bight, which was, in fact, the last evening of John's leave, that Mr. Emmanuel reported to the Coopers the promise he had made to Bruno. He was not quite sure why he had withheld it till then. The fact probably was, he realized, he was a little nervous about it. In the first place, John and Rose as likely as not would be rather cross with him. In the second place, they would try to stop him from going. And nobody and nothing in the world was going to stop him. What for? A British subject all of a sudden can't go on a visit to Germany? Who ever heard from such a thing?

He waited till all the young people had gone to bed. It was quite late. Last nights were allowed to draw out a long way beyond the normal bed-time. He lit a cigarette with such excessive casualness that it dropped out of his mouth. He replaced it.

"Oh, there's just one thing I should like to tell you," he announced. "About Bruno."

"Yes?" said the others idly. "What is it?"

"He is going to be a good boy."

"Well, of course. He's being a perfect angel."

"I mean he is *going* to be a good boy," he floundered. "I mean . . . no nonsenses, like at Roman's Bight."

"Yes," said John shortly. "I should think so. Gave him a bit of a fright, I shouldn't wonder."

"No," said Mr. Emmanuel quietly. "It did not give him a bit of fright."

"Well?" Rose asked uneasily. "What were you going to tell us?"

"I was going to tell you I made him a promise. And he made me a promise also."

"That he was going to play the game from now on," John supplemented. "Good kid!"

"That's right. Because I promised him I should go to Germany to find out."

"What?" They both sat up in their chairs.

Mr. Emmanuel misunderstood them.

"Find out what? About his mother, of course! What has happened to her! Somebody must know. It is the uncertainty that has been killing him!"

"No!" said John Cooper. "It's absurd! You can't go!" He reached for the whisky-decanter. "Never heard of such a thing!"

"It is lovely of you, lovely!" said Rose in a softer note. "But you mustn't think of it!"

"I am going!" said Mr. Emmanuel. "Excuse me, please!"

The tone frightened her.

"Dear Mr. Emmanuel!" She got up from her chair and came over and sat down on the arm of his. "It does you great credit. But as you know, the fullest possible inquiries have been made. It seems quite impossible to get any information, of any kind. You know that. It will be a lot of trouble and a lot of expense and all for nothing."

"What do you mean, trouble? For me it will be a great pleasure. You say inquiries have been made. Yes. Inquiries by letters. Letters here, letters there, what are letters? Who says you must answer letters, if you don't want to? Don't I know? Is it for one week I was secretary to the Board of Guardians? But when you ask in person, it's not the same thing. One time they say nothing, a second time, a third time. A fourth time they will answer, believe me!"

"If anybody could find out anything, it would be you!" said John. "I haven't any doubt of that!" His tone was not very pleasant. Mr. Emmanuel looked a little ruffled.

"John!" Rose remonstrated.

John ignored her.

"But you're not going, Mr. Emmanuel!"

"How do you mean it, I'm not going?"

"I won't let you! I'll clap you in irons or something. I'll find a way."

"Please! We must not quarrel!"

"You're not going, because it's dangerous!"

"Dangerous? An old man asks a question what has happened to a boy's mother, he is dying of a broken heart, he throws himself into the sea he should drown himself, and he says it is dangerous. I will make them cry till they do not know is it today or yesterday. I will make them run round, in this place, in that place, like chickens with heads chopped off. Dangerous? Such an idea!"

John regarded Mr. Emmanuel coldly, almost with a touch of hostility.

"Excuse me for being frank, Mr. Emmanuel. Are you really foolish, or are you only pretending to be?"

"John! Really, John! You mustn't talk like that to Mr. Emmanuel. He's not your second mate or second engineer or something!"

"Oi, such a business!" wailed Mr. Emmanuel.

"Don't *you* see, either?" John turned testily on Rose. "A funny old Jew from Doomington goes over to Berlin. He goes about poking his nose into things which don't concern him! Things which already look rather fishy! No, it's not dangerous? Don't be ridiculous, Rose! We mustn't let him go!"

"Do you think *I* want him to go? I know it's all wrong. You mustn't think of it, Mr. Emmanuel, you mustn't!"

Mr. Emmanuel felt he had announced sufficiently often and clearly that he did think of it and was, in fact, going to do it. He sat nibbling at his lower lip and tugging at his beard. He drew out his handkerchief and blew his nose into it vehemently.

"The fact is," announced John, *"I'm* going!"

Rose gasped. Mr. Emmanuel looked up sharply.

"Oh, yes," John continued, "I'm going! If I hadn't kicked the kid out of the house, he wouldn't have tried it on. You'd both have been here to help him over his disappointment when that damn letter didn't come. Quite clearly, it's up to me."

"But you're joining your ship tomorrow, John."

"Yes. I mean, of course, after the return trip, six or seven weeks from now. It's too late to do anything this time."

"Six weeks from now?" whispered Mr. Emmanuel. "Seven weeks from now?"

"Time enough. Six weeks one way or the other won't make much difference to the kid."

Rose sat fidgeting with the buckle of her belt. Mr. Emmanuel sat silent for a minute or two, contemplating the situation. Then, placing together the tips of his fingers, his head inclined quite a few inches from the perpendicular, he spoke. His voice was firm and quiet.

"Six weeks from now I shall have gone, Captain Cooper. Perhaps also I shall be back. I do not know. Six weeks for that boy, from now on, till I come back with news, will be like six years." John snorted impatiently. Mr. Emmanuel resumed. "You are a good man and a kind man. I know that. But this business is for me, not you. Who was it promised the boy he shall go? Was it you, Captain Cooper? It was not. You have other things to do. And me? What is there left for me? Palestine? It can wait. You say there is danger? I do not believe it. For why? But let it be danger. Again that is a thing for me, an old man, a widower, with his two boys grown up. It is not for you."

"O.K.," said John, with considerable disgust in his voice. "Have it your own way!" He was silent for a moment. "But look here—" he started off again; then, as if at last he realized how useless it all was, he relapsed into silence. "More whisky!" he demanded grumpily, reaching his glass forward towards Rose. She unstoppered the decanter and dutifully poured out more whisky.

"You, Mr. Emmanuel?"

"No, please. It makes my head swindle."

Rose poured out her own brand of drink for herself, a thimbleful of whisky, a gurgle of black cordial from a medicine bottle, and the rest soda-water.

"Rat-poison!" announced John.

"Sorry!" murmured Rose. She lifted her glass and drank. "Forgive me, Mr. Emmanuel," she began diffidently. "There's one aspect of the matter I'd like to bring up. If you'll let me——"

"Please!"

"It's going to cost something. It might take longer than you think. Are you . . . will you be able to manage?"

"Thank God," murmured Mr. Emmanuel. "You see"—he hesitated—"I have in October a policy coming. It will be all right."

John turned suddenly.

"So you won't leave till November?"

"Perhaps next week," Mr. Emmanuel replied mildly. "I have a great friend, his name is Silver. He lives in Oleander Street. Do you perhaps remember, Rose?"

"With the five daughters? Of course I do. I used to know Esther quite well." She seemed about to continue her reminiscences when some thought came up suddenly in her mind and brought her up sharp. "Yes," she said. Her tone had altered completely. "You said Mr. Silver."

"Only a few weeks ago one night he came in. He said if I wanted the money in advance I should go to Palestine, he would arrange. I said no. For why hurry? Is Palestine running away? Well, this is different. When I go back I ask him he should arrange. Then I go. It should be with luck, please God!"

Rose clasped her hands and closed her eyes. "Please God!" she murmured and her shoulders swayed slightly from side to side.

Would you believe it! Mr. Emmanuel thought. Like her own dear mother, peace be upon her! You could think it was a *yomtov,* a holiday, in the women's section of the synagogue.

"But when you *get* there," Rose was saying. "When you *get* there." Her eyes were still closed as if she were keeping out images of terror. John kept his back turned away from both of them, as if he washed his hands of the whole matter. He was fingering a weekly journal, but it might have been Chinese for all the attention he paid to it. He was, in fact, listening intently.

"What I shall do when I get there?" Mr. Emmanuel repeated. "You mean if I have difficulties? I have thought of that. Do you want to know what I shall do? I shall tell you. I said I shall ask my old friend Mr. Silver, he shall help me. Yes?"

"Yes."

"When I am in Berlin, if it is necessary, I shall ask help from another member of his family."

Rose remained quite motionless for several seconds, her eyes still closed. Then she opened them again. There was an expression of dismay in them, and of horror. John's fingers were fastened like steel clamps round the edges of his magazine, which stood rigid before him like a block of wood.

Then at last Rose spoke. The words were almost inaudible.

"Do you mean," she began, "do you mean . . . *that woman?* How can you? No, no, Mr. Emmanuel! You must not! You dare not!"

John flung himself round in his chair.

"What woman?" he rapped out.

"I mean . . . Elsie Silver!" said Mr. Emmanuel.

"Elsie Silver!" he repeated. *"Elsie Silver!* Do you mean Brockenburg's woman?"

"She is the daughter of my old friend," murmured Mr. Emmanuel, his head bowed as with the shame of a whole race.

"Elsie Silver! Elsie Silver!" John kept on mechanically repeating. "I knew she was Jewish," he said, as if to himself. "I heard she came from Doomington. But somehow I never connected up . . ." Then suddenly a gust of passion swept over him. He banged his fist down on the table, so that the glasses rattled and one fell over, dribbling its contents onto the carpet. "The bitch!" she shouted. "The bitch! And that's the woman you're going to ask for help, Mr. Emmanuel?" His eyes sparkled with anger. "You're crazy, I tell you! You oughtn't to be allowed out without a keeper! Damn this glass!" He righted it. "I haven't any more to say!" He switched round again in his chair.

Mr. Emmanuel addressed his remarks to Rose.

"I know he is right," he said. "It is a shame a Jew should ask a favour from that woman! She is a bad woman! She has shortened by years the life of her father and mother. She is a shame to our town and to all Jews . . . to all Jews that have been and are today.

"But just the same, if it is necessary, I shall ask her. I will forget she is the fancy woman of Brockenburg. I will forget she is a traitor to her people. I will remember only she is the daughter of my old friend, Sam Silver. I will remember she is a woman. She has not herself had a child; maybe for that reason there will be some place in her heart for Bruno. I will ask her to use her position to find out what I am asking. She will not refuse. She cannot refuse. No human being is so bad like that." He stopped. He could continue no longer, his words had been barely intelligible. "Forgive me, Captain Cooper. I know it is your last night. It has not been for you a nice time. Forgive me. It is like that now with the Jews. Good night. Good night, Rose."

He went off unsteadily to the door. They made no effort to stop him.

"Good night!" they called out bleakly after him.

A silence fell between them. Neither felt like disturbing it for minute upon minute. At last John Cooper let himself go again.

"Elsie Silver, eh? Elsie Silver! I used to see her at the Tivoli, you know, smacking her bottom with a cane! Oh, the bitch!"

"It was a strange houseful of daughters," said Rose,

more mildly. "I used to meet them at Mrs. Poyser's shop, when I was a little girl. You wouldn't have known Susan, would you, the next older one? No, you wouldn't!"

"Why shouldn't I?"

"She was as plain as a pikestaff. You never heard about her, did you?"

"I don't suppose I did."

"She married a young fellow who used to hang about the place, a certain . . . Polednik. Yes, that was the name. He became a Bolshevik Commissar later. She became Mrs. Commissar! I told you once. I'm sure I did."

"I don't remember! By God, *what* a crew! Are they still Mr. and Mrs. Commissar, or have they been"—he placed an index finger horizontally against his forehead—"liquidated?"

She shrugged her shoulders.

"I don't know a thing about them. I've not thought about them for years!"

"Grrr! *What* a crew!" he repeated. "Give me another drink, Rose! You've upset me. A stiff one!"

V

It was some half-hour later. A line of light glowed under Mr. Emmanuel's door. Presumably he was not yet asleep. Rose knocked at his door.

"Can I come in, please, Mr. Emmanuel?"

"Who is that? Rose? Come in, please."

Rose entered. She stood hesitantly by the door.

"Please, Rose, what is it? Is anything the matter? The boy"—he made a movement as if to get out of his bed.

"No. He's perfectly all right. We've been talking things

over, John and I. We think you're grand, Mr. Emmanuel. But it's not that I've come to talk about. I've not come to argue, either. I just want you to agree to one thing."

"Yes?"

"You've written to London. I've seen the letter. You've not written to Berlin."

"That's true."

"John and I think you ought to write to the authorities in Berlin before actually going there."

"The Committee in London said——"

"Yes, I know what the Committee in London said. But after all, they've got a great many people to deal with besides Bruno. So have the authorities in Berlin. We think you ought to make a serious effort to extract some information direct. Perhaps they've heard something since the Committee wrote. Perhaps they know something they can tell a private individual which they couldn't tell to a committee. You've got to write, Mr. Emmanuel, before you do anything else."

"And if they don't answer!"

"If they know anything they'll answer. You might even tell them you propose to go over if you don't get satisfaction. That'll rouse them, I think. They won't want you poking about over there, if they can help it."

"But supposing they *can't* help it? Supposing they can't tell me anything?"

"Then you will go, my knight-at-arms. Then you will go."

He turned his head away, blushing.

"You shouldn't talk such nonsense, Rose. A bit of a holiday in Berlin, she talks like going to hunt in Africa wild animals."

"I have your promise, Mr. Emmanuel?"

"If it is not for Bruno a disappointment there should be such a delay."

"It will be all right with Bruno. I can promise you that. Good night, Mr. Emmanuel. Sleep well."

"God bless you, Rose."

But Mr. Emmanuel did not sleep well that night. All night long he was haunted by visions of Elsie Silver. He had put up something of a show when mentioning her name, opposing, or attempting to oppose, to Rose Cooper's horror a certain equanimity. But deep inside he had not felt like that. It was only now, as the dark hours went by, he realized how deeply she had wounded him and all the people of his race; for now was the first time during the three years that had elapsed since the establishment of Herr Hitler's regime, that he, or anyone of his acquaintance, had permitted himself to speak overtly of her existence.

He remembered her vividly in the years just before the War. She had already begun her equivocal career as a vaudeville artist, a male impersonator in the tradition of Vesta Tilley and Hetty King, who anticipated the technique of Lillie and Dietrich. He had seen her once or twice at the Tivoli in Doomington, but more frequently in her father's kitchen among the "anarchists," as those rather callow intellectuals insisted on calling themselves. She was the fourth of the five Silver daughters. She had disappeared quite early in her career from Doomington, and during the War had married a wealthy baronet, to whom she was still married, for all anyone knew to the contrary.

She had left her baronet and gone to live in Berlin during the inflation period, where she made a new reputation in the Kurfürstendamm cabarets. It was in Berlin, as certain travellers reported, that she had met her life's *grande passion,* a certain Oskar von Straupitz-Kalmin, a ruined nobleman, it was said, an habitué of the circles of the Crown Prince. Her father, the little rainproof manufacturer from Oleander Street, had become immensely rich at this time, owing to the extraordinary partnership between his own radiant naïveté and the incomparable astuteness of one of his sons-in-law, Alexander Smirnof, who had married Esther, the second daughter. Elsie's allowance was as prodigal as she cared for it to be. Elsie, therefore, gave up the cabarets for von Straupitz-Kalmin the Crown Prince. She lived with him, and he on her, in a state of immense mutual satisfaction.

Then Alexander Smirnof committed suicide, for the same reason as a Whittaker Wright, a Kreuger. Sam Silver saw no alternative but to strip himself of every penny to pay off the creditors of the various companies. It was at this point that Elsie Silver for the first time since her marriage swung back into the Doomington orbit. She and three of her four sisters swooped upon their father from widely spaced points of the compass and sought to restrain him from, as they deemed it, his monstrous folly. Even Susan came over from Moscow, the one married to Polednik, at that time a high official in the Commissariat for Foreign Trade.

The women were not successful in their mission. Sam Silver returned to his old home in Oleander Street, for it so happened he had bought it in his wife's name at the beginning of the starry rise of his fortunes. Elsie Silver, now a poor woman, returned to Berlin and to cabaret.

But not, the moralizers grimly pointed out, to the arms of Oskar von Straupitz-Kalmin. It was her money, more than her favours, he was partial to.

But von Straupitz-Kalmin apparently understood as little of the situation as the moralizers. He realized that, money or no money, the Jew woman's favours had become necessary to him. She resumed him with delight and no recrimination.

Then the smoky planet of Adolf Hitler came glowering upward into the troubled heavens. Even before his appointment as Reich Chancellor, rumours that were pronounced as preposterous as they were odious, began to link her name with the name of Wilhelm Brockenburg, one of Herr Hitler's closest associates, friend of Goebbels, Röhm, Hess, special intimate of Göring, Nazi member of the Reichstag. The *passion* for von Straupitz-Kalmin was not so *grande,* after all, or it could not withstand the lure of an intrigue at once more profitable and more highly spiced. The rumours went about in Berlin, London, Warsaw, Paris, Doomington, wherever Jews were. Many who were not Jews were intrigued by a situation more piquant than the situation in which for years the names of an Eastern European royalty and a red-headed lady of Jewish descent have been linked together. Some who were not Jews were not only intrigued but shocked; so were all Jews everywhere in the world who heard the incredible tale, and would not credit it.

If, however, a treachery so black were thinkable, it was decided on all hands that with the triumph of Herr Hitler's regime the liaison must inevitably come to an end. The traitress would be pushed bag and baggage across a frontier, or something worse would happen to her. As for her lover, he would renounce her, or share her fate, whatever it was.

Nothing of the sort happened. Brockenburg retained his high place in the inner councils of his party. Elsie Silver remained his private solace. It was, of course, anomalous that the mistress of one of Herr Hitler's right-hand men should be a completely non-Aryan lady, and one, moreover, whose sister was married to a high Soviet official. The anomaly was pointed out on more than one occasion by an indiscreet chatterer in a café, sometimes by a slightly puzzled burgher in the fancied security of his home. But condign measures followed swiftly on such indiscretion: the S.A. cellar, the concentration camp.

It was not for mere rhetorical purposes, or by way of oblique compliment to his friend, now General Göring, that Wilhelm Brockenburg incorporated a famous dictum of his in one of his most widely broadcast speeches. *"Wer Jude ist bestimme ich!"* pronounced Herr Göring, now a General and Prime Minister of Prussia. "I decide who is and is not Jewish!"—the reference being to complaints regarding the "blood-purity" of a certain highly placed soldier in the Air Force, who had once been instrumental in saving Herr Göring's life. *"Wer Jude ist bestimme ich!"* repeated Herr Brockenburg, the reference being not to a gentleman but to a lady; and the broken eyebrows moved up and down, and the fist came thundering down on the table.

It had been decided, apparently, that Elsie Silver was "Aryan." But she was, in fact, the daughter of a little Jewish rainproof-worker in the Longton district of Doomington in England. She is the daughter of Sam Silver, my old friend, mourned Mr. Emmanuel in his bed that night at Shipscar in the New Forest. How could she *do* such a thing? How could she think it is not far better to be dead, or a beggar at back doors begging for crusts?

It is a bad taste in my mouth, thought Mr. Emmanuel, trying to swallow it, but without success. It is like bells in my ears. Please God I should not have to ask her she should help me.

But if I must, I shall go to her. It is for Bruno. Can I help it?

4

I

MR. EMMANUEL spent quite a lot of the following morning drafting and writing out a letter to Berlin. By the time it was finished, John Cooper was pretty well ready to go. The family was going with him. It was a pleasant drive to Southampton and back again.

"You will post this letter for me, Rose?" bade Mr. Emmanuel. "You will not forget?"

"I won't forget," Rose assured him.

"Good-bye, tough guy!" John smiled at him. "I hope you don't get further than Liverpool Street."

"Who knows?"

John drove off, sucked as a straw in the wind towards his world of dock, ship, wheelhouse, and the vast sea. Mr. Emmanuel spent most of the rest of the day with Bruno, roaming about the nearer woods. Bruno had his mouth-organ. He played *"Drei Lilien," "Morgenrot,"* all the favourites. And, of course, he sang *"Pimpanulla."*

Die geliebte Pimpanulla
Schreit einmal Hula! Hula!

It was as if there had been no Roman's Bight, no moonlit excursion to the floundering silver porpoises. They were very happy.

Mr. Emmanuel left two days later for Doomington. He was, after all, a man of affairs. He could afford to neglect them no longer. He had a great send-off at Salisbury station: the five Cooper women, the Cooper boy, Bruno Rosenheim, Tessa the spaniel, two other dogs, or, if you count a Pekinese that Sarah had suddenly acquired from somewhere, three.

Mr. Emmanuel stood at the open carriage window, his head floating in the frame like a buoy.

"Good-bye, everybody. Good-bye. Good-bye."

Bruno stood rigid, his arms extended straight down along his thighs.

"Good-bye, Bruno. I hope I see you again soon."

The boy tried to reply but could not. His mouth shaped one word, and then another. *Good-bye. Thank you.* The guard by the engine whistled and lifted his green flag. The train hissed and sneered and charged off.

"Are you coming, Bruno?" asked Mary junior, tugging at his sleeve.

"Leave him for a moment or two," her mother whispered. "Get me a paper, will you, darling?"

II

It was on a Wednesday, the fourth of September, that Mr. Emmanuel returned to Doomington. He got busy at once. The first thing he did was to write a letter to his son Moisheh, in Palestine, explaining that he had volunteered to do some work in Germany in connexion with German refugees. That is to say, if it was necessary. It might not be. He hoped, if he went, that would make no difference to the date of his intended departure for Palestine. Moisheh knew already he was waiting till the insurance company paid up his endowment some time in the middle of October. He hoped to arrive in Palestine, in a lucky hour, some time in November. If the work he was going to do in Germany held him up at all, it might not be more than a week or two.

Mr. Emmanuel wrote that way because he relied on receiving before the end of September some sort of answer to his letter to the Berlin people. During this time he wrote letters every second day to Bruno, both at Shipscar and at his school in Haslemere after the term started. They would not be the letters for which the boy's heart had once yearned with such dreadful intensity, and to the non-arrival of which he seemed now to have reconciled himself with a more dreadful resignation. But they would be letters, at least. And though they contained the minimum of reference to Mr. Emmanuel's proposed excursion, they were an earnest of his fixed intention to go, as soon as it was clear there was no alternative.

The end of September arrived and with it no reply from Berlin. Simmering with impatience and quite sick with misery, he gave them one more week. Still no word came. Then he let himself go. He wrote such a scarifying letter, he reported to Rose, it will be a strange thing it shall not burn up all the other letters in the same letter-bag. They expected help from the various committees in London, in Doomington, in Leeds, and this is the way they treated Isaac Emmanuel, late Secretary to the Doomington Jewish Board of Guardians. He would make a complaint to the Board of Deputies in London, to the New York Board, he would show them up, such manners like they had, they should be ashamed of themselves.

The letter to Rose reporting what he had written was

posted at the same time as that same letter to Berlin. Within an hour he was suffering acute pangs of conscience. He was afflicted with the distressing faculty of feeling things, and in so brief a space of time, from the other person's point of view much more acutely than from his own. Have they got nothing more on their mind in Berlin that they should go answering interfering old men that have not got even an official position any more? If one boy is unhappy about his mother, are there no other boys unhappy about their mothers, and mothers about their boys? He sat biting his nails in his home in Magnolia Street, wondering whether this time they would reply, and if they did, in what language it would be couched.

A letter came on the Friday morning, four days later. It was a formal letter, but there was a tired ring about it. The Community office had already done everything in their power at the request of the Refugee Committee in London. In response to Mr. Emmanuel's plea they had, however, once again addressed an inquiry to the proper quarters in Berlin. Their letter had been returned, underlined three times: *"Ohne Interesse für die Jüdische Gemeinde"* (Without Interest for the Jewish Community). They begged Mr. Emmanuel to suspend his activities in the matter, and particularly urged him not to carry out his stated intention to come to Berlin in person to continue his inquiries.

Mr. Emmanuel duly reported to Rose that an answer had at last arrived from Berlin. It was not satisfactory, and he proposed, therefore, to leave for Berlin on Monday, by which time he would have everything in order. He would have left sooner, if the following day had not been the Sabbath. He wrote to Bruno to the same effect.

His passport was, of course, already in order, a completely virginal passport. But he thought an hour or two well spent that Saturday, studying the map of Berlin, with the assistance of a Herr Zittau, a refugee from that city, a glass manufacturer who had once been in a big way and was now trying to start again in a couple of rooms in Oleander Street. He felt that if he knew something about Berlin in advance, it might shorten his stay there, and he was not pretending he was looking forward to it as a holiday. The Rosenheims used to live in the Motzstrasse, in West Berlin, and it seemed to him that the neighbourhood would be as useful a headquarters as any.

There was a Jewish pension, Herr Zittau informed him, the Pension Kahn, in the Bambergerstrasse, which ran straight into the Motzstrasse. Mr. Emmanuel addressed a letter there that same evening, requesting them kindly to reserve a room for him for the following Tuesday. Mr. Zittau further warned him to descend at the Zoo station when he got to Berlin, as the principal station, the Friedrichstrasse, carried him a good distance away from the pension. On the other hand, the Friedrichstrasse was much nearer the Community offices, where he proposed to conduct his first inquiries.

But Mr. Emmanuel did not, in fact, leave for Berlin the following Monday. After writing to the Pension Kahn that night, he went to Garden's Travel Bureau to make final arrangements, and on his return was caught in a tremendous downpour. There was no Mrs. Emmanuel to see to things when he got home, and Ada Hummel, Rose's sister, when she came in to make a meal for him next day, found him in a state of high fever. She at once sent for Dr. Shulman, who found complications, of which the most serious was pleurisy. A district nurse was called in, and the Magnolia Street women, from both sides of the street, behaved, it was reported, like angels.

But that did not seem enough to Rose Cooper, over in Shipscar, to whom Ada very early sent the news of Mr. Emmanuel's illness. She handed Dick over to his aunt and left the three girls in the charge of the housekeeper under Aunt Mary's general supervision. Two days after the receipt of Ada's letter, an exchange of telegrams having in the meantime confirmed the gravity of Mr. Emmanuel's illness, she came to Doomington. She drove straight to Magnolia Street, having not set foot there since her departure to marry John towards the end of the War, nearly two decades earlier. She had sent orders to Ada to prepare Mr. Emmanuel's back bedroom, and with her sister's aid proceeded to install herself with no ceremony and little sentiment.

She was less moved than might have been expected by her return to Magnolia Street after all these years. Perhaps that was partly because she had lived a full and happy life since then, fuller and happier than is the usual lot of the dwellers in such streets. She had a pleasant home, four children she loved, a husband she adored. Perhaps she was in some ways a not very sensitive woman. The fact remains, and it is hardly a discredit to her, that for her the important thing about her return was that now dear Mr. Emmanuel would have somebody efficient, as well as devoted, to look after him. To the people of Magnolia Street, the women rather than the men, those who had been her contemporaries and those who had been brought up on her legend, her return was at once curiously thrilling, curiously bewildering.

Hers had been one of two marriages between young

people from opposite sides of the street which had captured the imaginations of a whole generation of its inhabitants. One had been between Benny Edelman, a carpenter, and a Jessie Wright, a green-eyed siren of a widow. That marriage had turned out disastrously, and in course of time the young man, minus the leg he had lost somewhere in France, came crawling back to his mother. He still lived with her at number seven, a grim old lady, who had mourned him as dead during the time of his defection, and had permitted him to return from the dead, not only, or even so much, because he was her child, as because he must henceforth be a living witness to Israel of the iniquity of intermarriage.

It was true that the Gentile harlot had stolen from Benny Edelman his youth, his good name, his chance of rearing a Jewish family to the glory of Jehovah; even the blame for the loss of his leg was insensibly transferred from the Great War to the green-eyed siren. But Rose Berman's marriage to John Cooper had involved her in no such calamities. On the contrary, it was known she was a happy woman, with a quiverful of blessings. It seemed to the more dispassionate residents that as exemplars or warnings the two intermarriages ruled each other out.

But Mrs. Edelman was not dispassionate; nor was her lieutenant, Mrs. Poyser, of the grocery shop. They had no doubt that Rose's cupboards were crammed with skeletons, her husband was faithless to her in every port he called at, her children were bags of sicknesses. What if Rose's sister, Ada, who had never denounced the relationship, tearfully denied these allegations? They looked at her coldly, and turned their shoulders upon her, busying themselves with the pound of sugar or packet of candles which one had come to buy and the other was there to dispense.

The women of the Jewish pavement were on the whole inclined to take the Poyser-Edelman view of these matters. The Gentile women, on the other hand, who remembered clearly enough the Edelman-Wright and Berman-Cooper affairs, were less disposed to think of them as instances justifying, or not justifying, an abstract principle. They judged affairs like these strictly on their merits. One had been a failure, one a success. That was all there was to it.

With the advent of Herr Hitler's regime and the promulgation and execution of his racial policies there was an uncomfortable readjustment of views on the Jewish pavement. In all conscience Mrs. Edelman had made trouble enough about this question of intermarriage. But Herr Hitler was making a great deal more. His view was seen to be curiously similar to that of Mrs. Edelman, though the Chosen People of her conception were not identical with the Chosen People of his. The very fact of this identity of views made her lose a certain amount of ground.

It was true that with a chill fury she argued that Herr Hitler's regime was a direct consequence of, and punishment for, the behaviour of Germany's Rose Bermans. In the same way she had earlier argued that the Great War was the Lord's reprisal against those evil Jews who committed the sin of riding in tramcars upon the Sabbath. But now, as then, it was felt that there was some disproportion between the offence and the punishment, it was altogether too much of a bad thing.

The sentiment was vague. Among the dwellers on the

Jewish pavement it might not reflect itself in conscious thought for two or three generations, though in what philosophic or physical weather they might find themselves in two or three generations was beyond surmisal. But vague though the sentiment was, it expressed itself in a certain shy welcome to Rose Cooper which quite surprised her. She recalled how an invitation had been sent her to that great Magnolia Street Party held some five years ago which had formed the subject of frequent reminiscences on the part of Mr. Emmanuel during the evenings at Shipscar. She knew Mr. Emmanuel had sent the invitation not in the hope that she would accept it, but because he could not bear to miss anybody out of anything.

She had sent back a charming little note saying how sorry she was, but what with the new baby and one thing and another . . . And, of course, she had not entertained the idea for one moment of accepting the invitation. She wondered whether, after all, she might have accepted, whether it would have been so embarrassing as she had imagined. John was at sea at the time, but Ada, her own sister, would have been there, and John's sisters, Mary and Enid, and all the Emmanuels. She would have seen again all these lovely funny people, Durbinses and Billigs, Poysers and Tawnies.

She was wrong, of course. She had lived too long away from all this to have a delicate sense of it all; it would have been really rather embarrassing for everybody five years ago, if she had been there. Since then, however, a great deal had happened. For instance, the Reichstag, in Berlin, had been burned down. Even in the kitchens of Magnolia Street the smell of the burning was very perceptible. . . . But she really did not have much time, at least by day, to think of those things. She had a good deal to do. She was at least as skilful a hand as the district nurse with Mr. Emmanuel's poultices, and rather better than Ada, or any of the other women who came in to give a hand, with the invalid foods that were put to the patient's lips every hour or two: the arrowroot, the beef tea, the chicken broth.

But at night, as she sat drowsing in a chair beside the fire, thoughts like those would not be gainsaid, thoughts in which place and time and people were confounded. Now she recalled how old Mother Tawnie had come in, only an hour or two ago, with a great bunch of hothouse grapes. Now it was Mrs. Seipel, Mrs. Shulman, Mrs. Billig, coming in processionally with egg-cakes and *knishehs;* but the person lying in the bed a few feet away was no longer Mr. Emmanuel; it was her own mother, dead long ago. She recalled Benny Edelman, but he still had both his legs; she passed the time of day with Nellie Tawnie, of the public house, but she was not a grown woman yet; she was a little blue-eyed slip of a thing, with blue eyes and a pink ribbon in her hair.

Yet one image haunted her imagination more persistently than any of these, though he had no connexion at all with Magnolia Street. It was a boy some fifteen years old, with unruly chestnut-coloured hair and green eyes with brown specks swimming in them. It was, in fact, the boy Bruno Rosenheim, awaiting down southward in Haslemere the fulfilment by Mr. Emmanuel of a pledge sworn to him. Strangely enough, the boy's age and appearance did not remain consistent. There were times when he seemed much younger, only five years old. His face was squarer, there was a cleft in his chin, his hair lay on his forehead in a fringe. He was, in fact, young

Dick Cooper, her own son, who also, like Bruno Rosenheim, was the offspring of parents of whom one was Jewish and one not.

Even more by night than by day she felt her duty a twofold charge. She must do all she knew to nurse Mr. Emmanuel back to health for his own sake, for she loved him; also for the sake of Bruno, who, if Mr. Emmanuel died, would die too, a child slain by his own hand.

It is possible that Mr. Emmanuel would not have fought so bravely to recover for his own sake alone. But he, too, knew he was fighting a twofold fight, and he pulled through at length. It was hard going.

A strange thing happened about this time. Magnolia Street added to its roster a citizen who had never set foot there nor, it seemed more than probable, ever would. It was this same German refugee boy, Bruno Rosenheim, from the Motzstrasse, in Berlin. It was not from the lips of Mr. Emmanuel himself they had learned about him, though he had been by no means shy about spreading the news when Rose had issued her original summons, requesting his help with her clutch of boys. There were people about, he gathered, who thought he was at the end of his tether, merely because he was getting a bit old for his job at the Board of Guardians. Well, this Rose Berman affair would show them. If there was a job about that needed tact, it was still Isaac Emmanuel they called on. Yes, he made no secret of it at the synagogue, the Lithuanian Brotherhood, and elsewhere.

When he returned from Shipscar, however, he was not quite so expansive. He let it be known there was a chance of his going to Germany shortly on refugee business, but he kept the name of Bruno out of it. There was a sort of delicacy about the boy and about the mission which made it desirable that the teeth of tittle-tattle should not be allowed to nibble at them.

Rose Cooper, however, was not quite so sensitive as he. Also, she felt there was something rather grand about the spirit in which he had vowed himself to this journey, its simplicity, its nonchalance almost. She told Ada the whole story and Ada told the street. The street was immensely affected, both the Jewish folk on the one side and the Gentile folk on the other. "Poor little doveling!" they said on one side. "Poor little mite!" they said on the other. He was Mr. Emmanuel's Bruno and Rose Berman's Bruno. He became Magnolia Street's Bruno, too. They took him to their bosom.

The street, too, prayed for Mr. Emmanuel's recovery for Bruno's sake as well as Mr. Emmanuel's. When once the old fellow had recovered, he would go to Germany and show them what was what. Mr. Emmanuel was not the sort of person who would be put off by soft phrases, or hard knocks, either. He'd get to the bottom of this business of Bruno's mother, good and quick. He was clever, was Mr. Emmanuel; he could argue the hind leg off a horse. They'd *have* to let him know what had happened to the poor woman. What? She might be in a concentration camp? That wouldn't stop him. He'd get through to the Governor somehow, and talk and talk and talk at him till the wretched fellow would have to release her if only to stop Mr. Emmanuel talking.

No doubt the Governor would be a bit sticky at first, for Mr. Emmanuel was a Jew, of course. But then he was an Englishman, too. That would make them keep a civil tongue in their heads. If anybody could get Bruno's mother out of a concentration camp, it was Mr. Emmanuel. And if she wasn't there, in other words, if she was dead—well, the sooner the boy was brought out of his misery the better.

All that was necessary now was for Mr. Emmanuel to get better.

He took a long time about it, despite the help of Dr. Shulman, and Ada, and Mr. Silver, who was ready to act as errand-boy at any hour of the day or night. And, of course, of Rose, who managed to put in a whole fortnight with him, up there in Magnolia Street. It was a good month, however, before he could sit up for any length of time, even though he had been steered clear of the graver complications of pleurisy.

Towards the middle of December, Ada was given the job of taking him down to Bournemouth, where Dr. Shulman knew of a nice Jewish boarding-house that took in convalescents. It was universally known that Mr. Emmanuel would not come back again to Doomington before his projected journey to Germany, so there was quite a to-do in the street the day he and Ada left for Bournemouth. Of course, he was anything but strong, and Dr. Shulman was very firm about his not getting excited. Otherwise there would have been real goings-on.

"Good-bye, Mr. Emmanuel!" they called out to him from both sides of the street, as the taxi made off to the station. "Give that there Adolf one for me!" "Tell Bruno's mother she can come here! *We'll* look after her!" "Good-bye, Mr. Emmanuel! Good-bye! Good-bye!"

He leaned back in the taxi and wiped away a tear. It should only be so easy like they think, he said to himself. And why should it not be easy? What am I going to try and find out, after all? How to make diamonds out of lumps of sugar? Well, please God, it should be in a lucky day!

Rose and Mary drove over quite a number of times during his convalescence to see how he was getting on. But it was not until the second week of the New Year that the doctor there finally let him go, and Rose drove down to carry him off to Shipscar. It was the school holiday time, and to his great joy, Bruno, too, was at Ringwood. But he was not at Shipscar most of the time, for Captain Cooper was away, and Mary had both Dick and Bruno staying with her at Wain Cottage, partly so that they might keep each other company, partly because she felt Rose already had enough on her hands.

Mr. Emmanuel was straining on the leash to be gone all the time he was at Shipscar, but Rose kept a tight hand on him. She tried rather forlornly once or twice to get him to drop the whole idea, though she knew quite well she had no chance of succeeding.

"It's not because you're getting on in years a bit," she would urge. "It's not even because you've had a bad illness lately . . . it's because . . . it's because . . ." She did not quite know how to express her idea.

"Well?" he asked with a patient smile.

"Don't you *see?* It's as if something is trying to get in your way . . . trying to stop you! As if . . . as if perhaps you *oughtn't* to go! Do you see what I mean?"

"My sweet one," he said indulgently. "Perhaps it is trying to stop me till I should arrive just in time for good news? Why shouldn't it be like that, eh?"

She sighed and shrugged her shoulders.

It was actually not until the last day of January, the year being now 1936, that Rose and Mary went up to town with him, to see him off at Liverpool Street station.

Bruno was not there, of course. He was back at school. But he had something of Bruno to take away with him, a photograph or two, and a cigarette-holder; you never saw such a cigarette-holder—real amber with a real gold mouthpiece. The boy must have spent all his pocket-money on it, for months back and months to come.

It was the ten o'clock boat train for Harwich Mr. Emmanuel was taking, for the Continent via Flushing.

"I want you to write to me regularly," Rose enjoined upon him. There was more than a hint of tears in her eyes. "I'm going to be very worried about you, you know."

"Worried? What should you be worried about? Of course I'll write you. Why not? Every day, if you like."

She suddenly seized his hand.

"I know it'll be an awful nuisance," she urged. "But, please, if you only would . . . write every day, I mean. If it's only a postcard."

"I promised Bruno I shall send him a postcard every day. Why not you as well?"

"Thank you, thank you. You won't worry about Bruno, will you?"

"I will not worry about Bruno. He trusts me. I trust him."

"Yes," she said. "I trust him, too, as I trust you or John."

He smiled at her.

"You are a good girl, Rose." He turned to Mary. "You are a good girl, too, Miss Cooper. Thank you, both of you, for that lovely rug and that lovely cushion."

The porter banged his door to and locked it.

"Keep warm!" they cried. "Wrap your things well round you! Good luck! Good-bye!"

He blew a kiss towards them.

"Good-bye, my Magnolia Street girls! Good-bye!" he cried, and, as the train pulled away from the platform, he leaned from the carriage window and waved his pince-nez in the air above his head, as some centuries earlier Don Quixote had waved his lance.

5

I

MR. EMMANUEL snuggled down into his corner, with the nice soft rug that Rose had bought for him spread over his knees and the small of his back pressed up against the cushion Mary Cooper had made for him.

He was not an experienced traveller. He had been to London a few times on committee work, and had done a lot of jogging about Lancashire and Cheshire to enlist the support of wealthy patrons in connexion with one cause and another. But since his original arrival in England in his early teens he had never left the country. He did not know, for instance, how useful a rug and cushion can be on a long journey, and had not provided himself with them. Rose and Mary made up the deficiency. John Cooper, who had received orders to sail for Sydney, sent a note requesting Rose to buy him a pocket flask. He had a nice new suitcase with some nice linen in the rack above his head, also a nice new attaché-case. They were all going to come in useful later, on the longer journey to Palestine.

He felt the pocket flask snug in his trousers pocket. Rose had filled it with brandy. He thought of taking a swig at it to try it out, but decided he would wait till he really needed it. His hand was not too steady and he would probably spill it. Instead, he patted reassuringly the bulge in his waistcoat on the left-hand side. Yes, it was all there in the special pocket he had had sewn onto the lining—the wallet with his loose notes, his ticket, and his letter of credit, and the passport.

Above all, that nice passport, bound in good blue cloth, tough as a book, with its gold embossed seal, its pages like skin, and that wonderful personal letter from Sir John Allsebrook Simon, requesting and requiring in the name of His Majesty all those whom it might concern to allow the bearer to pass freely without let or hindrance and to afford him every assistance and protection of which he might stand in need.

It was very snug there, snugger than the cushion, the rug, the pocket flask. It was really, in a way, more stimulating than any brandy. He plunged his hand into the special pocket, brought out the passport, and studied it lovingly. It was good and firm, like England itself. He had seen other passports, in his office in Doomington and elsewhere, but they were often poor things, sometimes shoddy, sometimes flashy, like the countries that had issued them.

Like those people in the other corner, for instance, the two nondescript men, and the woman with the black hair falling all over her face. She was the wife of one of the men, perhaps. The two men might have been brothers. Who were they, poor things? What sort of passport did they have? He had no idea what language they were speaking; it was not even a Slavonic tongue, he thought. Something further away, perhaps Asia Minor somewhere. The material their clothes and shoes were made of was not much use, either.

He was himself no Clark Gable, of course. His overcoat was a little shiny, maybe, in places, but the stuff was good, it was English. Like his passport.

A fine lot of use it would be, he said to himself, if poor foreigners like those should want to go to Germany to find out about Bruno's mother. He turned the virgin pages of his passport lovingly, then came to the regulations printed on the back flyleaf. He read them through, not with interest but with devotion, rather, as one reads the obscure lines of a ritual; then he closed his passport and stuffed it carefully away into the special pocket. He drowsed off. It had meant getting up very early that morning to reach Liverpool Street in time for the day boat train. He did not awaken till the train slowed down on the outskirts of Harwich.

There was a good deal of the North Sea, Mr. Emmanuel thought, and all of it disagreeable. He was glad to get out upon terra firma again. His customs examination was of the simplest, but he was a little nettled to find at the passport barrier that the most inept-looking little passport carried exactly the same weight as his own stout document, not a milligramme less. The train was not crowded and he found a corner seat without difficulty. Two large, stout gentlemen were already in occupation of the two further corners; a woman soon after occupied the seat facing him. They were all German, he gathered. The two men were speaking German to each other, the woman was carrying German newspapers. Besides, they looked German. Oh, yes, he was en route for Germany right enough.

He turned the pages of one of the magazines he had with him. He found he could not concentrate, not even on the pictures. He was conscious of a tingling excitement all the way down to his toes. Why am I so excited? he asked himself. I am going to Germany. I am going to Germany. The pounding of the wheels took on the rhythm. I am going to Germany.

He realized suddenly that Germany seemed to him a long distance away. But it had not always seemed so to him, had it? When, in fact, it was not very far, no further than the next country to Holland and Belgium, just across the water. He had himself as a youth come from Russia, a country a great deal further away, in terms of the time it takes to make a journey.

Well, why did Germany seem so far? Yes, it was clear enough. It was three years now it had seemed like that, a place so strange, so utterly outside the mind-workings of a dim clerk, living in a dim street in an English provincial town.

The large, stout gentlemen on his left were talking hard. They had a lot to say to each other. They had rather military, peremptory voices. They were speaking German, of course, and Mr. Emmanuel understood quite a lot of what they were saying. The nature of their background was not very obscure, either. They were business men, agents for certain business products which they had been marketing in England. They were not in a big way, or they would not be travelling second-class. They talked business for some time, consulting and comparing papers they extracted from big leather portfolios. Then they put their papers away and the conversation became personal and domestic. Then they talked about beer, from this brewery, from the other brewery, how light it was, how heavy it was, it foamed too much, it foamed too little.

There was nothing occult, nothing frightening, in

their conversation, yet Mr. Emmanuel was frightened. They were so big and strange and inscrutable. He remembered, by way of contrast, the nondescript little group in the train between London and Harwich. He had no idea who they were, what they did for a living, what their relations were with each other. He had not understood a single word they were saying. Yet he knew they were the sort of people who would be sad over such things as made him sad, rejoice when he rejoiced, though their home was in the lee of the last mountain of Asia.

It was not so with these Germans from across the North Sea. They seemed almost of another species, whether it was the egg-baldness of their skulls, the deep pleats in the back of their necks, or the bottle-green opacity of their eyes. Or all these together, with the harsh staccato of their voices and the rigidity of their preoccupation with their theme.

Beer, Spatenbräu, Hackerbräu, Patzenhofer, Dortmunder . . . the art of *lagern,* keeping the beer . . . the art of *ausschänken,* pouring the beer out, so as to know exactly how much froth to get; a certain beer from Munich, it was still *Judengift,* Jew-poison; a *dunkles,* a dark beer from the Grabo Brauerei in Mecklenburg, there was nothing to equal it. . . .

They were at home, they were happy, the cigars flared like Thor's torches in the sides of their mouths.

The picture magazines lay disregarded by Mr. Emmanuel's side on the close-cropped plush seat, dull green, dark grey. The woman opposite was of a milder, slighter build. It did not seem easy to believe she could be the wife or mother of men like those. She sat with her head turned, looking out into the dark country. There were four photographs in framed panels above the seat, flanking a central mirror . . . German holiday places of one sort and another; a town with an old-fashioned market-place, a town hall, a fountain; a spa with fine hotels, a tree-shaded road; a lake with a small steamboat on it; a strip of sand, with a few hotels, a line of firs, a level sea.

That, then, was Germany. The moon, after all, was an odder place. Southport, Matlock, Buxton . . . they were not hopelessly dissimilar. The photograph nearest to him, immediately above the woman's head, was the strip of sand, with the few hotels, the line of firs. He craned his neck forward and screwed up his eyes to see what place it was.

It was Föhr.

Föhr? he asked himself. He had heard the name of that place. Föhr? Then he remembered. It was the place where Bruno had been on holiday once or twice with his parents. It was an island, with some pine-woods. They had swum and gone for long walks and eaten great meals. They had had a lovely time. The small boy, the mild intellectual, the gold-haired mother, who sang like a rosewood music-box, with dancing ladies and gentlemen painted upon it.

Mr. Emmanuel thrust back into the corner of the carriage. He felt cold all of a sudden, though there was ample heat in the pipes. His eyes moved from the picture of the strip of sand, to the lake with a steamboat, the spa with hotels, the old-fashioned market-place. They seemed very far again, further than Archangel or the Canadian Rockies, in a country very far and cold. The man came round and said food was ready. He got up and found the way to the restaurant-car. He was not interested in the food much, but he was thankful for the cup of hot soup and the coffee afterwards. He went back and dozed for a time till the Dutch frontier officials woke him again. They looked at his passport, they examined his luggage, they were quite satisfied. The train stopped. The train started again. A passport official in another uniform appeared with a colleague in attendance.

"Heil Hitler! Ihre Pässe, bitte!"

Mr. Emmanuel handed over his passport. These, too, were quite satisfied with it. I am in Germany, Mr. Emmanuel said to himself. It is like going to Altrincham on the tram. They say *"Heil Hitler,"* like "Good morning" or "Pleased to meet you." What should they do? They should eat you up?

"Have you any foreign currency, gentlemen?" The German gentlemen and the German lady had not. Mr. Emmanuel had some pound notes, as well as his travelling-marks and his letter of credit.

"Get it registered in the office there!" the officials bade, and walked on to the next carriage. Mr. Emmanuel looked about him in bewilderment. They had said something in Doomington, at the travel bureau, about having to register your foreign money at the frontier; he could not clearly remember what they had said. The two merchants, grumpy for sleep, looked stonily through the window.

"Bitte, Herr!" said the little woman opposite, addressing Mr. Emmanuel for the first time. She took him in hand, shepherded him through the examination, brought him back again.

He wanted to tell her how grateful he was, but he was so tired his German eluded him. He mumbled a few words. She smiled, made the ghost of a curtsy towards him, and retired into herself. The officials came and looked through the luggage, and at length the train started again.

I am in Germany, the wheels went. *I am in Germany. I am in Germany.* And why not Germany? Such a nice kind little woman, a real Jewish heart, God bless her! Like Queen Victoria! Why not in Germany? Why not in Germany? He was asleep soon.

He awoke with a start. He did not know whether half an hour had gone by or five hours. One tiny jet burned in a ceiling-lamp, obscured by a dark blue shutter like an eyelid. Each lay back in his corner, each of the two merchants, his belly vast and round, his throat stretched, his mouth open. They were enormous, they seemed to fill nearly the whole carriage, they seemed to be sucking in most of the air as through two funnels. The little woman opposite was, in fact, nearer to him than they were, by a foot or two. Yet she seemed further off, immensely further off. Her kindness seemed a delicate, remote, irrelevant thing.

All his fright reasserted itself. What have I got to be frightened of? I am tired. I am not used to long journeys like this. Rose was right I should take a sleeping-berth. Have I got money I should waste on a sleeping-berth? Do I want I should arrive a pauper to my son's colony in Palestine?

He had no idea how many miles further off Berlin was, twenty or two hundred. He knew there was as little chance now of his not getting to Berlin as there was of his not drinking a cup of coffee sooner or later. He knew he wanted to get to Berlin exactly as much as he had always done, ever since he had made his promise to Bruno.

But he knew he was in a state of panic; for no reason

at all. Or rather, for an exact and quite idiotic reason. Because there were two German business men in the carriage beside him, with shaven polls and creases in the back of their necks.

A fine reason. You should pick yourself together, Isaac Emmanuel. What is the matter with you? You should be ashamed of yourself.

Well, ashamed or not ashamed, shall I make a holiday of it? I promised Rose I should go straight to the boarding-house when I get to Berlin, and have a few hours' sleep before doing anything. Well, I shall instead go straight to the Jüdische Gemeinde, the Community office. For Bruno also the quicker is the better. Is that not true perhaps?

He took out his watch and screwed his eyes up to try and make out the time. He could not see.

"Tscha!" he muttered.

"It is about six, I think," the dim little woman said in the corner opposite. "We shall be in Berlin in one hour."

How faint and far her voice was, from another century.

They duly arrived in the Friedrichstrasse station an hour and some minutes later. It was very early, only seven-twenty. How very foolish of me, he thought. I might as well have got off at thc other station and gone straight to the Bambergerstrasse. I will, in any case, have to kill a couple of hours before I can hope for any attention in an office.

I am in Berlin, Bruno's city. Perhaps his mother is at this moment in some cellar less than a mile away, lying on a straw mattress. Perhaps she is staring through a prison window, her knuckles holding the bars. Perhaps she is five hundred miles away, in a big concentration camp, with fences round it and big lights shining down. Perhaps, perhaps . . . *Do not be afraid, Bruno. I shall find her for you.*

A hand brushed by his elbow.

"Guten Tag, Herr," a faint voice said. He did not even see her face again. The little woman was gone.

"Gepäck?" the porter asked.

"Danke schön!"

He put his suitcase away, not the attaché-case. It looked so English. He felt better with the attaché-case. He went into a lavatory and had a wash and brush-up. That took up half an hour.

I shall go out now and get a cup of coffee. With a bit of a walk and a cup of coffee it will be almost time. And I will feel much better as well. I feel quite good already. I did not see those two business men. Where did they go? They got down maybe at the other station? Two men big like that should disappear like soap-flakes? Well, well, I should break my head about them.

A sweet little woman. He was walking down the station-ramp towards street-level. A sweet little woman, God bless her. In Germany there must be millions like her, and men also. He was out in the street now. It was daytime, but it smelled a bit like night. It always smells like night near railway stations—the smoke and the tunnels. It is cold. He was grateful for his warm coat and scarf and his fur-lined gloves. But it was cold round the ears. He raised his scarf and pressed his hat down.

Which way, left or right?

What does it matter? Let it be left. I stretch my legs a bit, then I have some coffee. It will be good, a cup of coffee, and a roll with butter. Then I will be like a horse. There was not much traffic yet, and the people had hardly started arriving for the shops and offices. He passed under the steamy vault of the railway bridge and a little distance further came to the black waters of a canal or river. Beyond the water were small hotels, rather shoddy-looking in the black air. I will keep to this street, he thought. There is some life in it. There are windows with lights and people going in and coming out.

He crossed the water still on the left side of the street and continued till he came to a corner. Karlstrasse, he read. There is a light over there. Yes, it is a café. He walked for another twenty yards or so, then turned in. He pushed aside a heavy leather portière and the warm air puffed against his face. The steam condensed on his glasses and for a few moments he could not see. Then the steam cleared off. There were small round tables on his left, mostly empty. Over on his right was a glass-topped counter, on which stood baskets of rolls and cakes. A pleasant smell of coffee and fresh rolls came out from an inner room.

A woman stood behind the counter, her hands clasping her elbows, her fair hair pulled back from her forehead and screwed up behind into a bun. He had advanced within a yard or so from the counter when for the first time he noticed there was a placard pasted up behind the woman's head. Two words were printed on it in neat, large capitals: JUDEN UNERWÜNSCHT. *Jews Not Wanted.* He stopped as if his ribs had come up against an iron bar. He blushed. His head seemed to go all to pieces, bits of it floating this way and that.

He looked up with incredulous eyes into the woman's face. She did not seem, somehow, a bad woman, a woman who would put such an affront on a tired old stranger, with a dry throat from the soot and stale air of a long train journey. And, in fact, she was not. She parted her lips wryly and shrugged her shoulders. None of my doing, old Jew. Don't blame me.

He turned round and shuffled back towards the leather portière.

"*Zweite Ecke rechts,*" she called out after him, just loud enough for him to hear. "Second corner on the right."

He left the café and looked round before crossing the road. You are a big silly man, he told himself. You are not in Doomington any longer, you are in Berlin. You have got to look out for such things. They will happen to you all the time. That glass manufacturer told you—what is his name?—Herr Zittau. And have you not been reading newspapers? Look! Look at that shop window! Nothing in it but two big swastikas, and a few pairs of boots! Those men in brown uniforms, they are S.A. men. Look, this is swastikas on their arm-bands! Swastikas everywhere! And once, when you saw one swastika on your front door, it was like somebody had smacked you in the face. That was Doomington. This is Berlin. Remember, Berlin, Berlin.

Yes, this was the second corner on the right. There was a café there; doubtless Jews owned it. He entered and ordered breakfast. There was no embarrassment. Though he lingered as long as he could over his cigarette, it was still not quite nine by the time he had smoked it.

"Oranienburgerstrasse, please. Where is it?" he asked. He was, in fact, there already. He got up and walked back towards Unter den Linden, then north again to the Oranienburgerstrasse. It was half-past nine now. He had no difficulty in finding the offices.

He entered, gave his name, and asked for the Secretary,

the Herr Walther with whom he had had correspondence. He was taken into a waiting-room where there was a great air of activity. People were moving about with papers or standing about talking busily in groups; others sat about on benches. The same air of gloom hung over them all, whether busy or idle. He got through to the Secretary a considerable time later. That gentleman already looked very tired and worried, though the day had just begun.

"Good day. Yes? What can we do for you?"

"I wrote to you from England, Herr Walther. You don't remember my name?"

The Secretary reached for the slip of paper on which Mr. Emmanuel had written his name, then looked up swiftly.

"From Doomington? The Board of Guardians? You're *that* Mr. Emmanuel? So you've come after all! You're mad, Mr. Emmanuel!"

"I am sorry I should be a nuisance. I had to come. I promised that boy. I could not help myself."

"What boy?" He passed his hands through his hair. "Oh, yes! I remember! It'll do nobody any good, Mr. Emmanuel!"

"He would have killed himself if I had not come here!"

"Well? Boys are killing themselves every day!" He touched a pile of papers as if the statistics were all ready to hand. "It'll do nobody any good!" he repeated sombrely.

"Please, I beg you! If you have kept back anything, please tell me! I am not going to rest till I find out!"

Herr Walther lifted his fist as if to bang it down on the table, but the fist relaxed in mid-air. He bit his lips. His nerves were very much on edge.

"Mr. Emmanuel, it is as I wrote you." He rubbed his hand across his forehead wearily. "I do not know. Nobody knows. It is dangerous to try and find out." He looked shortly to left and right as if fearful somebody might have overheard him utter so critical an observation.

"Why, please, is it dangerous to try to find out?"

"All we have to say has already been said to you, in letters. I cannot explain any more. I will not argue. It is dangerous for us to have you here. It is not fair to us. Lord God!" he exclaimed, a break in his voice. "Have we not enough on our hands already?"

"You can give me no advice, no advice at all?"

"You are from England. You can go back again any moment. Do you know what that means?" He paused. A look of immense grief came into his eyes. "You are not far from the station," he resumed. "You want my advice? Go straight back there and take the next train home."

Mr. Emmanuel said nothing for some time, then at length:

"Will you be kind enough to take this address?" he requested. "I am going to stay at Frau Kahn's pension in Bambergerstrasse, number 38."

"I will not have your address, Mr. Emmanuel. You can put it on file with your consul. We cannot take any responsibility for you."

"Then there is nothing more to be said, Herr Walther?"

"Nothing more to be said." The man looked dejected to the point of tears.

"Good day, Herr Walther."

"Good day, Mr. Emmanuel."

Herr Walther bent down to his desk again. Mr. Emmanuel stood about unhappily for a moment or two, then he turned and went. I am painful in the neck to him, he thought, but can I help it? I am tired. I will take a taxi and get my big bag, then I will go to the Pension Kahn. I think I need a little rest, maybe.

It was quite a long drive, all told; first back to the station, then to a big tract of park, with statues in lines and circles, and stagnant black water in cement conduits, and bare patches of thin, nipped grass; then among streets again, newer-looking than those round the Friedrichstrasse, smarter shops with more chromium-plate lettering and bigger sheets of plate-glass. They got to a big church with towers at the intersection of several streets, with fine cafés in the offing and modern cinemas. A few minutes later the taxi stopped. They were in the Bambergerstrasse, at number 38.

It was a good thing to have no more luggage than you could carry yourself. He entered the vestibule, in one hand his attaché-case, in the other the suitcase with the rug and cushion strapped to it. He stood there uncertainly a moment or two, wondering how many floors he would have to climb; then a window snapped open on his right. A grizzled close-cropped head poked through.

"*Jawohl?*" a voice asked gruffly.

"Pension?" Mr. Emmanuel asked. "Frau Kahn?"

The window snapped to again. The glass pane, the lace curtain behind it, looked about as friendly as a sheet of ice.

They do not make things easy in this town, reflected Mr. Emmanuel. He could see no indication there was a Frau Kahn's pension on the ground floor. He climbed up a flight of stairs, then another. Here it was, her name on a glass panel, in a door parallel with the street. He rang.

A few seconds later a woman opened the door, dark-looking, a Jewess probably. She had a brush and duster in her hand.

"Yes?" she asked. She peered beyond Mr. Emmanuel's shoulder, as if she wondered whether someone were concealed behind him.

"Emmanuel is my name," he explained. "From England. I have written to Frau Kahn."

Another woman came into view, from the corridor that dived down towards the rooms on the left. She gave the appearance of having been waiting out of sight while she ascertained what sort of caller this was. She seemed reassured, evidently.

"I am Frau Kahn," she announced. "Please come in, Mr. Emmanuel. We were expecting you. Trude, take the bag." She herself took hold of the attaché-case, with a hand that trembled so much she could hardly hold it. She was a small woman, with misty blue eyes and a pointed nose. There was an odd old-fashioned collar to her dress, and her hair was piled up in a mode that seemed decades old. She wore a big cameo-brooch and big earrings and a big gold cable-chain looped two or three times round her neck and falling before her in a great arc. All her jewellery was too big for her. It did not seem at all the right get-up in which to supervise the morning chores of a pension; it seemed rather designed to indicate to the stranger that Frau Kahn still was, as she always had been, a woman of substance.

Trude went first and turned left, Mr. Emmanuel followed, Frau Kahn took up the rear.

"*Bitte,* Mr. Emmanuel. We have prepared one of our best rooms for you, Mr. Emmanuel." Perhaps she had never had a Mr. Engländer in her pension before. It seemed to give her pleasure to insist on that Mister, as if he were someone from Oxford College, and high up in the Foreign Office.

Trude opened the last of the doors parallel with the landing. It was a good room, with two windows. There was, however, too much furniture, and all of it too big —the bed, the secretaire, the vases, the plant-pots on occasional what-nots, the plush-clothed centre table, the plush-upholstered chaise longue, the plush easy chairs. Perhaps there was too much plush.

"An agreeable room, no?" asked Frau Kahn. "Very warm, no?"

The two women put the cases down on the chaise longue.

"Indeed, indeed," Mr. Emmanuel agreed. "A nice room!" He was a little fearful lest the cost of this plush splendour was going to be rather out of his schedule. "But a telephone, please? Is there a telephone in this room?" He looked round and saw none. He had hoped to do his telephoning in privacy. He did not want to economize on that. There was a silence. The silence became so marked that he wondered if he had quite got the word right. Surely it was the same in both languages. "I see there is no telephone in this room," he said again.

"And why, please? And is there any reason why there should be a telephone? Is it not perhaps a good room without a telephone? Please, if it is not good enough——"

He looked over towards Frau Kahn quite bewildered. Her pointed nose had become quite white. The colour seemed to have gone out of her lips. Her whole body was shaking.

"I beg your pardon," he said hurriedly. "If not, then not."

"There is no reason in this house for private telephone-calls. Show him, Trude. Look please. Only a yard away in the corridor." Trude opened the door again and showed him the instrument on a small table quite close. He went back into the room, and now another excitement came up. A door he had not noticed had been opened at the opposite corner of the room, a communicating-door, evidently, between this room and its neighbour. A slatternly woman stood grinning in the open doorway. She was quite old, but she seemed anxious to look as young as might be. Her raddled cheeks were daubed with rouge. Her clothes were considerably too young for the scrawny neck and the fallen chaps. The skirt on one side was pinned up six inches or more, showing a red flannel petticoat.

"This room has been done already!" Frau Kahn was crying. "What are you doing in this room again?" Frau Kahn turned on Trude. "I told you the doors between the rooms should always be bolted! Aren't you ever going to learn? All right! Drive me quite mad!" She seemed on the verge of tears. Trude went up to her and patted the back of her hand. Trude seemed a good sort. The old woman stood sniggering for a moment or two longer then went off, closing the door behind her. Trude crossed over to that end of the room and opened the door again, as if to make sure the old creature had gone. She was gone, it seemed.

"Come here, come here, please!" whispered Frau Kahn, motioning Mr. Emmanuel to the centre of the room. He went over. "I must apologize. I must explain." Both hands hung from their wrists, trembling, like aspen-leaves from their stalks. "You see, she is the only Aryan woman we have. Her name is Kati. She comes in to scrub the floors. She came a year ago. The house-porter said we must have her. I do not know what is the connexion between them. Perhaps nothing. Perhaps only he sees she makes us unhappy. Also, we are afraid. Sometimes one moment she is in one end of the apartment, then in the same second she is behind your shoulder. She is sixty, seventy; no one knows how old she is. But she says she is thirty-eight. How old do you think she is?" It seemed a question that had already been debated more than once in Frau Kahn's pension.

Mr. Emmanuel put out his hand on one of the plush chairs to steady himself. He was very tired indeed. He felt called upon to give a judicial answer.

"Some women are older than they say they are," he murmured.

But Frau Kahn was not really interested in his reply.

"So for us in one way the Nuremberg Laws came like a blessing. Do you see? If she is thirty-eight, let her be thirty-eight. No Aryan woman under forty-five is allowed to work in a non-Aryan place. So we said she must go, we were sorry. And what happened? The house-porter came up. Did you see that house-porter?" Her voice fell to a whisper.

"Yes, I saw him," admitted Mr. Emmanuel, without enthusiasm. "But not much of him."

"He came upstairs here. He said she was not thirty-eight, any longer. She was turned forty-six. He said it would be better for us she should be forty-six."

"I see," Mr. Emmanuel murmured. "I see." He was not sure that this was quite the right moment for an exposition by Frau Kahn of her domestic tribulations. "Perhaps if I could have a bath now and rest for a few hours . . ." he suggested.

"A bath? Yes, of course, a bath! In the other corridor, please! See Mr. Emmanuel has a bath, Trude! Whatever you wish, Mr. Emmanuel. Only please ring that bell, Mr. Emmanuel." Frau Kahn bowed to her Mister once more, her loops of cable-chain clanking. Then she disappeared.

II

Mr. Emmanuel was not in the habit of sleeping by daylight, and it was hardly two o'clock when he woke up again. He had a sense that a meal was in progress somewhere along the apartment, but he did not feel like tackling a tableful of strangers. He was not very hungry, either. He stayed on in bed and turned the situation over.

The Community office had been anything but helpful. Of course not. He told himself he had never expected anything else. What was the next stage? There was only one next stage and one next stage after that. To ask and ask and go on asking. He must first of all go along to the Motzstrasse, and ask there. The Rosenheims had lived there for years and years. The mother had gone on living there, after the father had . . . after the father had passed out of the picture. It must be possible to find something out at the Motzstrasse. People are not like soap-bubbles. They can't just disappear into nothing and leave not a trace behind.

He admitted to himself he would have been a little happier if the pension he had got into had been cosier. He looked round his bedroom. All that grand furniture, like the Lord Mayor's parlour. And so much plush. It was a bargain what he was paying for it, dirt-cheap, but it smelled a bit musty, like the air and sun never got to it.

That woman, too, Frau Kahn. A real bundle of nerves she was. He would have liked to ask her a question or two, how to go about things. But she didn't seem the sort of woman who likes to answer questions. She was afraid of her own shadow; even that painted lump of old flesh that had come in through that door there had frightened the inside out of her.

That door there. . . . Had Trude locked it, after all, as Frau Kahn had asked her to? He got out of bed and went to see. It was all right. Trude had locked it.

I will not get back into bed, he thought. I will dress slowly. There is no hurry. Then I will go and have a bit of dinner, if anything is left. Then I will go . . . I will go to Bruno's house. Bruno's house, he repeated to himself incredulously. Do you know you are only a few yards away from Bruno's house, here at this moment? Perhaps I will have luck even today, the first day. Please God!

He found his way to the dining-room, a long dark room on the inward flank of the house. The meal had been cleared away, but several people still sat about the place. Two were playing a card game, with a ferocious hopeless air as if there were nothing left in all the world but to play card games. Another had a reading-lamp on the table before him, by the light of which he was studying dozens of flimsy bits of paper, invoices and receipts perhaps. It seemed a complex job, whatever he was at. At a small table beside the window, a woman with big dark eyes, in a blue Chinese peignoir, was listlessly polishing her nails. In the darkest corner of the room, nearest the door, a small man with great owl-like eyes sat perched up in a sort of pulpit, doing accounts. He jumped down as Mr. Emmanuel entered the room, landing on both feet with a bird-like precision. He extended his hand to the stranger, announced in a thin high voice he was Herr Kahn, jumped up into his pulpit again, and rang a small handbell.

It was all done with the utmost economy of time and movement. He is the brains of all this, decided Mr. Emmanuel. The other one, the wife, she remembers too much she was a lady. She looked less like a lady when she appeared now. All the jewellery was gone. The hair had gone to pieces. Something to eat, Mr. Emmanuel? But certainly, what would Mr. Emmanuel like? Some eggs? *A la coque* or in glass? With pleasure, Mr. Emmanuel. There was as much insistence as before on the Mister, perhaps more, for there was an audience. But the others did not seem impressed. Herr Kahn in the pulpit and the business man at the table went on with their accounts. The card players went on with their card playing.

The exotic lady doing her finger-nails yawned and left the room. Perhaps the Herren had been Herren in their native land for so many centuries without any profit coming to them that they were not so impressed as they might have been by an English Mister who looked like any immigrant East-Jewish tailor from the Berlin ghetto. Perhaps they were merely disconsolate, and the appearance of a de la Pole or a Montmorency in their midst would not have quickened their heartbeats. Mr. Emmanuel finished his meal, uttered a small blessing, and rose to go. Herr Kahn jumped down from his pulpit, with a form in his hand. "Please register!" he bade. Mr. Emmanuel registered. "Thank you!" said the other, then handed him a key, as if the award of the key had been contingent on the signing of the form.

Mr. Emmanuel went back to his room and put his warm things on. It is not likely they will help me much here, he thought. I will go out now. What should I wait for? The Inspector of Police should come and tell me everything I want to know? I will go at once. He descended the two flights of steps and halted a moment in the vestibule. He had a feeling that the curtain in the porter's window on his left quivered a little, but he was not sure. An icy blast blew down the Bambergerstrasse. Thank God for my warm scarf. He lifted it round his ears. Beyond a lesser turning, the street ran into a much bigger street not many yards away. Perhaps that is Bruno's street, he thought.

It was. It was the Motzstrasse. It seemed a very large impersonal street to have housed so small and distinctive a child. It was heavy-jowled, with protruding bay-balconies like teeth and scrolls of heavy decoration over archways like scars. He turned left, in the direction where the road widened out into a sort of square. The Viktoria-Luisen Platz, the name of the square was. The number he sought was further away. He crossed the square and two more corners. Here it was at last, number 65, towards the left end of a block. He halted on the pavement outside the archway and peered in. Up and down that flight of stairs, left or right, the boy Bruno had run in the old days; in the morning to school, not more unwillingly than most boys, in the evening, with almost a lover's ecstasy, back to the gold-haired mother he had loved so poignantly.

You should not have been so beautiful for him, Mr. Emmanuel censured her. It is not sensible. To make a person love too much is a bad thing, a very bad thing.

He heard the sound of descending feet on the right-hand stairway. A moment or two later a woman appeared. He could not see much of her face; her fur collar hid a great deal of it. But she was a woman of middle age. She was quite probably a wife, perhaps a mother, too. Perhaps there, behind that line of forehead was all, or a good deal, of what he wanted to know. Can you tell me what has happened to Frau Rosenheim? Have they got hold of her? Is she dead? If you could tell me something, even if it is not good news, it will be *something*. We will know where we are.

His heart made a movement towards the woman, but his feet did not. She lifted her fur collar higher about her ears and was gone.

He passed into the vestibule out of the cold. The house-porter's little window was directly opposite him. The bell beside the window, the curtain behind it, seemed identical with those in the house in the Bambergerstrasse. It seemed almost as if he were still there, in the Bambergerstrasse, in the moment after his arrival there. The window had not yet snapped open, he had not yet found his way upstairs to Frau Kahn's pension. He waited for the click of the catch, but there was no sound. It is not the same place, he told himself. Are you silly? This is Bruno's house. He removed his wallet from his breast-pocket and took out a crisp pound note. It will be useful, maybe. His heart was banging fearfully behind his ribs. He took three steps forward and pressed the bell.

The window clicked open, as if the hand which pulled it had been at the handle all the time. The sound was the same as the sound in the Bambergerstrasse; the head of the porter that poked through was the same, grizzled and close-cropped.

"*Jawohl?*" the voice demanded.

"Please. I am Englishman," explained Mr. Emmanuel.

"Yes? And?" The information did not seem to have a shattering effect.

"I want to ask something, please." He wondered at what moment he might most suitably slip his tip over. Now, to ease the passage? Later, when he had some value in hand? Now, he thought. Anything to soften a bit the hard lines of that jaw. He looked round, as if he were committing a felony, then placed the pound note on the window-sill before him. The porter lifted a hand and took the note, held it a moment towards the light, then hand and note disappeared.

"Ja?" he asked again, exactly as if no transaction with a pound note had taken place.

"I am asking after the mother of a small boy. He is now in England. I am helping to look after him."

"What name? What do you want to know?" The voice had no invitation in it whatsoever.

"The family name is Rosenheim. The boy has not heard since——"

"Quiet!" the man roared. "This is a Jew-thing! You say you are an *Engländer?* You are a Jew, also?"

"Yes!"

"Verdammtes Judensau!" the man exclaimed. "Get out of here!"

"But, please——"

"I tell you, get out of here! If ever I find you nosing round here again, you'll get more than you bargained for! Pig-Jew! Get out!" He pulled the window to. The whole thing rattled in its frames.

Mr. Emmanuel turned out into the street again. His knees trembled so violently he had to lean up against the wall for support. What is it so terrible I am doing? he asked himself. Asking about a poor little boy, where his mother is. Is it terrible? No, no, he sighed deeply; it will not be easy. Maybe God will help me. Maybe He will make help come quick. Who knows? He could not bear the thought of turning in after so swift and smart a failure. And now—what now? He shut his eyes. The view inside his mind was as blank and featureless as the view outside it, the heavy length of the Motzstrasse. It is cold. I must keep moving. He walked the length of the street and came out into a big square, the Nollendorf Platz.

It was not a bright square, with the Elevated Railway striding across the middle of it, but there was a café or two and one or two show-houses. It would be nice, he thought, to go in and have a cup of coffee and some sweet cakes, and read the papers; perhaps there would be someone I could have a game of dominoes with. Then he remembered with a sinking of the heart his experience of that morning. *Juden Unerwünscht.* Yes, of course, I have got an English passport. So I will open the door with one hand and hold the English passport with the other. Please, I am an Englishman. Give me a cup of coffee, please. The idea did not seem attractive to him.

There would certainly be cafés round here, too, where Jews could go without trouble. And cinemas, and so on. They would tell him all about that at the pension. It was their duty. It is too cold to stand about here on the pavement of the Nollendorf Platz. I will go back home and talk to Frau Kahn.

He returned and rang the bell and asked might he speak to her. She came. She seemed to be in a much calmer frame of mind than she had been in that morning. It might have been that the elderly Kati was out of the house. In fact, she said as much. We all feel so much better when she goes home, Mr. Emmanuel, even if we have to set to and do her work all over again. Is there anything we can do for your comfort, Mr. Emmanuel? We do so want our guests to be comfortable. Would you like another table, perhaps, or another bureau? We have a very fine one, in number 4, with a rolling top.

Mr. Emmanuel thanked her. No. He could not be more comfortable. But it was something outside he wanted to talk to her about. He recounted his experience that morning at the café in the Friedrichstrasse. Her eyes filled with tears. She shook her head sadly from side to side. Even with an *Engländer,* she murmured, even an *Engländer.* She would not permit herself a more extended comment. But there are some cafés round here in the West, he asked, where a Jew can go to? Just to slip in now and again and listen to the music, if there is any, and play a game of dominoes, perhaps. Of course, we always have wireless here, over in the dining-room, the *sogenannte Berliner Zimmer,* she paraphrased it, as if it were a local architectural specialty well worth scrutiny. There is a piano, too, and chess and draughts and dominoes. She was sure Mr. Emmanuel could be very comfortable in the dining-room.

But if he wanted to go out sometimes, why not? (What does she think? he asked himself. I have come to Berlin specially to sit and listen to the wireless in her dining-room, and play chess with the other boarders?) She enumerated a few cafés where he could take his ease. There was the Café Hahnen, only out there, in the Nollendorf Platz. There was the Café Adler, about the same distance away, at the Wittenberg Platz; then further west, on the Kurfürstendamm, the Café Dobrin, the Café Wien. . . . (And play chess with the other boarders? Perhaps it is a good thing I should tell her straight away. For sure they are all asking each other already what I am doing here. If I tell her, there shall be no nonsenses. And she looks so nice and quiet tonight, it is perhaps the best thing.)

"Frau Kahn."

"Yes?" She looked up suddenly.

"I should like to tell you what I have come for to Berlin."

"Why?" she exclaimed. "It is not my business. I have enough on my hands."

"I am a stranger and an old man. Please, I should like your advice. It is so simple. It is nothing."

She hesitated a moment, looking up furtively from under her eyelids.

"All right," she said. The sooner it was over, the better. She got up and walked towards the door, as if to make sure no one was behind it. "Oh, it's all right," she remembered, her hand at her heart. "She's gone home already."

"It is like this," said Mr. Emmanuel. He told her, quietly, earnestly, what his quest was. Several times she tried to interrupt, but he was launched into his tale, and he would not let her. At length he stopped. He saw her face was deathly pale, and her hands shaking uncontrollably. She tried to speak more than once, but it seemed beyond her now to utter a single word.

"Are you ill, Frau Kahn?" he asked miserably. "Please, what is the matter?" He knew too well what the matter was.

At last she managed to speak. Her body seemed so frail and frightened, he almost thought he could see the heart thumping behind the dress.

"We will not be mixed up, Mr. Emmanuel. We have trouble enough of our own. This is a pension. It is not

. . . it is not a detective bureau. You can stay here if you like . . . but you can go if it doesn't suit you. We can have no question-asking—not from us, nor our guests either. Do you understand? We can't have it." She folded her hands piteously, like a woman praying. "Don't you *see,* Mr. Emmanuel, how it is with us? We are poor, my husband and I. We need your money. Things are not too well with us. Yet I ask you . . . wouldn't it . . . wouldn't it be better if you went back home?"

He was silent for some seconds. Then he spoke again. "All right," he announced. "There will be no questions, nothing to make you unhappy. I promise you that. What is that café, please, in the Nollendorf Platz? The Café Hahnen, you said?" He reached for his hat.

"You look so tired, Mr. Emmanuel. You look as if you are ready to drop. Won't you stay in and have a little *Abendbrot* and then go to bed?"

"I will not be out long, thank you, Frau Kahn. A little change for a few minutes would do me good." He passed his hand across his forehead. "Besides," he said, "there is something I want to buy." It had been on his mind all day. There was something he wanted to buy. What was it? Oh, yes. Postcards. He had promised to write every day—had he not?—to Rose and Bruno. He must buy post-cards, and send them off, to Rose, to Bruno, to one or two of the Magnolia Street folk, to old Sam Silver. He asked where he could buy them, and where he could buy stamps.

She told him, and went to the door; then, with her hand on the handle, she turned again. Her face was very pale and severe. The pointed nose was dead white.

"Understand! No questions!" she commanded. Then she went out.

In the Café Hahnen he thawed out a bit, heart and skin. People here were not dancing about on tables, but they did not look as if tomorrow it would be an operation. He spent quite a happy half-hour, writing out his postcards, saying what a nice journey he had had, and hoping it found them as it left him at present.

Finished the first day. A fine first day, eh? What do you expect on your first day? It should come to you with a carriage and six horses? Cheer up, Isaac Emmanuel! It's another day, please God, tomorrow!

He let himself into the pension an hour or two later. He proposed to go straight to bed, not feeling he wanted any dinner on top of the cakes he had had at the café. As he opened the door, the door of a room opposite on the right opened too, and Herr Kahn appeared. It looked as if he had been waiting for Mr. Emmanuel's appearance. He raised the index finger of his left hand and wagged it sharply to and fro. The gesture was firm and business-like.

"Understand! No questions!" he exclaimed. It was like an echo that had been stored up, waiting for its moment of release. Then he shut his mouth tight, bowed sharply, and turned back into the room from which he had emerged.

So ended Mr. Emmanuel's first day in Berlin. This day was Friday, the thirty-first of January. On that day another obscure Jew, not English but Yugoslavian by nationality, also made a journey, a much shorter one, within the frontiers of the small country where he was a resident at that time. The country was Switzerland, the journey was between Berne and Davos, the name of the obscure Jew was David Frankfurter.

This Frankfurter was less than half Mr. Emmanuel's age, being twenty-seven years old. His family, a race of rabbis and scholars, lived in a small town in Yugoslavia, but they were German Jews by origin, having borne their German name some hundred and fifty years. Mr. Emmanuel was a Russian Jew of similar origin, from one of the Dnieper villages. He had emigrated to Doomington, in England, in his eighteenth year, and had become a British citizen in his early thirties. He had never left England since that time. The two men, David Frankfurter and Isaac Emmanuel, were as unaware of each other's existence as two pebbles on the opposite shores of a sea.

Frankfurter was a medical student, and during the last four years had been enrolled successively in the Universities of Vienna, Leipzig, and Frankfort. He did not do well in his examinations; partly because he was a chronic invalid, partly because his heart was more in philosophy and theology than in medicine. But perhaps the principal reason was the triumph of the Nazi regime, which filled him with bitterness and despair. He found it impossible to stay in a university which officially sponsored a set of theories according to which all Jews, himself among them, were deemed something half-devil, half-brute. He moved to Berne in October 1933, where he endeavoured to pursue his studies. Between that time and the end of 1935, while his personal sufferings did not diminish, the sufferings of his people in Germany increased immeasurably, reaching both a fresh climax and a fresh starting-point with the promulgation of the Nuremberg Laws.

During all that period, the German regime had spared no efforts to establish its philosophy in the countries with which it had a common frontier, not least in Switzerland. The leader of the movement in that country was a certain

Wilhelm Gustloff, at one time a bank-clerk from Mecklenburg, later an employee of a scientific institute in Davos. In 1923 this Gustloff became a member of the Nazi party, and during the years that followed fought unremittingly on its behalf. After Herr Hitler's accession to power, Gustloff was appointed "National Leader of the Swiss Group." He was a devoted servant of his master's cause. When asked by an important Swiss official how seriously he took his Nazi duties, he replied: "I love my wife and my mother more than anyone else in the world; but if the Leader ordered me to kill them, I should obey." He established in Switzerland virtually a state within a state, with its headquarters in Davos, where his home was.

Towards the end of December 1935, Frankfurter had bought a revolver. About that time he addressed a letter of farewell to his father, in which he wrote: "I leave this life without bitterness, convinced you will not doubt my love for yourself and my dear mother. I have lost faith in myself and in humanity. I can't hold out any more." Perhaps he had already made up his mind to take Gustloff's life as well as his own. That is not known. Either then or later his being was flooded with the determination to strike a symbolic blow against the power and system he abominated. He was not restrained by the thought that such a blow often recoils in incalculable directions, with an unpredictable increment of force. On Friday, the thirty-first of January, he set out from Berne to Davos, to strike a blow at the idea called Adolf Hitler by the murder of his agent, the man Wilhelm Gustloff.

6

I

WHAT day is it? Mr. Emmanuel asked himself. It seemed days and days since he had got into the train at Harwich. Would you believe it, I've been here only one full day? Yesterday was Friday, wasn't it? It's Saturday, the Sabbath.

He was no stayer-in-bed for breakfast. He rose and washed and went over into the dining-room, which was rather gloomier by day than by night, for at night the electric light livened things up a bit. It was the Sabbath. He looked round, almost unconsciously, for the white tablecloth, the brass candlesticks, the brass beakers that graced the Magnolia Street tables on the Sabbath. They had never been missing even from his own bereaved table; Ada Hummel had seen to that. But they did not go in for that sort of thing here in the Bambergerstrasse. It might have been Tuesday. Well, what do you expect? They are not orthodox. Well, am I orthodox? It seems like in Germany here they get all the kicks from being Jews but none of the halfpennies.

Maybe there aren't so many halfpennies, either.

He had his breakfast, and asked where the nearest synagogue was. It was not far. Perhaps it will do Bruno good I should go to the service this morning. He is a little

Christian, I am an old Jew. But it is the same God, I think. He felt quite at home in the synagogue there, though they were all talking German, and in his own synagogue they always talked Yiddish.

Should I ask them can they perhaps give me a bit of advice? Let it be. They have puzzles of their own already, how they should make a living, how they should get out of this country. God should help them like He should help me!

There was one quite smart-looking gentleman in a seat near the Holy of Holies, with curly hair and a small brown pointed beard. Perhaps an artist, eh? I think Bruno said his father had a brown beard like that, with curly hair. Would it be easier, maybe, to try and get some news about Bruno's father? They might know about him at picture-dealing places, and if anybody knows about him they might know about her also.

For God's sake, Isaac Emmanuel, keep your head screwed up the right way. With him it has been some real monkey business, God knows what. But he is dead, and not in a clean way, either. It is different with her. She was living on in the Motzstrasse a long time after her husband left Germany. If it is so hard to find out about her, is it sensible to try and find out about him? Forget about him, Isaac.

The service over, he found his way back towards the Motzstrasse, crossing the road to be on the opposite side to number 65. Well, and now? I will walk up and down the street, perhaps I will get an idea, perhaps something will happen. It seemed a forlorn prospect. What is going to happen in the middle of the Motzstrasse, it should teach me anything I want to know, on a cold Saturday morning in February? Yes, it is February already. How long ago was it I promised little Bruno? My God, it was in August, late on in August. It is a long time already. It is like something was trying to hold me back all the time. Am I never going to get to know anything?

A woman emerged at that moment from the doorway of number 65. She looked like a resident. She had a shopping-basket over her arm. She crossed the road straight away and turned right, towards the Viktoria-Luisen Platz.

I will ask her, proclaimed Mr. Emmanuel, I will. She comes from Bruno's house. Perhaps she even knew Bruno's family. Perhaps even she knew about Jo the rabbit. Can she eat me up?

He hurried after the woman, and touched her lightly on the shoulder. She turned.

"Please to excuse me; I am a foreigner, an Englishman. You live in 65 there, no?"

"I do. Can I do anything for you?" Her manner was quite pleasant.

"I want to find out the present address of a friend of mine who used to live there, first floor. A Frau Rosenheim?"

"How long ago might it be?"

"Oh, till last March certainly."

"I am sorry. I only moved in last September. Good day." She went off quite nonchalantly.

Mr. Emmanuel turned back again and rubbed his gloved hands together. He had got a civil answer, without any hint of menace or panic. He felt quite happy for a moment or two, as if he had made a definite step forward. Then the happiness went. No, he could not say he had moved forward exactly. And he had not moved back. He was where he had been.

Perhaps with the next woman I will have more luck, he assured himself. Perhaps she has lived there from a long time before March. Perhaps she has known Bruno even—can you help noticing a nice little boy like that? The next person who appeared was a man, not a woman, a chubby, snub-nosed little man, with a green hat and a feather in it. He was leading a small boy by the hand, his son probably. The small boy was younger than Bruno, some ten or eleven, but he was even more likely to have known Bruno than his parent. Maybe they went to the same school together. The man and the boy turned the angle of the block and went directly up the Lutherstrasse. It took Mr. Emmanuel all he was worth with those rickety old legs of his to cross the road and catch up with them. Mr. Emmanuel touched the man on the shoulder. The man turned.

"Please to excuse me," began Mr. Emmanuel as before; "I am a foreigner——"

The man turned again.

"Come, *Bubi!*" he said. He hurried the small boy off.

"——an Englishman!" called Mr. Emmanuel desolately after him. "I—I—I—" But the man seemed about as interested in him as if he were an empty match-box. The small boy's legs were positively twinkling now, like sunlight on ripples.

Mr. Emmanuel returned down the Lutherstrasse and was about to cross the roadway of the Motzstrasse, when he paused suddenly. The house-porter at number 65, he remembered. . . . If I walk up and down there, on that side of the street, opposite the entrance, he will see me. Perhaps he has already seen me. Why should I make extra troubles for myself? I will wait a bit here, in the Lutherstrasse. On the other side the pavement goes out a few yards further than this side. I will be able to see better there if someone with a kind face comes out.

He crossed the road. There was a little cigarette kiosk on this other pavement, a rather gimcrack affair. This will be a help, he thought. If that porter should come out, and look at me with a bad face, well, I can just go up to the kiosk and buy a pack of cigarettes. Such a year on him! What harm am I doing him or anyone else? Perhaps even now a cigarette will be a nice thing. He fumbled for his cigarette case and brought it out. A pity. It was empty. What am I near a cigarette kiosk for? He went up to the little counter and asked for a box of Turkish cigarettes. He liked Turkish cigarettes.

"What sort, please?" a gentle voice asked. "There are several sorts, you know."

Mr. Emmanuel had not been aware of anything more than that there was an old man serving in that kiosk. It had not occurred to him to be more interested. But the quality of the old man's voice was such that it at once impressed you. It was gentle, cultured, surely even distinguished, even to a person who was no great expert in the language it spoke. Mr. Emmanuel looked up. The face exactly matched the voice. The lines of it were gentle; so was the expression in the eyes. There were culture and distinction in the broad brow and the thin arched nose. Selling cigarettes? A man like that, with such a voice, such a forehead? It is upside down, the whole world!

"I would be glad if you could perhaps recommend me—" Mr. Emmanuel started. Then all of a sudden he remembered, with a sick feeling, it was *Shabbos,* the Sabbath. He was not orthodox, but he did not, as a rule, smoke on the Sabbath. Somehow, he wanted to be extra careful in such small things, here in Berlin. It might help. You never can tell. Who can argue this way or that way about such things?

"Oh, I beg your pardon, please," he stammered. "I forgot. You see, it is——"

"It is *Shabbos*," the old man said quietly. "Please do not disturb yourself."

"You, too, are . . . are Jewish? I did not think——"

"Yes, I too am Jewish. When you are ready to smoke, may I suggest this brand? R 6 the name is!" He held up a yellow packet from the little store beside him. He talked like a scholar who recommends to a student one learned variant of a text as opposed to its rivals.

"Thank you, it is so kind of you. When *Shabbos* is out, Herr . . . Herr——"

"Herr ex-Professor Sachs," the other informed him, with the ghost of a smile. "Of the Faculty of Classical Literature in the Friedrich Wilhelm University, here in Berlin."

"Yes, oh, yes, of course," said Mr. Emmanuel hurriedly, as if it were the most natural thing in the world for an ex-professor of the Friedrich Wilhelm University of Berlin to be peddling packs of cigarettes over a kiosk counter. "Good day, Herr Professor."

"Good day."

It is upside down the world—it *is*, it *is!* A man like that, a professor, should be selling cigarettes so many pfennigs a time! Mr. Emmanuel, after all, crossed over to the opposite pavement of the Motzstrasse. He felt if he stayed in the ex-professor's immediate vicinity a minute longer he would be somehow associating himself with the unspeakable humiliation that had been inflicted on that courteous and delicate man.

I am dreaming this, he assured himself. It cannot be. He looked back as if to assure himself that the kiosk was really there. Yes, it was really there. Ex-Professor Sachs was serving a customer with great alacrity.

Then suddenly he remembered. Didn't that Herr Zittau, over in Doomington, say that quite a lot of university professors and specialists who had been turned out of their jobs had been allowed, as a special favour, to set up street kiosks for the sale of cigarettes? A special favour! He shivered as if a cold wind had found his shoulder-blades.

I will not think of it. I must put it out from my mind. There is a young woman coming out of the doorway of 65. She, too, is carrying a shopping-bag. Where is she going, then, to do her shopping? He followed her with his eyes. She descended into a sort of basement grocery shop further down the Motzstrasse, on the side he had just come from. He crossed the road again and descended into the shop after her. There she was. There was no one else in the shop but her and the man attending her. One or two of her purchases were already on the counter before her, a packet of rice, a packet of sugar. She consulted a list she held in her hand. A packet of macaroni, please. Thank you, yes. And a pound of coffee. Yes, grind it for me as usual.

Now, if ever, was the opportunity, now while the man poured the beans out into the funnel, now while he was turning the handle of the grinding machine. The woman looked round idly. "*Guten Tag,*" she positively said to him. He tried to say "*Guten Tag*" back to her, but the words would not leave his mouth.

He has very nearly finished grinding the coffee. He has finished now. He is pouring it into the bag. What is the matter with you, Isaac Emmanuel? She is a nice woman. She has said *"Guten Tag"* to you all by herself. Have you got no tongue in your head?

He could not speak; a sort of paralysis had fallen upon him. Perhaps it was the business of the ex-professor that had so demoralized him. Perhaps all of a sudden he was afraid. He could not speak. The woman crammed away into her bag the rice, the sugar, the macaroni, the coffee. The man totted up her account and transcribed the sum to his own book. The woman said *"Guten Tag"* a second time and climbed up the stairs onto street-level. Mr. Emmanuel's eyes followed her with the profound melancholy of a dog that is not, after all, going to be taken out by his master. The grocer was tapping impatiently with his pencil on the counter. Yes, please? Yes, please?

Mr. Emmanuel shook his head hard. What did he want? He saw before him an advertisement for a brand of sardines. Sardines! he demanded. The sardines were wrapped up and handed over. He paid for them and went out.

Pick yourself together, Isaac Emmanuel! A real mummy, I should live so! How far do you think you're going to get, eh, behaving like that?

He made one more effort that day—it was afternoon now—to get something done. He followed another woman, an older one, into a shop—a greengrocer and fruiterer's nearer the Nollendorf Platz. He stationed himself beside her at the counter. There were three or four other people in the shop.

"Please excuse me, *gnädige Frau,*" he started. The words gaggled in his throat like geese.

The woman looked at him stonily.

"Excuse me, I am *Engländer,*" he began again.

"*Und auch Jude, vielleicht?* And a Jew also, perhaps?" She turned slowly away from him, her shoulder poking into his ribs. A deathly silence fell on the place. The man had been weighing apples. He stood stock-still. Nobody spoke for half a minute or more.

"Excuse me," murmured Mr. Emmanuel. "I think . . . perhaps I have . . . made a mistake." He turned and went out of the shop. He went straight back to the pension, though he moved very slowly, he felt so tired. Perhaps I have done enough for one morning. Perhaps it will be more luck later on. Please God, I need it maybe.

He had his lunch with the other boarders at Frau Kahn's establishment, and took part in a certain amount of rather indeterminate conversation. What were the chances of Sir Mosley's party in England? Were they a serious threat to the Government? What were the prospects for new industrial undertakings in the Doomington area? He answered to the best of his ability, though for the most part he found himself out of his depth. He was aware of a curious lack of cordiality; they seemed for some reason or other to resent him. What right had he, by origin a ghetto Jew from the Pale—they somehow sensed that—what right had he to lord it over frontiers, while they, Germans whose families went back perhaps for centuries, must pad to and fro like beasts behind bars?

I am only thinking like that, because I do not feel happy inside, he assured himself. What should they feel funny with me for? I will finish my lunch and lie down in my room for a bit. Perhaps I can read and doze off. Then I shall write postcards. Write? On the *Shabbos?* No, I will not write. I will tell them why tomorrow. They will understand.

He went to his room, drew the curtains, and lit his bedside lamp. He could not read, so he switched the lamp off and lay back, trying to doze. But he could not do that, either. He became more and more aware how profound was the abyss of gloom he was plunged into. On both sides of him soared black unscalable cliffs. They were quite smooth, like glass. There seemed no faintest shadow of a hand-hold in them. What hope was there, ever, of climbing clear, into the air, the sunshine? He remained suspended, as it were, for he did not know how long, between the black smooth walls; then a picture formed itself in the polished basalt, as it might be a soothsayer's crystal.

He stood in an ambulatory behind a row of heads curving away in an arc; beyond the row was another, and another, and another. He was in the well of a theatre. Beyond the rows of heads a line of lights was drawn like a string. Beyond the lights there was someone dancing against a backcloth of dim gigantic heads. It was a girl, though she wore a top-hat and a male dress suit. How elegant she was, the manikin, twirling her cane and puffing her cigarette!

Elsie Silver, her name was. She was the daughter of old Sam Silver, his friend. The lights gradually suffused the whole stage and both illumined and revealed the features of the colossi on the backcloth—Herr Hitler with the flash of black hair, Herr Goebbels with the long upper lip and the pursed mouth, the broad cheekbones of Göring, the humped eyebrows of Brockenburg.

No, Elsie Silver, Mr. Emmanuel murmured in the darkness and melancholy of his room; *please God I should not have to ask any help from you.*

II

He had a feeling it would be something of a comfort to go and attend the evening service at the synagogue he had been to that morning. But he was in a queer state of lassitude, and by the time he had risen and drunk a cup of coffee, he felt he could hardly arrive before the service was over. I cannot do anything tonight, he told himself resignedly. I will go out to the Café Hahnen, maybe. Or why not that big cinema, just around the corner of the Motzstrasse? Is it a law I should not go to any cinemas?

He put his things on and went out. At the corner of the Motzstrasse and the Lutherstrasse there was quite a press of people. Oh, yes, there was a big music hall round the corner, the Scala. Perhaps he might go instead to the Scala? He turned and found himself a yard or two away from Herr Sachs's kiosk. Of course, cigarettes. The Sabbath must be pretty well over now. He would buy that packet of Turkish cigarettes the Herr ex-Professor had recommended. What were they called? R 6—yes, that was it.

It is a pain and a shame a professor should sell cigarettes like a gutterstripe. But is it any sense I should go and give somebody else my custom?

And then suddenly another idea struck him. How long had the professor had this kiosk? Even if he had acquired it since last March, wasn't he as likely as anyone round here to know something about the Rosenheim story? He seemed a kind old man. You would have thought he would have been a lot more embittered by what had happened to him. But he wasn't. He was a philosopher. Why not, poor man? What else was there for him to be?

There was a customer at the kiosk. Mr. Emmanuel

waited till the customer had gone, then he stepped almost jauntily up to the counter.

"Good evening, Herr Professor," he said. "Those cigarettes. You remember? R 6. You recommended them to me this morning."

"Oh, yes. Good evening. Those cigarettes. Here they are. One mark, please."

He didn't seem at all the same old man as he had been this morning. He seemed anxious. He seemed furtive. His eyes roved from left to right as he spoke.

He is different. Something has happened. I cannot let this chance go. What harm am I doing? I am buying cigarettes, what else? I must ask him my question. I must.

"Herr Professor, please." He bent forward. His voice and eyes were alike piteous. "I must ask you for advice. It is only a simple question. I want to——"

"No, no, no!" the old man forbade. "Please! Not here! Wait! Let me think!" He stooped and brought from under his counter a fresh supply of R 6 cigarettes. "Tomorrow evening!" he whispered. "At nine. Under the clock at the Zoo station!" Then, raising his voice: "Matches? Certainly, Herr! Five pfennigs. Good night!"

"Good night!" said Mr. Emmanuel, and blinked, and turned away.

On second thoughts Mr. Emmanuel decided against a visit to the Scala music hall. He had already been to one music hall performance that day, though it was but a phantom show. He played with the idea of going instead to the big cinema on the Nollendorf Platz. But the posters indicated it was some sort of big feature Nazi film, with a good deal of orating and marching of men in uniform. He went to a café on the Kurfürstendamm, sat there quietly for a time, then went home again.

Tomorrow evening, he said to himself, *at nine, under the clock at the Zoo station.* I have got somewhere to go to. I am not standing still any more, thank God! I am going somewhere.

Where? What does it matter where? Who knows? I am going somewhere.

So it finishes for me, he said to himself, my second day in Berlin. It has been *Shabbos.* You would not believe it. No, you would not.

Over in Davos, in Switzerland, a long way south and west, the Sabbath day drew to a close for another Jew, as lonely as this one.

It is the Sabbath day, this Jew, David Frankfurter, said to himself. Thou shalt do no murder, said the Lord God.

I am driven by the dæmon within me to slay this man Gustloff. As Moses was to slay the Egyptian, as Jael to slay Sisera, as Judith Holofernes.

I shall slay the man Gustloff as they slew Rathenau, as they slew Erzberger.

But not upon the Sabbath day.

Observe the Sabbath day, to keep it holy, said the Lord.

I cannot do any other thing than slay the man Gustloff. If there is any pollution, it is myself I pollute. But I can choose any other day for the slaying. I will not pollute the Sabbath.

Until tomorrow then, sad murderer. Until tomorrow.

7

I

THE next day was Sunday. The air outside was bright and fresh. Even the *sogenannte Berliner Zimmer* wore a less funereal aspect.

Frau Kahn was quite chirpy this morning. How was Mr. Emmanuel? Had Mr. Emmanuel slept quite well last night? Was he quite sure he wouldn't like still another feather-bed? Mr. Emmanuel was very grateful for the kind attentions. No, he felt he could get along without another feather-bed.

"Good morning, Fräulein Pfeffer!" smiled Frau Kahn. "Going out for a little *Ausflug,* an excursion?" The remark was addressed to the lady of the blue Chinese peignoir and the very black eyes. She was wearing quite a smart going-out costume now. The lady with immense deliberation removed a plug of chewing-gum from one side of her mouth to the other.

"Ja!" she said, and went off.

"You see?" said Frau Kahn, as if Mr. Emmanuel had been arguing against going out. "It is a beautiful day, you know. We often have fine weather like this after a few days of drizzle and cold, here in Berlin." It all sounded like one of the extra amenities thrown in by the Pension

Kahn. "And why doesn't Mr. Emmanuel go out for a little *Ausflug,* too?" she asked, almost archly.

A little *Ausflug,* reflected Mr. Emmanuel. A little *Ausflug*. Why, that was exactly what he would do! He would make the excursion to the Spreewald, to Haus Anna, the Rosenheims' bungalow at Lübbenau! What a good idea! There was nothing he could do, or wanted to do, in Berlin for the time being; not until tonight, at nine o'clock, when he might get something, or he might not, from the ex-professor. Really, he had had enough hanging about the Motzstrasse. He would start attracting attention if he hung about the place much more, touching people on the shoulder and pursuing them into shops.

Of course he would go to Lübbenau! Who knew how much information he might pick up there? Besides, over there it was the country. People are always so much nicer in the country than the town, are they not?

"As a matter of fact," confided Mr. Emmanuel, "I had already made up my mind to go on a little *Ausflug,* Frau Kahn!"

Her expression changed at once.

"Really!" she exclaimed. "Really! Who'd believe that now?" Suspicion had cropped up on her again like a cock's hackles. "I suppose it would be too much to ask where you are planning to go, Mr. Emmanuel?"

He looked at her a little quizzically. He remembered her dour insistence, so tartly reiterated by her husband: "Understand! No questions!" But he was not a Berliner. He came from Doomington. Questions did not frighten him so much as them.

"As a matter of fact, I thought of going to the Spreewald; a German friend of mine in Doomington has often spoken to me of the Spreewald."

"The Spreewald? Indeed! That's a long distance away! Two hours, perhaps three hours, each way! Why the Spreewald? You might not get back in time! There might be inquiries!" Her voice began to take on the quickened tempo of alarm.

"Please, *mein Schatz!*" her husband's voice came down sharply from his pulpit. "If the Herr wishes to go to the Spreewald, it is his own affair." He addressed himself to Mr. Emmanuel. "It might be a little awkward, you know, if you have to stay the night there."

"Will you perhaps let me see the time-table? If the trains don't work out right, I won't go. I have an appointment here in Berlin tonight."

The trains worked out all right. Mr. Emmanuel found his way to the Görlitzer Bahnhof, and installed himself in due course in a third-class carriage, making for the Spreewald country.

I am in Germany. I am going to Lübbenau. I am in Germany. I am going to Lübbenau. It is extraordinary what a variety and complexity of rhythms you can impose on the simple reverberation of a train's wheels. He rearranged them. Lübbenau. Lübbenau. Bruno's Lübbenau. Lübbenau. Lübbenau. Bruno's Lübbenau.

So you see, Bruno, he mused, you see I am not falling asleep. I am an old man. Who says I am not? But I go from one place to the next place, I do this thing, I do that thing, a young man could not do any more, I think. I am going to Lübbenau. That will surprise you, Bruno, eh, when I tell you? Perhaps I will send you a picture postcard from Lübbenau. Shall I? What do you think, Isaac? It will pain him, maybe? We will see what it is like when we get there.

Königs-Wusterhausen? Where the wireless station is.

Yes, so it is. I am going to Lübbenau, Lübbenau, Lübbenau, going to . . . Oh, the devil should take it! They will think I am mad, the people in this carriage, shaking my foot like I am a band conductor. They are looking at me funny enough already.

Lübben? He got up from his seat in alarm. There is not some mistake? This is not the same place Lübbenau? Not at all, old man. Take your seat again. Next station, five kilometres further on.

It was half-way between the two places that a sudden distressing thought gripped him. The Rosenheims only went there for holidays, you silly old man. Haus Anna is a bungalow all among the rivers. In winter it will be cold and damp. The people who have the place now will not be there. It will be all shut up. It is wasted, all this time and money. A whole day wasted.

He quickly turned back upon himself. Well, and what if it is? What is a day and what is a few shillings? You cannot afford to leave no stone upturned. Say Haus Anna is empty just now, well? Perhaps someone will tell me where they live, the new people, and they might even be friends of the Rosenheims, they might have bought the bungalow from them. Or perhaps they are there, after all, who knows?

The crispness had gone out of the day for him, none the less, by the time the train stopped at the Lübbenau station. Not many people got into the train or out of it. He descended to the platform and looked round and up. The station seemed small, the sky large, Germany large. He felt thin and frail, like a single reed in a vast sheet of water. Which way do I turn? I will get lost. Nobody will put me on the right track again.

He followed in the wake of a group of people, peasants

they doubtless were, very stiff in their Sunday best. They had not much to say to one another. They showed passes or gave up their tickets, and went out through the turnstile into the roadway. They did not seem the sort of people who would answer very graciously if questioned. The ticket-collector? Oh, yes, he might well know.

"Excuse me, please. Can you tell me the way to Haus Anna?"

The ticket-collector thought a moment or two.

"Haus Anna?" he repeated. "Haus Anna?"

"Yes, if you please!"

"Look here! What are you up to?"

"Nothing! I am only making a little *Ausflug.*" It had occurred to Mr. Emmanuel the fellow might quite likely know something about the Rosenheims. Lübbenau was not the sort of station where the personnel of the staff changes very rapidly. He might even remember Bruno himself, fussing around the hutch of Jo, the famous white rabbit. He had had it on the tip of his tongue to bring up the Rosenheims by name. But the fellow's tone and his words were not encouraging.

"Oh, you just want to make a little *Ausflug,* do you?" The porter shrugged his shoulders. After all, he was no detective, he was just a *Beamter,* an official of the railway. "Well, look here. You don't know Fritschke's mill, do you?"

"No. I'm a stranger." As a matter of fact Mr. Emmanuel knew Fritschke's mill well by repute. He had often heard Bruno talking about it.

"Anyhow, Haus Anna is one of the bungalows by Fritschke's mill." The fellow had a strange accent, not at all easy to make out.

"Is it far from here, please?"

"If you knew your way, it wouldn't be. Down there's the town, no? Not much of it, I must say," he conceded. "Then you turn left there on the main cross-road." He gave certain other directions, but it would be easier if he asked again two kilometres farther on, at the Schwarzer Adler. "There's a cab outside, if you'd like it," he added indifferently.

"Thank you. It will be nice to have a walk. Good day."

The porter muttered something between his teeth and walked off to the station office. Mr. Emmanuel went out into the station approach, and down into the main street of the village. It was rather a scattered place, its houses nestling in big gardens dominated by their trees. The Spreewald had clearly covered all this territory at one time. He turned left at the cross-roads and continued between grey-green fields and black woods, intersected by steel-grey channels. It was all very bleak and rimy, despite the unclouded sun.

The thought even of Berlin seemed friendly here; there were streets there, cafés, shops. Even in England the country was strange to him. The German countryside was stranger; it was like a sheet of paper covered with an indecipherable writing. By the time he came to the Schwarzer Adler, he felt sorry he had not taken the cab that had been suggested to him. But at all events the inn was there right enough, standing back from the roadway, a rambling log-built affair. The man at the station had not sent him chasing for a wild goose.

Mr. Emmanuel entered. It was quite hot inside there; wood was cheaper in these parts. A good deal of the place was taken up by a clay oven, and there were stuffed fish and animals in glass cases all over the walls. He wiped his glasses, and looked round. "Good day," he said to the large gentleman in shirt-sleeves at the bar, who was evidently the landlord. There were three other people sitting at a table, but these respectfully had their coats on. "Good day," the man in shirt-sleeves answered. The others did not turn their heads. "Good day," they muttered under their breaths.

Mr. Emmanuel asked for a glass of beer; a glass of beer was set down before him. He drank a mouthful or two, but could not go on; he was no beer-drinker at the best of times, and this was strong stuff. He wiped his lips with his handkerchief, as if to wipe the taste from them.

"You don't like it?" the landlord said somewhat truculently. "It's easy to see you're a stranger. It's the best beer in these parts, isn't it, *meine Herrschaften?*" The worthies rumbled assent in their throats.

"Yes," agreed Mr. Emmanuel timidly. "It's very good indeed. I'm from England," he added, as if that might explain why he was not such a connoisseur as he ought to be.

"Oh, from England, eh? What's it like over there?" the landlord asked.

"It's not bad, you know. A bit quiet. Please, can you help me?" he demanded suddenly. He did not feel this was the moment to enter into a long disquisition on the internal condition of his country. "I was told at the station to ask here. They said you would know. Can you please tell me where Haus Anna is?"

"Haus Anna?" The landlord's voice was raised a note or two. "Haus Anna?" The men turned their heads.

"Yes, please." Mr. Emmanuel felt a faint stir of fear. "Some friends of mine used to live there."

"He's asking after Haus Anna?" the landlord announced. He was addressing his customers where they sat silent at their table. "Some friends of his used to live there."

"At least I know their small boy, Bruno," Mr. Emmanuel corrected.

"So you would like to pay a visit to Haus Anna?"

"Yes, please. I am making a little *Ausflug*."

"Is there any reason why the Herr Engländer should not pay a visit to Haus Anna?" asked the landlord. From the noises his friends made, it was to be assumed they saw no reason against it.

"Of course you may pay a visit to Haus Anna! It is not far, across the fields. We will tell you how to get there!" Suddenly the landlord burst into a loud roar of laughter. The others followed him, an octave or two lower, like thunder lower down a valley. Mr. Emmanuel was beginning to feel uncomfortable. He did not quite see what was so funny about it all. Either they were going to tell him where Haus Anna was or they weren't.

"Please," he said. "I have not too much time. I have a train to catch back to Berlin this evening."

"Beg the pardon," said the host. He slipped his coat on and came out from behind the bar. "Come, I will show you myself."

"Really, it's very kind of you," Mr. Emmanuel assured him. "Please not to trouble." And then it occurred to him he might as well get another question in. "Oh, and could you tell me, please, is there anybody living there now?"

The landlord stopped. He bent forward a little and placed his hands on both thighs. He repeated the question. "Is there anybody living there now? Yes," he said. "There are people living there now. A Herr and Frau Ratte." His face was entirely without expression.

"Thank you," said Mr. Emmanuel, "very much indeed." He paid for his beer, opened the door, and went out, followed by the landlord. As the door closed behind them, Mr. Emmanuel thought he once more heard the sound of laughter from among the worthies at the table. But if he did, it was not a thundery rumble now; it was not more than a titter.

"Come, this is the way," said the landlord. He turned left and walked for some fifty yards, then pointed out a lane across the road. There he gave certain directions, not too complicated. Mr. Emmanuel would get to Haus Anna, he said, in ten or fifteen minutes. *"Guten Tag, Herr Engländer,"* he wound up. *"Viel Vergnügen.* Much pleasure." He turned and strode back to his inn again.

Herr and Frau Ratte, mused Mr. Emmanuel. That was an odd name. The man was not making fun of him, was he? He passed through a hazel-wood and two or three minutes later came out upon the waterside. Oh, yes, that must be the thin bridge the landlord had spoken of, a hundred yards further on. The landlord was not making a fool of him, anyhow. There was a bridge where he had said there would be one. Across here, across the black water. It was a spindly sort of affair. It has thin legs like me, thought Mr. Emmanuel, a little knobby at the knees. Here on this side were fields of grass; very pale and sour the grass looked now. Perhaps in summer the grass grows rich and tall.

Are these the fields where Bruno went haymaking? And Bruno's father sent out drinks for the haymakers, beer for them and sweet cider for him? And are those the barns and stables Bruno would go to, and talk to the horses and cows and brush the flies from their faces? Oh, yes, just as the landlord said—here is the first bungalow, where the trees begin again. I suppose the main road swings out over on the opposite side, beyond those farms. Here is a bungalow, just ahead. It is not Haus Anna, this first one. Not yet. Not yet. This one has a tarred roof. It was another sort of roof for Haus Anna. How did Bruno say? A roof with red tiles . . . like little waves running up on the sand, Bruno said. . . . Do you remember?

Here was a post stuck in the ground. Die Drei Bären. And there the three bears are, three garden ornaments sitting round a flower-plot, half-way down the garden there. The people are not living there now. Not during the week, anyhow, though the furniture's still there. I think the landlord said Haus Anna was the second one. Herr and Frau Ratte. That is a funny name. Well, they must be funny people living there, in all this damp and cold, in February. He *did* say they are living there now. He surely did. Perhaps they have nowhere else to live, do you think?

The next bungalow was some distance away, but it was Haus Anna right enough. At least it had those red curved tiles Bruno had spoken of; you could just see them through the dark trees. He walked on, his heart beating faster and faster. Three minutes later he had reached the post outside the little wicket-gate. The words "Haus Anna" stood out black and clear on the post. Haus Anna, Bruno's Haus Anna. Or you might say it had *once* been Bruno's Haus Anna.

There was not much left of it now. It had been smashed and looted and set fire to. The fire did not seem to have caught on, though the place was made almost entirely of wood. Perhaps the rain had come down and put the flames out. But it was a pretty complete wreck, none the less. There was not a pane of glass in the windows and the doors had been wrenched from their hinges. Most of the flat red tiles in the veranda seemed to have been carted off bodily. The mess within was so soggy and beastly you did not want to see it any more clearly. They had not been able to do much with the two forms and the dining-table they flanked, where the Rosenheims would sometimes eat alfresco, when they did not take their meals in the punt with them. But the garden beds looked very pulpy, like a skin patched with sores, and most of the trees in the garden had been cut down. Perhaps that row of stumps on the left side of the lawn were the pear trees that Bruno had spoken of. When the petals fell, they got into your hair, said Bruno, and you looked like the Christmas Man.

There were several deep holes in the roots of the trees, quite deep, as if some beast had dug them. Yes, truly, a beast had dug them. Mr. Emmanuel bit his lip and fought back his tears. The white rabbit Jo, that hero, that paragon, had seemed till now too large to be strictly true. He was true, right enough. There in the roots of the trees and by the posts of the fence yonder were the holes he had dug, his signature, the attestation of his valorous feet.

Jo was dead, doubtless. His master Bruno was not truly alive. His master's father was dead. His master's mother —where was she? And there the house stood now, between the trees and the water, a forlorn and gutted thing, that had been so happy once, housing an artist with his brushes to hand, his pipe, his glass of beer, a fair-haired woman singing, a boy with his red Indian and cowboy dreams. A shell now, like Bruno's boyhood, like the felicity of that small family, like the good name and well-being of a people that had gone about for centuries harmlessly upon its business. Between the trees and the water. A gust of wind made the dry branches click like bones.

There was a soft plop of something sliding into the water. A stone? Some small beast, perhaps? A rat?

Oh, yes. Herr and Frau Ratte lived in Haus Anna now.

Mr. Emmanuel found his way back to the main road again, not without a little anxiety, for his head was aching, and the way was not so clear now, with the chill mist that had come up from this land of two hundred water-channels. He kept his head averted from the Schwarzer Adler, fearful lest they should call after him from the windows. It seemed a long way back to the station, much further than it had seemed coming. He bought some rolls in a pastry-shop, for he did not wish to enter another inn in that countryside. The rolls were enough to keep him going. He was not hungry. His train was late, but it did not matter. He remained tied up within himself in the waiting-room. He would not have understood or answered if anyone had spoken to him.

The train arrived at length. He got in. Now it was Lübbenau, now it was Berlin. He knew hardly more of the journey than that. He had time to make some sort of meal at the Café Adler, then he went off to the Zoo station. He had an appointment to keep there. He arrived there punctually at nine.

II

The meeting was to take place under the clock at the Zoo station. The clock hangs forward towards the pavement. Professor Sachs was not there. Mr. Emmanuel looked anxiously left and right along the pavement of the Hardenbergstrasse, across the road towards the complex of corners at the Gedächtniskirche. The professor was not there. I cannot bear it if he does not come. Where will I turn? Where can I go? *No, no, not to her. Not to Elsie Silver. Not while my feet can drag from one place to another.*

You fool. Here he is. Not half a minute late. He should come running up in fire-engines?

Professor Sachs was coming up from round the side of the Zoo station, the blind side of the Joachimthalerstrasse, towards the Tiergarten.

"Oh, good evening, Herr Professor. How glad I am to see you! How kind of you you should come so punctual like this!" He reached forward his hand. The professor extended his till the fingers hardly more than touched, then he dropped them again.

"Please," he said, hurrying on into the subway approach. "Not to stand about here. Come straight to the telephone booths, please." He seemed very apprehensive, anxious to get the thing over as quickly as possible. He was an old man, at least as old as Mr. Emmanuel, but Mr. Emmanuel found it hard to keep pace with him. He talked in a low voice, his head straight before him, as if to create as far as possible the impression that he was not with Mr. Emmanuel at all. "It is a pity you have made yourself so conspicuous," he brought out. "There has been talk. The house-porter saw you at my kiosk. He has spoken to me. Make quite clear exactly what you want, please."

"Yes," said Mr. Emmanuel, "at once. I met a little refugee boy in England, Bruno Rosenheim. He used to live in the Motzstrasse there, number 65. He used to hear from his mother regularly till March last year. Then the letters stopped completely. His heart is dying because he does not hear from her. I want to find out where she is, or if she is alive at all."

They had reached the cluster of telephone booths up towards the blind end of the approach. The professor looked anxiously up and down to make sure no one was with earshot.

"It is the man, the husband," he brought out. "There is something strange about him. I am frightened. But to find out——"

"It is all over with the husband," Mr. Emmanuel assured him. "They think in London——"

"Quiet, quiet!" said the other, a note of anguish in his voice. "I do not want to know! Why have I come? I am foolish!"

Mr. Emmanuel's mouth quivered with unhappiness.

"Perhaps, if you do not want—" he started.

"We are here already," the professor broke in. "Let us get it said quickly. To find out the address of someone who has moved is simple. Why all this trouble? You go to the *Meldestelle,* the Information Post, in the nearest police station. For the Motzstrasse you will find the station in the Nollendorfstrasse. If they can't tell you, they will send you to the *Einwohner Meldeamt,* the chief registration office for addresses, in Police Headquarters in the Alexander Platz. You will fill up a form. You will pay a mark. It is simple. I have done it myself." The phrases succeeded each other without variation of pitch or tone. Knowing there could be no one behind him, the professor kept his eyes fixed forward the whole time in the direction of the exit. "I will go in now and make a call," he concluded. "I thank you. Good-bye." He made for the last booth, and held the handle a moment.

Mr. Emmanuel stood there, goggling.

"It is for me to thank you—" he started. But the old man made a gesture of dismissal, and closed the door to. He bent down as if to consult the book.

I cannot let it go like this, Mr. Emmanuel insisted to himself. I must say just one word of thank you. But perhaps, if he does not want——

But the thought was given no time to complete itself. In that same instant, the door of the booth was thrown open, the old man emerged, his eyes quite glassy with terror. His hands were shaking; it seemed as if his knees must give in under him. Mr. Emmanuel, his heart pierced with dismay, sprang forward to give him a hand.

"Go away! Go away!" the old man croaked. "Let me be!" He tottered down the passage, dwindling uncertainly beyond the staircase, the cigarette kiosk, the newspaper stand, and disappeared.

Mr. Emmanuel stood a full minute gazing after him, his mouth open, a hammer thumping behind his forehead. What has happened in there? What have I done to him? The old man did not hear anyone speaking? He could not, he did not lift off the receiver. What has happened? Is there a corpse inside there?

He went into the telephone booth. There was no corpse there. The telephone book was open on the ledge in front of him. Scrawled in red crayon, in great letters that ran across both pages, were the words:

ROT FRONT LEBT

The crayon was fresh and powdery. The words had the appearance of having been written down quite recently. *Red Front Lives.*

Mr. Emmanuel shut the book to. He was aware that if the book remained open, it might seem, should someone come along within a moment or two to use the telephone, that the old professor had written down those words. Or perhaps himself. Why not? He shut the book with a bang. We have got nothing else to do, the old man and me, we should go about writing Red Front slogans in telephone books.

Would you believe it, these people, what a panic they are in! Is it anything simpler in the world than to shut to the pages of a book? Perhaps no one for weeks now will open the book at that page and see those words! Mr. Emmanuel sighed deeply, and stepped out of the booth, his head shaking violently from side to side. The episode had unnerved him considerably.

I must not buy any more cigarettes from that kind old professor, he realized as he walked slowly down the passage. It is not good for him he should be seen talking to me. Like I was a . . . a Prince Kropotkin, a big anarchist, somebody like that. Did you ever hear from such a thing?

That house-porter . . . do you think that house-porter is at the bottom of it? The old man said the house-porter had spoken to him. Ugh! Such a year should take that house-porter!

And now I shall not be able to buy any more cigarettes from the poor old man. Did you ever hear from such a thing? Such a shame! Perhaps he is the biggest man in all Germany for the literature of the Greeks and Romans, but now my custom for a pack of cigarettes is more important to him than all Homer and Virgil and all those people. A country, eh?

Then his heart leapt with a sudden thought. Perhaps I will not need to buy cigarettes here in Berlin much longer. You have not yet understood what has happened,

Isaac. You have got somewhere. You know something. Tomorrow you go to the local police station. If they do not know, you go to the big police station. You fill in a form. You pay a mark. It is easy. He has done it himself, the professor. Perhaps in a day or two I will know where Bruno's mother is. Perhaps in a day or two I will be able to speak to her. Are you listening? I say perhaps in a day or two I will be able to speak to her. Who knows? *Please God, it should be so.*

It is enough for one day, Mr. Emmanuel thought. He had a cup of coffee at the Café Hahnen, then went home to his bed. So ended Mr. Emmanuel's third day in Berlin.

So ends my third day in Davos, said to himself the young Jew, David Frankfurter. No, I must not reproach myself. It would not have been easy to kill him today, Sunday. He would not have been in his house. He would have been at his *Stammtisch* at the Nazi café, his regular table with the swastika banner on it, with all his cronies round him.

I must go to his house, as if I was one of his people. I must ask quite simply: Please, is Herr Gustloff in?

Tomorrow is Monday, a weekday. It will be all right tomorrow.

8

AT about ten o'clock next morning Mr. Emmanuel made his way to the district police post, in the Nollendorfstrasse. The place was not very imposing. A plaque on one side of the door announced: *Polizei Revier.* It seemed to occupy one or two floors of an ordinary apartment-house. The actual office he had been requested to ask for was on the first floor, the *Meldestelle.*

He put his hand up again to his right-hand breast-pocket. Yes, there it was, solid and trusty, his British passport. He knocked. There was no reply. He knocked again. A muffled bellow came out towards him. Perhaps you should not knock. Perhaps you should walk straight in. He entered. The room was a bare grey-washed room, with a number of closely printed posters on the walls. There was only one with an announcement legible at some distance. It faced you as you entered. *Deutsch Sei Dein Gruss.* German be thy greeting. There were two desks along that wall, and a door leading into an inner room. There was a third desk against the right-hand wall. Three police officials, hatless, but in carefully tended uniform, sat at the three desks. A wooden barrier, with a small wicket on a hinge, separated them from the public, for whose use there was a low form left of the door. The heads of the three policemen were bent close over their papers, as if to make clear to the public what industrious servants of the State they were.

"Guten Tag," said Mr. Emmanuel, after waiting a few moments. It was not as German a greeting as might be. The officials did not raise their heads. Mr. Emmanuel extracted his passport. He held it before him with two corners gripped tightly between thumb and forefinger of each hand.

"Excuse me, please! I am a foreigner, an Englishman!"

All three policemen looked up. Two looked down again. The third, the one nearest on the left, stared at him coldly for several seconds.

"Was wollen Sie, Herr? What do you want?"

"My name is Emmanuel. I am from Doomington, in England."

"What do you want?" the policeman repeated. The tone was quite impersonal.

Mr. Emmanuel related exactly what he wanted, having nothing to hide. He wanted the present address of Frau Hertha Rosenheim, if she were still alive. She had lived till March of last year at Motzstrasse, number 65. He was inquiring on behalf of her son Bruno, at present at school in England. The two other policemen went on shuffling with their papers. The policeman by the window raised his hand to his chin and stroked it reflectively for several seconds. Then he shrugged his shoulders. It was, after all, no concern of his if an Eskimo or a Brazilian came inquiring after an address in his district.

"What street? The Motzstrasse? We will see if we have the record." He rose and went into the inner room. Mr. Emmanuel stood there, his head dithering, his passport still clutched in his hand. A minute later the policeman returned, carrying a card-index file. He sat down and thumbed the index-cards till he came to the one he was looking for. He read carefully the entries on it, then, apparently, read the entries again. They seemed to interest him a good deal. He called both his colleagues over and they too read them. They went back to their desks. There was not a word from any of them.

Then at last the first policeman spoke.

"Excuse me, *Herr*. Will you take a seat, please?" He pointed to the form beside the door. "Perhaps it will be better to wait till the *Herr Polizeileutnant* comes in." The tone was quite polite, perhaps even a shade friendlier than before.

"Yes, very kind." Mr. Emmanuel sat down. "Will it be long, please?" It would have been pleasant if the matter could have been settled without reference to a *Herr Polizeileutnant*.

The policeman gestured with one hand. He did not know. The matter for the time being had no further interest for him. His pen started scrabbling over the paper. A half-hour passed, an hour. It was the sort of place in which half-hours merged insensibly into hours, hours into half-days. The sleepy routine of it was interrupted only by an occasional handing over of a paper or a brief disappearance into the inner room. It is a hard bench, Mr. Emmanuel thought. It is low for these long legs of mine. They are aching a bit. What does that matter? He will be coming soon, that police-lieutenant. At last he will tell me. My news is there, it is almost certainly there. Is it not strange? It is on that piece of cardboard only six feet away from me, the answer to the puzzle, the end of my journey. Well, wait in patience,

Isaac. If he is not here this morning, he will be here this afternoon. If he is not here today, he will be here tomorrow. What are you talking about? He is the officer here. He will be here in five minutes. There, what did I tell you? Someone has just gone into that inner room. The policeman is getting up; he has those cards in his hands. He is in there with him. He is talking to him. I can hear their voices.

Then, some five minutes later, the policeman reappeared at the door.

"This way, please!" he requested.

Mr. Emmanuel rose. The policeman opened the little wicket-gate for him. He was getting more courteous all the time. Mr. Emmanuel followed into the inner room, less forbidding than the one he had left, though there was less in it—a big desk, a few horse-hair chairs, a large picture of the Leader. The *Herr Leutnant* sat in a swivel chair. His uniform was very spick-and-span. He had a black pointed moustache.

"Guten Tag, Herr," he said. "Take a seat." Mr. Emmanuel sat down. "Would you be so courteous as to let me see your passport?" Mr. Emmanuel removed his passport from his pocket and handed it over. His hand trembled so much as he did so, he wondered how the officer could fail to notice it. His heart seemed to have gone a long way down, into the pit of his stomach. He remembered suddenly how exactly it was like that, when he used to swim in the Dnieper, as a boy. He was quite a bold swimmer in the shallow places, where he could put his feet down on solid earth the moment he wanted to. But not when there was no earth there, he was out of his

depth, the water was coming up round his nostrils . . . like here, in Berlin, in the *Polizei Revier,* the passport out of his hands.

My passport, please. I want back my passport.

"Thank you," said the officer. He took down a few details, then handed back the passport a minute or two later.

(You silly old man, getting into a panic like that. You shouldn't move five inches from the corner of Magnolia Street and Blenheim Road, if you can't control yourself better.)

"And where are you staying, please, here in Berlin?" the officer asked. He motioned to the policeman, who had not left the room. The policeman took out a note-book and pencil. Mr. Emmanuel tendered the information.

"And for how long, please?"

"That I cannot say," Mr. Emmanuel hastened to point out. "As soon as I find out about Frau Rosenheim, I go back at once."

"Frau Rosenheim. Exactly. We are coming to that." The officer turned to the policeman. "Bring in the *Herr Kriminal-Kommissar!*" he ordered. The policeman clicked his heels and left the room, by a door that led still farther into the building.

Mr. Emmanuel's body straightened. He held out his hands before him as if to ward something off.

"K . . . Kriminal?" he stammered.

"Please not to disturb yourself," the other said. "It is only a matter of routine. Perhaps you will kindly sit down again." Mr. Emmanuel sat down. A few moments later, the *Herr Kriminal-Kommissar* entered, followed by the policeman. The officer rose and extended his arm.

"Heil Hitler!"

"Heil Hitler!"

Mr. Emmanuel rose during the brief ceremony, as he would have risen if it were the "Marseillaise" or "God Save the King." He sat down again.

"Herr Kriminal-Kommissar," the officer began, "I would like your presence during this interrogation." The other saluted and brought his hand down smartly to his thigh.

"You are Mr. Isaac Emmanuel, of Doomington, England?" the officer stated, referring to his notes.

"You are by religion what?"

"Jewish."

"Please state for what reason you have come to the *Polizei Revier."*

Mr. Emmanuel did as requested.

"Herr Kriminal-Kommissar, I would like you to study the entries on the Rosenheim card in this index."

The *Herr Kriminal-Kommissar* came round and did as he was asked. Being asked for no comment, he made none. He returned to the side of the desk.

"Have you given us your sole reason for asking the address of Frau Rosenheim?"

"Yes, the little boy. He has not heard from her since March. It is killing him."

"You have no other reason for wishing to get in touch with her?"

"No, of course not. In August, or perhaps September, the little boy tried to drown himself and——"

"How long did you know this Rosenheim, the boy's father?"

"The boy's father?" Mr. Emmanuel asked, aghast. Was

the officer trying to trap him? "I have never known him," he said heatedly. "I only know he is dead."

"Who told you he was dead?"

"The Committee in London that looks after refugee boys."

"Why did you ask?"

"I did not ask." His brain was burning with a clear fire. (It is all right if only you stick to the truth. That is all. The truth. Now and always.) "I asked if there was any fresh news about Bruno's mother. They told me the little they knew about both parents. It is very little."

"Do you know anything about the circumstances of Rosenheim's death?"

"I know it was on the frontier somewhere."

"But you said you only knew he was dead!"

"I know what the boy told me. That he was an artist, and then he got mixed up in politics. But it is not my business. I am not interested. I only want to know if I can find out where the boy's mother is."

"For what purpose?"

"So as to give some news to the boy."

"You are hiding nothing?"

"Hiding?" Mr. Emmanuel's voice cracked. "What should I hide?" He held out the palm of his hands. "Please, *Herr Leutnant,* are these hiding anything?"

The officer got up from his chair, and leaned forward across the desk, resting his weight on the palms of his hands.

"Mr. Emmanuel," he said. "I am perfectly satisfied. As far as I am concerned, I am ready to give you such information as we have here. I think, however, I ought just to refer the matter to my colleague. What is your view, *Herr Kriminal-Kommissar?*"

The *Herr Kriminal-Kommissar* straightened up. His eyes were glued on the panels of the door by which he had entered. His voice was quite toneless.

"It would be in order to refer the matter to the *Geheime Staats Polizei,*" he said.

The officer rubbed the back of his left hand across the palm of his right, as if, so to speak, he were washing his hands of the matter.

"Very well." He turned to Mr. Emmanuel. "I do not anticipate any difficulty. We have your address. As soon as we receive word, we will get in touch with you."

"Please," Mr. Emmanuel begged. "How soon might that be?" The fellow was so nice and friendly. A real Jewish heart.

"I don't know." He sounded quite cross all of a sudden. "Two or three days. Four or five. I don't know." He got down to his desk again without another word. The *Herr Kriminal-Kommissar* walked out through one door; Mr. Emmanuel was led out through the other.

He felt quite faint when he got out. He looked forward a lot to his lunch. I will have a nice lot of time now for my postcards, he said to himself. I will write to Bruno, to Rose, to Ada, to Mary Cooper, to my son Moisheh. It is about time I wrote a nice long letter to Moisheh. I must tell him perhaps, after all, I will be a week or two late, arriving in Palestine. There is also Sam Silver. Perhaps also to Sam Silver I should write a nice long letter.

He went home and lunched and rested for a little while. Then he spent quite a long time writing to his friends. He had in a fair stock of picture postcards. He knew they were anxious about him in Magnolia Street. In a day or two he hoped he would be himself receiving letters from the other side. When his writing was over, he made himself comfortable indoors for the evening. It was very cold outside. There was really nothing very much to go out for. He gave his letters to Frau Kahn, who said certainly she would see they got posted. He could rely on her. So ended his fourth day in Berlin.

Over in Davos, the fourth day for David Frankfurter ended, with nothing done. Long, long he sat at his window in his little pension, looking down the snow-hushed valley, at the stationary lights in houses and hotels, the fewer moving lights in streets.

One more day has passed. Well, then? You return to Berne tomorrow? I do not return to Berne tomorrow. I kill the man Gustloff in the good day.

The good day? You have forgotten. Tuesday is the good day, the third day of the Lord's week. You have forgotten how often our father would put a thing off till the good day came round. For (he would say) it is written in the Book that on the other five weekdays the Lord gazed upon the work of His hands and said that it was good, but he said it once only. On the third day, however, he gazed upon his work, and said it was good, once a first time, and a second time again.

Wherefore I will wait till tomorrow, the twice-good day. Please the Lord, my hand shall not falter.

9

I

FOR Isaac Emmanuel, the things he himself did the next day, which was Tuesday, the fourth of February, were of little importance, or none. He got up, breakfasted, wrote his daily postcards, went out and came back to lunch, went out again once or twice, then came back to settle for the evening. Of more importance to him was the thing David Frankfurter did that day, in Davos, beyond the frontier, some hundreds of miles away.

David Frankfurter well knew the road to Wilhelm Gustloff's house. A signboard, with the local leader's name and the initials of the party, pointed the way there. It was evening. The first stars were out. The snow was firm on the roadway.

It was a blue-painted house with a flat roof. Frankfurter was quite familiar with it. He had passed by several times already during these five days. He hesitated a moment at the front door, and felt in his pocket. Yes, the revolver was there. In the privacy of his room he had taken it out and contemplated it so often during these five days, his brain had almost ceased to register what the thing was, as the brain sometimes ceases to remember what a word means, if the tongue of the mind too often repeats it.

It was a revolver. A revolver to shoot Gustloff. The Leader's delegate; leader in Switzerland of the N.S.D.A.P. He knocked at the door. A servant came.

"Herr Gustloff, please!" he demanded. His voice was calm. He aroused no suspicion.

"Step straight in!" the servant said. He followed into a reception room. Directly before him, a large portrait of the Leader stared sombrely down upon him. There were other portraits of the Leader on the other walls, portrait challenging portrait.

"Kill him! Kill him! Kill him!" moaned the heart of David Frankfurter.

"I will tell Herr Gustloff at once!" the servant said, and disappeared through a door into a passage.

There was a desk in the room and on it a ceremonial dagger. Not a dagger to kill with. No dagger is sure enough. A revolver. A revolver. There in my pocket. Four bullets for him, four to make quite sure. Then for myself the fifth. A voice was talking, as it seemed to itself, out in the passage there. No. Talking on the telephone. There were intervals between the sentences. Whose voice? The voice of the Enemy? What words? *All Jews and Communists, we'll show them, the swine. . . .* Do I hear them only in my own brain? Do I hear no voice at all? The click of the telephone on the receiver. There was a voice out there. There is none now. Heavy feet come marching forward, the feet of the brown hordes.

The door opens. A huge man stands framed in the doorway; it is surprising how huge he is. I had no idea. The man's mouth opens to ask a question. Don't stand dithering there. Out with it. The revolver is pulled from the pocket. The man makes to lunge forward. The trigger! To the heart! Pull! Once, again, again, again! The body crashes downward, with a splintering, a rending, like a tree.

Out now. At once out. You must not die in this place. It is infamous. It is abominable. He rushes out into the street, runs hither and thither for some moments, as if he has discharged the fifth bullet into his own heart and this running were only the reflex action of a dead thing.

But he has discharged no bullet into his own heart. His spirit's stored gunpowder has exploded once. It will not explode a second time. The panic running stops suddenly, like a toy run down. There is a telephone booth, he remembers, not many yards away. His feet drag wearily under him over the piled snow. Give me the police. Is that the police? My name is David Frankfurter. I am a foreigner. I have just murdered the Nazi leader, Wilhelm Gustloff, in his house. I am coming round at once to give myself up to you.

A few minutes later he was at the police station. They asked him for a statement. "I have not committed the murder," he said, "for personal reasons, but because I am a Jew." Later he supplemented the statement with these words: "No one drove me to this deed. No one inspired it. No one knew of my idea."

At that moment in Berlin, some hundreds of miles north and west, in the Pension Kahn, in the Bambergerstrasse, the woman in the blue Chinese peignoir was teaching Mr. Isaac Emmanuel a new card game. She was really quite a nice person when you got to know her; a bit moody sometimes. But which of us is not?

II

Mr. Emmanuel did not get up very early next morning, which was the morning of Wednesday, the fifth of February. He had nothing much to get up to. It was nearly ten o'clock by the time he got into the dining-room for his breakfast, a time when the room was usually pretty empty.

Ten o'clock, he was saying to himself! Ten o'clock! Such a lazybones, eh! What will they do to me, I should like to know, if I start getting up in Ain Charod, in the colony, at ten o'clock. Such an idea!

The dining-room was not empty this morning. Most of the guests were still sitting about the place. Even Herr Kahn was not perched up in his pulpit. He was down at the table with the others. The table was littered with the loose sheets of newspapers. Frau Kahn sat in the easy chair by the window. She looked pale and miserable. The lady in the blue Chinese peignoir looked hardly more cheerful.

"Good morning!" exclaimed Mr. Emmanuel jovially. He had felt much more at ease the last day or two. He had scrupulously obeyed Herr and Frau Kahn's request to ask nobody any questions; similarly, nobody had asked him any. That was really a funny thing; in Berlin here, he supposed everywhere in Germany among the Jews, human nature wasn't the same any more. Nobody asked anybody any questions. Perhaps it was like that among the Gentiles also. He gathered that the people in the pension had been given to understand he was in Berlin on refugee business for the Doomington Board of Guardians. Well, it was true, if it wasn't quite so official as that.

"Good morning!" he exclaimed. "What is it here? A funeral?"

"Bad news!" said the industrious student of invoices and receipts. (He had them with him at the breakfast table.) "Bad news!"

"It is enough already with bad news!" Mr. Emmanuel objected with forced heartiness. "It is time it should be good news already!"

"Over in Switzerland there has been a murder," another guest said, a one-time architect from Cassel. "The leader over there of the Nazi Party! A Jew did it!"

Frau Kahn rose from her chair as if someone had touched her with a hot cinder. Her eyes were directed, not towards the group at the table, but towards the door by which Mr. Emmanuel had just entered. Everyone turned. The elderly maiden Kati stood framed in the doorway there. She had slapped more paint than usual on her cheeks. She was wiping her hands vigorously on her sacking apron, back and palm, back and palm, as if she had just been paddling them in a pail of slops. She stood there tittering, as if something very funny had tickled her fancy. Then she turned and shut the door behind her.

"No politics, please!" implored Frau Kahn. "I must insist! No politics!"

"Quatsch!" exclaimed the one-time architect, addressing Frau Kahn. "It's not politics!" (He had not been licked into shape yet.) "It's news! It's here in the newspaper!" He slapped the paper with the back of his hand.

"Can I see that paper, please?" asked Mr. Emmanuel diffidently. He felt almost as if he were butting in on a family quarrel. The one-time architect handed it over. It was the *Berliner Tageblatt,* morning edition. It was not quite the paper it used to be, but Berlin Jews took it from force of habit, that and the *Jüdische Rundschau.* Mr. Emmanuel adjusted his pince-nez and read the messages, from Berne, from Geneva: *With respect to the murder of the National-Socialist Landesgruppenleiter, Wilhelm Gustloff, the murderer, the Jew David Frankfurter, born in 1909* . . . He sighed deeply and shook his head from side to side, again and again.

"A Jew, eh? A Jew! He should not have done such a thing, poor boy!"

Then he stopped. Herr and Frau Kahn did not like his talking about public affairs.

"God damn him!" a voice brought out from somewhere down the table. "He should roast in hell!"

The violence took everyone by surprise, at this time and in this place where people knew how to keep the bit on their tongues. No one spoke for some seconds, and then once more it was the foreigner, this Emmanuel, who gave tongue. There was a tiny spot of colour in his cheeks. His eyes were glittering behind the pince-nez. (If these people shall have no pity in their hearts, no understanding, who shall? A shame someone should talk like that, and no one give back an answer!)

"Perhaps," he said softly, "perhaps he was feeling it in his heart like a knife, his father dead maybe in a concentration camp, he does not know where his mother is, how can you say what—?"

"He was not a German Jew!" snapped the student of invoices and receipts. "He was a foreigner, a Yugoslavian. As if we had no troubles of our own!"

A silence fell. It was more than a silence, almost as if a cold wind had entered the room, or as if it were there already. No one spoke for half a minute. Then at last the lady in the blue Chinese peignoir lifted her voice.

"You never know with a thing like that," she complained. "You never know who it's going to hit."

"Now! Now!" This was Herr Kahn. He brought the flat of a knife down sharply on the table, almost like a chairman bringing down his gavel. It was clear he considered there had already been too much conversation along these lines. "You'll be wanting your breakfast, Mr. Emmanuel? Eggs, yes?" He always knew which client took eggs, which sausages. "In glass or fried?" He knew quite well Mr. Emmanuel liked them in glass.

"In glass!" suggested Mr. Emmanuel meekly. His self-confidence had quite gone out of him.

Herr Kahn went up to the door that led towards the kitchen.

"Trude!" he called. "Trude!" He knew Frau Kahn would be helpless for the rest of the day. "Two eggs in glass for Mr. Emmanuel!"

Mr. Emmanuel hardly lifted his eyes from his plate all the way through breakfast.

"The paper?" someone suggested.

He reached his hand forward, then dropped it again.

"No, thank you, no paper! I have a bit of a headache this morning."

He felt lonely and friendless among these people, a stranger a long way from his own place.

III

The next few days would have been slow going for Mr. Emmanuel if not for the fact that his letters from England began to come in. There was a letter from Rose, one from Mr. Poyser, two from Bruno (which included a photograph taken in football kit at Greystones), one from Sam Silver, and a big envelope of oddments forwarded by Ada. It was nice getting that photograph of Bruno the footballer. He added it happily to the collection of photographs he had in his wallet—his own family, Rose's family, one or two others.

However, there was quite a lot of the day which could not be filled with letter-writing, and that weighed heavily. On the second night after his interview at the police station, he made up his mind to go to one of the big cinemas on the Kurfürstendamm, the Marmorhaus. What could they do to him in there? Could they eat him? There was a Clark Gable film showing, with Constance Bennett. He was no great cinema-goer, over in Doomington, but here in Berlin Mr. Gable and Miss Bennett were like old friends. The name of the film was *Nach Büroschluss.* He hoped, in a way, he had seen the film already, though that was not very likely. It would make him feel twice as much at home. The newsreel was showing when he went in, and that was really very frightening. It was all brown troops, and regular troops, and tanks, and the seven heavens flapping with swastikas, and the Leader declaiming into a microphone. Nothing in the minor key seemed to be happening in Germany. Even the snow-spread mountains of Garmisch-Partenkirchen, where the Olympic winter sports were just due to begin, seemed to have been caught up into the mechanism of Nazi publicity, like washing in a terrific mangling machine.

Mr. Emmanuel would have liked to creep out during the newsreel, but he was afraid he would attract attention to himself if he went so soon after he came in. It might be interpreted as a sort of disrespect. It was, however, in the long interval, between the second feature and the big film, while the lights were up and they were projecting animated advertisements on the screen, that he felt really unhappy. There was no question at all but that people were turning towards him and pointing him out and talking about him. He wished he had not come. He vowed he would not come again. But while I am here, he said to himself, I stay here. I am not going to let them chase me out. Is my money maybe not so good as theirs? And what are they, after all? They are Germans. I am an Englishman. He saw the big film through, but it was dubbed in German dialogue. He did not enjoy it at all.

He walked, he sat in the Jew-owned cafés, he read newspapers. There was not much more about that shooting in Davos, he was glad to notice. It was the sort of thing the authorities could make a lot of trouble over, but the winter sports seemed to be occupying people's minds a lot more. Thank God for that! Back in the pension, he played card games with the lady in the blue Chinese peignoir. She was still in the blue Chinese peignor. She was hardly ever out of it. The boarders began to make funny remarks about them both. But the truth was, the poor lady was a bore. The pension was a bore. All this hanging about was a bore. He would have liked to be of some use to the Community office, but he did not think they would give him much of a welcome. On the fourth day, the Friday, he got so impatient, he went and called at the *Polizei Revier* in the Nollendorfstrasse, to see if they had any news for him. But they were scarcely civil. The policeman went into the inner office, obviously to consult the *Herr Leutnant,* and when he came out again his face was quite unpleasant. Hadn't the *Herr Leutnant* said he would be informed when there was any news? Well, there wasn't any yet. Clear out of here! There was nothing to do but to clear out.

He went to the Friday evening service at the synagogue, and that made him feel a lot better. Tomorrow is *Shabbos,* he told himself. I will get up in good time and be in *shool* for the beginning of the service. I will ask them to wake me up at eight o'clock. It is a shame how lazy I am getting. Like a big soprano from the opera, I should live so!

But he was, in fact, wakened a good deal earlier than eight o'clock next morning.

IV

It was not quite half-past five, when a large Mercédès drew up in the Bambergerstrasse, opposite number 38. Half-past five is the time when even the most inveterate stop-out is back in his bed, and the earliest riser has not yet risen from it. Two men got out. The taller one rang the bell, keeping his finger continuously on the bell-push. In less than a minute, the door opened before them; the house-porter, dressed only in his night-shirt and slippers, despite the intense cold, stood obsequiously awaiting inquiries. You are in no doubt what callers they are who call at five-thirty, and you are well advised to waste no time over your toilet before rising to let them in.

"Pension Kahn?" the taller man rapped out.

"Second floor!" the house-porter replied, with the vigour of the sergeant he had once been. The two men advanced to the staircase and disappeared. The old man went back to his room. They've been a long time raiding that roost, he thought.

The door-bell of the Pension Kahn rang so long and loud, there were few people there it did not awaken. Whom is that for? they asked themselves in one room and another. They have no doubt, either, who calls at such an hour. Please the Lord God it is not for me! Please the Lord God it is not for me! they repeated, their teeth chattering, their bed-things drawn up over their ears.

Herr Kahn was at the door, he, too, only in his nightshirt. No one delays when these callers come.

"There is a Mr. Emmanuel here, an Englishman?"

"This way!" said Herr Kahn. He went ahead of the men, turning left to the last door on the passage.

"Get out of it!" said the shorter man.

You do not argue with these callers. What is there to argue about? Herr Kahn turned back along the passage to his own room.

The taller man knocked once at the door before him, so violently that the door shook in its frame. Then he turned the handle. The door was not locked. He entered, feeling for the switch in the wall on his right. He found it, and stepped into the room, the stouter man following him.

An old man was sitting bolt upright in his bed against the left-hand wall. His mouth and eyes were wide open with astonishment. The hairs of his small white pointed beard were faintly tugging in the draught that found its way in through the open doors.

"Your name Emmanuel?"

"Yes—I—I——"

"Gestapo! Get up! They want you!"

"But I—I—I am an Englishman. I——"

"Get up!" The taller man made a step forward. "You can tell them that over there!"

"Where?" Mr. Emmanuel breathed faintly. "There is some mistake. I——"

The taller man stood by the bedside now.

"You want us to take you as you are?"

Mr. Emmanuel pushed his bed-eiderdown aside. He moved his long limbs down towards the floor. His feet sought for the slippers. There seemed hardly any sensation in his limbs.

"Come on, come on now! We've not got all night!"

Mr. Emmanuel rose and staggered over towards the chair where his clothes were lying. It was painful to him to have to get out of his pyjamas and into his underclothes with these two men standing by, looking on. He would even turn away from his wife, and she from him, while they got into or out of their night things. He hoped the men would look somewhere else. But they did not. They stood regarding him with their pale hostile eyes.

But there *is* some mistake. It *cannot* be there is no mistake! It is the wrong house! It is. . . . *Hear me, Lord God, open their eyes that they may know of their mistake!* It is only for little Bruno! I have come to find out where Bruno's mother is, because his heart is dying for her. Is there anything wrong in that, please? What will Bruno say, when——

His head was buzzing dreadfully. It is no joke to be awakened suddenly by a bang on the door; it is like the Day of Judgment. And then the central light is switched on suddenly and it is blazing down on you. And two men are standing there, like Angels of Death.

Do you understand what they have said? *Gestapo!* Secret Police! For *me!* They have come for *me!* What for? Are they mad?

He had just slipped his braces over his shoulders. He turned to the men sharply.

"You cannot do this! I am an Englishman! I will show you my passport!"

"You can show it to them over there!"

What was he an Englishman for, eh? What was it he had read in that passport, eh, coming in the train from Liverpool Street Station?

". . . *to pass freely without let or hindrance and to afford him every assistance and protection of which he may stand in need.*"

That was not only words. Oh, no! It was the request of Sir John Simon himself, in the name of His Majesty the King.

"I want to ring up my consul, please! At once!" Mr. Emmanuel requested.

"You can ring them up from over there!" The taller man looked as if he was losing his temper. "Get dressed, will you? I'll give you five more minutes!"

Mr. Emmanuel opened his mouth to speak again, but as he did so the taller man advanced two steps and lifted his fist as if to bring it crashing down on Mr. Emmanuel's skull. In the meantime the stouter man had got down to work on the apartment. Swiftly, expertly, he turned the mattress, separated the bed-clothes, thrust his fingers into the crevices of chairs, looking for papers. He opened every drawer, every cupboard. He found nothing at all, except a few letters, answered or to answer, lying inside the blotting-pad; also, a few picture postcards. He thrust the letters and cards into his pocket.

Mr. Emmanuel tied his shoe-laces, got into his shirt, put on his tie and collar. He was worried about his studs. Sometimes they eluded his fingers altogether even when he had all the time in the world. And now . . . he only had five minutes now.

Perhaps, yes, they would let him ring up the British consul over there, where they were taking him. They could not, dare not, try to prevent him. An Englishman! Do you know what that means? An Englishman?

The studs and collar and tie went quite well. He slipped on his coat and waistcoat. He suddenly felt very miserable and ashamed. Those poor Kahn people, bringing all this trouble and scandal upon them! It was a shame! She, Frau Kahn, had felt it in her bones from the beginning, the poor woman! The sooner this is over, the better for everybody.

He turned to the two men.

"What shall I bring with me, please? How long shall I be away!"

The taller man shrugged his shoulders.

"Put what you want in there!" he said, indicating the attaché-case.

Perhaps he was only going to be away a day or two, perhaps only a few hours, just time enough to explain the mistake someone was making. He transferred a shirt and a change of underclothing from the suitcase to the attaché-case, just in case of emergencies. That left room only for his toilet things and slippers and a book or two. He had his papers with him, of course—the passport, the travelling-marks, the letter of credit. They were inside the secret pocket of his waistcoat. They were better there. In his wallet he had his photographs to keep him company.

"I am ready now," he said. There was the ghost of a smile on his face as he turned to them. After all, it was not their fault. They were here only because someone had sent them.

The stouter man advanced straight towards him, as if to knock him down. The smile went from Mr. Emmanuel's face, like mist from a mirror. He lifted his hands as if to protect his glasses. His mouth opened, but no sound came from it!

"Ruhe!" said the stouter man, and knocked Mr. Emmanuel's arms down with the blunt flat of his hands. He was a strong man, and it hurt. Then deftly he passed his hands down Mr. Emmanuel's pockets, side and hip. It was all right, it seemed. He nodded to his colleague and advanced to the door.

"Go!" said the taller man, pointing.

Mr. Emmanuel picked up his attaché-case, the attaché-case he was so proud of, that looked so English with its bright chromium locks. He stood for a moment and looked round the room, with grief and incredulity. His eye hesitated for a moment on two objects: the lovely plaid rug that Rose had given him, hanging over the foot of the bed, Mary Cooper's travelling cushion, sitting in a chair. They would hardly want him to take a cushion with him, but a rug—why not? It was very cold outside.

"I can take my rug, please, no?"

"Yes!"

He took up the rug and went over to the door. The taller man followed. As the three men passed along the passage to the front door of the pension, you would have thought it was a house of the dead, so dreadfully quiet the whole place was.

The boots of the three men made an astonishing clamour on the empty staircase. On street-level the door was still open. They walked over to the big black waiting car, its bonnet pointing northward, towards the Tauentsienstrasse.

A driver sat motionless at the wheel. The taller man got in beside him. The stouter man opened the rear door.

"In there!" he directed. Mr. Emmanuel got in.

The driver pressed the starting-button. The stout man pulled the blinds over the two rear windows. The car moved off.

Such a car, thought Mr. Emmanuel. I have never been in a car so grand like this in all my life before. Like I was going to the Lord Mayor's Party at the Town Hall. The Lord Mayor and all that pertained to him were Mr. Emmanuel's standard of grandeur, though he knew that was a foolishness; there were grander people in England, even than the Lord Mayor of Doomington.

It is almost like travelling in a box, thought Mr. Emmanuel. He could see nothing on both sides of him, and not much ahead, for the taller man was quite burly too. I would not know much, he said to himself, even if I could see. They crossed a broad street, and a few moments later they were in a park. It must be the Tiergarten, he thought. He had come that way on his arrival just over a week ago. Just over a week ago? Is it possible? That is all, just over a week ago. They were out in the streets now; perhaps they were those streets round the Friedrichstrasse. Oh, yes, it was northward they were going all the time. He could make out the chill glow eastward, right-handed from the taller man. To the east lies Jerusalem. A Jew knows, even if he is blind, which way lie the dawn and Jerusalem, for he must turn that way to prayer.

Where are they taking me to? What for?

"Please, what for?" he asked aloud, in a small plaintive voice.

"Shut your jaw!" the stouter man said.

It was very quiet, the streets, the men, the car too. So quiet, Mr. Emmanuel said to himself. Like the Lord Mayor's hearse going to the cemetery.

10

I

IT was not till the Thursday of the following week that Rose Cooper, over in Ringwood, in England, began to get worried. Mr. Emmanuel had been very punctilious about that daily postcard she had got him to promise her. Once or twice it had been a fat letter. He had reached Berlin on a certain Friday, the last day of January. He had written that same day, and she had received his card the following Monday. She heard again next day, though he himself had missed a day; for he had not written on the Sabbath. She heard from him every day after that, till Saturday. There was no post on Sunday, and she did not hear on Monday, but she did not give the matter a thought, for once again the Sabbath had intervened, the day on which he did not write. When she heard nothing on Tuesday, she still thought nothing about it. After all, she told herself, it *is* a bit of a nuisance to have to write every day. She did not hear the next day, either. That was Wednesday. She did not like that. On the Thursday, there was still no word from Mr. Emmanuel. She went about all day, unhappy and distraught. It would have been different if he had not been so punctilious with his cards. But he *had* been. What on earth could have happened? Was he ill? After all, that bout of pleurisy had been no joke, and he wasn't a young man any more. But he was not the sort of person to let his correspondence come to a full stop merely because he was ill. He would scrawl a word or two, however ill he was; or, anyway, he would get someone else to write a note for him. If he wasn't ill, what on earth was the matter with him?

After lunch, she felt she couldn't stand it any more, so she drove over to her sister-in-law Mary Cooper, to find out what she thought about it. Mary asked her to be sensible. Mr. Emmanuel might all of a sudden be so tied up in things, she said, he simply hadn't a moment to spare for postcard writing. It was, in a way, rather unkind to have bound the old man down to writing every day, wasn't it, now?

Rose was not at all sure Mary was right. Mr. Emmanuel had obviously enjoyed writing his letters and postcards. He had had practically nothing to say all the time he had been in Berlin, but he had liked saying it. He seemed to like seeing himself write, almost as much as he liked hearing himself talk.

Quite so, Mary admitted. But there was another thing. Perhaps he wasn't in Berlin just at the moment. His quest for Bruno's mother might have taken him afield somewhere. What was the name of that place the boy so often talked about? Where his people used to have a bungalow? Lübbenau, Rose reminded her. Yes, that was it, Lübbenau. Perhaps old Emmanuel had gone to Lübbenau, and from there somewhere else, perhaps.

But how would that affect the situation? Rose wanted to know. Couldn't he write from Lübbenau, or wherever else he might be?

Mary thought that Rose was a little dense. Didn't she see that in certain circumstances it might be better for Mr. Emmanuel to give up writing home to England? It might be awkward . . . somehow.

In *what* circumstances? Rose pressed.

"I don't know," said Mary, "don't ask me. All I say is, don't go and get panicky because an old gentleman hasn't got down to his fountain-pen for a day or two." Then another thought occurred to her. "By the way," she asked, "have you heard from young Bruno?"

"He sends me a weekly letter," replied Rose, "as you know. Yes, I've heard this week. On Tuesday, I think."

"I wonder if *he's* heard anything from Mr. Emmanuel?"

"Yes, I wonder. The old man might stop writing to me for a day or two, but he'd hardly stop writing to Bruno. Not unless there was some very good reason for it. I think I'll drop Bruno a note and ask him when he last heard from him."

Mary hesitated.

"Don't you think it might alarm Bruno? I mean, if he sees you're getting worried . . . won't he get worried too?"

"Not if he's heard. And if he hasn't . . ."

"Well . . . and if he hasn't?"

Rose shrugged her shoulders.

"I don't know. I don't know. What do you think?"

"Well, wait a day or two before you write to the boy, won't you? Wait till over the weekend."

"All right," said Rose. "I'll wait a couple of days longer. I'm not very happy about it." Her face was full of trouble.

She was back again next morning, quite soon after breakfast. Mary was in her armchair, reading the morning paper. She had not cleared away the breakfast things yet. The dogs lay about like rugs.

Rose entered. Tessa got up and began pawing at her dress.

"Down, Tessa! What is it, Rose? You look awful!" Her face asked a question she did not give words to. What news was there? Bad news?

"No," said Rose. "It's not bad news!" She opened up her handbag. "In a way," she added grimly, "I'd prefer bad news. Look at this!" She handed over an envelope.

"A letter to Mr. Emmanuel? But . . . but . . . it's your own handwriting, Rose! What's it all about?"

"That's what I want to know. You see these two words on the side here? *'Adressat Unbekannt.'* Addressee unknown. They make out they don't even know him, at that pension he was staying at. It's ridiculous. I've written to him there, and I've had an answer back again! What on earth does it mean, Mary? It's worrying me sick!"

"Really, you must pull yourself together. Probably all it means is that he's gone somewhere and forgotten to leave his address behind."

"No," said Rose shortly. "It doesn't say *address* unknown. It says *addressee* unknown. I've looked the words up!"

"Yes," Mary agreed. "It does look a bit funny. I'm sure the explanation will be perfectly simple when once we get it."

"What am I to *do,* Mary? I don't like it! Ought I to ask somebody? We can't just sit down——"

"Now you're going to do no good to anybody by fussing. In the first place, write to Bruno. Find out if *he's* heard anything. Then send a registered air mail letter to that pension. It ought to be in German, I think. Old Major Townley will give you a hand. His German's quite good, I believe. After that . . . well, we'll see. Now you're here, you can help me bring in some weekend shopping from the village. Pull up your socks, Rose! Do you hear?"

With the aid of Major Townley, Rose got her letter written to the Pension Kahn. She herself wrote to Bruno. It also occurred to her she might as well write to Ada, up in Magnolia Street, in case she had heard, for one reason or another.

Her letter to Bruno crossed a letter from Bruno to her. The boy had been very worried, too. He had had no word all week from Mr. Emmanuel. And now, that morning, Friday, he had got back a letter he had himself addressed to the Pension Kahn: *Adressat Unbekannt.* Had Rose heard? Why hadn't Mr. Emmanuel written? Was he ill, or anything? The boy seemed anxious and miserable.

A further consultation with Mary followed. It was agreed that the people in Berlin must be given several days to answer the air mail letter. Perhaps they were very busy. Perhaps this, perhaps that. Probably they didn't feel much like writing, anyway. In the meantime, they might well get word again from Mr. Emmanuel himself. To Bruno a not entirely truthful letter was written, conveying the information that Mr. Emmanuel had warned Rose he was going to be very busy for some little time to come. With respect to the letter she had sent him, which had crossed his to her, she had merely been wondering whether, after all, Mr. Emmanuel had found time to scribble a note to Bruno.

The days passed. A week passed. No word came from the Pension Kahn. It was impossible that Rose's registered letter had not been received there, unless the place had gone up in smoke. And if they had received it, they seemed to have no intention of answering it. Why? It was a very straightforward letter. That week passed. The half of a second week passed. Two and a half weeks had gone by since word had been received from Mr. Emmanuel. No, Ada had heard nothing either. No one else had heard anything, Ada reported, among Mr. Emmanuel's cronies in Longton.

"What are we to *do?*" Rose wept. "What are we to *do?*"

"I think it doesn't look too good," Mary Cooper admitted dourly. "Let's go and talk it over with old Major Townley. He's a dear!"

They talked it over with Major Townley. He scratched his head and thought hard a good long time. He helped himself to three whiskies and soda, one after the other.

"You say the chap's a British subject?" he asked. He pushed forward his deaf-box for the reply.

"Yes, he's been a British subject for years and years. He's a saint," said Rose tearfully.

"It doesn't matter if he's a saint or a scoundrel!" the Major said belligerently. "He's a British subject, isn't he? Damn monkey-tricks!" He growled. He helped himself to another whisky and soda.

"He's not been up to any monkey-tricks!" Rose insisted defensively. "It's all as open as the day! All he wanted——"

"I don't mean *his* monkey-tricks! I mean *theirs!*" he snapped.

"I'm sorry," Rose said humbly.

"What?" He pushed the contraption forward.

"I'm sorry."

"Oh!" He drew the box back. It had not been worth the effort. "There's only one thing you can do, you know," he said suddenly. His whole expression had changed. The mouth was firm and quite implacable. The eyes were gentle as Mr. Emmanuel's own. "You'll have to tell them about it in the Foreign Office."

"That's what I've been thinking for some days," said Mary quietly. "It's rather a long job, though, isn't it?"

"A long job!" wailed Rose. "A long job! While poor Mr. Emmanuel . . . *Anything* can have happened to Mr. Emmanuel! Oh, why on earth did I ever let him go!"

Major Townley put out his hand and patted her gently on the arm.

"You're forgetting the youngster, aren't you?" he murmured. "I met him, you know; a nice lad. You're forgetting the old man, too. The sort of man he is. No," he decided. "It won't be enough to write to the Foreign Office. Somebody'll have to go down there and shake 'em up a bit!"

"I'd go tomorrow," said Rose, "if I thought anybody'd see me."

"Tell me, Mrs. Cooper, how long will it be before your husband's home again?"

"A good three weeks."

"Three weeks, eh? Too long!" He shook his head. "Don't worry!" he murmured. "I know a chap named Face-ache. That's what we used to call him at Wellington. Scuddamore, his name is. He's in the Foreign Office. How about driving down tomorrow, Mrs. Cooper?"

"You mean . . . you mean that you'll take me down to the Foreign Office and . . . Oh, Major Townley, it's simply too lovely of you!"

"I can't hear a word you say!" he shouted. "Why don't you talk up?" He seized the decanter. "Come on now, both of you, have a drink! Come *on,* now!"

II

Major Townley was quite a person with the gentleman he called Face-ache. The gentleman he called Face-ache was quite a person at the Foreign Office. There was a certain amount, during the next two days, of going to and fro along corridors and into thick-carpeted rooms. The rooms had suave gentlemen in them, wearing wing-collars and herring-bone trousers.

"That's all right," announced Major Townley, when the two days were over. "They're going to get going at once. I think I'll stay on in town for a day or two. What about you?"

Rose took hold of his two hands. "I'll have to go. You forget I'm the mother of a large family. I don't know how to thank you. I feel very silly. I want to cry!"

"Don't!" exclaimed Major Townley in horror. "I'll be coming on you for some of these indigo pansies of yours this year! Don't worry! They'll soon find out about the old chap. And if they don't . . . my God, there'll be trouble!" His blue eyes darkened with the anger that swept across them. Then they lightened again. "Give my love to that gang of daughters you have! Good-bye, see you soon!"

"See you soon!"

Don't worry, old Emmanuel, wherever you are! (So Rose took counsel with herself.) *You're not alone in the world, old fellow. You're not forgotten. There's still England . . . Face-ache, Townley, whatever its name is!*

III

In the course of several days a chit was sent round from the British Embassy in Berlin to the British Consulate. It stated that a certain Isaac Emmanuel, of Doomington, a British subject, had arrived in Berlin on the morning of Friday, the thirty-first of January. He had taken a room in the Pension Kahn, in the Bambergerstrasse, number 38. He had written to his friends in England daily during the whole of the following week. Then his correspondence had ceased abruptly. During that week he had received and commented on letters received from England. Since then, however, letters to the Pension Kahn had been returned: *Adressat Unbekannt*. Direct inquiries regarding the whereabouts of Mr. Emmanuel had been ignored. It was requested that an inquiry should be made at the Bambergerstrasse.

Next day a young man from the British Consulate presented himself at the Pension Kahn. It was impossible to extract any information with respect to the present whereabouts of Mr. Emmanuel, or even as to whether he had occupied a room there. The woman who ran the place, Frau Kahn, was almost speechless with fright. Her husband kept his head, but he was nearly as terrified. The young man returned to the Consulate, convinced that things were not at all well with Mr. Emmanuel.

The day after a more responsible official from the Consulate turned up in the Bambergerstrasse. It was perhaps helpful that Herr Kahn was not in at the time. An attempt was made to shut the door in the official's face, but the official put his foot in the door. He peremptorily stated he must see Frau Kahn immediately. On seeing her, he informed her that if she and her husband persisted in withholding information which he was legally entitled to demand, the consequences would be very grave. It was not without danger of serious international repercussions that officers of His Majesty's Consular Service, sent at the instance of His Britannic Majesty's Ambassador, were trifled with in this fashion. On the other hand, he gave Frau Kahn his guarantee that no harm of any sort would befall her if she replied to his inquiries in a simple and straightforward manner.

The woman broke down completely. Sobbing pitifully, she told the whole story of Mr. Emmanuel, so far as it related to herself and her pension. She gave the official certain facts already in his possession, namely the nature of the business which had brought Mr. Emmanuel to Berlin, a thing he had not attempted to hide. The important fact that emerged, and a fact by no means unsuspected by the British authorities, was this: that for some reason known to themselves, Mr. Emmanuel had been apprehended by the Gestapo. Two agents had called for him at five-thirty on the morning of Saturday, the eighth, and carried him off. Nothing had been heard of him since.

The woman relapsed into a further paroxysm of weeping. The official was grieved to have caused her such distress. He left, and presented his report.

The next day His Majesty's Consul-General addressed a note to the head of the Gestapo, stating that he had received a report to the effect that a British subject, a Mr. Isaac Emmanuel, had been arrested by two officers of the Gestapo, on such and such a date at such and such a place. He respectfully requested to know whether there was any truth in the report, and if there was, what were the grounds for Mr. Emmanuel's arrest. No reply was received to that letter, nor to a similar letter that succeeded it, several days later. His Majesty's Consul-General therefore deemed it necessary to request a personal interview at Gestapo Headquarters in the Albrechtstrasse. He was received with the utmost courtesy by a high official of the Gestapo, who explained that his letters had not yet been dealt with owing to the negligence of a subordinate, who would be properly reproved. The matter would receive the earliest consideration.

A further week passed by, and it became clear that the Gestapo authorities did not intend, for so long as they could help it, to give the matter any consideration at all; or, to put it properly, to let the British authorities have any information with regard to it. In a state of considerable annoyance, His Majesty's Consul brought to His Majesty's Ambassador the dossier of the transaction. His state of mind was not helped out by the arrival on the scene, there in Berlin, of a certain Mr. John Cooper, a captain in the British merchant-service, whose truculence and impetuousness threatened to complicate matters seriously. Captain Cooper had brought his ship back to Southampton from Capetown some days earlier. That same evening he had learned from his wife of Mr. Emmanuel's disappearance in Berlin; they had both been friends of Mr. Emmanuel for a great many years, having all been neighbours at one time in Longton, in Doomington. He had left the very next day for Berlin. He had almost pulled the roof off the walls at the Consulate, and this bull-necked man was, from every point of view including his own, a dangerous man to have roaring round the streets of Berlin.

Some two or three days later, Captain Cooper was received at the Embassy by one of the principal secretaries. He was, for some reason, in a more subdued mood now. He seemed almost a little frightened, as if he now perceived the matter was even more serious than he had suspected, seeing that the British Consulate had failed so completely to get to the bottom of it. The secretary was charmed by Captain Cooper; but the extraordinary thing was that he was even more charmed by a personage who was not there at all, namely the unfortunate Mr. Emmanuel, who, though Captain Cooper was obviously not addicted to rhetoric, emerged from his account as a gallant and lovable gentleman.

His Excellency now took the matter in hand. At the Gestapo he was treated with an almost hypochondriac courtesy not in the common tradition of that institution. The authorites had not yet come upon any trace of the individual concerned, he was informed, but an especially vigorous inquiry had been ordered. His Excellency permitted less procrastination than his colleague in the less august service. After three days, during which his subordinates repeatedly telephoned, or paid repeated personal visits, to the Gestapo, all without avail, His Excellency brought the matter to the notice of the Wilhelmstrasse. He pointed out that his patience was taxed to breaking-point, and unless the matter of Mr. Emmanuel was satisfactorily cleared up within three days, he would be forced to make serious representations to the British Government. The authorities at the Wilhelmstrasse were desolated to learn that His Excellency had been put to so much trouble, and promised that if any facts were available regarding the *affaire* Emmanuel, these would be rendered within three days. A note from the Embassy was sent round by hand forthwith to the effect that the reply was unsatisfactory. Facts *must* be available. The qualification was untenable.

On the third day a very high official at the Wilhelmstrasse rang up His Excellency and stated that he was glad to be in a position to say that the man Emmanuel had at last been located. He was under arrest, in a place concerning which the high official had no information, with respect to an offence regarding which he could supply no details. He begged His Excellency to preserve patience for one more day. He promised that at twelve-thirty next day he would himself get in touch with His Excellency and provide him with a full statement of all facts.

His Excellency waited till twelve-thirty next day, and at twelve-thirty-five he lifted the telephone from the receiver in order to ask for a line to the Wilhelmstrasse.

At that moment one of his secretaries entered, the one who had been most active in the Emmanuel affair. He held in his hand an early edition of the *Beobachter am Abend.*

"Excuse me, sir, I think this is important," the man said.

His Excellency replaced the receiver, took the newspaper, and adjusted his horn-rimmed reading glasses.

"Thank you, Mallam."

A huge headline ran across the page—underlined by a thick red line like a puff of flame:

ACCOMPLICE IN GUSTLOFF MURDER
ARRESTED

A second headline proclaimed:

INTERNATIONAL ANGLO-RUSSIAN JEW SPY
UNMASKED

The facts contained in the story itself were few. A certain Isaac Emmanuel, a Jew from Doomington, in England, had been arrested for complicity with the international Yugoslav Jew spy, David Frankfurter, in the murder of the *Landesgruppenleiter* Wilhelm Gustloff, in Davos. The unveiling of this criminal was a signal proof of the existence of that widely ramifying net of international Jew murderers to which the Leader had drawn the world's attention in his funeral oration over the martyred body of Gustloff. It had been established that the Jew-murderer Emmanuel had landed in Berlin with the intention of carrying out his nefarious instructions, on the same day as the Jew-murderer Frankfurter had arrived in Davos. It was understood that in course of time this Emmanuel would be brought to trial in a place and at a time to be announced later. As in the case of the Dutch communist van der Lubbe, the Reichstag incendiary, and in accordance with the magnanimous practice of National-Socialist justice, the best defence lawyers in the country would be placed at the disposal of the said Emmanuel.

A rider was added in small type below the news-paragraph: *Citizens, beware of the international Jew-death that creeps among you.*

His Excellency removed his glasses and put them on the desk beside him. He brought the tips of his fingers together two or three times.

"I see," he said reflectively. "I see."

He said nothing more, nothing more at all, for several

minutes. The secretary wondered whether he had been forgotten.

"Any immediate instructions, sir?" he asked tentatively.

At that moment the telephone bell rang.

"Answer that, please."

"Yes, sir." He lifted the receiver to his ear, and listened. A voice spoke. At this end the secretary made no statement, as none seemed to be expected from him. He replaced the receiver.

"It is the Wilhelmstrasse," he stated.

"The Minister?"

"No, sir. It is one of the officials. He is asked to state that all known facts relevant to the Emmanuel matter are published in this afternoon's press. It is regretted that it was not found possible to let us have the facts before the press had them from the Propaganda Ministry. Apologies are tendered."

"Yes . . . yes . . . yes . . ." murmured His Excellency, at long intervals.

"Anything I can do, sir?"

"Ask them to give me the Foreign Office at once, will you? But I am afraid it will be no good, Mallam. I am afraid it will be no good."

IV

John Cooper was sitting in the lounge of his hotel after luncheon that day moodily sipping at his coffee, when an Englishman whose acquaintance he had made that same morning came up to him, holding a copy of the *Beobachter am Abend.*

"Queer business, this," said the Englishman. "Could I

cadge another of your Players from you? I've not tasted 'em for three months."

"Certainly," said John. He held out his cigarette case. "No, I'll smoke my pipe. What's a queer business?"

"This," said the Englishman. He opened up the front page of the newspaper. Then he looked round to make sure no one was within earshot. He had been in Berlin for three months. "About this poor old Jew fellow. What a ramp, eh?" He pointed to the huge headline underscored in bright scarlet.

"Read it," said John. "I can't read the lingo!" His heart was thumping like an engine.

The Englishman began to translate: Accomplice in Gustloff Murder Arrested. International Anglo-Russian Jew-Spy Unmasked. A certain Isaac Emmanuel, a Jew from Doomington, in England . . .

"By Christ!" roared John. He brought his fist down so violently to the table that the coffee-jug toppled over and rocked from side to side in the tray, spilling its contents onto the carpet.

The Englishman stopped reading and looked up. The broad-shouldered fellow's face was red as a raw steak. The eyes were like water chopped and vicious under a wild north-easter. The Englishman's mouth opened and shut again.

"By Christ!" the bull-necked one shouted again. "I'll . . . I'll . . . I'll . . ." He could, for the time being, bring out nothing else.

"Do you know this fellow?" the Englishman brought out at length.

"Do I *know* him?" shouted John. "Do I *know* him? I'll bloody well show them whether I——"

He stopped. The other fellow had got up from his side.

He was gliding across the lounge and into the corridor where the lift was, like a shadow; it was a movement swift and silent, like a fish's in a tank.

The porter was looking surprised and attentive across from his desk. The eyes of the page-boy at the door were round with speculation. The lounge waiter for some seconds stood quite rigid. Then the moment snapped. The porter resumed his study of the time-table. The page-boy sprang forward to open the door. The waiter on swift, flat feet reached the table, righted the coffee-jug, mopped the carpet with his napkin.

John rose and walked over to the porter.

"Have you got an evening paper?"

"Yes, sir. The *Beobachter am Abend?*"

He took it. Yes, it was the same paper as the fellow had been translating from.

"Tell me what all this means."

The porter translated, very dryly and dispassionately, like some sort of mechanical instrument.

"Anything else, sir?"

"No, that will do."

He strode over towards the door.

"Taxi, *Herr?*" asked the page-boy.

"Yes. Tell him the British Consulate!"

He went to the British Consulate, but already on his way there was fully sensible that the matter was something beyond their power to tackle, beyond the power, doubtless, of the British Embassy. It was a matter for London, for the British Government. Surely to hell . . . oh, the bloody fakers . . . surely to hell the British Government would not stand for this bleeding, screaming frame-up. Surely to hell . . . He stopped.

"This visit is going to be quite useless!" he said to himself aloud. "I'll go in, but it'll be quite useless! I must get back to Rose! Today! This very bloody day!"

He had an interview with one of the people at the Consulate. It was as he had expected. They saw no use in his staying on in Berlin. They had, in fact, seen no use in his coming to Berlin at all. He returned to his hotel, packed, sent a wire, and took the first train home.

V

John found Rose waiting for him in Liverpool Street. He kissed her, then held her away from him and took her face between his hands. "There are rings round your eyes. You were crying last night."

"Yes, darling. All night."

"You shouldn't have come, darling. I could have managed."

"No, darling. There's a lot to do. What can you tell me?" She gave the taxi-driver the name of the hotel they usually stayed at in London. John gave her his bleak report.

"It's dreadful, darling!" she cried. "Dreadful! Dreadful!" She was sobbing against his chest.

"Come now. Come now!" He jutted out his lower lip. He did his strong-man turn. But it lacked its usual conviction. "Pull yourself together!"

She took out her handkerchief and wiped her eyes.

"Of course I knew you'd come back alone. I was frightened for you, too."

"Rubbish! How did you get to know?" He answered the question himself. "The wireless, of course?"

"Yes, it was on the afternoon bulletin. But I heard earlier. The old Major happened to be in Southampton;

he saw an early edition of the evening paper; he didn't want me to have the shock of first learning about it on the wireless, so he phoned me up. He's been an absolute brick. He understands."

"Understands what?"

"How I feel about it . . . responsible, I mean. If it hadn't been for me . . ."

"Rose!" he said slowly. "None of that now!"

"All right!" she said wearily. "I won't!"

"Because if you once start, there's no stopping! I could say, if it hadn't been for me, the kid would never have gone to camp; he'd never have chucked himself into the sea; old Emmanuel would never have——"

"All right, John! All *right!*"

"Very well, then. I just wanted you to understand. What are we going to do? What does Townley think?"

"He got through to his friend Scuddamore at the Foreign Office—the one he calls 'Face-ache.' He's arranged for me to see him tomorrow. You'll come with me."

"Any good?"

She swallowed hard.

"You can't tell. The Major drove me over to Salisbury this morning. He's in such a state of fury we nearly crashed half a dozen times. His lips were quite white, John!" She turned to him suddenly. "John! Is it *very* bad?"

"Not good," he admitted surlily. "Not good! That reference to van der Lubbe . . . did you see?"

She shuddered. "Yes, I saw. It's in all the papers."

"Of course. The papers don't like it, do they?" His jaw set. "Those skunks over there! My God, there'll be hell to pay! If the whole country doesn't get up on its hind legs and make them disgorge, I'll . . . I'll . . ." It seemed for the moment as if he would go about breaking taxi windows.

She passed the tip of her finger along his thigh.

"Do you think it's likely?" she asked plaintively. "A little old Jew? Born in the Pale of Russia?"

"God damn it!" he shouted. "He's English now!"

"That's the point, isn't it?" she said quietly. "I mean that's their point!"

John sobered down. "You mean it's a try-on, eh?"

"There can't be any other reason for it. This is how old Townley works it out. They saw their chance, he says, when this thing happened—this thing in Davos. Here was an old Jew prowling about, born in Russia, too . . . that means he's a communist . . . and they pounced. If they can get away with this, they're sitting pretty."

"That's about the size of it," said John sombrely.

"Major Townley thinks it's as clear as day," Rose went on. "Next time it'll be an ordinary Englishman, any Englishman they don't like. The moment they can put their hands on him."

"They haven't got this one, yet," said John grimly. "Look here!" He turned to her brusquely. "There's another thing we have to think about."

"The boy? Yes, darling," she said quietly. "We *have* thought about it, Mary and I. Mary's become awfully fond of him, you know."

"I've no doubt." He dismissed the matter. He was always rather embarrassed by the expedients with which Mary sought to fulfil the morose vacuum of her existence. "Well?"

"I got on the phone this morning to Mr. Forsyte—that's the headmaster at Greystones."

"Yes?"

"He was very worried. The place was besieged with reporters, he said."

"God Almighty! Already?"

"It's *news,* John," she said mournfully, "it's *news!* As if it isn't bad enough for the kid already!"

"Think he'll try and make a fool of himself again?"

"No, John. You don't begin to understand that boy."

"What did the old fellow say?"

"He didn't know what to say. He wondered whether the boy ought to come to us for a few days, or whether he ought to try and stick it out over there, at Greystones."

"Has it occurred to him to put a man with a gun at the school gates?" John growled. "That would keep 'em away! Reporters—ugh!"

"Mary's gone over to Haslemere," Rose continued. "The Major's taken her. We're to ring her up tonight. She'll be at Shipscar."

"You think of everything, you women!" he grudgingly admitted. "Damn nice chap, Townley! Well, how are the children? All right?"

He took it for granted they were. They talked of other things for a minute or two, but by the time the taxi drew up at their hotel, once more the theme was Emmanuel, Bruno, Bruno, Emmanuel.

"Hello, is that you, Mary?"

"Yes, it's me. Is that you, Rose?"

"Yes. Everything at home all right?"

"Yes. How's John?"

"He's fine. Well, how was Bruno?"

"He looks months older since he left us. But he's fine. He's keeping a straight lip."

"Did you take him back with you?"

"No. Mr. Forsyte was quite ready to let him go, but Bruno said he'd rather not. He said he was sure Mr. Emmanuel would rather he carried on."

"Do you hear that, John?" Rose turned to her husband.

"Of course I didn't hear that!" John said crossly.

Rose turned to the telephone again.

"Hold on, Mary. I'm just telling John." She told him. "He says the kid's got guts, Mary."

"Yes, Rose, he has."

"Well, that's all then, Mary?"

"Yes, Rose!"

"Kiss the children for me! Good night, Mary!"

"Good night!"

"One moment. You're *sure* it'll be all right with Bruno?"

"Yes, Rose. I'm quite sure."

"All right, Mary. Good night."

"Good night."

There was a click of replaced receivers, in Ringwood first, and then in London.

Scuddamore at the Foreign Office was very guarded. He permitted himself to say that he considered there was going to be an unholy stink about this Emmanuel business all over the country. He understood the member for North-West Doomington was going to raise the question in Parliament. He would rather not say more about the matter at present. He was very charming. They left him, feeling sick at heart, and made their way to the station, where they had already deposited their bags.

VI

Within a few minutes of the appearance on the Berlin streets of the afternoon editions announcing Mr. Emmanuel's arrest, the news was being telephoned to the English newspaper offices. In London, in Liverpool, in Glasgow, it was just news, though it made a startling story on the front pages of the evening editions. But it was something more than news in Doomington, for it was a Doomington man that had been arrested.

"Speshul!" cried the newspaper boys. "Speshul! Doomington man arrested as spy in Germany! Speshul!"

But the clamour was more insistent in the Longton district. The vans had had instructions to drop extra big loads at the local newsagents'. The newsagents pounced from their doorways to seize every delivery-boy available. In Longton the announcement became more specialized.

"Speshul! Longton Jew arrested as spy in Germany!"

Along the central thoroughfare of the Blenheim Road ran the newspaper boys, darting into the streets of the flowering shrubs on their left and right hand. Into Acacia Street, Oleander Street, Laburnum Street, Mimosa Street, they ran, their straight hands stretched alongside their mouths as a sounding-board, the thin soles of their boots pattering on the stone slabs. They ran into those streets, but they walked out, for the newspapers had been torn from under their arms with a sudden grey flurry and squawk of snatching men and women, as of seagulls pouncing in a ship's wake.

One of these newspaper boys was a resident of Magnolia Street, where he lived on the Gentile pavement. Like the other newsboys, he had had half a second's time to glimpse the nature of the stop-press news which had sent them careering round the city selling a special edition. But to him the news had meant more than to those others.

Emmanuel, English Jew from Magnolia Street, Doomington, Alleged Spy, Arrested in Berlin. Complicity Claimed with Gustloff Murder.

It had meant more to him than to those others. Mr. Emmanuel? But that was the funny old man from number 13! The funny old geezer with the 'ead bobbing up and down like a balloon! The one who always 'ad a stock of bull's-eyes for the kids in his back pocket! Arrested? *'Im?* For being a spy? They were balmy on the crumpet, that's what they were!

But in the golden moments involved in the marketing of a special edition, no newspaper boy can afford himself the luxury of weighing the political imponderables of a situation. The boy hurled himself out of the newsagent's shop. He raced along the Blenheim Road like the wind. As he turned shouting into his native street, his proclamation was entirely specific.

"Speshul! Mr. Emmanuel arrested as spy in Germany! Speshul!"

He paused a moment, several yards from the corner. Well, where were the customers? Where were they? There were women going in and out of the public bar of the Lamb and Lion. There were women going in and out of Mrs. Poyser's grocery-shop. There were people walking up and down the pavement, on both sides of the street, Jewish and Christian. Well, where were the customers? What were they all doing gaping there, the gawmless gowks?

"Speshul!" the boy cried again, his voice shrill with vexation. "Mr. Emmanuel arrested as spy in Germany!"

But the potential swarm of customers still stood there, doing nothing, gaping. The boy looked round, bewildered, apprehensive. He spotted old Bill Huxtable, standing half turned on one of the steps leading up into the public bar of the Lamb and Lion. Old pals they were, him and Bill Huxtable. He ran forward and pressed a copy of the paper into Mr. Huxtable's hand.

"Mr. Emmanuel! Arrested!" he said again, as if he had not been saying it very loudly for several minutes. The man on the steps looked blank and hostile. He did not look one bit like his old pal, Bill Huxtable. "It's the old geezer!" explained the boy, on the verge of tears. " 'Im from number 13!" The golden seconds were slipping between his fingers like profitless grains of sand.

"Jigger off!" exclaimed Mr. Huxtable. "Doan't try any of thy bloody larks on me!" He turned and climbed into the public-house, and slammed the door sharply behind him.

The sound broke the trance that had fallen on Magnolia Street.

"Coom on, then!" said a voice at the boy's ear. "What the 'ell's all this about?" The boy found a penny in the palm of his hand. He felt the copy of the newspaper he held snatched from between his fingers. It seemed to him that within fifteen seconds the whole sheaf of papers under his arm had been torn from him. The customers were here right enough. Oh, yes, they were here now. They came streaming out of the public-house, the private houses, and over from the grocery-shop. Here was Mr. Clausen the hairdresser, with his crimped gilt hair, from the Pompeian Rooms. Here was Benny Edelman clumping up on his wooden leg. Here was old Steve Tawnie. Here now were certain old men with dim beards and rheumy eyes, old men from the synagogue at the corner of the street. Like leaves they came, rustling dryly along the gutters, sucked as by a wind into the vortex of the excitement.

"What is this?" their old lips went quivering. "What new thing is this, dreadful to hear?" But they did not speak aloud. The centuries had schooled them to the cautious asking of questions only at the right time and in private places.

But the newspapers were all gone by the time these greybeards had reached the corner of the Gentile pavement. They heard a name again and again. Emmanuel. Emmanuel. They had thought, down there at the threshold of the Lithuanian Brotherhood, they had thought that was the name they had heard the newspaper boy proclaiming. But that was clearly a mistake. What born Englishman can make out the words shouted out by newspaper boys? It was a mistake. What connexion could there be between their friend Emmanuel and a boy shouting at street corners and newspapers flapping in the air?

But all these people, gathered together in groups, separating, joining again, kept on repeating that same name. Emmanuel. Emmanuel.

"Please, please," the least timid of these old men asked, pulling at someone's sleeve. "What is this for a business with Mr. Emmanuel? It is not our Mr. Emmanuel, no? From the Board of Guardians?" He pointed towards number 13 with his beard.

"Well, auld cock!" said the gentleman addressed. "I knaw about as mooch as tha doos! Luke for thasel'!"

He pointed out the blurred lines of stop-press news, and seeing the old man was fumbling for a pair of spectacles, he read the news aloud. Emmanuel . . . alleged spy . . . arrested in Berlin.

"Bah goom!" he proclaimed. "They'll be arresting Lord Mayor next! I'll be jiggered if I can maake 'ead nor tail of it!" With that he turned, and strode off towards the steps of the public bar, wiping his lips with the back of his hand. "I feel thaat dry," he said to himself, "I could sup a 'ole ruddy gallon!"

"The bloody sauce!" he muttered. "Did you ever 'ear? I wonder what the 'ell they'll be oop to next!"

When the newspaper boy came round into Magnolia Street shouting his news, Mr. Poyser was standing behind the counter, serving, and Mrs. Poyser was up in the first floor back, which she kept as a store-room, digging out some lines of grocery which were going short downstairs. She heard the muted clamour of the boy shouting, but paid no especial attention to it. They made a special edition out of anything these days: Doomington Girl Chosen to be Cotton Queen; Heavy Fighting in Abyssinia. She collected the stuff she had come upstairs for, and then went down the narrow staircase into the room below. There she found her husband sitting white as a sheet in the chair up against the backyard window, and a knot of women gathered together, looking at each other without a word, not one of them paying the slightest attention to poor Mr. Poyser.

"What's the matter?" cried Mrs. Poyser. "What's the matter with Isrol?" She ran over to him and took his hands into hers, and called his name. "Isrol! Isrol!"

Mr. Poyser opened his eyes.

"Nothing!" he said faintly. "I'm all right! It's not me!"

His wife turned on the women. "What is the matter?

Did he faint? Couldn't you do nothing for him?"

The women remained silent; one uttered a deep groan, opened her mouth as if to say something, then relapsed into silence again. Mrs. Poyser stared from one to the other. What were they doing in here? They belonged on the other side of the counter. She turned towards her husband again, then her attention was taken by the clang of the bell. It was the bell which rang when someone pushed open the shop door. She strode over to the door that led into the shop. Through its glass panels she saw there was another group of women there, beyond the counter. They too stood dark, unmoving, as if suddenly stricken dumb.

One of the women behind her suddenly gave tongue.

"Mr. Emmanuel! He's in the newspapers! It is a special edition!"

For the first time she noticed there were several copies of the evening paper in the room. Two women each held a copy. There was a copy beside her husband's feet.

"Mr. Emmanuel? In the newspaper? What should he be in the newspaper for?"

There was a faint note of asperity in her voice. She thought Mr. Emmanuel had rather a tendency to get himself a little too prominently into the limelight.

"It is a lie!" exclaimed her husband suddenly. "It is a mistake! It is some other Emmanuel!"

"What? What? Are you all *meshuggeh?* What is he in the paper for?" She stooped and picked up the paper near Mr. Poyser's chair. *"Nu,* where is it? Where?" One of the women turned the paper round and showed her a couple of lines of blurred type in the stop-press column. "What does it say? For God's sake, what does it say? Where are my glasses?"

"It says," her husband explained quietly, "it says they have arrested Mr. Emmanuel in Germany for being a spy. It says he was mixed up also in a murder."

"What? Is it a joke somebody is making?" She lifted her hand to her heart. Her heart was none too good these days.

"Not a joke!" Mr. Poyser insisted. "Who would play such a joke? A mistake, I tell you. It will be made right in the next edition!"

"Oi!" one of the women sighed. "Oi!" the other women sighed, after her. "Oi! Oi! Oi!" they went in unison. "Oi! Oi! Oi!"

The door-bell clanged. Mrs. Poyser, for the first time in the thirty years or more she had run that shop, took no notice of it. Her head was turning like a top, round and round. She went over dizzily to the dresser and fumbled for her glasses. She fixed them on and read the lines of stop-press news:

> EMMANUEL, ENGLISH JEW FROM MAGNOLIA STREET, DOOMINGTON, ALLEGED SPY, ARRESTED IN BERLIN. COMPLICITY CLAIMED WITH GUSTLOFF MURDER.

"It says Magnolia Street," said Mrs. Poyser dully. "It says Emmanuel! Do they mean *our* Mr. Emmanuel? Are they mad?" Her voice rose. Colour rose in her cheeks. "What for a game is this? Arrested? In prison?" Her voice was getting shriller and shriller. "A spy? A murderer?" She turned and flung open the door and stood there for a moment or two, her fists clenched, looking far off somewhere, beyond the street, beyond the door, beyond the sea, to another town, another street, to a huge dark building there, with an iron-studded gate and barred windows.

"A spy? A murderer?" One half of the upper lip had drawn itself up, so that the teeth were showing. She looked in that moment as if her intention were, then and there, losing not a fraction of time, to project herself upon the leaders of the German State, and, like some cat of the woods, to tear the flesh from their cheekbones and the eyes out of their eye-sockets.

But she did no such thing. They were a long way off, and she was not a strong woman. The heart had been very troublesome lately. She slid to the floor in a faint, and it took the women quite a long time to bring her round.

The later editions of the paper left the matter in no sort of doubt. It was this same Magnolia Street, it was their own Mr. Emmanuel. Towards dusk the greybeards began to gather at the portals of the synagogue. Normally they went straight in and after some minutes there would be a *minyon,* a quorum of ten, gathered, so that the evening service might begin; and if there were not, the beadle would go out into the street and impress one or two old men passing by, or as many more as were needed.

Today, however, they hung about with a dim trouble on their faces, and some who went up into the synagogue came down again. But it was getting late now; the evening service should have begun; the beadle looked worried, and his old fingers fluttered like bedraggled moths in the air before him.

"It is fitting," said some old man, "that on this day of mourning, the Rabbi should be summoned from his house that he should say the evening prayer with us, here in the synagogue."

The other old men nodded their heads, and the beadle went off down the street, his greeny-black coat lifting about him as he moved. The door of number 5, where the Rabbi lived, was open. The beadle pushed it before him and entered. Five minutes later he was out again, the tall Rabbi following him, hanging over him enormously, his great white nose like a bird's beak, his beard like its raddled wing-feathers. From what far place of metaphysical speculation he had been summoned, not even those greybeards, learned though some of them were, were instructed enough to divine. It seemed some aerie, high in a cliff's perpendicular face, whither only such wings could aspire as are rarely fastened upon men's shoulders. Even now at dusk his face still streamed with the water of that windy sunshine into which it had been lifted all day long.

So the Rabbi went up into the synagogue and the greybeards went up after him, and the evening service was said first, as was proper. And when it was over, the greybeards came together—all but the Rabbi, who stayed on in his corner beside the Holy Ark—swaying and whispering, communing, as it were, with almost audible voices, like reeds by the edge of a lake. And one of the old men took up the Bible, and turned the pages, till he came at last to the Book of the Prophet Daniel, and read these words concerning the Prophet:

And when he came to the den, he cried with a lamentable voice unto Daniel; and the king spake and said to Daniel, O Daniel, servant of the living God, is thy God, whom thou servest continually, able to deliver thee from the lions?

Then said Daniel unto the king, O king, live for ever.

My God hath sent His angel, and hath shut the lions' mouths, that they have not hurt me; forasmuch as before Him innocency was found in me; and also before thee, O king, have I done no hurt.

Then was the king exceeding glad for him, and commanded that they should take Daniel up out of the den. So Daniel was taken up out of the den, and no manner of hurt was found upon him, because he believed in his God.

And that old man having concluded this passage, the others turned towards each other, muttering in their beards. There is nothing new. Be of good cheer, brothers. To us all things have happened before, even the den, even the den of the lions.

Yet doubt was in their minds, and grief in their hearts, for Daniel was long ago, and it was now, at this very moment, while they stood in the beloved place, free men, turning the pages of their Holy Book—it was at this very moment their friend was in a prison-cell, in worse plight than Daniel; for lions, when the Lord does not restrain them, do their work quickly.

So they took, all that were there, the Book of Psalms into their hands, saving only the Rabbi, for he had in his head all holy words that ever were written down. And there began then an intoning of Psalms that went on hour upon hour, all night long; as it may be that elsewhere in Europe, in small dark synagogues, there was an intoning of Psalms all night long, for old Emmanuel's sake. And the old men swayed to and fro, chanting, clapping their hands, in the belief that though the words of the Psalmist might not pass through the stone walls of their friend's incarceration, they would not fail to reach the ears of the most High and incline His mercy towards the captive, so grossly accused, so innocent. So they chanted, for their distress was grievous:

Deliver me from mine enemies, O my God: defend me from them that rise up against me.

Deliver me from the workers of iniquity, and save me from bloody men.

For, lo, they lie in wait for my soul; the mighty are gathered against me; not for my transgression, nor for my sin, O Lord.

And the words of comfort arose from the pages, as water-springs do, and the flowers in the edges of their hollows.

Great is the Lord, and greatly to be praised in the city of our God, in the mountains of His holiness.

Beautiful for salvation, the joy of the whole earth, is Mount Zion, on the sides of the north, the city of the great King.

Till at length the injunction came:

Walk about Zion, and go round about her: tell the towers thereof.

Mark ye well her bulwarks, consider her palaces; that ye may tell it to the generation following.

For this God is our God for ever and ever; He will be our guide even unto death.

So all night long the chanting continued, the swaying to and fro, the clapping of hands. Till at length the eastern window of the synagogue whither the old men turn, as looking over towards Jerusalem, became smeared over with the grey pallor of dawn. And the old Rabbi, not having spoken a word, at least in their hearing, all night long, got up from his place beside the Holy Ark and said to them: "For *our* sins, children, not for *his*, is this thing fallen upon our brother. Let us then utter the prayers that go before the *Selichoth*, the Propitiation."

And he took from its place on the reading-desk before him the velvet and gold-embroidered bag in which he kept his praying-shawl, and with this he went up into the pulpit. Then, taking out the praying-shawl, he placed it about his head so that it veiled his eyes, and gathered up a handful of its substance, and pressed it to his mouth, breathing a prayer in so doing. That concluded, he recited, the others following him, the especially sacred medley of prayers and Psalms called *Ashrei*, which is an overture to the prayers for atonement sung nightly for several nights preceding the High Festivals. Gradually the voices took on another timbre, till in the concluding prayer there was so strange a prolongation of syllables, so dizzy a spiralling of melody, it seemed almost another speech, spoken in an age long gone by.

The Lord is righteous in all His ways, and holy in all His works.

The Lord is nigh unto all them that call upon Him, to all that call upon Him in truth.

He will fulfil the desire of them that fear Him: He also will hear their cry, and will save them.

The Lord preserveth all them that love Him; but all the wicked will He destroy.

The Rabbi ceased, and stood there silent for some time, only his lips moving, his body bowed towards the reading-table before them. Then one of the greybeards there, who happened to be commemorating on that day the anniversary of the death of someone close to him, rose and intoned the *Kaddish*, the prayer for the dead. Then all prayer and chanting of Psalms was over for the time being. Dawn was poking like a grey old charwoman with her broom into the recesses of the synagogue. The greybeards rose and left, and went home to their beds. There would be time for two or three hours' sleep before the day's work began for them. Only the Rabbi did not leave. He stayed on in his place beside the Holy Ark, his lips moving, his body swaying slightly to and fro.

11

I

IT is no use, I can't see anything, Mr. Emmanuel reflected. And if I could see anything, what should I know about it? I should know it's Berlin, that's all. Sit back, Isaac. Make yourself comfortable. For why not? It is a mistake. They will soon find out it is a mistake, and they will send you back again to Frau Kahn. Poor Frau Kahn! Perhaps she will not have me again! Ah, well! I shall have to find some other pension, that's all.

He leaned back against the black upholstery of the car and tried to make himself more comfortable. But it was no use. He was aching all over. Is it a joke, he demanded, to wake up an old man at half-past five in the morning, an old man sixty years old? Sixty? Well, perhaps a little more than sixty.

The suburbs dwindled and disappeared. It was country. Between the two heads in front and on both sides of them you could see green fields. It is springtime beginning in the fields. Is it sheep with lambs over there? Or is it just barrels of something? A fine picnic for a springtime day!

I wish they would say something, these men. Do they think, perhaps, I have got something against them? For why? They are only doing their duty. Somebody has told them to go and fetch me. But for why has somebody told them to go and fetch me? For why? For why? For why? What are you shivering about, Isaac? Thank God for the rug my dear Rose gave me, and my thick winter coat. You remember—you bought it from old Hyman's last year, on Begley Hill Road! If he should see his coat now, old Hyman, that he sold me, he would have a fit!

I wish they would say something to each other, these men, one word! What are they thinking of? Are they thinking of me? Don't you believe it, Isaac! You are to them a sack of coal, you are a bundle of newspapers, luggage. Have they got wives? Have they got children? Are they wondering when they shall have breakfast-coffee? How long have we been travelling now? It is not long, really. How long? He took out his watch. Would you believe it? Forty minutes.

Hello, here is a village beginning! That must have been a cart on the right there. Did I not catch a sight of horses? There are people on the road up there, a woman, a man. What do people think when they see a great big black car like this coming in from Berlin? Perhaps they think it's a millionaire, he is going to shoot animals for a day on his country estate. There, that's it, Isaac! You are going to shoot animals on your country estate!

What is that big building over there, straight up the road? A prison, maybe? No, I think a castle. Yes, it is a castle, from the old-fashioned times, with that funny fat cannon in front of it. It is *my* castle! I am going to shoot animals here!

He was not entirely incorrect. That was, in fact, the building they were making for. The road swung away right-handed from the workhouse, or castle, or whatever it was. The car drew up with a sudden screech of brakes by a massive iron-studded gate. The driver got out and rang a bell. Half a minute later there was the sound of a key turning, then of another. A man in an old blue uniform opened a small door in the gate. The two men got out of the car.

"Get out!" exclaimed the taller man.

Mr. Emmanuel got out, stiff and stooping.

"Excuse me, please!" he said, and reached behind him for his attaché-case and rug. He turned, the case in one hand, the rug over the other arm.

"Drop that!" requested the stouter man, bringing the iron-like flat on his hand down on Mr. Emmanuel's arm. It was the arm with the rug over it. The rug slid to the ground. The stouter man tossed it lightly behind him into the car.

"Move on!" he exclaimed.

"Please, my rug!" Mr. Emmanuel protested. "It's from my friend——"

The stouter man landed his fist in the small of his back so forcibly that Mr. Emmanuel's legs almost gave under him and his hat almost fell from his head. The pince-nez on their black cord swung out wildly.

"Move on!"

The taller man had gone in. Mr. Emmanuel followed. The stouter man drew up the rear. The man in the old blue uniform clanged the small door and turned a key, a second key. The sound of the key turning set up a sudden jangling in Mr. Emmanuel's nerves, like the tip of the tongue poking a chip of something into a diseased tooth.

"What is the matter? What have I done? For what have you brought me here?"

Once again he felt that fist like an animal's hoof in the small of his back. His teeth rattled like dice shaken in a box.

It is better I should not talk to them, to ask any questions. I will see the high-up one here, soon, at once. I will tell him what a mistake it all is. An Englishman, I ask you, an Englishman!

They were in an arched gateway, paved with an old style of rounded cobbles. This, in turn, was shut off by a gate. Beyond the gate was a courtyard, flanked by a gloomy wall, set with rows of small windows. Men in black uniform passed in and out of doors.

The man in the old blue uniform opened the second gate. The taller man advanced and turned to the right, the stouter pushed Mr. Emmanuel after him. They entered a vestibule in the ground floor with several rooms leading from it.

"In there!" said the taller man.

They passed through one of the doors into a sort of reception-room. Two men in black uniforms were yawning and lounging over desks. They looked as if they had been up a good many hours. They straightened up momentarily to give the Hitler salute, then they slumped again. The two men in plain clothes went up and handed over a document, which was initialled and stuck into a clip. Then they all talked to each other for a minute or two. Mr. Emmanuel may or may not have been the subject of their conversation; no one looked in his direction, or paid any attention to him at all. Then the two men in plain clothes said *"Heil Hitler"* again and went off, as if they had just come into the place to leave a rubber stamp and had no more business there. Besides the two chairs at the desks, the room contained only one chair, within a foot or two of the door. A few moments after the departure of the two men in plain clothes, a man in black uniform entered, saluted, and took possession of the chair; he was evidently on guard. He straightened his tie, straightened his Sam Browne belt, played about with his revolver-case. He was evidently on good terms with himself.

Why do they not say a word to me? Mr. Emmanuel asked himself. Why have those others gone off like that and left me? A pity there is not another chair. I also would like to sit down. They are not busy. They are not doing anything. When are they going to take any notice of me?

He addressed himself to the men at the desks.

"Please, can you not tell me—?"

One of the men rose and roared at him, all the stuff of his throat flapping.

"*Maul halten!* Shut your face, Jew! Wait till you're spoken to!"

It is no use hoping for manners from people like that. They are only under-people. Look, they have brought out cigarettes. It is a damp air in this place. It makes you think you want to smoke without even thinking. Shall I ask can I also smoke? He felt in his pockets. Yes, he had a pack with him. Oh, where is my lovely amber cigarette holder that Bruno gave me, with the gold mouth-piece? I must have left it on my bedside table. I hope no one will touch it. Such a boy, he should not have spent all that money on it. The three men were eyeing him narrowly. No, perhaps it is better I should not ask can I smoke. Perhaps they will not let me. Besides, a cigarette will not stay still in my mouth. Also it is the Sabbath. Have you forgotten that? Wait, Isaac, wait. They have gone for the high-up one. I will ask him for an explanation. When I know what they have brought me here for, it will be different. I will say: Do not forget, please. I am an Englishman. I want to see my consul. I have a right. Also a lawyer. You should never open your mouth if there is no lawyer there. I will show them. They cannot make such a fool like this of me.

He looks very comfortable, that one sitting down in the chair by the door. I would like also to sit down. My legs are not so strong like they have been. It would do no harm someone should ask an old man to sit down. He shifted the weight of his body from one foot to the other.

The man by the door fumbled about pleasantly with his revolver-case. The minutes went by, ten, twenty; a half-hour had gone by; it was more than half an hour. Mr. Emmanuel leaned up against the wall. Anyhow, they did not try to prevent that. He would have liked to get down on the floor; his feet were as tired as anything. But he did not fancy it. It would be like truckling to these people, like getting down on his knees to them. He was not going to do that to such low-lives. S.S. men. Yes, of course, that was what they were, with those black peaked caps and black coats and black breeches; very smart, too. The place was livening up with them; they kept on coming in and going out. Those two were getting quite busy at their desks. No one took any more notice of him than if he were a crumpled ball of paper. Yes, very well-cut. Old Hyman, if he could make suits with a cut like that, they'd be coming to him from all over Doomington. It was a bit frightening, wasn't it? That cap-badge, a skull with crossbones.

Do you know—it is an hour and a half since I have been standing here. What are you talking about? It is two hours and a half. Would you believe it? You can get so tired, you don't even know how tired you are. He rings a bell there, the man at the desk. Again a man comes. Again he goes. It has nothing to do with me. When will they have pity on me? Pity, what for should I ask for pity? Not from anybody! Again he rings a bell, again a man comes. This time the man goes into the room behind there. Yes, I thought I heard someone go into that room. Perhaps yes, perhaps no. I am hearing boots, I am hearing bells, all sorts of noises and swindlings in my head. It is in the small of my back mostly, my tiredness. He comes out again. He is walking straight over to me. To me, yes. To me. Thank God. Yes, please, I am coming. I will be able to tell them the mistake. They will make an apology. . . .

Mr. Emmanuel followed in the direction indicated by the switched thumb, through the door between the two desks, into the room behind. An S.S. officer sat behind a desk, facing a portrait of Herr Hitler. He was completely bald and had several sabre-cuts across his cheeks, yet somehow he looked very elegant. He did not raise his eyes from the paper he was scrutinizing. The other men stood by in attendance.

"Up!" the first S.S. man shouted, giving Mr. Emmanuel a shove that nearly sent him to the ground again; he was, it is true, all over the place. The officer did not lift his eye, not for five, not for ten minutes. The two other men remained motionless. Then at length the officer reversed the paper before him. It was, in fact, a newspaper. He continued reading for another few minutes, then lifted it delicately and put it on one side. He brought another document forward and examined it for some moments. Then at length he lifted his eyes. They came to rest on one of the S.S. men. They were cold green eyes, rather protuberant. There seemed no human emotion in them at all; none the less they succeeded in asking some sort of question: Is this the individual involved in this memorandum?—something of that sort.

"Zu Befehl, Herr Standartenführer!" assented the S.S. man.

The officer moved into place a chart, it might have been, studied it for a moment or two, then announced crisply:

"Third floor! Number 23!"

"Zu Befehl, Herr Standartenführer!" the S.S. man exclaimed again. Then he clicked his heels and gave the salute. The officer, having decided he had not got from the newspaper all it had to give him, unfolded it again neatly.

"'Raus!" one of the men exclaimed. The other went to the door. Mr. Emmanuel stood there trembling, his mouth trying vainly to shape words. The man yanked him towards the door by his coat-collar.

"No!" cried Mr. Emmanuel, finding tongue at last. "No! Leave me alone!" He drew from somewhere within him a jet of strength and pulled his collar from the man's grip. He ran for several yards back towards the officer at his desk. The movement was so comic, with the skirts of his coat flying one way, and his head bobbing up and about and his hat under his arm, and his beard like a half-built bird's nest, that everybody there burst out laughing—a sudden peal, sharp and ominous, like a storm at the edge of the sky. Everybody but the officer. The green convex eyes hardly swivelled in their sockets.

"I am an Englishman!" cried Mr. Emmanuel. "You

have made a mistake. I only came to Berlin, a little boy, he did not hear from his mother——"

The officer raised his hand and pointed towards the door with all five fingers. They were curiously white fingers, with a sort of mother-of-pearl glow on the skin; they seemed to have no bones in them. Mr. Emmanuel heard feet scuffling up behind him. A pair of hands seized his left arm and swivelled him round. Another pair of hands seized his right arm. The fingers bit so deeply through the overcoat into the scraggy muscles, he cried out with pain.

"This way, pig-Jew!" one of the men shouted.

He was frog-marched out of the room, down several corridors, out into a second and grimmer courtyard overlooked by row on row of small iron-barred windows. With the fingers still biting into his arms, he was pushed up a stone stairway and flung at length into a room facing the first landing.

"Clothes off!" the older man shouted.

Mr. Emmanuel took his overcoat off.

"Clothes off!" the man repeated. The overcoat was not enough.

Mr. Emmanuel looked up incredulously, but the eyes he looked into were not friendly. He stared round the room. There was nothing in it but a single bench.

"In here? It is so cold! Please, you can see for yourself——"

There was no argument with eyes like those. He removed his coat and trousers; not his waistcoat, with its sad passport, its little hoard of money. Why do they look on like this? he asked himself. Isn't it enough they bring me here for nothing? Must they make me ashamed also? A moment later the waistcoat was gone, too. The younger man had caught the back lining and ripped it off with a swift tearing of cloth and explosion of buttons. He turned it inside out.

"Ah!" he exclaimed with satisfaction. They were men of few words and simple vocabularies. He dived his hand into the inside pocket and removed its contents.

"No!" Mr. Emmanuel cried, with an almost animal yelp of fright. "You cannot take that! It is mine! It is English!"

The older man pushed his hand against his face so that he fell backward on the floor, landing hard on his thin haunches.

"Quiet!" he roared. He stood towering over him with his huge fist clenched. Mr. Emmanuel said nothing. A minute examination of the clothing followed. Everything was removed, except a few trifles, a copper coin or two, a handkerchief. The wallet was gone, the wallet full of England, Magnolia Street, Ringwood, Haslemere.

"On again!" the men bade.

Mr. Emmanuel put his clothes on.

"Come!" The men led the way.

Treading hard, uncertainly, like someone walking under water, Mr. Emmanuel followed. At a right-angle round into a corridor. Another corridor. Men in black uniform, lounging, smoking; older men in blue uniform, prison warders, doing chores. Up a flight of stairs. Another flight of stairs. An old man coming towards him. Himself, it was himself. He was looking into a mirror.

It was not himself. It was another old man, long-shanked, with a beard all awry, his eyes as dull as cobwebs, two warders coming up behind him. Coming whence? Going whither? The old man disappeared. There were doors further along, massive doors, with covered spy-holes at eye-level. There were people behind those doors, or behind some of them. Somebody moaned, long and soft and low. Somebody laughed; very amused that person was. On the right hand the wall was bleak as death, except for the thin slats of windows high up towards the ceiling, through which the paltry light came. A warder advanced, jingled a bunch of keys, chose one, and opened a door.

"Get in!" he said.

Mr. Emmanuel stood hovering on the threshold. His knees were stiff as the gnarled joints of roots. He did not know how to unstiffen them, but the flat of the warder's hand unstiffened them for him. He found himself toppling headlong through. The door was banged to behind him, the key turned in the lock once, then a second time. A bolt went squeaking along its groove.

He remained for some time on all fours, in the posture of a Moslem saying his prayers. When he lifted his head again, he could not see, partly because it was so dark in there, partly because his eyes were dimmed with tears. He shook his head hard, and the tears fell like warm thunder-drops on his cheeks. Slowly and painfully he rose to his feet, his arms winnowing in the air about him. A few paces from his right leg was a wooden truckle-bed, with a dirty straw palliasse bunched up on it and a couple of coarse blankets. In the left-hand corner was a table with a dented enamel pitcher and basin, and a pail below. There was a chair by the bed-head. The heating came from a single pipe running close to the ground along the wall facing the door. A small window high up in the same wall gave the room what light it had.

Pick your hat up and sit down, Isaac Emmanuel, he

commanded. It is no good standing up being puzzled and excited. You're tired. Sit down. Sit down. It's no good telling me to sit down. I want to go away from here. I don't belong to here. Don't be a fool, Isaac. Pick your hat up and sit down. *Sit down,* I tell you! That's better. That's sensible. Think it out now. What has happened? They didn't like the way you went poking about, asking questions. They thought you were a spy, eh? Yes, that's it. They thought you were a spy. That porter in Bruno's house, in the Motzstrasse . . . is he at the bottom of it? A bad life, an enemy of Israel, a black year should take him! A spy! Me! Isaac Emmanuel, late Secretary to the Doomington Jewish Board of Guardians!

Bruno's house! Poor little Bruno! Of course he mustn't ever get to hear of this! Why should he? I'll be out today or tomorrow, when they find out their mistake. He'll never get to know.

Now don't be a baby, I tell you. Don't hide anything from yourself. What have they brought you here for? Because you were asking questions? Yes and no. Who were you asking questions about? Bruno's mother. What has happened to Bruno's mother? Nobody knows yet—only those people. But Bruno also had a father. You know what happened to Bruno's father? He ran away. He tried to come back again, and they shot him. It is all written down, everything's written down in this country. It's written down in books, in card-indexes, even on walls. Do you see? A lot of writing there, all over the walls. From a lot of people, different handwriting all over. Look! Ever so high up! How did that one get there? He must have been a very high man. Everything written down, waiting, waiting. Then I come to this country asking questions, and they take out the card, there is a black mark there. What?

A foreigner, a Jew, he is asking questions about a family with a black mark? Get hold of him! Take him away! We'll show him, asking questions!

You see, Isaac, you see? But why should you worry? Is it a crime to ask questions? Do I hide it why I ask questions? I am an Englishman. Nothing can happen to me. If only they let me talk to my consul, or see a lawyer, talk to consul, see a lawyer, talk to consul, see a lawyer, talk to consul, see a lawyer . . .

He was walking up and down the cell, between the wall and the door; talk to consul, see a lawyer, talk to consul, see a lawyer . . .

It is not much room in here, he told himself ruefully, for a high man with long legs like me to go walking up and down. My case, oi, my beautiful little case! Where is it? It has my slippers in it! I should like to change into my slippers! Take it easy, Isaac. There is time. They will bring you your things later. Lie down on the bed, why not, is anyone stopping you? It costs the same money. He turned to the bed and tried to make it comfortable. He shook the palliasse and spread out the blankets. There was no pillow. What, no pillow? You expect they should give you sheets, as well, and maybe a hot-water bottle? Thank God, it is not cold in here. He took his greatcoat off and folded it up for a pillow. He lay down and stretched out his legs. He sighed deeply. A fine place they've taken me to, eh? What sort of a place is it? It looks very old-fashioned. Like an old castle, or an old barracks for soldiers. I think that is perhaps right. A barracks for soldiers, and this is the prison for the barracks. It is very quiet. I do not like it it should be so quiet. What's that? Someone banging at his door, downstairs, perhaps one or two stories below. Bang! Bang! Bang! What does he want?

Why don't they come to him and answer him? Oh, there they are, they've come at last! Oi, what language, what terrible language! He did not understand it all, but the little he understood was bad enough. *"Shut your bloody jaw, you bloody communist swine, or we'll rub you up a bit more! Understand?"* The banging at the door stopped abruptly. The mournful silence prevailed again.

I should complain because it is quiet? Perhaps I'll be able to get a bit of sleep, even. It is like lead, my eyelids. A cup of coffee would be nice. And something to eat as well. Perhaps they will be coming round soon with something. Well, if they come, I will hear them. Maybe they will waken me. It is not bad in here, after all, under these blankets. They will find out their mistake soon, perhaps already this very morning, see a consul, see a consul . . .

He drifted off into sleep. He had no idea how many hours later it was when he woke up again, or if it was hours at all. It did not seem lighter or darker in the cell there than it had been.

It is a funny taste in the back of my mouth. Did they come round with something while I was sleeping? Perhaps they didn't wake me up because they could see how tired I was. I would like something to eat now anyhow, something to drink. I am so stiff all over. They should not knock about an old man like that, they should have respect.

They do worse things than that to old men, Isaac Emmanuel. His stomach made a half-turn within his thin carcass. You mustn't start getting funny ideas in your head now. At the beginning, yes, maybe there was a lot of funny goings-on. And now as well, maybe; for communists and freemasons, and people like that. But they are Germans. They would not touch a foreigner, when he is innocent like the new-mown lamb. Not an Englishman, anyhow. What? Is it a joke, an Englishman?

They would not dare to lay one single little finger upon you, Isaac Emmanuel. They would not dare. It would be such a row in the Foreign Office in Whitehall. . . . Oh, you have other things to think about. You must be sensible, Isaac.

A drink. I am thirsty. What time is it? He slipped his fingers into his buttonless waistcoat. No watch. They have taken my watch as well. But that is robbery. How can they take from a man his watch? Perhaps they do not want me to know how the time passes? Well, what good does that do them? Is it after dinner-time? They must bring you food round in this place. They can't want to starve you. Never mind eating, I am thirsty. What shall I do? It will save my life a cup of coffee. Shall I go and bang on that door like that man was banging? Will they hear me? I have not got strong fists like that one.

He got up and went over to the door, beat at it a few times, waited a minute or two, then beat again. He went on like that for some five or ten minutes. What? What is that? Down the corridor he heard the sound of feet advancing.

"Please!" he called out. "Please!" The feet stopped.

"Hi! Is anybody there?"

"Jawohl!" a voice croaked back. *"Da bin ich! Schon lange Zeit!* I am here. A long time already!"

"Who are you?"

The voice did not answer again. The feet that had stopped did not resume their movement.

"Please!" Mr. Emmanuel cried. He banged at the door again. His weak fist made little alarm on that stout timber. "I am thirsty! Can I have something? Perhaps some coffee?"

There was no sound, except a sigh that seemed to come from nowhere at all, or somewhere down below, or somewhere above his head.

He turned back into the room. Well, it is not time yet. In places like this it runs with a system. I must wait till the next meal-time; please God I shall not be asleep. His eye caught sight of the blue pitcher bulging against the wall. Is there water in that? There was. It is a bit old and warm. Well, in the Sahara Desert they would think it champagne. He drank deeply and sat down on the chair again. Then he got up. It is not comfortable, this low chair. Better on the bed. He lay down on the bed again, and waited. An hour passed by. Or it may have been an hour; he had no means of measuring. Another hour passed by. Another hour. It was not merely the darkness of the cell all round him now, it was the darkness of evening. There is not going to be anything now any more, no food, no drink. The thought took possession of him, like the wind in a bleak place. They must have come round with food when I was sleeping. What a pity! Could you believe it, they should not trouble to waken me up?

What? There is a key turning in a door downstairs! And another, not so far down! There are feet coming round into this corridor! I can smell something! It is something to eat, it may be soup! I can smell it, I tell you! There, they are opening a door down there! The old man says something, someone answers! A little nearer now! That is the cell where the laughing man lives. Do you hear? He is laughing again now! I shall laugh also when my soup comes to me. What sort of soup is it? Bean soup, meat soup? Maybe you would like some soup from skylarks, in prison? That is the cell of the other one, the sad one. *Is anybody there? I am here! A long time already.* Now in one minute, the hot soup, with little lumps of meat maybe, and with cabbage. . . .

What? He stops there! What are you stopping for? I am hungry and thirsty! My soup, please! All day I have not had anything! He is walking again! Not *to* me! Away *from* me! He jumped off the bed and put his mouth to the blind spy-hole.

"You, there! Another one is here! You have forgotten me!" The feet stop. The feet move on again. They have moved round the corridor onto the landing. They move away somewhere out of earshot.

Mr. Emmanuel banged at the door again, and again, and again. The laughing man further down laughed like a tittering bride.

"Nichts zu machen!" the sad voice declared hollowly. "It is no use! No one will come to you!"

"You, there!" cried Mr. Emmanuel. "What do they want of me? I should not eat? I should not drink? I should die, then?"

There was no reply. The sad voice had withdrawn into its tomb again.

"You, there!" Mr. Emmanuel cried more loudly. "Please! Please! Will you not answer! What do they want of me?"

Feet came marching up the corridor. They did not stop this time till they reached Mr. Emmanuel's cell.

"Hold your trap, pig-Jew, or you'll get what's coming to you!" Then the feet marched off again.

I think I know. Suddenly he had come to understand. They want to weaken me down. They want to weaken me down. He removed his shoes and chafed his feet. How swollen they are! I should have taken my shoes off before now. They want to weaken me down, when they ask me questions, I should give silly answers. They will see. He took one of the blankets off the bed and put it under his feet, for the stone floor struck cold. Then he stood up and, having placed his hat on his head, addressed himself to his evening prayers. Which way it is east, I do not know. God will perhaps forgive me. Forward and backward he shook, forward and backward, now and again striking his bosom. So they shook at that moment, so they struck their bosoms, in many a small synaogue in Europe. So over in the Lithuanian Brotherhood, in Doomington, so they were at that moment saying their prayers. His prayers said, he lifted the rug from the floor and spread it on the bed. Then in his turn he spread his own lanky body down. Soon he was asleep. There was a smile on his face, as if it had been a quite pleasant day.

Morning came. It was morning in so much as it was less dark in the cell than it had been. He allowed sleep to fall from him as a boy buried in sand by his companions allows the sand to fall. He was awake now. There was a certain briskness along the corridors, if anything could be called brisk in that doleful and timeless place. There was again an unlocking of doors, a clinking of cans, a scraping of plates. There was again a smell of food in his nostrils, so sharp that it almost made him sneeze. The can and plates, if that was what they were, again stopped some distance down the corridor. They did not advance as far as Mr. Emmanuel's cell.

I know now, he murmured to himself, that phantom smile once more upon his face. I know now there will be nothing for me till have they asked me questions. Well, let them ask. If I had anything to hide, maybe I should be frightened. But what have I to hide?

The long, the interminable, morning began, continued, and did not end. If I had a pencil, I should also write on those walls, like those others. If I had a match, I would burn it and write with a match. It is funny, people in prison cells always write on walls. Never mind writing, I am hungry. I would like to eat. What are you saying, hungry? You are so hungry now you do not want to eat any more. Your stomach could not hold it. Well, thank God, there is still some water in that blue jug. He got up from his bed, and almost fell back again, he was so weak. He advanced feebly to the table and was about to lift the jug to his lips, when he stopped suddenly. What a *goy* you are, Isaac Emmanuel! You have not said your *Shachris* yet, the morning prayers!

He said the *Shachris,* standing the whole time, though he did not know how it was he did not fall for weakness, unless, in fact, it was God's own hand that held him up. He broke his fast then with a draught of that stale water and lay down on his bed. The morning at length became midday. There was again a turning of keys in cell doors, a clinking of cans, a scraping of plates. He knew now they would not come to him. The cell doors were locked again. Again there was silence, except for a sudden shout somewhere lower down, and a titter from down this corridor. Apparently there were not very many people in this place. Only very special people, maybe.

I am very dizzy. Oh, yes, I am dizzy. Should I lie about it? It is a bad smell in here, too. Is that my fault? I am so weak, sometimes I think my heart is not beating any more. I am weak, yes. But not in the way you want. Oh, no! I am not weak like that!

He heard feet turn round from the landing into the corridor. Not one pair of feet only; another, and another. The feet did not pause at any intervening cell door.

For *me?* he asked. For *me?* It is not possible. I am not wanted. I am at the edge of the whole world, where nobody comes. The feet paused at his cell door. There was silence for a moment or two, then the jingling of key against key. A key hit blindly upon the substance of the door, then scraped towards the key-hole.

Like a shrill sound piercing the ear-drum, a wild excitement pierced his heart. The door was opening again, the world was opening again. They could not keep him in that cell, like a criminal, any more. They dare not. They were going to take him to a question-place and ask him questions. Well, let them ask questions. Did they hope he would give foolish answers? They would see. It was they who believed foolish things, so foolish you could crack your ribs laughing at them. He would look them straight in the eyes, he would talk firmly to them, as man to man. Look here, do you really believe—?

The key turned in the lock, once and a second time; the bolt squeaked back along its groove. The door opened. In the doorway stood a warder, behind him two S.S. men, very trim and dapper, the light concentrated on their black leggings and the black, shiny peaks of their hats.

"*'Raus!*" ordered the warder.

"I am ready, gentlemen!" It was as much as Mr. Emmanuel could do to raise himself from the bed. He felt very feeble.

"*Keine Frechheiten!*" the warder growled. "No cheek now!"

Mr. Emmanuel resented that. How had he been cheeky?

"Can I take my coat, please?"

One of the S.S. men made a negative gesture.

"Out!" the warder said again. Mr. Emmanuel went out. The warder thrust him to one side, and led the way. The S.S. men drew up the rear. Down one flight of stairs, down another, along a corridor, down another flight of stairs. They were on ground-level now. At this point the warder went off. It seemed as if the prison staff had nothing to do with the running of this part of the building. In the passage ahead a number of S.S. men lounged about, as if they might be detailed for duty at any moment. The two S.S. men led the way and halted in front of a door. There they waited for some minutes. The lounging S.S. men stared a brief moment under their eyelids at the unkempt old man, his head bobbing about so absurdly, then they turned indifferently away. They had seen his kind before. The door at last opened from within.

"Get in!" one of the men gestured with his thumb.

He entered. The two others came after. Someone closed the door. Along one side of the room ran a long, low form, where some four or five S.S. men sat. Against the opposite side was a dais with a desk on it. Against the wall facing the door stood a low, thick-legged table, bone-clean, as if it had been recently scrubbed. Nothing happened for some five or ten minutes. That did not perturb Mr. Emmanuel. He was becoming well accustomed to these pockets of dead time. He was not asked to sit down, of course. He did not mind that, either. His feet were not so swollen as they had been. He only hoped he would be able to last out. It would be childish to fall in a faint before all these men. It would be a great joke to them. Everything seemed very small and far, like things seen through the wrong end of a telescope—the dais with the desk on it, the table, the black, outstretched leggings of the waiting men. Suddenly the leggings thrust backward upon themselves, boot-toes touched the ground, the bodies were rigid from the knees, arms raised.

"Heil Hitler! Heil Hitler! Heil Hitler!"

He turned. A man in civilian clothes had entered the room. He was mounting the dais. He had seated himself at the desk. An S.S. man who had come in after him bearing a portfolio respectfully laid it down before him and extracted the papers in it. He was a small man, dark, rather monkey-like, but evidently a personage of great importance to be treated with such deference, even though he wore no uniform. He took his spectacles out of a case, breathed on them with great deliberation, and wiped them. Then he blew his nose, long and exhaustively. Then he regarded his papers for a minute or so. The men had remained standing. He made a gesture; they sat down again. He continued his study of the papers, chewing them, as it were, his mouth munching as his eyes went up and down the lines behind the glinting glasses.

The monkey-like face suddenly plunged upward; a voice, like the forked tongue of a lizard, shot from between the yellow teeth.

"Your name?"

"Please, I would like to say——"

A fist hurled itself into Mr. Emmanuel's back. The lips of the small man rolled back, revealing the yellow teeth to the gums.

"Your name?"

"Isaac Emmanuel!"

"Place of birth?"

"Sveksen."

"Where's that?"

"It's in Russia, on the Dnieper!"

The small head nodded vigorously. A really damaging admission had been elicited, at the first sally.

"Date of birth?"

"Well, on my English certificate it says——"

"Date of birth?" The repeated words were like the hissing of a lathe.

"May 1871."

"Jew?"

"Yes, I'm a Jew. But I'm also an Englishman—" began Mr. Emmanuel, heatedly. The blow in the small of the back was repeated. The man on the dais smiled.

"To us you're just a Jew!" he said softly.

There was silence for several seconds. Then suddenly the head thrust forward, craning on its neck like a hen on its roost. The eyes glittered.

"Why have you been arrested?" he screamed. *"Why?"*

Mr. Emmanuel reeled as if someone had caught him a blow on the chin. He tried to speak, but the sounds his throat produced were like the babblings of a deaf-mute.

"Why have you been arrested?" the man screamed again. He brought his fist down on the table. But it was a small fist. It made no noise.

"I—I—it is just that question—" Mr. Emmanuel brought out at length. "I want to know . . . ever since they wakened me . . . I have asked a consul should . . ." It was hopeless. There was no coherence either in thought or in speech. *"Please, for God's sake—"* he begged.

"All right!" the monkey-faced man said sharply. He got up from his chair. A moment later Mr. Emmanuel was out of the room, and on the other side of the door. They were shoving him back again, corridor and staircase, corridor and staircase, back into his own cell. The key turned twice, the bolt went home. Mr. Emmanuel was alone again with all those ghosts, the man who had scratched the verse of a hymn on the wall, the man who had made dirty drawings, the high man who had got up near the window somehow, God knows how.

He sat down on his bed, and stayed there a long time, for he was very feeble and the excursion had broken him up a good deal. Only one thought was in his head, as only one foot is in a sock. What have you been arrested for? What have you been arrested for? Are they perhaps stark, staring mad? he asked himself. No, no, he decided. They are very clever, very clever indeed. Please God, I should also be clever. And why clever? Let me hold fast by the truth, God, I ask only that, God, please.

They gave him a meal that evening, a hunk of bread and a bowl of soup, which tasted chiefly of soda—the soda which they put into the food of prisoners to repress their animal desires. He slept without trouble of erotic phantasms, though he had retained little either of the soup or of the soda in it. Next night was more disturbed. Once, far off, for about half an hour he heard a shrill, sharp howling as of someone being hideously ill-treated. Then the howling was closer somewhere; it might have been from within a cell in the same building. It had almost no human quality at all.

The second examination took place the day after that. It was cursory, and very pointless; or so it seemed to Mr.

Emmanuel. But he may have been incorrect in that. The ritual may quite well have been following an exact and venerable rule.

"You again?"

Mr. Emmanuel hung his head.

"Stand straight!"

The attendants saw to it he stood straight.

"How much currency have you smuggled abroad?"

"I swear, sir, none!"

"None, eh?" The lips drew back, the upper and lower teeth told each other what a good joke it was.

"And that German girl you debauched last week! Where did you take her?"

It seemed to Mr. Emmanuel as if he must retch then and there.

"Oh, how *can* you, sir? How *can* you? An old man like me!"

"You're the dirtiest of them all, you old men!" The little man was enjoying himself. He rubbed his hands together delightedly. "And the dirtiest of all old men are Jewish old men! Take him away! He makes me puke!"

It was not until the next examination, namely the third, that they really got down to business. This again was two days later. He had been allowed just enough food and drink to keep the life inside his body. But he felt even more demoralized by dirt than lack of food and drink. There had been no soap in the cell, practically no water in the ewer. He felt sticky and unclean.

"Emmanuel, eh?"

"Yes."

"You still deny the charge of smuggling?"

"But——"

"And of rape?"

"But of course! How——"

"When did you last meet Norbert Rosenheim?"

The question was like a pellet sharp and round between the temples.

"Who?" The name for a moment or two did not register anything at all in Mr. Emmanuel's mind.

"You know!" The lips tightened. "When did you last meet Norbert Rosenheim?"

"I tell you, sir, I–" Then awareness was switched on in him like an electric light. The blood came rushing up into his cheeks. "Oh! You mean Bruno's father! But I have never met him in my life! I swear to you! I only met the boy——"

"You never arranged to meet him in Schaffhausen?" The examiner's stumpy index-finger prodded the air.

"Schaffhausen?" Mr. Emmanuel repeated, in a tone of bewilderment. "Schaffhausen? Where is that, please?"

"Very pretty!" said the other admiringly. "Oh, very well done indeed!"

"But, please. That place you said. I do not even know what country——"

The examiner changed his tack abruptly. The amused irony had quite gone out of his face.

"What did you come to this country for? Who wanted you? Who asked you?" The voice was full of fury.

"Only the little boy, the son of the man you said, Rosenheim. You see, he has not heard from his mother since last March, and I met him in the house of an old friend of mine——"

"Whom've you been in touch with since you got here?"

"I have only been trying to find out about Bruno's mother, where she is, if I can——"

Again the examiner pounced on his sentence as a cat waiting by a mouse-hole pounces on the issuing mouse.

"So you admit you have engaged in espionage activities? You admit you have been approaching innocent citizens and trying to compromise them? You admit you visited the town of Lübbenau in the Spreewald to see what you could find out there? You admit all that or you do not?"

"I have been trying to find out if anybody could tell me where——"

The examiner brought his fist down violently on the table.

"You admit all that or you do not?"

(He is trying to trick me. I should admit lies and foolishness. He will not frighten me. He can hit me with sticks and stones, but I will not say yes to lies.)

"I do not admit what you say."

"Very well." The small man seemed almost mollified. He cast his eyes down on his papers. He studied them for a little time, then he raised his eyes again. He regarded Mr. Emmanuel almost amiably for a moment or two. Then suddenly the face set again. It was as if a sudden gust of wind had struck athwart the eyes. They were odious now, and furious. He jerked up from his chair, like a thing on springs. He thrust his arm forward and pointed his finger, not as with an accusation, but as with a ratification, of guilt.

"When were you last in touch with David Frankfurter?" The voice rose to a scream.

Again Mr. Emmanuel's face was blank with bewilderment.

"Who is that you say? Who?"

"None of your damned lies, you filthy Jew! *When were you last in touch with David Frankfurter?*"

(It must be that this place has made my head fluffy like cotton-wool. Who is he talking about, who?)

"Who are you saying? I do not know who you are talking about."

The examiner dropped back into his chair again. His eyes fixed Mr. Emmanuel's very intently.

"So you do not know who David Frankfurter is, eh? You do not know who David Frankfurter is?" His eyes remained unblinking, like a serpent's.

Mr. Emmanuel felt the fluff of the cotton-wool seeping like a fog into the remotest recesses of his brain. Like in Doomington, the way the fog is in the Blenheim Road, and the trams can't move, and they keep on clanging and clanging like fire-engines, and the fog is in the house, and it is in the scullery, and you would think it is the steam of washing-day, but it is not; it is fog, and the trams are clanging and clanging, and then you cannot even hear the trams, the fog is like cotton-wool, it is like big bolsters with all their feathers coming out. . . .

He dithered uncertainly for some moments, his whole body jigging, not merely that thistledown head on its neck. Then he was on the floor, crushed and crumpled, like a piece of paper thrown away among a press of people, and trodden on.

The small man took his spectacles off, and put them away in a case, while a clerk collected his papers for him and stowed them into a portfolio. The salute was given, the small man came down from the dais and walked delicately towards the door, avoiding the prostrate old man like a lump of carrion. He had his handkerchief to his nose, as if the thing smelled.

II

He was lying on his bed when he came to his senses again; and when that happened, he discovered to his astonishment that the whole of his jaw was distended in a monstrous grin.

I am laughing, he informed himself with astonishment. What for should I be laughing? Am I maybe in Blackpool, and it is Wakes week? And looking up into the ceiling of his cell, the thing he was laughing at took on its lineaments, the thing so preposterous that if the sky suddenly rained peanuts it would be less silly, or if the ranked trams in a tramway-depot lifted their voices and sang.

So I know David Frankfurter, eh? When did I get into touch with David Frankfurter? Let me see now. Where from was that young man? What did the paper say? Czechoslovakia? Yugoslavia? I have been to the North Pole, also, perhaps. Also to Honolulu. Is it possible someone should ask such a question? Is it possible? Such wickedness, it is like a lump of lead, lying hard in my stomach.

Do you know what that question means, Isaac Emmanuel? Do you know what they are trying to join together? Of course, you do. It is better you should not put words to it. How can there be people like this in God's kind world? Oh, yes, I know also Norbert Rosenheim. Well, at least I know Norbert Rosenheim's son. But that poor Frankfurter, the mad one, the silly one. . . . Where did I arrange to meet Rosenheim? How did he say it? Schaffhausen. Yes, that is how he said it. Or was it there I arranged to meet Frankfurter? I cannot think. My brain is swindling.

It is a mistake, of course. It cannot be on purpose, it

cannot be. It is a terrible, terrible mistake. Someone has made a mistake, and he is now frightened to admit it, so now they are asking mad questions, I should answer mad answers. If they would only give me a chance for one minute, and let *me* ask a few questions! If they would only let me get in somebody, a lawyer, a consul, a lawyer, a consul . . . His mind switched itself with difficulty from the compulsion of the hypnotic syllables. But they will not allow it, that is clear now. That man will be shown up the mistake he has made. I must not lose hold of myself. Whatever is waiting for me, I must trust in God. If I trust Him, He will take me out at the end of it.

I know what those men are waiting for in that room. I know what that table is there for. He remembered certain verses out of the Psalms, as Jews always do in the time of trouble, these as often as any. He muttered them over to himself swiftly, once, and then once again:

> Deliver me from mine enemies, O my God: defend me from them that rise up against me.
> Deliver me from the workers of iniquity, and save me from bloody men.
> For, lo, they lie in wait for my soul; the mighty are gathered against me; not for my transgression, nor for my sin, O Lord . . . nor for my sin, O Lord . . . nor for my sin, O Lord.

He was treated fairly tolerably the next two or three days, if such food could be considered tolerable, if it could be considered tolerable to remain immured in a cell a few feet square for twenty-four hours out of twenty-four. But he received his meals regularly, he had his ewer replenished, he was allowed to tidy up his cell a bit. It was as if the authorities wanted to let him see that things could be made easier for him, if only he would do the right thing by them, that is to say, if only he would admit the allegations made against him.

On the third afternoon, he was taken out once more to be examined. The same monkey-like gentleman was in charge. The proceedings started off fairly placidly. Mr. Emmanuel was asked whether he still persisted in denying the fact that he had ever met Norbert Rosenheim. When he stated that that was so, the small man did not jump up and scream at him. He merely recorded the answer. Did he still insist he had never been to Schaffhausen? Yes, he still insisted. He refused to give any information about his dealings with David Frankfurter? But, please, in God's name, he had none to give. Not even the invocation of the God of Israel affected the tranquillity of the proceedings. The examiner closed his eyes. For a minute or two it almost seemed he was asleep.

I do not like this quietness, a voice whispered in Mr. Emmanuel's heart. It is frightening. I am not so frightened when he is standing up and shouting at me and pointing his finger at me. What is he thinking about under that sloping-back forehead? How funny that hair is, standing up stiff and short! Where have I seen hair like that? Wire . . . on a brush . . . Slatta used to have a wire brush like that, in the scullery sink to scour out the frying-pans. . . .

The questioner opened his eyes. They were very sombre and ominous. A cold chill seemed to have fallen upon the room. When he spoke, it hardly seemed the voice of the same man.

"I warn you. You must weigh your answers carefully. You will pay heavily for every lie you tell. Our dossier regarding your political activities is being rapidly completed. Our agents are this moment concluding their researches in your own headquarters." (*Headquarters?* What did he mean, headquarters? The Board of Guardians in Doomington? The Refugee Children's Committee in London? What was he talking about?) "We expect to receive our final documentations within a few days. You must be in no doubt of what I am saying to you. Do you understand?"

"Yes, I understand." (Such a year upon him if I understand. Talking and talking . . . like a record on a phonograph.)

The man's eyes were black and beady behind the shining spectacles. The voice bit and jumped like a drill.

"Is it true that you have for many years frequented a band of communists in your town? Is it true, or is it not true, that you are one of their principal leaders?"

"I tell you it is foolish, you should ask such a question." Mr. Emmanuel's voice quivered and cracked. "I am not a political man. I know nothing from politics. A communist? I was Secretary of the Jewish Board of Guardians. What for should I have anything to do with communists? No, please, it is nonsense!"

The questioner let him speak out his protest to the end. Then he waited a moment or two. It seemed part of his method, to wait a little while before, from another angle, darting to the attack with some new name or fact.

"You declare you have no acquaintance with Samuel Silver, the communist leader? In the face of this letter"—he lifted a sheet of notepaper and waved it before him—"you persist in denying you are an accomplice of Samuel Silver, the communist leader?"

Mr. Emmanuel was very angry. His cheeks were fiery red.

"What are you talking about, communist leader? Did you ever hear such a thing? My old friend and neighbour, he lives across the entry from the back of my house——"

"So you do *not* deny your acquaintance with this Silver? You do *not?*"

"Of course I do not!"

"He wrote this letter to you?" He sent the letter over by one of the men. Mr. Emmanuel did not look at it.

"Yes, he wrote letters to me. What for should he not? My old friend——"

"And you wrote to him in your turn?" He held up another letter and once more sent it down with one of his men. Mr. Emmanuel brushed it aside.

"Please, sir," he appealed. "What are you trying to prove? Of course we write letters, me to him, him to me. He is my friend. He was once a rich man, but now, like myself, he is a poor man, he is a nobody, in a little house with his wife——"

The man on the dais rose to his feet. He opened his mouth. His words were like hammer-strokes, hard and sharp.

"What are you lying for? Have you never heard the name Polednik, Commissar Polednik? You don't know he married the daughter of this same Silver? You don't know they are both among the principal leaders of the Communist Party in Russia?"

Mr. Emmanuel's eyes were staring from their sockets. His hands were making frantic movements in the air about him, like a bird beating against the bars of its cage.

"What are you talking about?" he shouted. "Is it Sam Silver's fault what his daughter Susan does? Is Susan his only daughter? Is it Sam's fault if his daughter Elsie—?"

But it seemed that the mention of Sam Silver's daughter Elsie was displeasing in these circles. The man who had been standing nearest Mr. Emmanuel during the inquiry suddenly smote Mr. Emmanuel's open mouth with his fist. Mr. Emmanuel, whom a strong wind could have blown over, fell, his mouth streaming with blood. Two or three teeth rattled to the ground as he fell.

"*Abreiben!*" commanded the examiner. "Rub him up!"

The table against the wall was brought further down the room. Mr. Emmanuel was lifted and his limbs pinioned. Then the men got to work. There had been a number of lengths of lead piping under the benches they sat on. Mr. Emmanuel was not a very satisfactory subject, for he fainted almost at once, and twice again during the proceedings. But on each occasion a jug of cold water revived him, and they got to work again. The examiner looked on, interested, but a little impersonal, as one might look on at the clipping of someone else's dog. At last he raised a finger. The flogging was suspended. Mr. Emmanuel was carted back to his cell.

III

For a long time before Mr. Emmanuel remembered who he was, where he was, and what had happened to him; he was aware of the pain bound tightly round him like the wrappings of a mummy. As the wrappings relaxed a little, he became conscious of those other matters. He became conscious, too, that a light was burning high up in the ceiling. It was very friendly of them, he thought, to switch on a light so that he might see his pain with his own eyes. There was even a bowl of mush on the floor beside his bed, and half a loaf. He saw them because his head happened to be lying on the right cheek, not the left; otherwise he would not have seen them, for he found it better not to move even a finger. The pain was dreadful if he lay quite still; if he moved the fraction of an inch it was intolerable.

But I can at least say my evening prayers, he told himself. They cannot stop that. It does not maybe show respect to God to say them lying like this on my stomach, but He will forgive me, I think. He recited the evening prayers in a low voice, prolonging them as much as possible. He made quite a business out of them, for, quite apart from God or anything, they brought the time nearer when the pain would be less frightful. He heard steps coming along the corridor when he was half-way through, but that seemed no reason why he should suspend his prayers. Nothing, however, was wanted from him or said to him. A warder came to switch the light out.

He could not sleep, however, with the pain gushing in gouts, like blood from a severed artery. He found himself chanting a Psalm, not a Psalm that he had thought out because it was relevant to his condition, but just the first Psalm that came to his lips. How very strange! he told himself, as the verses proceeded; it is as if there was Germany in the time of David too, and they had cast David also into prison, innocent as a white flake of snow.

In Thee, O Lord, do I put my trust; let me never be put to confusion.

Deliver me in Thy righteousness, and cause me to escape; incline Thine ear unto me, and save me.

Be Thou my strong habitation, whereunto I may continually resort: Thou hast given commandment to save me; for Thou art my rock and my fortress.

How very strange! he said again. Like I myself might have written it on these walls, if I had a pencil, and if I could get up and write. He remembered another Psalm and another. There was not one verse, one word, which might not have been distilled from the anguish of his own heart and body, from the exultation which possessed him in the knowledge that the Lord held him in His keeping. At first he did no more than mutter the Psalm under his breath. As the night went on, and his pain somewhat receded, he lifted his voice and chanted them, as he had often done among his cronies in the synagogue, both in Doomington and many years ago in the Dnieper village where he was born. He realized with a thrill of pride that he knew the Psalms by heart, almost all of them. He was very surprised; he had not realized it before. In course of time he even turned over on his other side, the Psalm had made the pain so much less, or so much easier to bear. He heard a warder come up and tell him to shut his filthy squalling. But he disregarded him. All they could do was to take him off to give him another flogging. If it was no worse than the last one, he could ease his hurt with Psalms. If it was worse, he would die . . . and that would not be so bad, either.

There was one element in the situation from which he drew some comfort. It was very probable that no one in Germany, except these people, knew where he was. It was therefore certain that no one anywhere else in the world knew anything about him, where he was, what was happening to him. They did not know in Doomington, in Ringwood, in Haslemere. Above all, thank God, Bruno did not know. The others were grown-up, they had people to look after them. But Bruno . . . please, Lord God, keep him from knowing.

How *could* Bruno know? Yes, my postcards are not coming to him any more; nor to Rose, either. Perhaps they are beginning to get a little anxious already. Well? Perhaps soon Bruno will be writing to Rose: have you heard from Mr. Emmanuel, please? She is clever, that Rose. She will say perhaps Mr. Emmanuel is ill; perhaps it is better for a week or two Mr. Emmanuel should not write postcards all the time. And after that? Well, after that, we shall see. God is with me, here in my cell; like when they call me up to stand before the Ark on the High Festivals, and the curtains are drawn, and the doors open, and the Scrolls are leaning back in their skirts of gold and velvet. He is no further than that.

If God is with me, what other help do I need? You remember what foolishness you had in your head once? That woman, you said, if it is necessary, I shall ask help from that woman. You know better now, maybe. It was when you mentioned her name, it was then they started on you, and knocked your teeth out, and there are not too many in your head already. You see? That is the help you can expect from Elsie Silver.

I will say of the Lord, He is my refuge and my fortress: my God, in Him will I trust. Elsie me no Elsies— I ask you a favour.

Next day was a red letter day. The liquid they gave him for breakfast was piping hot; it had a positive taste of coffee, too. Afterwards, they took him to the prison doctor, who eased his torn flesh a good deal. Then they let him totter up and down the corridor for a few minutes.

It was a good day. That night he chanted nothing like so many Psalms, he was asleep so soon. The day after, they took him off again to be questioned. His friend, the small monkey-faced man, looked him over for some time, and was satisfied, it seemed, with the result of his scrutiny. He addressed him in a brisk, almost a friendly, tone, whole sentences at a time. He was sure Mr. Emmanuel, having had time to think things over, was not going to make any more difficulties. All Mr. Emmanuel was expected to do was to give straight answers to straight questions. If by any chance Mr. Emmanuel still remained obstinate . . . but that was a contingency there was no need to discuss. The small man lightly stroked the tip of his nose.

Mr. Emmanuel stood in the centre of the room, his fingertips pressed close against each other. He looked up to the small man on the dais, curiously, almost dispassionately. Did that man also have a mother, he asked himself, or are there perhaps human beings who can happen without mothers?

"Will you talk, then, or will you not talk?" the voice from the dais was saying.

Mr. Emmanuel blinked, and shook his head. He gave up trying to remember whether it was in a science book, or a fairy-tale book, he had read of a sort of big lizard, it is born without a mother out of the stones by a riverbank. . . .

"What do you want from me?" he asked quietly.

But there was something in the gentleness of the tone that outraged the small man more than any insolence. His face was suddenly cloven with anger, as with an axe, left to right.

"I'll show you what I want from you, you lump of Jew-muck! Get hold of him, you two!"

Two men got hold of him by the forearms and twisted them behind his back. Rosenheim, Schaffhausen, Silver, Frankfurter; the questions jetted out like squirts of poison. But Mr. Emmanuel said no word to this man to whom he had no word to say. During each interval of silence, the two men twisted his arms more and more insufferably. The sweat ran down his cheeks in thick streams.

An interval of silence followed, during which the twisting slightly relaxed—an interval long enough to give Mr. Emmanuel time to think better of it, if by now he was so disposed. He was not. Green globes and daggers of red fire juggled against his eyelids.

"Rub him up!" exclaimed the small man.

The effort to break down Mr. Emmanuel's resistance went on for some time. He did not know how long, for he and time had no connexion with each other; there were no days or nights to it, no hours or weeks. He was taken to another cell all on its own somewhere, where, if they saw his eyes closing, they made a great clatter outside the door to keep sleep from entering; and if, at last, the iron-heavy eyelids drooped, they diverted upon him a ghastly beam of light to prise them apart again. They starved and beat him. They lodged him in that ingenious cage where a man can neither lie down, nor sit down, nor stand up. But they could not break him down.

They could not induce him during this timeless time of agony not to sing songs. If they slapped his mouth till the blood came, the songs still flowed with the flowing blood.

It was hardly a singing of songs; it was for the most part a low, barely audible chanting, still audible enough to infuriate his torturers; until at last, being convinced that so long as he was alive at all he would continue to chant in that God-damned lingo, which they correctly took to be Hebrew, they let him be. His mind could not now compass whole Psalms at a time. It picked up a verse here, a verse there, as a child picks up haphazard beads from a plate. But sometimes it was in some other language than the Psalmist's he was singing. Now it was English, the songs of the Edwardian music halls, for capriciously his mind rejected all the war-time and post-war stuff. *I've got diamonds in Amsterdam, Amsterdam, Amsterdam.* Or earlier still: *Good-bye, my bluebell, farewell to you. One fond last look into your eyes of blue.* And then one day, to their astonishment and annoyance, the dithering pig-Jew launched out into German:

Die geliebte Pimpanulla
Schreit einmal Hula, Hula!
Und flugs ist sie im Walde
Und hakt den Schnabel ein.
Hula, Hula, Hula!
Sie hakt den Schnabel ein!

He and young Bruno were walking together down the green rides of the New Forest, under the spread canopies of the beech-leaves. Bruno had his mouth-organ at his lips. Isaac Emmanuel supplied words to the tune, keeping time with his pince-nez. A jay chattered suddenly out of the high branches. A butterfly tossed over and over drunkenly in a honey-gold clearing.

But they were not to know that, and it would have made no difference if they had. What? A foreign pig-Jew venturing to sing in the Sacred Tongue? They slapped his mouth right and left, right and left, till the boy no longer went swinging under the beech trees and the butterfly lay with a broken back in the cart-ruts.

It was during this period of torment, elaborately contrived to break down his virtue, that his virtue was at its most lambent; that is, during the intervals, when he had command of himself for a time. When it had slipped from him, he was a feverish child, or an old man only just alive, hardly within a moral category.

In the lucid interspaces, he had a consciousness of God such as he had never had an inkling of before. He was certain that the limits within reason of his own resistance and fortitude had long been overpassed; he felt he was strong not only with his own strength, but with the strength of his race accumulated over many times and lands; and with more than that—with the strength of God, without which all else is as a straw in the wind.

In those intervals, too, his intelligence burned more brightly than hitherto. He had begun to recover from that series of shocks, which, but for God's grace, he told himself, must surely have unhinged his mind: the visitation in the Pension Kahn, the bang at the door, the light switched on, the two men standing there; the impounding of his darling passport; the monkey-faced man on the dais, the lounging men on the form, the fabulous questions launched at him, Rosenheim, Silver, Frankfurter—above all, Frankfurter, the Frankfurter question, with its lunatic innuendo. At length he was beginning to recover from these shocks; and though here, in his isolated cell, they knew how to shock his body with new and incredible outrages, they could not possibly so astonish his soul again.

His intelligence burned more brightly than hitherto, though he remained convinced that all that had happened to him was a mistake; in that respect he remained the fool, or the saint, in the sense in which they are the same thing. But he was intelligent enough to see through the compassionate lawyer who visited his cell one day, a mild-voiced and soft-eyed man. I have heard of your case from a nephew of mine, the man said, who works in the office here. With infinite difficulty I have prevailed on the Governor to let me come in and talk things over with you. The authorities are getting a little frightened, you know. After all, you are an Englishman, there might be trouble. But you see their difficulty, too, don't you? It is impossible for them to confess themselves entirely in the wrong. These people have their *amour-propre* to consider. Why not confess to one or two of the minor charges, why not? They will have something to try you for. They might sentence you to a month or two's detention, doubtless taking into consideration the time you have spent here. Then it will be all over. Don't you think that that would be a sensible way out for you all? Please, I beg you, do not make up your mind now. I will come in again, and see how you feel about it tomorrow, or the day after. Good day, my dear sir; believe me, I feel for you from the bottom of my heart. Please. Not one word. Good day. Good day.

The compassionate lawyer did not return for four days. That is to make me say to myself: Oh, why did I not say yes at once? Perhaps he will not come again; perhaps I have lost my chance. Ah, well, they are not so clever like they think. I will sign my name to no lies. I am in God's hand.

The compassionate lawyer came at length. I am so

grieved that I have not been able to come as early as I had hoped. And have you thought the matter over, my dear sir? I would be so happy to be of some use, if you would permit me. You are a kind gentleman. I will sign my name to no lies. You refuse, then? I refuse. Think again before you answer. You refuse? Absolutely. Go and choke yourself, you stinking Jew!

He did not need the compassionate lawyer. Now at length he began to see that it was impossible for his friends not to come to his aid, if God chose. He had written to two people daily from Berlin, to others almost daily. The time had come, or rather, the time had already gone by, when the expected postcard had not arrived, in Ringwood, in Haslemere. He worked out with astonishing correctness for how long his friends would remain unperturbed, how soon they would become anxious. It would be funny, he thought, if Rose would write to Bruno and Bruno would write to Rose, on the very same day, to ask if the other had heard from Mr. Emmanuel. At last they would set to work—in Doomington, he hardly doubted; in Ringwood, he did not doubt at all.

There would be representations made in higher quarters, in the highest quarters. He was not merely old Mr. Emmanuel, a not very learned, not very substantial, retired clerk from Magnolia Street in Doomington. He was English, of a land where to be English is all, to be of this race, this creed, is neither here nor there. There would be, he would not doubt it, a question asked in Parliament. He was conscious of a throb of pride and pleasure at the thought. Isaac Emmanuel! Would you believe it? A question asked about him in Parliament! What would they say about it, he wondered, when they read about it in Magnolia Street? A pity his wife would not be there, too. In one way a pity. In another way it was not so sad.

It was queer how certain he was that Rose was working for him, working night and day like a black man. For Bruno, too, as well as for him. Poor little Bruno! It is sad how life sometimes works round the same way a second time, when once is already bad enough. Like with Bruno and the letters—the letters that come regularly, then stop, then do not come at all. Once before it had happened to him and now a second time. Do not worry, young Bruno. Some day, please God, it will not be only letters, Bruno, that will come across the sea to you. It will be an old man, your friend, and he will have with him the news you have been waiting for.

What? What's that? Don't be foolish, Isaac Emmanuel! I tell you I heard the voice of Captain Cooper! He was outside that other door at the end of the long passage which leads from the other building! He was pulling and shaking at the door, and shouting: "Mr. Emmanuel! Mr. Emmanuel! Don't give up hope! We're coming! We're on our way!" I heard him plain as plain!

Pick yourself together, Isaac Emmanuel! Such foolishness! Say a few passages from Psalms, it will be better for you! What shall we say, then? Yes, yes!

O Lord, how great are Thy works! and Thy thoughts are very deep.

A brutish man knoweth not; neither doth a fool understand this.

When the wicked spring as the grass, and when all the workers of iniquity do flourish, it is they that shall be destroyed for ever.

But Thou, Lord, art most high for evermore.

IV

The situation began to be further complicated by the fact that Mr. Emmanuel had somehow got it into his head that they were from time to time dropping some sort of powder into his food. Sometimes he would eat; sometimes, after a mouthful, he would spit out his food at once. He had developed an altogether too fastidious palate, here in Schloss Kastanienburg. He would sometimes be seen pinching his flesh, what there was left of it, to make sure that there was still some sensation there.

It was decided that, on the whole, the effort to break down Mr. Emmanuel's resistance had failed. It would take very little more to kill him, but there seemed no way to get him to forswear himself. He was therefore restored to his former cell for a couple of weeks, during which time he was kept under the doctor's observation, and was given quite edible food, none of which aroused those ludicrous suspicions. Then one morning he was taken to the room where they had kept him hanging about for so many hours on the morning of his arrival, and there given back his attaché-case with the things in it intact. His wallet was not restored to him, neither were his passport and money, which had been extracted from his secret waistcoat pocket that first morning. He was then conducted to the Black Maria, the *grüne Minna* they called it, waiting outside the gates. The conveyance was not so luxurious as the one that had brought him to Schloss Kastanienburg, but there had then been no ghost of a smile on his face, as there was now. He saw the sun in those brief moments, he saw a glint of grass between houses, he saw children trundling a hoop a long way down the road, he saw small clouds high in the sky. But it was not only because of those things he smiled.

V

After his experience at Schloss Kastanienburg, the Moabit Prison seemed like a holiday. There were nights when he found himself screaming, and all his nightmare was that he was still at Kastanienburg. Here at Moabit he was away from the immediate control of the Gestapo and their special S.S. guards. He was in the hands of the regular prison authorities. There were certain rules and regulations which were more or less faithfully observed. The food was eatable. He could supplement it from the prison canteen, for he had been given some of his money back. He had a sink and flush-system toilet in his own cell. He could apply, if he wanted them, for certain books, by such writers as the Leader himself and the philosopher Rosenberg.

Above all, there was companionship. Though he himself was lodged the whole time in a one-man cell, perhaps because he was adjudged a more dangerous prisoner than his fellows, many of the cells contained two, three, even four prisoners. In Schloss Kastanienburg, he had hardly ever set eyes on the face of a fellow-inmate. He had no notion how many there had been, or for what crimes they had been incarcerated. They had been to him nothing but a company of invisible presences, sighing like gusts of wind in a chimney, tittering like churchyard ghosts. Here he saw them face to face, he smiled at them, grieved for them, and they sometimes in their turn smiled back at him and grieved for him. Once a day he even talked to them, if the more amiable warders were on duty, when the prisoners were allowed to take an hour's exercise tramping round and round the corridors.

The grand times were, of course, when they were shepherded into the open courtyard and were allowed to walk round under the blue sky, the flying clouds. For it was now the full tide of springtime. Out there, in the open, you could almost smell the woods and waters of the Tiergarten on the other side of the Spree; you could almost smell the little warm loaves on the counters of the pastry-cooks'. Round and round the prisoners went, in two rows, an outer and an inner, so that quite a good deal of secret winking and nudging and conveying of messages went on. The suggestion of military dispositions gave a certain pleasure to the Governor at that time, as well as, for another reason, to the prisoners. To those who would some day be released it could do no harm. It could do no harm, either, to the prisoners about to die.

Mr. Emmanuel had not been in Moabit more than a day when he became aware that he was a celebrity. He was more than that, he ascertained, the blushes deepening on his cheeks. He was a world-figure. He was front-page news in the great newspapers. There had been times when the idea of fame had been agreeable to him, partly for its own sake, but chiefly for the sake of the causes he espoused from time to time, for a famous man can promote causes with more chance of success than an obscure one. But fame as he had conceived it in his most ambitious moments went no further than this—that in his own town people should point him out in far-off districts, and say: "Look! Do you know who that is? That is Mr. Emmanuel!"; or when he went to address meetings so far afield as Leeds or Liverpool, the hotel-porter should recognize his name, and say: "Yes, Mr. Emmanuel, the Secretary is waiting for you in the Tudor Room."

But such fame as was his now, he had not courted. The prisoners were aware of it, the warders, the high officials. He felt naked, and blinked in the excessive light as a bat or an owl might, exposed in a cage in a market-place at noon-day. This was the man whom the State accused of being an accomplice of the Yugoslav Jew David Frankfurter, in the assassination of the Nazi leader Wilhelm Gustloff. This was the man whom the State declared it had unmasked in the preparation of an international Jew plot aimed at the destruction of a whole group of national leaders, of whom Gustloff was only the first and the least important victim. This was the man who had been the subject of several sharp questions in the House of Commons, and of several representations on the part of Whitehall to the Wilhelmstrasse, each more vigorous than the one before. He was the man concerning whom the State Prosecution was assembling its complex and cumbrous machinery, though no man could say, or would say, when the levers would be depressed and the wheels start revolving. It was, indeed, a heavy load of fame for such bowed and skinny shoulders to support.

To the greater number of his fellow-townsmen in that dark town of Moabit, both prisoners and officials, the accusation was a monstrous joke, on a par with the other not less monstrous joke by which responsibility for the burning down of the portentous mass of the Reichstag was laid to the charge of the little Dutch half-wit van der Lubbe. And if it had seemed fairly funny while Isaac Emmanuel was merely a name in the newspapers, a counter pushed to and fro by the State authorities and between

Whitehall and the Wilhelmstrasse, it became side-splitting lunacy when Mr. Emmanuel emerged from whatever darkness had entombed him, into the comparative open day of Moabit. A man so gentle, so delicate as this, with such eyes, with a head that bobbed up and down so comically—no, it was not such a man who was the weaver of complex plots, the accomplice of assassins.

There were, however, some there at Moabit who were quite disposed to believe in his guilt. These included the professional criminals, a large proportion of the warders, whom experience had often taught that faces are nothing to go by. They included also a small element of Nazi wrongdoers, who had been conditioned to believe that any Jew was capable of anything and, whether guilty or innocent, was better dead than alive. But whether they believed him innocent or guilty, there were few there, or none, who believed that, having gone so far, the State would not go the whole way, for the very reason that had made it set out at all. They remembered van der Lubbe. They were convinced that for the head of Isaac Emmanuel, too, the hallowed block was waiting, and the headsman's axe.

Only one person was not of that opinion—for a time, at least—and that was Isaac Emmanuel himself. He believed that his transference from Schloss Kastanienburg to Moabit was as near to an admission of his innocence as the authorities dared go; or not so much the authorities as that Sinister Person to whose catastrophic blunder he attributed all these miseries. The Person had thought it unwise merely to open the prison doors and let him go, as one lets a snared animal out of a trap. He, however, was not an animal. He was a man, an Englishman, with a tongue in his head and a passport in his pocket. Or there would be, when they had released him. He could make things very hot for them all. So he had been transferred to Moabit, to keep up the fiction of guilt for a little time longer. Then, when things had died down after a couple of weeks, they would let him fade unobtrusively out of the picture. Mr. Emmanuel smiled darkly. His fading would not be so unobtrusive as they hoped.

Well, here he was, in a cell which was positively a Lyons's State Café for comfort in comparison with the evil hole which had housed him in Kastanienburg. He had not only easy access to the doctor; he had even requested an interview with the *Herr Gefängnisintendant,* the Governor, and the Governor had granted it. It was true the Governor could say nothing regarding the probable date of his release, or—to be more technically correct—the probable date of his trial. But he was quite civil, and Mr. Emmanuel had heard that, with the majority of prisoners, civil was the last thing you could say about him. He had probably had orders from higher up to show a certain amount of respect. There was some point, after all, in being an Englishman. If Mr. Emmanuel had been able to stick out that scarecrow chest of his, he would have done so. Instead, he stroked with some satisfaction his wistful wisp of a beard.

What? They are going to make a trial with me? he asked himself. How can the high-up lawyers of a big country like this make such absolute fools of themselves? A hot chestnut, that's what I am. How pleased they'll be the moment they can let me drop from their fingers! With an Englishman you can't play about, even if he's a nobody like me. You see, I was right. They started working for me in England, and look where it led to. Questions in Parliament, notes between Governments, would you believe such a thing? An old man like me buried away in Magnolia Street. He bent down to fondle his little leather attaché-case, which they had restored to him on his entry into Moabit. It was the next best thing to having his passport to read and play with. He opened the chromium clasps, pulled out the expanding hinges, then shut the case again. It was English, good and solid. Everything would be all right again in a couple of weeks or so.

But a couple of weeks passed and it was not all right. That is to say, he was not released. A third week went by, a fourth, a fifth, and he was not released. The place was, of course, a treat compared with Schloss Kastanienburg, but it was very dull and miserable compared with anything else, even with the Pension Kahn. All the more when you are being kept there for nothing at all, nothing, while the man in the next cell to you raped a little girl twelve years old, and the man four cells away cheated the widows of a whole town of their life-savings. And it doesn't really get you very far in a prison being a celebrity; after all, nearly everybody there is a celebrity in his own way. What's more, a prison in a Nazi country is a Nazi prison, don't forget that. Quite a number of the prisoners and the warders managed to make you remember you were a Jew, such a year should take them!

It would have been different if he could send out letters, that is to say, the sort of letters you get answers to. Most of the other prisoners did. They wrote. They got replies. He also wrote, both to friends in England and to the British Consul in Berlin. But it became evident in a couple of weeks that his letters were either being destroyed as he handed them over or were just being pigeonholed somewhere. He went on writing for a time, because it was something to do, and then he dropped it. It was too disheartening. It was a bit painful, too, to see the other prisoners go off and meet their friends and relatives on visitors' day, and get parcels and bits of clothing and so on. But who was there, here in Berlin, to come and see him? Frau Kahn, perhaps, from the Bambergerstrasse? He would have liked someone to darn his socks, also.

So, instead, he scribbled messages on the wall to his sons Max and Moisheh, and his friends Rose and Bruno, and others, mostly in the idiom of the postcards he had earlier sent them. Here's hoping you are in the best of health as it leaves me at present. Sometimes the messages became more sentimental. As many fishes as are in the sea, so many kisses I send to thee.

And also, as before at Schloss Kastanienburg, he recited Psalms, sitting down on his bed and chanting those sweet words which had not failed him, even in the valley of the shadow of death; swaying backward and forward, backward and forward, till the warder at the spy-hole was quite dizzy—backward and forward, backward and forward, till the holy comfort was in his heart again, and his eyes shone.

A fifth week went by, a sixth week. They were certainly taking their time about it, both the high-up ones in England and the authorities here in Germany. He told himself unhappily he must readjust his views somewhat. There were people in this same prison who had been held without trial for months and months, though their cases were, of course, not so transparently simple as his.

It might still be, he admitted, two or three weeks before they released him. But that they would release him, either before or after trial, he had not the slightest doubt at all. *Truly,* he murmured, *my soul waiteth upon God: from Him cometh my salvation.*

And then came that episode in the prison yard which changed all this.

The prisoners in Mr. Emmanuel's block were taking their open-air exercise one certain morning. It was good to be stretching one's legs. It was good to be looking up into the sky. It was good to catch an occasional glimpse of one of the women employees of the prison, a canteen waitress, maybe, or a laundress, on her way between one building and the other. The prisoners were employed in these and other avocations, conveying messages to each other, spotting a new face, working out what old face was missing, perhaps because a prisoner was ill or dead, perhaps because his sentence was up. Round and round they marched in two opposed files, like beasts in a treadmill. But they were not blinkered. They had their eyes open. Their nostrils twitched. Heigho, the April day! Or was it not May now?

"Stop jabbering, you, there!"

"Pick your feet up, you!"

A flock of birds chattering like anything in the gutters!

Music, music, all of it, this good spring day!

Round and round, and once again. Who is that old man, Mr. Emmanuel asked himself, in the opposite file, coming towards me again? I have seen him once before. Where have I seen him? What have they done to him? What pain there is in that face! He can hardly lift his feet up. Who is he? Where have I seen him before?

He is coming towards me again now. He comes nearer and nearer. He is looking towards me. His eyes are upon me now. Why does he stare at me so? Does he know me?

What have I done to him? He looks at me as if I had killed his son or daughter!

And in that instant, as the man came abreast of him, as the man turned away the profound melancholy, the intolerable reproach, of his eyes, there was an explosion in Mr. Emmanuel's brain, by the light of which he saw who that old man was, and his own guilt.

The same broad brow, the same thin arched nose, the same gentle mouth, but drawn now with how much anguish! The little cigarette kiosk at the corner of the Lutherstrasse and the Motzstrasse! Such a man as that, with such a voice, such a forehead, selling cigarettes? It is upside down, the whole world!

"I would be glad if you could perhaps recommend me a brand of nice Turkish cigarettes. . . . Oh, I beg your pardon, please. I forgot. You see, it is——"

"It is *Shabbos*. Please do not disturb yourself!"

"Thank you, it is so kind of you. When *Shabbos* is out, Herr . . . Herr——"

"Herr ex-Professor Sachs. Of the Faculty of Classical Literature in the Friedrich Wilhelm University, here in Berlin."

The approach to the Zoo station, by the Joachimthalerstrasse. The telephone booths at the blind end, towards the Tiergarten.

"Excuse me. I will go in now and make a call. I thank you. Good-bye."

"It is for me to thank you——"

What has he run out for, his whole body shaking like leaves, his eyes like glass?

"Go away! Go away! Let me be!"

Is there a dead body inside there? No, there is no dead body. Only a telephone book open on the ledge. Scrawled in red crayon, in great letters that run across both pages, the words:

ROT FRONT LEBT

The crayon is fresh and powdery. The words have the appearance of having been written down only just now.

"He did not write them!" Mr. Emmanuel was screaming at the top of his voice, there in the prison yard at Moabit. "He did not write them! He had nothing to do with it! He had nothing to do with it! I only asked him just a simple question!" He stood there shaking his fists at the armed warders, the barred windows, the regime that had treated so sorely two innocent old men. His eyeballs rolled in his head, a froth was seething at the corners of his mouth. "Bandits! Butchers! Murderers! How can you—?"

But by this time the warders had recovered from their extreme surprise. From various corners of the yard swift feet came crunching over the gravel. The butt-end of a gun came dully down on Mr. Emmanuel's skull.

"Cart him off!" a sharp voice commanded.

They took him off to an isolation cell to mend his manners, and kept him there a week on bread and water. But they did not have any call to complain of his manner again. Henceforth he was as gentle and timid as any servant girl. To his own doom he was perfectly reconciled now. His principal regret was that he could not have failed still further to compromise Herr ex-Professor Sachs. He had not seen the poor gentleman's charge-sheet, but he had no doubt at all that his trivial association with himself had been his sole crime. He was deprived of privileges for several weeks after the occasion of his lamentable outburst, and when he was allowed once more to take exercise in the prison yard, ex-Professor Sachs was missing. He had not dared to ask any questions regarding him, for fear of tying the old man to himself by still one more knot. But the news came to him not long after, that the ex-professor had been summarily tried by the People's Court and duly executed. He saw no reason why, in their good time, they should not treat him in exactly the same way.

Except, of course, they would not try him in the same way by a secret tribunal. They would make a great case out of him, a world-shaking trial, as they had made out of van der Lubbe. He saw everything in a fresh perspective now. He had not been arrested as the result of the machinations of some Sinister Person, over-zealous but stupid. The regime, its suspicions already aroused, and seeing in the Frankfurter-Gustloff episode a gift straight from those gods that had already been so bountiful to them, had pounced upon him as an eagle pounces upon a lamb. They had released him from Schloss Kastanienburg, because they would have lost their new van der Lubbe if they had kept him there only a few days more, and he was too precious to them for that. Here in Moabit he could stink and dwindle until their Day came. They would not let him die.

He said his prayers duly as before, three times a day, putting his hat on his head, and facing east towards Jerusalem. The only trouble was to decide which day was Saturday, which has its special litany, for all the days were so exactly like one another. They came and looked at him through the spy-hole and mocked him, but he did not mind that, he went on with his prayers. He remained as good a Jew as he had been, at all events since they had locked him up in a cell.

That was the trouble. When he had been a free man,

he had hardly thought of these things. He had been slack in his duties, self-centred, vain. Above all he had been vain, even here, in Schloss Kastanienburg and Moabit. I am an Englishman, he had announced, goggling like a turkey-cock. A fine sort of Englishman, a foreigner from a Russian village, he has signed a paper and paid a few shillings, and he thinks he is an Englishman like maybe Lord Derby. Perhaps also England will go to war for me, because an old nobody from Magnolia Street is locked up in Germany?

If I had not been such a foolish muddling old man, who says I would have been locked up, either? It is a pity, little Bruno, it was not a cleverer man than me who said he would go to Germany and find out for you about your heart-breaking. A great pity, Bruno! Now you will never know what has happened to your mother, why she stopped writing and still she does not write.

What? Do you listen to yourself? Because *you* are too stupid to find out, because you go about it the wrong way like an old hen-woman from the market, do you think nobody else will find out? But it will not be me, Bruno, whose face is so like my dead son's face. It will not be me.

God is not pleased with me, Bruno. I have been a vain man. I said God is with me in my cell, and I talk to Him and He listens. It is to bigger men than me, and better men, that God comes, to judges and kings and prophets. Say over the Psalms to yourself, Isaac. Why not? Does it cost any more you should say over the Psalms?

He sat down on his bed, and recited Psalms. His voice was so thin and small he could himself hardly hear it. Then for long hours he would be silent. Then he would start again. It passed the time away.

12

I

THE little rainproof factory where Mr. Sam Silver worked was tucked away in a side-street off the Blenheim Road, under the lee of the clay-crofts. They heard the boys shouting "Special!" along the main road, but paid no particular heed to it. They did not know what the shouting was about, till an errand-boy came in with the paper a couple of hours later.

"Ee, bah goom!" the youth exclaimed. "I bet yer can't guess 'oo they've been and gone and locked oop in Berlin? A pal of yours, Mr. Silver! That old geezer Emmanuel, from Magnolia Street! They'll be lockin' oop Lord Mayor next!" The news so prostrated Mr. Silver that the errand-boy had to take him home as soon as he was able to get on his feet again, a good half-hour later.

By that evening, at least four out of Mr. Silver's five daughters heard the news, and were greatly affected. The fifth, namely Susan Polednik, the one married to a one-time Bolshevik Commissar and some-time high official in a Soviet ministry, can hardly have heard the news that same evening—that is, if she were still there to hear it—if only because in Russia the news would probably have been of next to no importance. In a country where one evening you may be the guest of a major political figure, and the next morning learn that he has been arrested overnight as an implacable enemy of the people, the news of the arrest of an obscure English Jew in Berlin for alleged political activities would not have seemed so odd as elsewhere.

The other four daughters, three of whom were in England at that time, and one in Germany, were all very shocked. They had all known Mr. Emmanuel, who used to live just behind them in Magnolia Street, their back doors facing each other. He was such a mild old gentleman, who would not hurt a fly, even though he was such a talker he could talk the hind leg off a horse. For some reason the old fellow had gone to Germany, where he had gone and got himself arrested. They were accusing him of being an accomplice in a first-class political murder . . . something or other that had happened in Switzerland; there had been something about it in the paper only the other day. . . . Oh, yes, a Jewish student who had murdered the local Nazi leader. He was not only a murderer, apparently. The old chap was all tied up with an international spy-ring as well. Old Emmanuel! He had about as much wickedness in him as a three-week-old kitten! It was ridiculous! It was infamous! What on earth would they be up to next, those raving cut-throats in Berlin? That night three of those four Silver women wrote frantically to their father.

One did not.

That one was Elsie Silver, who was in Berlin herself at that time, and had been a good many years now. For several years no word had passed between herself and her father, or with anyone she had once known in the pre-Berlin years. This was that same Elsie Silver to whom reference has several times been made in the pages of this narrative, Elsie Silver, still by title of law Lady Malswetting, but now, as she had been for five years, intimate friend of the celebrated Nazi leader, Wilhelm Brockenburg.

Elsie Silver at this period lived in an elegant but discreet flat in the Stadtpark. When the early edition of the *Beobachter am Abend* appeared with its news of the arrest of the elderly Jew-spy-and-murderer, she was taking things easy preparatory to her afternoon canter at the Beerman Tattersall, in the Hardenbergstrasse. She had just had her breakfast, or you might call it lunch, for she had only one meal in the earlier part of the day, a thin wafer of toast and a faint cup of China tea without sugar. Elsie Silver was not so young as she had been, and she had to manage her diet carefully. She was delighted to find that if she reduced the amount she ate and drank before dinner to a fragile minimum, she could eat almost anything at dinner, even potatoes, even an occasional dollop of cream, which she adored.

She was not so young as she had been. Willi, that is to say, Wilhelm Brockenburg, her lover, assured her she did not look a day over thirty, perhaps a fortnight less. Even her enemies could not believe she was over thirty-five. And whether in fact she was older than that was a question on which, even in silence and solitude, she saw no reason to meditate. She was still a most attractive woman. There was hardly any opulescence of those almost male lines which the taste of the Kurfürstendamm theatre in the late twenties and very early thirties had found so specially agreeable. Those smoky black eyes, those petulant, bright lips, were as alluring as they had ever been. Certainly Willi Brockenburg found them so, despite the Nuremberg Laws.

Mere self-denial was not enough to achieve so brilliant a protraction of youth. Elsie Silver went and had an hour's exercise almost every day at the Beerman Tattersall. It brought so pretty a flush to her cheeks, and gave so gallant a swing to her shoulders, that really (Willi Brockenburg said to himself) she did make those other women, pure Nordics though they were, look like a lot of old cows. They were both very attached to the Beerman Tattersall, for it was there that he and Elsie had first met, in 1928, when Elsie was at the apogee of her career as a star in revue and light opera, and Brockenburg, not yet having found his footing among the Berlin sand-banks, had accepted a position as a gentleman riding-master. He had not stayed there long, but long enough for Elsie and the new riding-master to get the measure of each other.

On the day of the announcement of Mr. Emmanuel's arrest, Elsie Silver duly went off to do her hour's canter round the circus. After her exercise she did a little shopping, then she returned to her apartment, to rest a little and to take a cup of China tea; she felt she could permit herself the extra stimulus of a cup of China tea. Willi was coming in this evening, she believed. There had been a meeting of the party leaders all day, but he had telephoned to say he hoped they would be through in time for dinner; in that case, their date at Horcher's, in the Lutherstrasse, would stand.

Elsie Silver's Lisa piled up the cushions on the divan behind Elsie's back. Over in the kitchen Lisa's Hansl was making tea. Hansl had been a waiter in a hotel in

Bournemouth, and knew exactly how to make tea in the most English fashion. Lisa and Hansl were a devoted and efficient married couple. They did for her perfectly.

Lisa moved up the low tea-table to the divan. She took a cigarette from the box, put it in her mistress's mouth, and lit it. She opened up the evening paper and laid it beside the Frau Gräfin's hip. Then she withdrew with a curtsy. She never forgot that while her mistress was an ex-actress of great distinction, she was also an English lady of quality. She withdrew. Her part of the ritual of five o'clock was accomplished. This was the time of day when Elsie did her Malswetting stuff. She thought it screamingly funny; but she was very serious about it, too. It helped.

Elsie Silver languidly opened the newspaper. A headline ran across the page, underlined by a thick red line like a puff of flame:

ACCOMPLICE IN GUSTLOFF MURDER
ARRESTED

A second headline proclaimed:

INTERNATIONAL JEW-SPY UNMASKED

"Hello," she murmured. "I wonder what they're up to now." She was not really very interested.

Then she read the text of the story. A certain Isaac Emmanuel, a Jew from Doomington, in England, had been arrested for complicity with the international Yugoslav Jew spy David Frankfurter in the murder of the *Landesgruppenleiter* Wilhelm Gustloff in Davos. The unveiling of this criminal was a signal proof of the existence of that widely ramifying net of international Jew-murderers to which the Leader, etc., etc. There was a note in small type appended to the story, giving such biographical details regarding the arrested man as were already to hand. Isaac Emmanuel, a communist emissary from Magnolia Street, in Longton, a Jew-infested section of the city of Doomington . . . Isaac Emmanuel, a communist leader from Magnolia Street, in Doomington . . . Isaac Emmanuel, a communist leader from . . .

Elsie Silver's heart pumped like a machine in a shed. Her eyes protruded like a stuffed doll's. The cigarette fell from her lips and lay smouldering on the white fleece carpet. It was fortunate that Hansl came in at that moment with the tea-tray, and noticed what had happened, or the cigarette might have done a lot of damage, for it was a very expensive carpet. He put down the tea-tray, raced forward, and picked up the cigarette apologetically.

"Bitte, Frau Gräfin, entschuldigen!" he begged.

She took not the slightest notice of him, not for two minutes, three, four. He felt very awkward. He did not know whether to stay or go. The cigarette burned closer and closer to his fingertips.

At length she turned round.

"Put out that cigarette!"

"Bitte sehr, Frau Gräfin!" He put it out.

"Go and fetch me a hammer!"

"A hammer?" he repeated incredulously.

"I said a hammer!"

His heart uneasy with alarm, he went off to his little tool-box in the kitchen and picked out a hammer.

"A hammer, *Frau Gräfin!"*

She took it from him with one hand, with the other lifted the delicate little Rosenthal cup from the tea-table beside her, then she smashed it to smithereens. She was very attached to that tea service. It had been a present from her previous lover, Count Oskar von Straupitz-Kalmin. He had certainly not been able to afford it, poor dear! not then, at least.

"I feel a bit better now!" she said to herself. Then she turned to Hansl again. "Go and get me another cup, will you, and pour my tea out?"

Hansl went off, his brain rocking dizzily, and got another tea-cup.

These English, these high-born ones, stark, staring mad, one and all. . . .

II

Elsie Silver first came to Berlin at the time of the inflation, liked it enormously, and settled there. She had run away from her husband, Sir Robert Malswetting, the eighth baronet, because she was tired of him, and because he cried in a dentist's waiting-room. She had a little money to be going on with—you did not need much in Germany during the inflation. Then she went back to her former profession, the stage. Her father had long since begun his spectacular climb to great riches, and was already a very rich man, but she did not draw on the old man's money-bags till she met, in a very odd sort of night club, her love, her darling, a certain egregious aristocrat, Count Oskar von Straupitz-Kalmin. He was not quite a pimp, though he was ready to live on her, but he was certainly something of a weed. None the less, he was exactly what she wanted; more than that, she had always wanted him.

She was absolutely convinced that she had seen his face several times already, at various periods of her life, in a sort of "spooky" foreseeing—the scar that went down from his nostrils to his chin, the fine blue eyes, the almost womanish mouth. She gave up the stage, because it meant taking up some of the time she might spend with Oskar. He was not doing anything in particular, so he, for his part, had nothing in particular to give up. The arrangement worked perfectly. She was wildly happy with him and he got all he wanted out of her. They got through old Silver's money at a great rate.

Then, after the suicide of Sam Silver's son-in-law and partner Alexander Smirnof, the old man developed his preposterous attack of conscience. He despoiled himself of his vast personal fortune in order to hand it over to the shareholders of his bankrupt firms, and went back to live with his wife in their old house in Oleander Street. Four of his five daughters, including Elsie, had assembled to dissuade the old man from carrying out his horrible intention, but it was no good. They all went back pretty well where they started from.

Elsie went back to Berlin. This was in November 1924. She and Oskar got through what she had over, then Oskar left her. She was not cross or disappointed. She had him weighed up to a "t." She did not respect her beauty-boy, she merely adored him. She knew he would come back again to her, and he did, only a month or two later. He knew that he needed her, if not quite in the same way, quite as much as she needed him. They did not now go to bed with each other anything like so frequently. But they were completely necessary to each other, as a mother and a son, as a sister and a brother, as an old husband and an old wife. It was a very special sort of relationship.

She went back to the stage, and in a year or two was one of the most successful artists at the Kurfürstendamm theatre, at a time when it had so brilliant and hectic a flowering that it was clear to all observers the flower carried within it the seeds of a speedy decay. Fritzi Massary was getting on a bit, Marlene Dietrich was just a novice, Margo Lion and Elsie Silver were the reigning queens. Marcellus Schiffer wrote the words, Mischa Spoliansky wrote the music, Barnowsky and Klein produced.

Nobody could say exactly what it was that Berlin found so irresistible in Elsie Silver. She did not dance very well. She did not sing very well. She was sometimes downright rude to her audiences. Perhaps it was exactly that. In one way or another, that always goes down well in Berlin. Besides, Berlin got to know she was the wife of Sir Robert Malswetting, holder of an ancient baronetcy; she was the mistress of Oskar von Straupitz-Kalmin, a Herr Graf of equally ancient lineage. By God, there must be something to the woman. The story of the Silver millions was well known too. She seemed to have been made for the Kurfürstendamm, and the Kurfürstendamm for her.

She first met Willi Brockenburg in the Beerman Tattersall in the Hardenbergstrasse. That was in 1928. It had occurred to her that if she did a bit of riding in the afternoons, it would do that figure of hers no harm at all. After all, she was Jewish by birth, a fact that the *Völkischer Beobachter* remembered, and she as a rule forgot. And you never know, she reflected, with the female Jewish body. One day as slim as a lath, and the next day—hey, presto, where on earth have they come from, those hips, those bosoms? If she got the way of her two elder sisters, for instance, little Oskar wouldn't like it. The managers wouldn't like it, either, though she didn't give a damn for the managers. But the public wouldn't like it, and she loved her Berlin public—not so much her immensely sophisticated Jewish public, which tended to take her with a grain of salt or two, but the "Nordic" public, the "Aryan" public, as those Nazi blatherskites phrased it. She loved their cow-like sentimentality, their bull-like brutality, the little girls with pig-tails, the square-headed men with chins at the back of their necks. She loved Berlin, adored Berlin. The Berliners knew it and adored her for it. Berlin was her spiritual home.

So she went out riding in the Beerman Tattersall to keep herself nice and shapely for her little Oskar and her little Berliners. The riding schools in Berlin are called Tattersalls, and some of them are big establishments with accommodation for a hundred and more horses. They all have a bar and a restaurant overlooking the riding circus. During the winter months a band plays in the evenings and on Sunday mornings. Sometimes they arrange gymkhanas. They are—or were—gay places. At that time the staff of *Reitlehrer,* or riding-masters, included a good many ex-officers, particularly, of course, ex-officers of the cavalry. They have other duties now. For several months during the year 1928 Willi Brockenburg was one of these *Reitlehrer,* in the school in the Hardenbergstrasse. He was happy to number Lady Malswetting among his clients. There, in the atmosphere of sawdust, polished leggings, and horse manure, it was felt proper to know Elsie Silver by her more equestrian name.

The career of Brockenburg is, in its main outlines, well enough known. The son of a Prussian Junker, he was born in Palmnicken, in 1890, joined the army as an aspirant to a cavalry regiment in 1908, and in 1914, when the War broke out, had just been appointed *Rittmeister*. When by the end of the year the mobile war had condensed into trench warfare, and officers of cavalry regiments were induced by better chances of advancement to join the air force, Brockenburg transferred too. He did service at many points on the western and eastern fronts, and in 1918 was transferred to the famous flying squadron, the *Jagdgeschwader Freiherr von Richthofen,* commonly known as the Richthofen Circus, whose commander was a certain Captain Göring. He proved himself an efficient and daring pilot, was appointed captain shortly before the Armistice, and with that rank left the army at the beginning of 1919, when demobilization was enforced.

He had a small pension and a certain small income from his capital, but during the inflation was reduced to a condition in which he could buy for his girl friends either ham sandwiches or silk stockings, but not both. There were many things he could do quite well: riding, shooting, flying; but there was no money to be made out of these accomplishments. He was therefore obliged to look round for more lucrative occupations, though the competition in these was enormous. There followed a period in which he floundered from one undertaking to another, without achieving success in any, except the last. He became an art dealer, a dealer in currencies (a *Valutaschieber,* as the indelicate phrase was), an agent for a newly patented parachute, a riding-master in a Berlin riding school, and, finally, the Berlin agent for a Rhine wine firm. In that occupation he definitely found his feet.

His political education had been developing all this time. He did not have an instinctive distaste for Jews, such as a number of his boyhood and army friends had, but he realized quite early what a useful counter they provided in the political game, how much could be achieved by stimulating hatred against them. He was not actually one of the "Mayflower Nazis," as they have been termed, but when Herr Hitler came out of prison, dissolved his party, and reorganized it with the assistance of certain potent industrial magnates, Brockenburg thought it would be useful to join too. By 1928 he had become *Oberscharführer* in the S.A. He had his uniform, which was useful from time to time—some of the women liked it immoderately. He also had an allowance. The party funds however, were still a long way from being ample enough to maintain many men like Brockenburg in whole-time jobs. He therefore took on a job as *Reitlehrer* in a riding school, where the emphasis was much more on his earlier history as an officer in a crack cavalry regiment than his present history in the S.A.

A few months later his birth and his political affiliations procured for him a much better job, as Berlin agent for one of the biggest wine firms in the Rhineland. For some time he became a habitué of the smart night clubs and restaurants, partly because he was happy in that atmosphere, partly because he could there engage in a twofold propaganda for his firm and his party. He would give the waiters enormous tips to recommend his wines, and, not so drunk as he pretended to be, proclaim his deathless devotion to Herr Hitler and the soonest possible damnation to Judah, Poland, France, and the world in general.

His connexion with two of the principal figures in the party was already close. He had served under Captain Göring in the Richthofen Squadron, and the men had remained great friends; and at this time, when Herr Göring and the Leader, Herr Hitler, were ceaselessly storming up and down the country, he saw a great deal of Herr Goebbels, whose duties as *Gauleiter* of Berlin, editor of the *Angriff*, and *Reichspropagandaleiter*, usually kept him in the capital. So, both eyes open in the night clubs, both ears open in the offices of the *Angriff* and the Propaganda Department, Brockenburg became a person of increasing importance in the high Nazi councils. In 1930 he was elected a member of the Reichstag in that triumphant election in which Herr Hitler captured 107 places. At the same time he was transferred from the S.A. to the S.S., where, being a person of good family, he was at once appointed *Gruppenführer*.

It was, however, only after Herr Hitler's accession to power in 1933 that Brockenburg was requested to give up his commercial situation and devote himself exclusively to the service of the party. The demand for men of Brockenburg's ability and experience was far greater than the supply. Within a few months he was appointed Minister of the specially created Department of Reconstruction. He was now universally recognized as one of the principal pillars of the regime.

The moment Willi Brockenburg touched Elsie Silver as he helped her mount into her saddle that day at the Beerman Tattersall in 1928 he knew that he was done for, that here was the woman he had been hunting for even more with the tips of his fingers than with his eyes and mouth during these many years of amatory exploration. He had seen her often enough on the stage, and she had attracted him a great deal, but not more than several other actresses. He was wary about actresses. It was by no means enough to see them behind footlights, for some had an immense skill in making something out of themselves between the dressing-room and the stage which had practically no relation with the woman who entered by the stage door. You have to know what the relationship is, if any, between these two women; and to Brockenburg, knowing them had a tactile basis, anything from shaking hands with them to sleeping with them. With Elsie Silver, all he had needed was to touch her with the tips of his fingers. He had needed no more than that. Here was the woman.

Elsie Silver knew immediately how the land lay; she never deceived herself in such matters. She had heard about the new *Reitlehrer* who had been appointed to the riding school, the ex-cavalry officer, the flying officer decorated with the *ordre pour le mérite,* the handsome buccaneer. She had a strong feeling that this Brockenburg had been more than once pointed out to her in the night clubs, a great handsome fellow, with broken eyebrows and fine teeth. "One of these Nazis!" they had said to her. "A follower of that madman Hitler! An officer in the S.A."

"One of the Nazis, eh?" she said to herself. "An officer in the S.A.? There's a fellow who's going to get somewhere, if that bloody movement's going to keep moving! I wonder!" she mused. "I wonder!"

She saw that the fellow had fallen for her, tail over tip. It was a real case. She knew, from the way he handled her, he wasn't going to treat her as a tart, or a Jewess, or anything not quite up to scratch. She was never wrong in that sort of thing. He was going to treat her as a lady—as Lady Malswetting, in fact. That was the way it had started, and that was the way it was going to go on. Oh, yes, he was going to be something to reckon with, in her own life, too, as well as elsewhere.

She could see in his face the fellow was clever and obstinate. So was she. After all, he was a Nazi. She did not like Nazis. She might just say to him then and there: "Get to hell out of it! I'm just a little Yiddishe, the daughter of a Yid tailor!" But she felt somehow he was not the sort of Nazi whom that would finish for good and all. He'd click his heels, and bow, and kiss her hand, and next day send her a bouquet of *recherché* flowers. She did nothing about it that day they first met in the Hardenbergstrasse; neither did he, for quite a long time. But they both knew exactly what it was all about within a month or two.

He knew, everybody knew, she was not really a blue-blooded lady out of the Domesday Book. She was a Jewess. Well, that was a pity. The fact might involve a little awkwardness now and again, much less than if she had not also been the wife of Sir Robert Malswetting, eighth baronet. You would have thought that that might be a doubtful passport to the affections of a school of gentlemen who were not only National but Socialist! To hell with all that! Love—had he not heard in some night club somewhere?—love will find a way. As for Oskar von Straupitz-Kalmin . . . the broken eyebrows beetled dangerously . . . that pimp had better keep off the grass . . . there is always something you can do to stuff the mouths of creatures of that sort, gold or lead, he was quite indifferent which.

The situation was a good deal more complicated with regard to Elsie Silver. First, of course, there was Oskar. Sooner or later Brockenburg was going to ask her to be his mistress. What was she going to do about that, seeing that Oskar was the one man in the world she had ever loved, loved now, and ever would love? She was, as she phrased it, "woozy" about him.

Well, what about Oskar? She knew very well he had had intrigues with other women since he and she had hitched up with each other—parlour-maid affairs, you might call them—but on the whole he had been pretty faithful to her. Yet the fact was she did not set tremendous store by his sexual fidelity. What did she want, then? She wanted him to love her, to be devoted to her, to be grateful to her . . . that was about all, but it was pretty well everything.

The circle worked round again to Brockenburg, this time Brockenburg the Nazi. The bloody Nazis were, after all, to be *the* party. She was sure about that. She did not need the confirmation of the 1930 election, when Hitler polled nearly six and a half million votes, a great portion of the total electorate. "Heads will roll," declared Herr Hitler sombrely. "They will," Elsie Silver repeated. She was a great deal cleverer than all the German Jews and a great many German Gentiles. "These are the boys!" she said to herself. "Blast their bloody eyes! They are going to pull it off!"

There were several reasons, besides an obvious one, why the thought of the impending Nazi triumph was detestable to her. In the first place, she knew it would mean the destruction of that extraordinary Berlin civilization which she found so enchanting. Berlin was an amalgam of, on the one hand, an immense sophistication and an almost psychopathic sensitivity; on the other, of an unexampled stupidity and brutality. It was that combination she found so piquant, whose endless permutations she could contemplate, even in a measure contribute to, with inexhaustible pleasure. The triumph of the Nazis would upset that fine balance, the stupidity and brutality would come galumphing down with a crashing resonance. Berlin would become the town of the gorilla.

Whatever happened to her—and on general principles it was easy to foresee what was going to happen to her—she was full of foreboding about what was going to happen to Oskar. He was, as much as herself, a flower of those febrile twenties. In the harsher airs which were blowing up, she feared things would go very ill with him. Except in her own heart, or nerves, or wherever you wanted to locate it, he had never managed to make a place for himself anywhere. He was well born. Apart from the negative period of an imprisonment in Russia, he had had a distinguished military career. He had always maintained some sort of contact with the circles close to the ex-Crown Prince; but whereas they managed to hold their own and, in some cases, to entrench themselves in firm positions, Oskar got nowhere; no one, except Elsie Silver, would have anything to do with him.

Poor Oskar! Poor Elsie!

She got some sort of insight into the position from Willi Brockenburg himself one day in the summer of 1930.

"You know what is wrong, Elsie, do you?" he asked. "With your friend Oskar, I mean?" He was twirling the slender stem of a wine-glass so restlessly between the tips of his enormous fingers, she wondered how he managed not to break it.

"There is nothing wrong," she smiled at him. "Nothing wrong at all. He is just perfect." But her heart went quite cold. She knew he had had something to tell her for a long time about Oskar. It seemed he judged that the fit moment to tell it had come now.

"He was very foolish," he said. "Very foolish indeed. He has a great faculty for doing the wrong thing."

"I would rather you did not criticize him."

"Have I criticized him before, Elsie?"

"It is true. You have not."

"It has become relevant. For his sake, I mean, as well."

As well as what? She said nothing.

"He never told you about that episode after the Armistice?" She shook her head. "Two and a half months after the Armistice, I think it was. It is all carefully noted down."

"Yes?" She did not raise her head.

"He has no judgment. He is also an incurable romantic. He thought the country would go communist. He put himself at the head of a small armed band of soldiers and sailors and went about frightening people. There was a certain amount of looting and a few deaths. There were other bands about at the time, of course. They hoped the troops would come over to them. They did not, as you know. They were suppressed very quickly. It was only because very high influence was brought to bear that Straupitz-Kalmin managed to get away with it. He disappeared for a time. But there are people amongst us with long memories. The affair has neither been forgiven nor forgotten."

Elsie Silver made no comment for a long time. It seemed to her that a good deal was explained. The poor silly fellow! The incurable backer of the wrong horse! The boy who would not, could not, get anywhere, any time!

"Please!" she said. "Put that glass down! You will

break its neck!" They were really very frightening fingers, very efficient despite their great size.

"I beg your pardon!" He put the glass down on the tray.

"Well?" she asked, after another long delay.

"You've been very useful to him in the meantime. But later . . . he'll need someone else, too. You will not be enough."

"Very well, Willi!" she said. "I must say you have handled the situation agreeably. You have been very *ritterlich,* very knightly."

He bowed his head.

"It *is* one of our wines?" he said. "I drink to you, Elsie!" She became his mistress a week later.

Quite soon after, she told her friend Oskar about it, reminding him that that was a great deal franker than he had been on a number of comparable occasions. He was very bitter, and full of reproaches. She let him have his sulks out, then a couple of weeks after that she went into the matter further. He was very scared when she brought up the matter of his *gaffe* in the immediate post-war days, the time he had played Robin Hood in red. He had pathetically hoped that by trying hard never to think of it he could make the episode seem as if it had never been. Alas, that is not so, she sighed.

I have not finished yet, she went on. She proceeded to make it clear that so long as this other relationship lasted, she proposed to be nothing more to him than his little sister. He got very offensive about that, slammed the door, and went off for another month. But the amount of play he had on his string was limited. He came back. For the time being, she said, he could come in for tea or cocktails. She would not receive him for hot drinks and a snack after the show.

They did not talk politics, she and Willi Brockenburg; they carefully avoided them. She was the stage-star and the English lady; he was the one-time cavalry and flying officer, the man-about-town. But the fact remained she was a Jewess, and he was a Nazi, sworn enemy of all things Jewish. How did they get right with themselves?

She saw at once that he had no difficulty at all and never would have, except the minor or major difficulties of inconvenience. She recognized four brands of anti-Semite. There was first the plain silly-ass type, whom you find in high places as well as low. He just believes what he is told about Jews, because it saves such a lot of mental trouble. There is the bad-man type of anti-Semite, to whom hatred of anything at any time is as the breath of his nostrils; it is usually the Jews he hates, because Jews are the most easily and universally accessible for hatred. There is the type who has the Jew fixation. In other respects he is sometimes completely sane; with respect to Jews he is completely mad. It might just as well be cats, or albinos.

Willi Brockenburg was not any of these. He was an anti-Semite for a fourth, the careerist, reason. In another time and place he might have been an anti-Scotsman or an anti-Italian. He could simulate the badness of the bad anti-Semite and the madness of the mad one. He knew exactly what he was doing.

In giving herself to Brockenburg for Oskar's sake, Elsie too knew exactly what she was doing. At that time the transaction was still to a considerable extent a private matter. The Nazis were still for most people, but particularly for the Jews, a bad joke, a joke that had gone a long way too far, but still a joke. If the entirely ridiculous could happen, and the Nazis could ever possibly get into power, it was universally agreed that they would not carry out the Jewish points of their programme, for the simple reason that they could not. The Jew-cry would have been to a great extent responsible for their getting into power, but once seated there, they would have to sing fresh songs. There were, after all, a few intelligent people even now among them. For a long time, then, the intrigue with Brockenburg was still a private matter. They were very discreet about it; she and Brockenburg and, even more, Straupitz-Kalmin, whose part in it was not a very gratifying one.

In so far as it began to be the talk of the cafés, people were, on the whole, rather amused by it, even if their amusement was sardonic. Brockenburg, was still, all the way up to 1933, a very obscure person compared with Elsie. If Elsie Silver wanted to do a topsy-turvy Delilah on this very non-Jewish Samson, well, that was Elsie Silver's business. She might even be a very good person to keep in with, if ever this Nazi show got really ugly. But of course it wouldn't. Hitler was certain to lose ground at the next election. Everyone said so.

There were also a certain number of people who thought her a harpy, and spat when she came anywhere near them. She looked at them humorously. She would be able to survive their displeasure.

The difficulty was not with them, or with Brockenburg, or with Oskar; it was with herself. But it was not until the Nazi triumph in 1933 that she really had to face up to it. Was she a Jew? she asked herself. In what sense? Her father had been a freethinker, in a raspberry-pop sort of way; there was nothing very Jewish about the Silver household. She knew very little more about things Jewish than about the customs of the ancient Peruvians or the modern Lepchas. Her sisters had learned something, at least, by staying on in a more or less Jewish atmosphere. She had cleared out of it at an alarmingly early age, to go and live among "professionals" in the theatrical section of Doomington.

What sort of Jew was she? All of a Jew the Nazis needed her to be, being the child of her parents. Well, it was true she was Jewish by race. She liked the old father a good deal, and was not indifferent to the old mother, though the old mother *was* a bit soppy. But if she got straight with herself, she admitted it wouldn't break her heart if she never saw the old folk again, never in her born days. So she couldn't call herself a Jew just because she loved her dadda and mamma so much. She had no great feeling for her four sisters, either, except the youngest one, May; but May wasn't much of a Jewess, either.

She wasn't a Jew then, out of family loyalty. Well, what then? What the hell? Why did she feel like scratching out the eyes of anyone who made a foul remark about Jews? She had been able to put up with it from Oskar, but that was Oskar; there was nothing she couldn't put up with from Oskar. He was her malady. She was, on the other hand, quite certain, in thinking back towards Bobby Malswetting, her dearly beloved spouse, that if he had made the slightest unkind remark about Jews she would have slapped his face and left him then and there; she would not have waited for him to start howling in a dentist's waiting-room. But her Bobby wasn't, in fact, that sort of person. He didn't quite believe that Jews really existed, any more than Nonconformists. Except the

Joels and the Barnatos. And Dizzy, of course, who got the Suez Canal for us and loved primroses. Damn nice fellah.

But now? How did she stand now? In nineteen thirty, thirty-one, thirty-two, with the brown tides sweeping up more and more menacingly? Aren't you a Jew any more, Elsie Silver? Have they frightened the guts out of you? Are you going to remain a little *Berlinerin* while the going is good, and then get out of it, with anything you can save out of the wreckage? Including your little fair-haired Count, of course, if they leave him to you? Well, Elsie Silver, how do you stand?

She knew exactly how she stood, even before that night in 1933 when Brockenburg came and told her that they had appointed him to one of the most important jobs at Nazi headquarters, that it was pretty certain they would appoint him to a higher place in the Government before many months were out.

"Well," she said to him, "you'll have to give me up, won't you?"

"I could as soon give up my two arms," he said. "I don't exist without you. I can't give you up."

"Do they know it?"

"They'll stand for it. They've got to. They need me, and I know too much."

"Give me till tomorrow, Willi, will you? Get back to your pals!"

She knew exactly how she stood, even before that night. She was a Jew, with something deeper inside her than race or creed. As for creed, she was as much of a Jewess as she was a Parsee. As for race, she could no more detach herself from her father and mother, her grandfathers and grandmothers, her great-grandfathers and great-grandmothers, than she could put on some other body and start walking about in it. With what was she a Jew, then? With whatever she possessed of virtue, every fibre of it. To be true to the Jew in her was the cabbalistic password with which she rearranged the parts that made her up, so that what was bad or trivial had merit in the new arrangement. It was the key by which she entered into herself. To be true to the Jew in her left her a tolerable human being, neither better nor worse than most. To be untrue was to be the rat that leaves the sinking ship (though even once again the ship might not sink after all). To be untrue was to be the snob, the smarmer, who is a derision both to the world he has aspired to and to the world he has scuttled from. It was to leave herself a harlot, exactly that, a lump of self-indulgent muck.

What should she do, then? She would have to give up the stage quite soon, with or without Brockenburg's protection. And after that? She could pack up her trunks and go off to Paris, or London, or somewhere, with little Oskar nestling in her muff. But she did not want to go to Paris, or London, even with Oskar. No good for Elsie, cadging her way from one agent to another, beginning all over again! And if she knew her Oskar, no good for Oskar, either; he would be doubling back to Berlin in no time, and they would be waiting for him!

What should she do then? There was a way out. She would not have to give up Berlin or Oskar or Brockenburg. On the contrary, she would have to stick to Brockenburg for all she was worth, every inch of her. It had nothing to do with her own career or comfort. It had only indirectly to do with her love for Oskar. It had everything in the world to do with this maddening thing, this wildly necessary thing—being a Jew.

It was for that reason she would have to stick tight to Brockenburg. It would keep her on the inside. She could be more useful, sometime, somehow, on the inside, than on the outside. She would have to pay one hell of a price for it! How they would loathe her, everybody, all Jews everywhere, from Oleander Street to the Dragonierstrasse, from the Porte St.-Denis to West End Avenue! How dreadfully ashamed old man Silver would be, and old woman Silver, and all the Silver sisters, God bless 'em! Well, she would have to put up with it, and so must they! She had always played a lone hand. Now she would have to play a pretty dangerous one, too.

I'm sorry about this, Willi Brockenburg. You've chosen your game. Mine has been chosen for me.

III

Elsie Silver drained her cup of China tea with lemon, then put it down on the low table beside her. Then she took up the copy of the *Beobachter am Abend* and read the Emmanuel story through once again, word by word. Then she filled her cup again, and rang for Hansl.

"Bring me the other evening papers!" she requested. "At once!"

"*Sehr wohl, Frau Gräfin!*"

They were with her three minutes later. They had no detail of any importance to add to the earlier account.

I can see exactly what they're up to, she said to herself. It's not very subtle, of course. They've had a Dutchman, a Czech or two, a Hungarian. Now it's an Englishman, of sorts. Next time it will be a pucka Englishman, all the way back to Ethelred the Unready. If they get away with it this time, the ball's at their feet. Nobody's safe, when they've once put a foot across the frontier. The other side of the frontier will do too. They're not so particular. But are they going to get away with it? They don't know the English. The English won't stand for it. Won't they? The Nazis have got away with a good deal, haven't they? Why shouldn't they get away with this . . . a poor little no-account Yid from Doomington? The English don't think that way. An Englishman's an Englishman. . . .

Oh, to hell! There's going to be a lot of talk this way and that way! To hell with the talk! *They're not going to get away with it!* Who's to stop them? *I'm* to stop them! *I,* Elsie Silver! Willi Brockenburg's going to stop them for me!

Now's your chance, Elsie. *You'll be more use on the inside than the outside.* That's how you worked it out. Well, what about it? It's about time you got going!

It just happens to be old Emmanuel, the poor sweet old dodderer! I can find out more about what really happened from Willi, I suppose. It just happens to be old Emmanuel, but it gives me my chance! If I don't take it, what am I? A whore. We've had it out already. That's that.

Don't worry, old Emmanuel, wherever you are! Things look pretty grim? *Don't you worry!*

IV

"Sorry I'm late, darling," said Willi Brockenburg, lifting Elsie Silver from her feet, and kissing her firm and full on the lips. "Can I have a drink? I rather hoped you'd be dressed already."

She poured out a glass of dry sherry for him. Everything in Lady Malswetting's flat was as English as it could possibly be.

"Darling!" She looked up at him apologetically from under her long eyelashes. "I hope you don't mind. I asked Lisa to make us a little meal; I don't feel a bit like going out tonight."

"Aren't you well?" he asked anxiously.

"Oh, I'm perfectly all right," she admitted. "But–" She sat down on the divan. He placed himself beside her.

"I *was* rather looking forward to going out tonight," he complained. "It's been the devil of a day at Headquarters!"

"Oh, darling, I'm *so* sorry! If you feel you'd like to have a bit of a change, why don't you go out without me! I'd be perfectly happy at home here, and perhaps later tonight——"

"Don't be a fool!" he said roughly. "What *are* you talking about? What's wrong?"

"I'm upset, Willi!"

"Upset?" His eyes glinted dangerously. "Has anybody said anything to you? Where? Who was it?"

"No, darling, no!" She placed her finger on his mouth. "It's not anything anybody's said. It's something I've read!"

"You've read? Where? In the newspapers?"

"Yes!"

"What is it?"

"You won't be cross with me?"

"What is it?"

"It's this matter of the arrest of the Englishman!"

"The Jew?"

"Yes! The fellow Emmanuel!"

He brought his fist down fiercely on his knee.

"To hell with it!" he swore. "As if I've not heard enough about that all day long! What's it got to do with you, anyhow?"

"I won't say a word if you talk to me like that!"

"I'm sorry, Elsie! Forgive me! I'm a boor! What on earth has the fellow got to do with you?"

"You can't have read the account properly. He comes from Doomington."

"Yes, of course. Doomington. Where you were born."

"Yes. He comes from a street called Magnolia Street, in a district called Longton."

"Well?"

"I was born in the next street, Oleander Street."

"Well, I suppose it *was* a bit of a shock to you. Well, forget about it."

"It's not so easy. The back-door of our house——"

He winced.

"Must you bring up that sort of thing?"

"You'll have to bear it. The back-door of our house faced the back-door of Mr. Emmanuel's. As a child I was always in and out of Mr. Emmanuel's house." Her eyes slowly filled with tears. "I've never told you how beastly my parents were to me, have I? Well, when they starved me and beat me, I used to creep into this old fellow's house, and he'd look after me, and sit me on his knee, and give me sweets, and rock me and soothe me. Then, when I was sound asleep, he'd carry me back home again. But sometimes, when they'd been particularly dreadful to me, he'd keep me in his own place all night. Willi, I loved that old man, I tell you. He was a saint. He can't have done this thing, he *can't!*"

"Of course not!" he admitted crossly. "Who on earth says he has?"

Her lips were quivering and the tears were on the verge of overflowing. She made a great effort to control herself.

"Willi," she said, "have I ever asked you for anything before? I mean, have I ever poked my nose into your affairs? Have I, or haven't I?"

"No," he admitted. He was looking thoroughly uncomfortable.

"Listen!" she cried. "I love that old man! He's the one thing I remember with any sort of feeling out of my girlhood days. There was old Emmanuel; then there was Oskar; then there was you. I suppose I had a bit of a crush on the old man, in a way, but it wasn't that. He made up for my father. You've no idea——"

"Oh, do be sensible!" he growled. "I'm not arguing about him. I'm perfectly sure he's everything you say. But what on earth do you want? What are you up to?"

She heaved a deep sigh.

"You know perfectly well what I want. You've got to use your influence with Himmler and the others. You've got to get him out of it."

"I wish you wouldn't talk about things you know nothing about. He's already out of Himmler's hands. He's in the hands of the State, awaiting trial. Anyhow, this is perfectly preposterous! I can't discuss it with you! Just because the miserable creature happens to have been nice to you when you were a little girl, you imagine . . . No, I forbid you to talk about it again! It's idiotic!"

"No, Willi, no! I'm afraid I can't agree. I've been perfectly honest. I've told you exactly why I want you to do everything you can to get the old man out of it. It'll be hard work, I'm ready to admit that, very hard work indeed. But you can do it, if you get Göring and Hess on your side. There's another reason, however, why you've got to do as I say, something that's got nothing to do with me at all. You yourself are involved in it, you're all involved in it. You've got to let that man go."

"What's got hold of you now?"

"You've always known I don't pretend to know anything about politics. But I do know something about the English. And that's more than you do, any of you. I don't say I like them, but I know them. You like them, but you don't know them. That's the difference.

"You can't do this thing, Willi. They won't allow it. If you insist, it'll put you back years and years with the English. They're a very strange people!"

"What perfectly horrible nonsense you're talking! The fellow isn't an Englishman, he's a dirty old Jew!" She winced, and drew away from him. "I'm sorry, Elsie, this is none of my asking. The fellow wasn't even born in England. He was born in Russia somewhere. He's a foreigner."

"No," she said. "No! The English don't look at it that way. It doesn't matter whether he was born in Brazil or China. He's an Englishman. Willi!" she appealed to him. "You might be able to bring off a scoop like this later. I don't know. It's possible. But you're a few years too soon. It'll be like losing a small war. Don't do it!"

"I've never heard anyone talk such rubbish! You're bleating like a schoolgirl! I strongly resent your mixing yourself up with affairs of this sort! Are you, or are you not, going to promise never to bring up the matter again?"

There was a long pause. "No!" she said at length, very, very faintly. A single large tear toppled over on to her cheek.

"All right!" he said. "I'm going home!" He made for the door, and paused there a moment, as if expecting she would utter a word bidding him stay. She did not. He closed the door behind him and went.

He was back rather more than an hour later.

"Have you had anything to eat?" she asked.

"As much as I want! Come to me!" he said. She went to him. Not a word passed their lips regarding the matter they had discussed earlier.

V

It was not brought up again till just over three weeks later. He looked very preoccupied all this time, as if things were not going at all well with him. He made an obvious effort to see as little of her as possible; at one time, when she had not seen him for five whole days, she concluded he was once again making the still more heroic effort not to see her at all. That had happened twice before, but on each occasion, as on this one, he returned to her a bundle of nerves.

"You little black-eyed fiend!" he murmured to her, covering her mouth, her neck, her bosom, with kisses. "I can't do without you! I can't. I can't! You know damn well I can't!" She was his alcohol, she was his morphine; she was the drug without which he was useless.

She placed her lips upon the ridges of his broken brows.

"Why do you try, silly one?" she said.

It was just over three weeks later that the Emmanuel matter arose once more between them. He had been with her for fifteen minutes already, hardly saying a word. There was something almost comic in the way the great hulk of a man fidgeted and squirmed in his chair, like a small child who has not done his homework properly in the presence of a stern governess.

She took pity on him at length.

"Come on now, Willi, what is it you want to say to me? Out with it!"

"It's this Goddamned Emmanuel business. The devil take it!"

"Well?" Her voice was very gentle.

"Well, Elsie, I hope to hell you've thought better of it!"

"How do you mean—thought better of it?" She raised her eyebrows.

"I've been exploring!" he exclaimed. "I've been nosing my way round! It's going to be quite impossible!"

"You must try again!" she said easily.

"Elsie, you're a fool!" She pursed her lips and inclined her head. "You don't know what you're up against!"

"Oh, yes, I do!" she objected quietly.

"What the hell do you want to drag me into it for?"

"Come, be reasonable! I couldn't get very far by myself, could I?"

"Why the devil you attach all that importance to a greasy, stinking old—" The word "Jew" did not actually leave his lips.

"You know why. That's one of the things I've always liked about you; one says a thing once to you, and you understand it. One doesn't have to repeat it over and over again. Like—like—" She too checked a name just as it was about to leave her lips.

"Elsie!" he appealed to her suddenly. "Are you absolutely dead-set on it? If I ask you, to please me—" He looked very appealing when he handed himself over to you like that, lock, stock, and barrel. "Look here, aren't there any of your Jew friends in Berlin we could do something for? Get them out of the country, help them to take a good whack of their money with them . . . you know, there are ways and means. . . ."

She looked at him coldly.

"I am not prepared to make a bargain for Mr. Emmanuel's head."

The inconceivable impertinence suddenly struck him like a blow in the face.

"*You* are not prepared, eh? *You* are not prepared? Who are *you* to talk of making bargains, or refusing them?" The depressions between the broken ridges of his eyebrows grew white, as they always did when he was very angry.

"If you are going to shout at me," she said quietly, "I am going to ask you to go home."

"And suppose I refuse to?" His fist clenched and unclenched on his knees.

She shrugged her shoulders. "Then I suppose you stay."

"I suppose you know what I could do with you if I just lifted my little finger?" His eyes were quite bloodshot as he glared at her.

"But, my dear," she said, "my dear. Of course I know. You can send me to a concentration camp. Well?"

"That would be one way out of it!"

"Would it?"

"What do you mean—would it?" The situation was becoming slightly ridiculous.

"You'd get yourself made Governor," she hazarded, "so that you could see me now and again."

"I'd get myself made Governor, eh?" he blustered. Then suddenly he snapped. He felt he couldn't go on with it a moment longer.

"Get me a drink, Elsie!" He sighed deeply.

"No, darling, get *me* one!"

He rose and lumbered over to the little sideboard.

"I'll see if I have any news for you in a week." He kept his head turned away from her. "My God, it's going to be a hard job! What will you drink, Elsie?"

"Danziger Goldwasser!" she said. "All those little gold leaves! *So* pretty!"

VI

There was no news for her in a week, nor in two weeks. It turned out to be a very prolonged tussle.

He came to her one night in early June.

"Take hold of this, Elsie!" He held his head between his hands, and shook it from side to side. "Is it still firm?"

She in her turn took his head between her hands.

"Yes, it's firm!" she decided.

"I'm lucky!" he told her.

"Well?"

He said nothing. He merely looked at her downwards and sideways out of the corners of his eyes, smiling faintly.

"Well?" she repeated.

It seemed to her that her heart had stopped beating. He did not play the fool in this way unless he had something of great import to tell her.

"It very nearly cost me this!" he said. Once more he was balancing his head upon his hands, the fingers along the cheekbones, the thumbs in the hollow of the neck. "But it's all right!" he went on. "He'll be out in two or three days; a week at most." He stopped. He saw the colour fade out of her cheeks.

"Are you sure?" she whispered.

He shrugged his shoulders. "He's sent through instructions himself!" There was no need to ask, or to tell, who "he" was. He saw the colour sweep into her cheeks again.

"Have I been good?" he asked.

"Good!" she cried. "Good!" She threw her arms round his neck and brought his mouth down to hers. "Kiss me!" she bade. "Kiss me! My love! My darling! My big black bear!"

13

I

MR. EMMANUEL sat on the edge of his bed, his hands upon his knees. His eyes stared straight before him, but there seemed no vision in them. His pince-nez dangled loosely over his unbuttoned shirt. It was queer how they had survived so much misadventure. But it almost seemed they had outlived their value. Those eyes did not seem as if it would interest them ever again to have their vision rectified. He had been sitting there, on the edge of the bed, one hour already that morning; or it might have been two. He would go on sitting there another hour, and another hour after that. He had not washed that morning, or the day before, or the day before. There was no heart in him.

He heard feet go to and fro along the corridor. He heard and did not hear. They had no message for him. Feet stopped at the door of his cell. The slat over the spy-hole was lifted and fell into place again. The bolt on the outside was shot back. A key found the key-hole and turned in it slowly, once and once again. The door swung open. He did not turn his head.

"Get up, Jew!" a voice bade, the warder's voice. He had heard it often enough before.

Mr. Emmanuel rose obediently to his feet.

The warder said nothing for some moments. He seemed to be studying the situation with more attention than usual.

"Wash yourself!" he commanded.

Mr. Emmanuel covered the few feet between the bed and the sink. It seemed a lot further than that. He took up the chunk of coarse soap he found there, turned the tap, and rubbed the soap upon his hands. It made next to no lather. Then he cupped his hands and stroked his face with them. He fumbled around for his towel, but it had slipped out of reach somewhere. He drew his sleeve feebly across his face.

"Collect your things!"

He collected his things. He moved so feebly, he took quite a long time about it, though there was little to collect.

"Get moving!" the warder rasped. "We've not got all day!"

It hardly occurred to Mr. Emmanuel to speculate why they had asked him to wash himself, to collect his things. A change of cell perhaps. A change of cell. The thought came and went dimly through his head. He shut the clasps of the attaché-case. They used to be so bright, once. They were like lead now. A pity about the attaché-case. They would certainly not throw it away, he said to himself. The thought was like a mosquito whining in his head. Such a good attaché-case, real leather, with chromium clasps and hinges. So English.

"Nothing else?"

Oh, yes. The coat and hat. He might as well take them with him. A change of cell? Another dim thought rose and condensed in his brain. Perhaps not a change of cell.

Perhaps they were taking him to the court-house. For the trial. It had been long enough in coming.

The warder gave him a shove.

"*'Raus!*"

He followed the warder along the corridor, and down the stairs, along another corridor, along another corridor. So many corridors in these prisons. Like in the Doomington Town Hall. He had once gone to make a complaint to the Chief Gas Office. Was it the Chief Gas Office? He could not remember now. Such a long time ago. So many corridors, such long ones.

They had come to a stop outside a door. Very handsome door. Oh, yes, he recognized it. The Governor's door. On a wooden plaque, the one word:

GEFÄNGNISINTENDANT

The warder knocked and entered. Mr. Emmanuel followed. The anteroom. He had been here before two or three times. More than that? Perhaps more than that. A warder came through. *Heil Hitler.* Then through the second door. The Governor. The Governor himself. Greater than God, greater than Hitler. Visitors or no visitors, exercise or no exercise, soap or no soap.

The Governor looked up.

"Emmanuel!"

It was not a question. It was a statement of fact. Yes, Emmanuel.

"I have some important news for you."

Important news? For him? There could for him be no important news.

"I have to inform you that I have received orders to release you. You are a free man. Your case has been dismissed."

It was as if he had been walking along a river-bank and someone had suddenly pushed him into the river, and it was very deep, and the top of the water was high, high over his head. He could not breathe; he could only swallow the green water with which his lungs were filled already. His ear-drums were bursting. He caught at his neck for breath.

He had come up to the top again. He gulped a mouthful of sharp air, choking.

The Governor was continuing. Something about one clear day to get out of here. Do you understand? One clear day to get out. If you are found still loitering about . . . He was not walking along a river-bank. He was walking along a road with trams. Begley Hill Road. Clang! Clang! Clang! Clang! Clang! Time and time again the tram-driver brought his feet down on the gong. Clang! Clang! Clang! Clang! Clang! He could not hear a word the *Herr Gefängnisintendant* was saying. What? . . . loitering around here, you will be immediately arrested. . . . You will receive no second chance. . . . Passport returned. . . . Go back to place you were staying at . . . received instructions . . . sign form . . . sign form . . .

"Don't you hear?" the man's voice soared high above the tram-gongs on the Begley Hill Road. "After you have signed this form!"

Mr. Emmanuel found a pen in his hand and a form under it. A finger pointed out a place for him to sign. The pen moved, making his signature. He was being shoved out of the room again, towards the anteroom. A sudden hideous suspicion swooped down on him like a vulture out of the turbulent sky. It was a joke, a trick. Like that lawyer at Schloss Kastanienburg trying to get him to sign himself away. What dreadful surrender had he put his hand to? He turned again towards the Governor, his mouth foaming with accusations. The Governor was no longer aware of him, any more than of the planks in the floor. He was screwing his eye-glass tighter in his eye. He had his face close down towards the papers.

It was no joke, no trick at all. They kept him waiting for another half-hour while they collected for him the things he had not been allowed to have in his cell. His pocket-knife, a batch of letters. His wallet with his photographs. His money. His passport, above all, his passport. A man had specially come over with it from Police Headquarters in the Alexander Platz. There was some more signing of forms, everything very meticulous. Then they led him to the gate of the prison. There was an unbarring, unbolting, unlocking. The lesser gate in the big gate swung hoarsely on its hinges. A small oblong hole opened out into Freedom. He stood there, his back arched, as if he did not want to go. They pushed him through. He was out beyond. The lesser gate in the big gate clanged to against Moabit.

There was too much world, it was too big, he was frightened. He was very weak, too; he could hardly drag one foot after the other. You would not think a little attaché-case could be so heavy. Had they put stones in it? For twenty or thirty yards he clung to the shelter of the great wall. A bell tinkled, a boy charged down on a bicycle, a basket slung over the handlebars. He laughed aloud. Of course there were bicycles still! How strange, he had forgotten all about bicycles!

A young man in a buttoned sweater and a cloth cap went past him, his hands in his pockets. He did not seem to see Mr. Emmanuel, as if Mr. Emmanuel were a ghost invisible in the daylight.

Am I so thin? asked Mr. Emmanuel. Is there so little of me?

A woman passed by. She went within a couple of feet of him. She, too, seemed to see no Mr. Emmanuel at all.

He saw himself suddenly with their eyes, shaggy, unkempt, ashen-cheeked, hollow-eyed.

"No wonder they are not seeing me," he murmured. "Twenty yards from that gate, too."

He heard a car coming up from behind him; then it slowed down. Then it crawled forward slowly, hugging the side of the pavement. Yes, it was a taxi, looking rather self-conscious about the job of scrounging for released jail-birds.

Mr. Emmanuel lifted his hand. The man saw the movement in his mirror. The taxi stopped. It seemed quite a long time before the fare got so far as the taxi-door.

"Where to?" the driver asked.

"Bambergerstrasse," replies Mr. Emmanuel. "Number 38." He felt quite proud of himself to have an address to give so straight off the mark. He got in and placed the attaché-case on the seat beside him. The taxi jolted forward. He whinnied incredulously. I am free! I am free! If I wanted to tell the driver to take me to the Nollendorf Platz, he would take me to the Nollendorf Platz. If I wanted to tell the driver to take me to the Motzstrasse . . .

His mind drew back cautiously, like the exploring antennæ of an insect. It was not ready yet for the Motzstrasse.

If I wanted to tell the driver to take me to the Rankestrasse, he would take me to the Rankestrasse. If I wanted to tell the driver to take me to the Kochstrasse, he would take me to the Kochstrasse. What nonsense you are talking! Try and talk sensible. In this street here there are more people. How clean they look, all of them! They have all washed themselves today, and yesterday also. He noted how men had white handkerchiefs in breast-pockets. How beautiful women were, with trim frocks and bright hats! Here were two children, a boy and a girl, walking solemnly hand in hand! Do you think they might be twins? How beautiful children are, and those leaves on those trees! Look, how open the leaves are! What? Is it nearly summer?

They were crossing the water now; now they had crossed it. There was a roundabout of greenness. The taxi had to slow down, and a youth—he looked, like a student, he had books under his arm—chanced to look in at the window. . . . An instant later he was looking elsewhere, as if he had intruded upon something not meant for his eyes.

Mr. Emmanuel thrust himself back as far as possible out of eyeshot. Did you see that clean collar? he asked himself. He looked down on his own begrimed shirt, his grease-spattered suit. No wonder, he murmured, he looks the other way.

They were in the big streets now, the cafés, the cinemas, chromium lettering, plate glass. There is a shop, all full of flowers it is, from floor to ceiling. How funny a man should want to *sell* flowers! If I were that man, I would want to keep them in my own cell.

What am I talking about, cell?

I am free! Do you know that? I am free! If I had not

said the Bambergerstrasse, he would not have taken me to the Bambergerstrasse. If, for instance, I would have said . . . He hunted about for the name of another street for a moment or two, but his head was aching like anything. I think I know this street, he roused himself suddenly. Yes, it is. It *is* the Bambergerstrasse. This is number 38. Here, driver, here. He had a moment's panic lest the driver should take him by mistake to another street, another house, to faces he did not know, and he would have to explain this thing, that thing. . . .

It is not going to be too nice at the Pension Kahn, either, he decided lugubriously.

He paid the taxi and entered the vestibule. There was no movement of curtains in the porter's little window. Let him be there, let him not be there, what do I mind? I have to inform you that I have received orders to release you. You are a free man. Your case has been dismissed. Do you know who said that? The Governor said that, the Governor himself. He was climbing up the stairs now; it was a very laborious business. Let anybody try and interfere with me, that's all. They put me in Schloss Kastanienburg and beat me with lead pipes and starved me, but they could not make me say I was guilty from anything. He stopped and drew breath on the landing. A reaction of gloom and rancour was setting in, after the blinding miracle of deliverance. They kept me for months in Moabit, and all the big lawyers in Berlin tried to make a case against me. . . .

He was half-way up the second flight when another thought cut across that one. And poor ex-Professor Sachs, they had against him such a strong case? And that prevented them from cutting off his head? What is to prevent them doing anything, when they can do everything? They can make a forgery from signatures, they can write whole letters for you, they can have hundreds of men swearing false witness. Is it a wonder with poor ex-Professer Sachs? . . . Oh, but he is a German! You are an Englishman, Isaac! And what benefit was it to you you were an Englishman? Your name was in all the papers. You were a question in Parliament. Did the English consul get through to see you, to give you an advice? Week after week you wrote letters. Did they get there because they had the consul's name on the envelope?

He had at last reached the landing of Frau Kahn's pension. He had not remembered it was so many stairs up. He had his finger on the bell-push, when once more a new thought came up from a new direction and held him motionless.

If it was not merely because he was an innocent man they had freed him; if consuls and lawyers had not succeeded in getting through to him . . . how was it he stood here, a free man who had to come to pick up his things and go back to his own country? How was it? How was it? He shook his head hard as if it were a puzzle-box and by shaking it he might get the answer to run into its proper place. But everything was confused. How his head ached! How dirty my finger-nails are! The dirt is in the lines of my hands like traced by a lead pencil. The first thing is a bath, and a shave, and a clean shirt. Oi, a nice glass of hot tea with lemon! With two lumps of sugar!

He rang the bell so long and hard, you might have thought he was a police officer. It was very queer how hollow the sound of it was, as if the whole place was empty.

II

It was Trude, the Jewish maid-of-all-work, who opened the door, a full minute later.

"Guten Tag," she said, with the suspicion of a bow, as if some great personage had come to call. But her face was very pale, and her lips not at all steady.

"Guten Tag, Trude. Is Frau Kahn in?"

"Very sorry. Frau Kahn is out."

"Is Herr Kahn in?"

"Very sorry. Herr Kahn is out."

"All right, Trude," Mr. Emmanuel said crossly. "Let me in. I'm not going to eat you."

"Oh, no, Herr Emmanuel, no. Your things are ready for you. They are just round the door there."

He entered and closed the door behind him.

"You knew I was coming, then?"

"Oh, yes, Herr Emmanuel, a . . . a man came and told us."

"Very well, then." He turned round the angle of the passage, where he saw his bag ready-packed against the wall. "I'll want a hot bath, Trude, first thing. Take that bag into some room somewhere."

"Oh, Mr. Emmanuel, a hot bath . . . I am not sure. . . . It would not be at all convenient. Frau Kahn said . . ."

He turned on her quite angrily.

"I don't care a fig what Frau Kahn said. You've had your instructions, haven't you? Do you want to get yourself into a bundle of trouble? Take that bag!"

He listened, astonished, to his own voice, ordering, hectoring. Like a warder! He would show them, he would show everybody, locking up an innocent old man for months and months! How many months has an old man got left in his life altogether?

"Would you like to go into the same room, Herr Emmanuel?" Trude was asking. Her voice was almost inaudible.

"Why not? Was there anything wrong with the room?"

She opened the door and put the bag down.

"How long would it be for, Herr Emmanuel?"

"I don't know. For a few hours. I'll tell you later! Trude!" His voice was kinder now. "Trude!"

"Yes, Herr Emmanuel?"

"While you are heating up the bath, will you make me a glass of tea with lemon? With two lumps of sugar?"

He saw a tear brim in the corner of her eye.

"Yes, certainly, Herr Emmanuel," she gulped. "At once!"

"A nice little woman!" he sighed. "But what is she so frightened of me for? What are they all so frightened of me for? Are they all in their rooms, shivering? Have they all gone out? You fools! You fools!" he shouted, and shook his fist. "I'm free! They've let me go!" And once more the mysterious question rose and curved over him like a wave. "What for? Who?" He sat down, or fell rather, into a great plush chair beside him. "I will feel better soon. A glass of tea, a bath, a clean shirt. Thank God I have another suit with me." He looked down with distaste at the one he was wearing. "What shall I do with this one? I will leave it here. It will be Frau Kahn's business."

Trude came in with the tea. There was a plateful of cakes too, garnished with chopped nuts. Would you believe it? Like my Slatta used to make them, the very same way!

"Thank you, Trude! You are a nice girl! It was not tea with lemon over there, Trude!"

"No, Herr Emmanuel!" Her mouth was working quite dangerously. "The bath will not be long, Herr Emmanuel!" She turned and ran from the room.

A pity Frau Kahn has not got a heart like that girl! A real good girl, I call her, with a heart! Well, what should I care for Frau Kahn! An hour or two, it depends upon the trains, I shall be saying good-bye to Frau Kahn, Pension Kahn, Bambergerstrasse, Motzstrasse. . . .

Once more it was like something lodged in his body, and if he bent a certain way, he could feel the point of the thing sticking into the lining of the lungs.

"I had some of that nice green hair oil in my bag," he remembered. "A whole bottle, not opened yet. Such a smell, like violets!"

He drained his glass of tea with delicate suckings through the cube of sugar planted between his teeth. He had several teeth fewer than before he went to prison; the performance was a little more difficult than it had once been. He ate a cake or two. Like snow-flakes melting on the tongue. No, Slatta herself would not have been ashamed to make cakes like these.

The door opened.

"Bath ready, Mr. Emmanuel!" said Trude, her face dimmed with steam. "You will find everything there!"

He beamed at her.

"Good girl, Trude. I will just take out my dressing-gown. It must be in here. A good thing I did not take it away, eh?"

She came forward and opened the big bag for him. The dressing-gown was lying on top.

"Here, Mr. Emmanuel!"

It was almost more than he could bear. He patted awkwardly her bun of greying hair.

"Good girl, Trude." He dropped the dressing-gown over his arm. "Thank you. Happiness should some day come to you, after all this." He made a comprehensive gesture, in which he included not only himself but Herr Hitler and all his associates. Then he turned and shuffled off out of the door and along the passage to the bathroom.

He bathed. He did not know how long he stayed in the bath, but he found it so difficult to get out, that for the first time the thought of time gave a tug of alarm at his heart-strings. You haven't all day, he told himself. Oh, yes, I *have* all day, that's just what I have. All day to clear out, you mean. But the point is: clear out of where? Anyhow, not out of the bath, that's certain. Don't be so foolish, Isaac! Clear out of where, then? Clear out of Berlin? Clear out of Germany? When do the trains go? You can gain time by going from the Zoo station, that's one thing. But there will not be trains every hour, like going to Southport. Oh, Trude will tell you the times of the trains. Did you have so many baths the last few months you should not enjoy this one? Besides, it takes a long time to get clean when you are in a state like this. You must be clean, above everything . . . you must leave it all behind you.

He got out of the bath at last, dried himself, and determined to leave every stitch of his prison clothing behind him in the bathroom, except for one or two oddments in the pocket. Frau Kahn should worry! She could burn it all!

He turned to his room and found that Trude had put everything out for him fresh and clean, fresh socks, fresh shirt and shorts, everything, including his other suit. He dressed. He looked at himself incredulously in the mirror of the wardrobe. Like a tailor's dummy from a high-class tailor, he told himself. Just one thing was missing, a handkerchief, here in the breast-pocket. Hadn't he brought that silk one with him, the one that Ada Hummel's boy Leo had given him for a going-away present?

He bent down and fished in his suitcase, and his fingers came up against a cardboard packet. What, a packet? Cigarettes, maybe. All along he had known something was missing, but he had so got out of the habit of smoking he could not give a name to it. He brought out the packet. Would you believe it? Gold Flakes! A whole packet of twenty; he had not opened them; he had left them there against a rainy day. English cigarettes!

"I might as well be home already!" he cried aloud. "I must find Bruno's cigarette holder—"

Then he stopped. For in that instant he realized what that thing was that was lodged in his body, and if he bent a certain way, he could feel the point of the thing sticking into him.

The packet dropped from his fingers. He fell down upon his knees, with his face among the spare shirts and socks in the suitcase.

"I cannot go home!" he whispered. "I cannot go home to Bruno without news of his mother, without any news at all. I cannot go home as if I had never come here, and made him hope. If only I could tell him whether she is alive or dead . . . it is that uncertainty that is killing him. I cannot face him with no news at all. I cannot, I will not, go home!"

He lay for a long time there. Then at last he raised himself and sat down again in the huge plush chair.

How quiet it is in this house! Is there no one in it,

not a soul? Is there no one who can tell me where Bruno's mother is? Is she dead? Is she alive? If she is dead, and he knows, he will empty his heart out, and slowly, slowly, it will fill up again. If she is alive, however bad it is, there is always hope. Was it so good with me, over in Moabit? Did it ever look like I should go about in taxis again, and put on clean shirts?

He bent forward, his elbows upon his thighs, his head in his hands.

If she is alive, and in prison, or in a concentration camp somewhere . . . You remember what wonderful ideas you had, back in England? You would talk to the high-up people, you would call on Governors, you would do this, you would do that. Oi, oi, Isaac, what a fool you were, eh? Perhaps she was under that same roof with me in Schloss Kastanienburg, how could *you* tell? And a fine use it would be somebody should go to those devils there and say: Please, you have a lady in there, she is the mother from a small boy in England. Let her out, please, or the small boy will die.

Fine ideas, yes, Isaac. If only she is alive, there is some hope still. If she is dead, she is dead. Who will tell me if she is dead or alive? You went so far and tried so hard, but you could not find her. You know where it took you to, looking for Bruno's mother? It does not matter. My life is nothing to me, if I have no news for him. My life is nothing to anybody, not to Bruno, or Rose, or Sam Silver, or my boy Max, the painter, or my boy Moisheh, the farmer, if I have no news. I am not worth anything. I am just an old man, a piece of potato-peel under the sink, a dark and useless nothing, if I have no news to give.

Who will give me news of Bruno's mother? Is she dead? Is she alive?

There was a knock at the door. He did not lift his head. After a long silence the door opened. It was Trude. She stood playing with her apron, squeezing it into her hand, letting it fall again.

"Please excuse, Herr Emmanuel. I was wondering about the trains. . . . I have been looking them up. There is one that goes in an hour and a half from now. It is a good train. . . ."

He lifted to her eyes so full of anguish she could not bear to look at them. She dropped her own eyes, and stood in the door there, screwing and unscrewing her apron.

"Go away! Please leave me!" said Mr. Emmanuel hollowly. She closed the door behind her.

Who will give me news of Bruno's mother? Is she dead? Is she alive? I cannot go back to Bruno without news of his mother. He sat there, his head upon his hands, for how long he did not know; it was as if a slow and cumbrous wheel revolved in the dark inward places of a water-mill. You could see nothing except the sheen of the slimy walls. You could hear nothing but the ceaseless drip, drip of the water, and the jerk and grunt of the mechanism as it jolted forward and upward and around again, upward and around again.

And then, in the nadir of his extreme despair, a name designed itself upon the blackness . . . a name pricked out in electric globes, as it were, round the rim of the glass marquee of a theatre.

Elsie Silver . . . Elsie Silver . . . the light in the globes went on, went off, went on again.

The moment has come, he said to himself. I must ask help at last from the daughter of my old friend. There is no one else in this town, or in this land, who can help me. She is a big lady here. A big man is her lover. I must ask help from Elsie Silver.

"God will forgive me!" he cried aloud. "It is not for myself! It is for another one!"

But for a long time the woman's name, so far from liberating him from the deadly lethargy into which he had fallen, seemed rather a spell cast upon him to bind him still more firmly to the chair he sat in. His trunk and limbs were like lead. His head, too, seemed like a stone thing, too heavy for the thin neck that bore it.

The day is going by. It is after midday now. One clear day to get out . . . if you are found still loitering around . . . Elsie Silver . . . the daughter of my old friend . . . I must go to Elsie Silver. . . . Where is Elsie Silver? Who will tell me where Elsie Silver is? Who will *dare* tell me where Elsie Silver is? It was suddenly as if he felt a cold blade at his ribs. Who will *dare* tell me where Elsie Silver is? Do you remember when once you mentioned her name—not even so much as that, you just made the shape of it with your mouth—do you remember how they hit you and your mouth bled, and the teeth came from it? How can I find out where Elsie Silver is? You fool! he said to himself, striking his forehead with his fist. How do you find out where anybody is? You look it up in the telephone book! Fancy not thinking of that before.

With enormous effort he raised himself from his chair and walked across to the door of the room. One-two-three-four-five-six . . . what a long way it is . . . seven-eight. There is a handle on this door. There is no handle on doors in prison. What a difference it makes, handles on doors. He turned the handle and stepped into the passage. The telephone was only a few feet further along, on a ledge, the telephone books on a small table beside it. Look up the name of Elsie Silver! See? Could anything be more simple! He turned the pages of the book with trembling fingers: P, Q, R, S. But even as he did so, with ashen certainty he realized the idiocy of expecting the name of such a person as Elsie Silver to be available alongside of any Herr Strumpff or Fräulein Schmidt in the pages of a public book.

He had attained now the Si's. His eye went mechanically down the Sil's from line to line. There were one or two Silvers, but they were not Elsie Silver; of course they were not. He shut the book and turned away, his eyes smarting. He shuffled back towards his own room, not lifting his feet from the ground at all. How shall I find Elsie Silver? Who will take me to Elsie Silver? The lines tinkled thinly in his head like a child's music-box.

He had his hand on the door-handle of his room when suddenly the telephone bell went, jangling harshly in the confined space.

How can you mock me? his heart cried; an old man who has done no one any harm? The bell jingle-jangled under its dome, like a live thing trying to get out of a box. It is so loud, it would awaken a dead man. Why does no one come? No one is here, that's why. They are all frightened. They are not even in the house. Trude is in the house. Why does not Trude come to answer it? Even Trude is frightened. She is hiding from the telephone in the kitchen. No one will answer the telephone in this house till I have gone out of it.

Still he stood there, muttering, his hand on the door-handle. Still the telephone bell leapt and spluttered.

Well, I will myself answer it. Such a headache it will give me. Can it bite me? I will tell them no one is at home.

He went back to the instrument and removed the receiver.

"Hallo, ja?" he cried.

"Bitte," a woman's voice said. *"Ist Herr Emmanuel noch zu Hause? Ich möchte Herrn Emmanuel sprechen.* Is Mr. Emmanuel still there? I want to speak to Mr. Emmanuel."

"What do you want of Mr. Emmanuel?" he asked, still in German. But it was, of course, not a native's voice or accent.

There was a pause, then the voice came back, this time in English.

"You are Mr. Emmanuel?" The voice did not wait for a reply. "Why have you not gone? Why are you still there?"

"Who are you?" Mr. Emmanuel cried. But he too knew the answer to his question even as he phrased it, with a sudden lightning flash before the eyes, and a sudden loud noise in the ears. "Aren't you—?"

But the voice broke in before he could say more.

"Be quiet! Have some sense!"

"It is you! It can be no one else! Why have you done all this?"

"Be quiet! I have done nothing. Why haven't you gone yet?"

"Listen!" he said slowly. "I cannot go! It is impossible! Are you listening?"

"Yes, I'm listening."

"I have come here to find out what has happened to

the mother of a small boy from Berlin; he is now in England."

"Yes. I know. I have been told."

"I will not go back to England, if I have not news to give him."

"Are you mad? Time is getting very short!"

"I wanted to ask your help! You are there! You have come to me! It is a miracle! Will you help me? Is she alive? Is she dead? I must find out that before I can go!"

There was no sound at the other end of the telephone. Minute upon minute passed—it seemed so long as that to him. No one was there any more. It was impossible anyone should still be there.

"Are you still there?" he called out in alarm.

"I am still here."

"Yes? Well? Tell me!"

"I am getting a pencil. Stay there. What is the woman's name? What was her last known address?"

"Hertha Rosenheim. Motzstrasse, 65."

"If I can find out, I can find out quickly. If I cannot find out quickly, I cannot find out at all."

"If you try, it is enough. I cannot hope for more."

"In one hour from now, you will be . . . let it be near where you are now . . . where you just said. A big black car will draw up. As it draws up, take your hat off your head, and he will know it is you. The driver will give you a piece of paper. It will have something on it . . . or nothing. Destroy it at once. Good-bye."

"Good-bye, and God should bless you!" he returned; but the receiver had already been replaced at the other end.

III

Mr. Emmanuel went back into his room and closed the door behind him. Then he stood there for several moments, leaning against the panels.

Why? Why? Why? he asked himself, striking his temples with his fists. Why did she do it? Why did she get me out of prison, when all the rest of the world could not help me? Why? Why? I was no friend to her. I hardly ever spoke to her. Was it because of her father, because he and I have been friends for so many years? But that is foolishness! Does she love her father so much? No, Isaac, she does not. If she loved him, she would have spared him that scandal, that terrible, terrible scandal which is making so bitter his last years.

Why? For God's sake, why? It is because . . . oh, no, it cannot be! . . . Is it because somewhere deep down inside her she has a bit of a Jewish heart, after all? There you go again, Isaac. Such an old fool like you are! Of everybody he thinks good! Haven't you learned a lesson by now?

Well? If not, why? Answer me that! There is no other explanation why, Isaac! Perhaps she is not so coal-black like she is painted. No human being ever knows everything that is in another human being's heart. Perhaps some day you will learn something about that woman, it will surprise you. It will surprise everybody. Perhaps, please God, I am not a fool! Perhaps also, please God, I am! I am like God made me!

He walked over to his two bags and began to get things straight. There was not much to do. One way or another he had got a good deal less to take away than he had come with.

Suddenly his heart stopped dead. You are not understanding what has happened, he told himself. I will perhaps, after all, find out what I have come to find out. I will perhaps have news for Bruno. It is a miracle from God! Only this morning you were sitting there on your bottom, thinking . . . what were you thinking? Nothing. You were like a lump of wood, a stone mummy, not like a human being at all. You should be ashamed of yourself, Isaac Emmanuel, losing hope like that! While there is wind in the windpipe no man should lose hope! It should teach you a lesson.

And if, after all, she is in a concentration camp, somewhere at the other end of Germany? Better to know something than nothing! It is better also, please God, she should be dead. What? Why should you say a thing like that? Did it look so hopeful for you only a few hours ago? And now you are a free man. Be patient, Isaac; in an hour you will know. No, not an hour, fifty minutes. I must be careful with the time. Thank God, I have still got my nice watch.

Elsie Silver! He was back to Elsie Silver again. Would you believe it? For years she has been the fancy woman of that terrible enemy of Israel, and now she acts like from God, one of His angels! Why? What for? Why? What for? He realized that was getting him nowhere, except to a great swindling in the head. He went over to the door and pressed the bell-push. It would be a good thing to find out about the next train, he told himself. What *did* the Governor say? Have I got a whole day to clear out from Berlin, or a whole day to clear out across the frontier? And what does he mean a whole day? Does he mean twelve hours? Does he mean twenty-four? You should listen properly when a man is saying important things like that. Listen! he says. Listen! When the whole head is full with fire-engines. . . .

"Ja, bitte sehr?" Trude was at the door. She was not out, after all.

"You have a time-table, please, Trude?"

"Ja, bitte sehr!"

"Then find out the time of the next train for Flushing . . . if there is one in two hours, maybe a little more."

"Ja, bitte sehr!"

The words, this time, seemed to have more life to them.

Poor Trude! Poor Frau Kahn! I have been painful in the neck to them all, like they say. Ah, well! he sighed. For me, too, it has not been a cakewalk.

Trude came back a minute or two later. There was a good train, she told him, at nineteen hours ten minutes. Thank you, please God, that will do fine, he said. She turned to go.

"No, stop a moment!" he called out after her.

She turned.

"Ja, bitte sehr?" she asked.

"It is not kind of you, Trude," he said, "you should *ja, bitte sehr* me like that. Tell me, Trude, you do not think I am a bad man?"

"No, God forbid!" she assured him, the colour coming up in her cheeks.

"Well, why do you treat me like you are frightened of me?"

She looked round before she spoke. Then, under her breath, she said:

"It is not you we are frightened of, Herr Emmanuel!" She dropped her eyes, as if she were ashamed.

"Are you frightened of that terrible old woman you had here—what was her name, Kati?"

"No, Herr Emmanuel. She has gone. One day, thank God, she did not come, and she has not come since."

"Ah, well. I suppose I know what you are frightened of. You know why they have all run away. Don't be frightened, Trude. No harm can come to you. They tried hard, but they could find nothing against me, so they have let me go."

"We all knew it was"—she dropped her voice again—"it was *Blödsinn,* nonsense! But it does not matter to those people! Nothing matters to them!"

"So you read all about me in the papers, eh?" He could not help feeling a slight thrill of pride. "Did it ever say what I really came to this country for?"

"No, not a word about that. Only that you were . . . a communist and a spy and a murderer."

"But you knew what I came for, Trude?"

"We all knew here. You made of it no secret, Herr Emmanuel."

"That is so," he murmured, "that is so. I know you would not have bad thoughts of me." (I have said enough. I must say no more, not even to this nice woman.) "Well, I am glad that old Kati is gone. It must feel happier in this place without her."

"Yes, Mr. Emmanuel." She hesitated a moment, then went.

There were still twenty minutes to get through, here in the house. No, not twenty, twenty-five. It is better not to go walking up and down the Motzstrasse. You have maybe done enough walking up and down the Motzstrasse. He smiled at the grim thought. An hour, Elsie Silver asked for, one single hour. She has a lot to do in a single hour. But perhaps it is easy, if these police people will only answer questions, it is easy to find out. You remember when you went to that police station at the Nollendorfstrasse? You remember the policeman took out a card? It was all written down there on that card, I suppose. But they didn't like an old Jew, a foreigner, asking questions, so they did not answer.

But if Elsie Silver sends somebody to find out, some big man from one of her friends? Or perhaps it would be only a telephone call. Hertha Rosenheim, last address Motzstrasse, number 65, what information have you got?

He was walking up and down the room, up and down, in his effort to see into the situation. You fool! What are you walking up and down for like an animal? Are you still in Moabit? Oh, those Gold Flake cigarettes! he remembered suddenly. I have not smoked one as yet out of that packet. Well, anyhow, there were no Gold Flakes in Moabit. He stooped and hunted around for the grand cigarete holder that Bruno had given him as a going-away present. Yes, it was still there, thank God! He stuck a cigarette in it and smoked it. Then he smoked another.

He looked at his watch. It was time to go now.

He reached down his hat and coat from the antler-stand. "But they are not my clothes!" he cried. "They are someone else's!" God bless her heart! It was Trude, of course. She had been at work on them while he had been taking his bath. He put the garments on, and paused a moment before opening the door. He closed his eyes, and stood as in prayer, as he had done so often before the opened Ark in the synagogue at home, before the blank wall of his prison cell.

"Please God there should be news! For little Bruno's sake! Please God! Amen!"

He opened his eyes and went out into the passage.

"Trude!" he called out. "Trude!"

She was not far off. He took her cheeks between finger and thumb.

"You are a nice girl, Trude!" he said. "With a real Jewish heart!"

She made a ghost of a curtsy.

"Bitte sehr!" she protested.

"I will not be very long!" he said. "I may perhaps have some food while I am out! Then I will come back for my things!"

"Please to excuse," she murmured unhappily. "There is almost nothing in the house. I am so sorry——"

"Please, please!" He waved her excuses aside. "I will not be a trouble much longer. You have been a nice girl!"

She opened the door for him and he went out, down into the Bambergerstrasse, out into the Motzstrasse. Here was the corner of the Lutherstrasse, where poor ex-Professor Sachs . . . He hurried across the roadway, with a constriction at the heart. The poor old man, he murmured, the innocent old man, like a lamb, a baby. He had crossed the roadway. He was on the pavement of the Motzstrasse again. Not many yards ahead was number 65. Here they were happy once, Bruno and Bruno's mother and Bruno's father, long ago. And Jo, the white rabbit! I must not forget Jo, the greatest of all the world's rabbits. Do not slow down here, Isaac; there are still two or three minutes to go. Go up the street a bit, then come down slowly.

He went up the street, then turned and came down slowly. A taxi was coasting along the street. It was not to be a taxi. It was to be a big black car.

The taxi turned into the Lutherstrasse and disappeared.

Here now, here! A car, a big black car! My heart is

not beating! It is slowing down opposite number 65. Take your hat off, Isaac, or he will not know it is you! Take your hat off!

He took his hat off. The car braked. He hurried forward, and the chauffeur leaned outwards from his seat. A hand shot forward. Mr. Emmanuel's hand shot forward to meet it. The car got into gear again and in its turn disappeared into the Lutherstrasse.

Do not open your hand yet, Isaac. Not yet. Walk a bit. You also walk around the corner. O my God, Thou art my rock and my fortress! O my God, Thou art my rock and my fortress! O my God, Thou art my rock and my fortress!

He turned the corner and walked fifteen yards up the pavement of the Lutherstrasse. Then at last he opened his tightly clenched palm and unfolded the slip of paper with fingers that had gone quite cold and numb. The slip of paper was not blank. There were words on it. Thank God, oh, thank God, there are words on it! An address written in pencil, in capital letters. News! News of Bruno's mother!

HAMBURG, ALTONA,
WEBERSTRASSE, 14, ERSTER STOCK

No more. But something, everything! News! He repeated the address in his mind, once, twice, a third time. Then he closed his eyes and memorized it, exactly as it lay on the paper, till he knew it was as safely couched in his brain as his own name. Then, as he had been enjoined to, he destroyed the slip of paper. He tore it into minute shreds, crossed the road, walked up the street, walked down again, releasing the shreds of paper one after another, every five or ten yards.

Hamburg, Altona, Weberstrasse, 14, erster Stock. So she is not dead! Thank God! Thank God! Do you hear, Bruno? Do you hear? She is not dead. She is not in a concentration camp. She is in a house in Hamburg. Other people live in that house. She lives on the first floor. *Erster Stock.* Do you hear that?

He was walking down the street like a bridegroom, like an athlete who has won races, when he stopped suddenly. A question came blundering up at him. She is in a house, is she? Well, why does she not write to her son? He walked on. Perhaps she has not been long at that house? Perhaps, after all, she *has* been in a concentration camp for a long time. Then it may be Bruno has heard from her, after all, while I have been in prison? Well, what happened to the letters he sent her all those months and months? Why did they not come back to him? Did they keep them? Could she get no one to tell her small boy what had happened to her?

He halted in the street, leaned up against a wall, and took his head between his hands. The mysteries seemed to assail him on all hands like flying cockchafers. The whole air whizzed with them.

What happened to those letters he sent her to the Motzstrasse? How long has she been in the Weberstrasse? Did she write from there, and they did not send on her letters? Is she ill? Maybe she has gone mad, poor woman, her sorrows have gone to her brain? Well, why did not someone answer Bruno's letters and say she could not write?

Why? Why? Why? He continued his journey down the Motzstrasse past the corner of the Bambergerstrasse, as far as the Prager Platz.

The tram-gong began to clang in his head again. Your

case has been dismissed . . . one clear day to get out . . . If you are found still loitering around here, you will be immediately arrested.

But don't be foolish, *Herr Gefängnisintendant!* Don't you see I've *got* to find out, whatever happens to *me?* I've got to find out, don't you see that? I can't leave Bruno in the lurch, just now, at the very last moment, when I have found out that at the Weberstrasse, 14, erster Stock, in Hamburg, Altona . . .

"What?" he suddenly shouted, so loud that one or two pedestrians who had already been observing him with some curiosity, the muttering old man with sunken cheeks and hollow eyes, were now quite convinced he was stark mad; and, guessing what sort of treatment it must have been to make him so, they hurried away, shuddering. *"What?* But I can go home from Hamburg! I can take a boat from Hamburg! I can go first to Altona, Weberstrasse, 14, and find out all I can! Then I can go home to Bruno! I shall have news!

"Thank You, God, thank You!" He had picked up his feet and was running as fast as his frail sticks would carry him, back towards the Bambergerstrasse and the Pension Kahn. "If I can get a boat tonight, well and good. I will find out from the information bureau as soon as I get to Hamburg station. If I cannot get one, and I am stopping too long in this country, well, let them lock me up again. I am going to Hamburg, to Altona! Just a little patience, Bruno! There will be news for you!"

He managed somehow to get to the top of the stairs. He rang. Trude opened for him.

"Quick, Trude, quick! Please, my bags. I am taking

an earlier train! Will you be a good girl, Trude, and help me I should get a taxi?"

"But, Herr Emmanuel, have you had anything to eat? And there *is* no earlier train!"

"I am going home by boat from Hamburg. I want to get to the station as soon as possible! What do I owe Frau Kahn, please? Tell her how sorry I am I have been such a nuisance! Quick, quick, Trude! I have no time to waste!"

He was in a taxi five minutes later, speeding out towards the Lehrter Bahnhof.

14

HE was in luck. He only had some fifteen or twenty minutes to wait before the departure of the afternoon streamline express. He got into the carriage and collapsed; perhaps his luck held there, too. If he had to give out, it was better it should happen in the railway-carriage, where there was a chance to recover and time to do it in; better than later, when there might be more call than he guessed for the shreds of endurance and vitality that were left to him.

There was a kind man in the carriage, blue-eyed and blond enough to be Wotan's own son-in-law. The kind man gave Mr. Emmanuel a nip of brandy out of a flask he had in his pocket and, when he had come round, saw to it that the waiter brought him a couple of sandwiches and a pot of coffee, as soon as he was ready for them. He insisted they should be egg sandwiches, too. He seemed to be thoroughly aware that Mr. Emmanuel was not one of his kinsmen in Wotan.

I am glad that this journey has begun and ended with kindness—if it is true that this is the end of the journey. (So Mr. Emmanuel communed with himself.) There was a kind woman in the train coming to Berlin. There is a kind man in the train going from Berlin. Perhaps I am not such a big fool like people say I am! Perhaps there is a lot more kindness in the world than we can guess, even here, in Germany, with all the shouting and the beating and the badness.

Why, when even Elsie Silver . . . But the return of his thoughts to Elsie Silver set all his nerves a-shudder again. The kind man with blue eyes looked up anxiously. He made a gesture towards the brandy-flask in his pocket.

"No, thank you, no!" the brown eyes of Mr. Emmanuel smiled. The blue eyes smiled back. The blue and brown eyes met across the dreadful abyss.

He was so nice and tired, it was so comfortable in that train, it seemed no time at all before they had arrived in Hamburg.

"Excuse me, please," said Mr. Emmanuel to the kind man. "Is it far from here, Altona?"

"Have you a lot of time to spare?"

"No, not much."

"Oh, I should take a taxi if I were you."

"Thank you, thank you. I was afraid it would be to take another train."

"No," the man smiled. "You're feeling all right now?"

"Fine, fine!" On a sudden impulse he reached forth his hand. "Thank you very much! You have made me happy!"

The other gave his hand warmly. Then he looked round to make sure no one heard him.

"Forgive us," he said, almost under his breath. "It is not all of us!" He picked up his bag and strode away.

"Where to?" asked a porter. "Luggage office?"

"Take me first to the information bureau! Then I will know!"

They went along to the bureau. He found out there

was a boat from Cuxhaven for Southampton that same night, as he had hoped. The boat-train left at eight-five.

"Perhaps, please God, I shall manage it," Mr. Emmanuel said to himself dizzily. "Like going round the corner for a packet of envelopes. A ticket for Southampton, please. *Southampton!* Two minutes from Rose! A ticket for Bruno, please! Thank you! How much?"

He turned to the porter.

"Yes, please, take my things to the luggage office. After that a taxi, please. Oh, one moment!" He felt in his pocket. Yes, of course, he had his wallet there, the wallet with the photographs. His little pile of letters was in the attaché-case. He opened it, and removed the letters he had received from Bruno while staying at the Pension Kahn. Perhaps, who knows? he mused. Perhaps there will be use for them. "Thank you! All right now!"

The porter put the things away and brought a taxi over.

"Where to?" the driver asked.

"Altona, please!"

"Where did you say?"

"Altona, please!"

"What part of Altona?"

Mr. Emmanuel swallowed hard. He hated giving up his secret, the secret it had cost him so many months and such sorrow to acquire. He hated giving it up even to the driver who must take him there.

"Weberstrasse," he whispered. "Number 14."

"Wha-at?" The driver put his hand round the back of his ear. The old bloke had a frog in his throat, or something.

Must I shout it out for all the people in Hamburg to hear? The man's deaf, that's what he is.

"Weberstrasse," he repeated, but his voice was only half a note louder.

"Oh, well, have it your own way!" The driver shrugged his shoulders and drove off.

Mr. Emmanuel leaned back in the taxi and shut his eyes. I don't want to see anything. I don't want to get excited. I must be quiet. I must be strong. In a few minutes I shall be there. In a few minutes I shall know something. After all this long time, after all I have been through. Perhaps I was not so wrong, after all, Bruno, in saying I might find out something for you. Don't be in such a hurry, Isaac. You don't know anything yet. Hold backward your horses. Why do my knees twitch like this, like a doctor was hitting them he should make my legs jump? No, lean back. Keep your eyes shut. That's right. Quiet, now, quiet. There, there. Now we have gone round a corner. Can I count one hundred slowly before we turn another corner? One hundred and six, one hundred and seven, one hundred and eight. There. We have turned another corner. Would you believe it? I reckoned the road out almost exactly before the next corner. I wonder how far I can count on this one before we turn. . . .

The taxi was slowing up. Yes, it was. He opened his eyes. A nice wide street, with trees, and strips of grass between the road and the pavement.

The driver screwed his head round.

"What number Weberstrasse did you say? You *did* say Weberstrasse?"

"Yes," replied Mr. Emmanuel faintly. "Yes. Number 14."

"Fourteen. Here we are, then. Thank you!"

The taxi stopped. Mr. Emmanuel got out. He was

afraid for a moment he would fall flat on his face, his feet refused so completely to support him.

"You are quite sure this is Weberstrasse? Quite sure?"

"Quite sure, old cock!"

"How much?" he quavered.

The driver told him. He handed over a note.

"No, no! No change! Thank you! Thank you!"

The chauffeur scratched his head. It was an enormous tip, a drunken tip. That's right! The old cove was drunk!

"Would you like me to wait for you, sir?"

"Go away! Go away! Do what you like!"

He turned and faced the house. The number 14 was painted on a gate-post, black letters in a white oval. It was a fine big house, old-fashioned, with a garden in front and behind. They were all big houses. Such a nice, quiet street, with trees in blossom everywhere. He turned to the house again.

Erster Stock. First floor. He swung the gate open and advanced along the flagged garden-path. There were three broad steps, with two big urns on the top one, standing on bases several feet high. Red flowers grew in the urns and hung like hair over their wavy rims.

What are you waiting for, Isaac Emmanuel? You want maybe a buttonhole?

He climbed the three steps and noted that in the right-hand lintel-post there were three bells, in descending order. Above each bell was a visiting-card in a frame. He bent forward and screwed up his eyes.

III. Dr. Ing. Paul Hüther
II. Emma Geigus
I. Karl Heinkes

He read the three names again. Dr. Ing. Paul Hüther. Emma Geigus. Karl Heinkes. But there was no Rosenheim there, no Frau Rosenheim, on the first or any other floor. But, you fool, what are you getting excited about? Perhaps it is some friend or relative she is staying with, this Karl Heinkes. Ring the bell. In ten seconds you will find out. Ring that bell, Isaac Emmanuel! What are you waiting for? You have perhaps not waited long enough?

He rang the bell. He heard it pealing a long way down the apartment somewhere. For fifteen seconds, twenty, he heard no other sound. A sudden panic beset him lest no one should be there; perhaps everybody had gone out for the day, including Bruno's mother, if she should be there. Why should she not be there? The paper had said Weberstrasse, 14. Perhaps this wasn't the Weberstrasse after all. Shall I ring again? Shall I go to the corner of the street to make sure?

At that moment he heard feet approaching down the passage.

Someone's coming! Control yourself, Isaac! They will think you are mad.

The door opened. A housemaid stood there, rather a fool of a housemaid she seemed, with a big slanting mouth and one shoulder higher than the other.

"Guten Tag!" said the housemaid. *"Sie wünschen?"*

"Please. Does Frau Rosenheim live here, Frau Hertha Rosenheim?"

"Who?"

"Frau Hertha Rosenheim!"

"No such person!" The housemaid began to shut the door.

"Please!" exclaimed Mr. Emmanuel, his voice rising

to a wail. "Please! There must be a Frau Rosenheim here. They told me so in Berlin! Very high-up people!"

The maid's lower lip began to jut forward sullenly. She advanced the door a few inches further.

"You can't do that, I tell you!" Mr. Emmanuel put his foot across the threshold. "I tell you I come from very high-up people! This *is* the Weberstrasse, isn't it?"

"Oh, yes, this *is* the Weberstrasse!" The girl seemed pleased to be able to see eye to eye on something with Mr. Emmanuel. "But no party by the name you speak of lives here. I can tell you that!"

At that moment there was the sound of a door opening in the wall just two or three feet behind the housemaid.

"Yes, yes, Lotte, who's that?" a voice called, quite a soft musical voice it was. There was the sound of slippers shuffling forward a pace or two. Then the face of a woman appeared above Lotte's shoulder, a pale face, not so much a face as a great disorderly cloud of golden hair.

Lotte turned.

"It's this old gentleman!" she exclaimed. "He's made a mistake. He's asking for a Frau Hertha Rosenheim."

The woman's face went ashen-grey. The fleshy lips began to quiver. She tried to speak, but could not.

He's made a mistake, the girl says. Oh, great God; oh, please, God in Heaven, let it be a mistake! Oh, God, why did you let me come out of Moabit, if I have not made a mistake?

That hair, which is not hair, but a gold cloud with silver and yellow in it! That voice, which is not a voice, but like a music-box playing! Why is her mouth going up and down, and no sound is coming from it, and that fright in her eyes, why is she so frightened of the name of Hertha Rosenheim?

Is it the ghost of your husband, Frau Rosenheim, you are so frightened of, or the ghost of your son?

"No," said Mr. Emmanuel. "I do not think there is any mistake." He spoke very quietly and with such melancholy as the wind has, in a field of dead men, after a battle. "Can I have a word with you, Frau Rosenheim?"

Lotte had moved a pace or two to one side. The woman stood more clearly revealed, an ample woman, fold upon fold of her, great hip and bosom, wrapped round in a green silk tea-gown. The light glistened in the caverns of her silver-yellow hair.

"I am not Frau Rosenheim!" The woman had found her tongue now. "There is no such person here!" How pasty her skin was, as if she never left this place from one week's end to another. She switched her eyes sideways towards where the maid stood dithering, then switched them round towards Mr. Emmanuel again. "I'm sure I don't know why you should make such a mistake." She made a movement as if to close the door. The conversation had been going on long enough.

This woman is frightened, Mr. Emmanuel told himself. It will not be hard to make a bluff with her. He had his foot in the door, he knew she could not close it in his face. He stared at her with profound consternation. It was not possible this woman could knowingly have let her son suffer such hells of anguish! It was not a bad face; it was a weak one, and a sensual one. How was it possible so poor a mass of femaleness could have mothered a boy so fine and taut as Bruno? Oh, surely, surely, it was, after all, a mistake. He would find out soon enough.

"I have a very important message for you!" he said. "I come straight from the office of a very important Government official!" That was no more than the exact truth.

She looked at him doubtfully. It is not likely, perhaps she was saying to herself, an old man like that can be a wandering confidence-man. If he tries any monkey-business, I can scream for police, or I can even myself manage him.

"I am Frau Heinkes!" she brought out. It seemed to be important to get that straight at all costs.

"I beg your pardon, Frau Heinkes! I am sorry! Can I come in now, please!"

She looked around miserably for one moment, as if there might still be a chance to get rid of this frightening old man. Then she gave in.

"Yes, of course. Why not? Come straight in here, please." She moved back a foot or two towards the door from which she had issued. "In fact you're the gentleman I was expecting, aren't you?" she added clumsily. There was a snigger from Lotte. That was too much even for her. She turned on the maid furiously. "What are you standing about for, like an ox on the mountain? Have you no work to do?"

Lotte turned, and shambled off, the one shoulder grotesquely higher than the other.

She has a fool here to look after her, Mr. Emmanuel noted. It is not for nothing. Why does she have a fool to look after her? The woman was holding the door open.

"In there, please!"

"Thank you, Frau Heinkes, thank you!"

He had no sooner crossed the threshold than he found his eyes taken and held by another pair of eyes, arrogant and contemptuous, that stared at him from a picture on the opposite wall. He turned his head swiftly away, for he had no reason to remember those eyes with anything but terror, and again he found those eyes confronting him. He turned his head once more, and once more they confronted him; from every wall, from every piece of furniture, from framed pictures behind glass, from pinned-up magazine photographs, the eyes of Herr Hitler stared out at him. For one moment a wild instinct of panic seized Mr. Emmanuel, to duck and run from the place while there was yet time. Into what den more deadly than Schloss Kastanienburg had he somehow blundered, this place flickering with the lightnings of those cold malefic eyes?

He felt a touch on his arm, and heard a soft voice speaking; it was a voice the rumour of which had many months ago travelled to his ears.

"What is the matter with you? Aren't you well?"

He blinked, and wiped the back of his hand across his forehead, as if a sweat had gathered there. She was, undoubtedly, a kind woman. There was gentleness in that touch. If she had no such quality, how else could she have been Bruno's mother, loved by him so consumingly?

"It has been a big day," he explained. "And seeing all those portraits of Herr Hitler . . . like a lot of mirrors."

"You see," she explained, "my husband is one of the party chiefs in these parts. He is hoping one day soon to be *Gauleiter*." There was a note of pride in her voice. He looked round for a portrait of the *Gauleiter*-to-be, but no image of any other creature, divine or human, had been permitted to challenge the bleak ascendancy. He caught sight instead of a sort of altar in a recess at the further end of the room, with a white fringed altar-cloth running along it. In the centre, in a heavy silver frame crested with a swastika, stood still another portrait of Herr Hitler, this time wreathed round with green vines;

it was flanked by candle-sticks at either end and vases of flowers in between. A glass cupboard below seemed to serve as a sort of *châsse,* or reliquary, of sacred objects, which included a couple of drinking-mugs, a boot, a number of swastikas in one design or another, a few medals in their velvet cases, a pair of spurs, and a whip.

"You are a foreigner, of course?" Her tone was still not unfriendly.

"Eh, what?" He turned to her. He was afraid she had already asked that, or some other question, once already.

"You are a foreigner, of course?" A certain suspicion began to manifest itself in her demeanour.

"I am," he told her. "An Englishman."

"Oh!" That seemed somehow reassuring. "Well? Perhaps now you will explain what you have come about? And please," she requested, "do not take too long about it. I am expecting my husband from his office shortly."

He put his hat down on a chair. She did not ask him to take his coat off, so he kept it on.

"Can I sit down, please?"

She made an indifferent gesture towards a chair. She was evidently getting uneasier from moment to moment. What did the old man mean by making himself at home like that? Had she nothing better to do with her time? She sat down on a chaise longue drawn up towards a huge white-tiled oven, where she could get the greatest benefit of its warmth during the cold weather. If the rest of the room might be deemed a chapel dedicated to Mars, this end of it was a boudoir of Venus. On a low table near the head of the chaise longue stood a handsome box of chocolates, the floor alongside being littered with their wrappings. On another table were a scent-spray, a manicure set, and a basket of coloured wools. The switches of a wireless were within reach. A number of picture magazines lay round and about.

He sat down on the chair indicated and examined her again, with a slow, intense scrutiny. Bruno's eyes were like that, exactly like that, green, with brown specks swimming in them. He had a full chin, too, the Greek style, they called it, did they not?

But why was Bruno's mother sitting here, a bride in the marriage chamber of Herr Hitler's lieutenant, with riding-whips, and scent-sprays and chocolates, while her boy across the sea ate no food which was not bitter like gall and drank no drink which was not salt like tears?

There has been some mistake, Elsie Silver. You have sent me chasing for a wild goose.

"Tell me, Frau Heinkes," he said casually, "why do you not wish it to be known you were once Frau Rosenheim?"

She gave up her position at once, though it could not be said she had till now defended it very brightly.

"Well, what do you think?" she exclaimed angrily. "Do you think this is a time when you want people to know you were once married to a Jew? The very idea!" A spot of colour burned in her cheeks. "Do you think *he* wants to be reminded of it, after all we've done to forget about it?" She made a movement with her head towards one of the portraits of Herr Hitler, but she meant her husband Herr Heinkes, of course. Perhaps they were in a sense, interchangeable.

"Yes," he admitted, "I quite see that. Nowadays it is disagreeable to be married to a Jew, and also to have been once married to a Jew."

"Well, then?" She tossed her head.

"But at all events," he continued gently, "you *were*

very fond of your other husband while he was alive?"

"And what if I was?" she said defiantly. "Not that I was so fond of him as all that! Look here!" A sudden suspicion had crossed her mind. "You've not come with any nonsense about his not being not really dead, have you?" That would have been one explanation of this preposterous visitation. "Anyhow"—she folded her arms —"my husband could soon put *that* right! What is that message you have got for me, anyway? I've not got all day, you know! Who are you? What's your name?"

He had no desire for any attention to be diverted towards himself. He ignored the question.

"No, it's not because of your husband I've come here! As far as I know, he's dead, like you say."

"Well, if it's not because of my first husband, what have you come for, then?"

Do I see, or do I not see, a little point of fright in her eyes, like the wing of a bird far off in the sky?

"I have come with a message from your son Bruno!"

It was as if an arrow had gone ping into her flesh. All the folds and flaps of it started shuddering.

"Bruno?" she cried. "My son Bruno? What are you talking about? He's dead!"

"He is not dead!" he said very quietly. "He is not dead!"

She pressed her hand to her bosom. Her breath came short and sharp.

"It's not true! He *is* dead, I tell you! He *is* dead! He died a long time ago! I saw the letter with my own eyes!"

Surely the woman was not lying? Surely there was truth in that anguished protestation? Her lips were working grotesquely, her fingers fluttering like hanging leaves.

"When do you say your boy died?"

"Last year!" she brought out. "Last year! February! March!"

He took his wallet from his breast-pocket, and two or three letters and postcards.

"I left England towards the end of January of this year. I was in Berlin for about ten days . . . then I had to go away. During those ten days I received these letters and cards from your son. I would like you to see them for yourself."

She stretched her hands out towards the letters, then pushed away the sight of them, and hid her eyes with her hands.

"No!" she cried. "It is not true! It is not true!"

"I have some photographs here," Mr. Emmanuel went on. He extracted them from his wallet. "I met him at the house of an old friend in a place called Ringwood in England. Here he is with some other boys from Germany. Will you look, please? It was taken last summer in the house of my friend. This is a later one. He sent it to me in the last letter I got from him over here, in Berlin. It is from his school. You know it, of course—Greystones. You have often written to him there. Do you see? It shows him in his football shorts. He is a real little Englishman now." The woman still had her hands before her eyes. She was moaning now, swaying from side to side.

"You had better look at them," commanded Mr. Emmanuel.

Slowly she let her hands fall from before her eyes.

"Where? Where?" she cried. Her eyes were staring, the little veins round the pupil bloodshot. He held the photographs up before her. The eyes seemed for a moment to make the effort to get the things into focus, for one moment only, during which the truth of the tale they told hit her like a blow between the temples. She seemed to reel before the force of it, then she collapsed, dissolved. She was a sweltering trough of tears.

"My baby!" A sound came out of the centre of it. "My Bruno! My little one! My Bruno! My sweet one! How could I— Oh, Bruno, Bruno, Bruno!"

He let her go on like that for some time; her face bloated with tears, her nose running. Even the marvellous silver-yellow hair seemed to have lost its lustre.

"My sweet one! My baby! My darling! My treasure!"

He began to get a bit sick of it. The dreadful feeling even came to him, to him who was no cynic, that the woman was, in fact, getting a sad horrible pleasure out of her grief.

He placed a hand upon the slithering traverse of her shoulder.

"Listen, Frau Heinkes! It is not so bad as all that! What is the matter with you? He is not dead! I've not come to tell you your boy's dead! Your boy's alive! He's alive and well! Do you hear? I'm going back to England tonight to see him! I'll see him in a couple of days! He's alive and well, I tell you!"

Her moans ceased. She dropped the edge of the tea-gown with which she had been stemming the flood of her tears. A look of bewilderment had come into her face.

"Yes, of course!" she said flatly. "He's alive!" Then another thought, also a very serious one, struck her. "What will Karl say?"

Mr. Emmanuel's lips were a thin grim line.

"Karl is, of course, your husband?"

"Yes," she said. "Of course."

A silence followed, broken only by the sound of the

woman's breath catching in her throat. She raised her eyes at length.

"Well, what do you want?"

"I want you to tell me now how this thing happened."

She looked right and left, right and left again, as if hoping that somewhere she might find a hole to creep through and get away from it all. But she saw none. She saw only the haggard old man with the stricken inquisitive eyes, and perhaps, between the old man and the door, she had the sense of another and younger presence. Suddenly she launched into her tale, as if the realization had come to her that it would be a comfortable thing to get it off her chest once and for all.

"You see, poor little Bruno was ill. You know he was ill, don't you? He had rheumatic fever. It wasn't the first time, either; he had it once before, when he was seven. It nearly killed him that time too. We were nearly driven crazy, my Busi and me." (Her mind had switched back without effort to the pre-Heinkes era, and to her pet name for her first husband.) "I do not say anything about the way they look after him in that school in England—how do you call it, in Haslemere?—but, poor boy, once again he gets rheumatic fever. As long as he is strong enough, he writes letters to me; such beautiful letters that boy always wrote, like a grown-up author, and I always write back, sometimes every day, twice a day even.

"I loved that boy, more than my eyes I loved him. And then . . . and then . . . he gets so ill, at last he cannot write to me at all, not one word even; the matron writes to me for him, and the poor boy can only put a cross to sign his name. And then he gets worse and worse; it looks like he is dying, and he cannot even put a cross any more.

And all this time Karl is there with me, he comes every day to help me through with my trouble, and Karl says to me, and is it not these days perhaps true——"

"I am sorry, Frau Heinkes," Mr. Emmanuel interrupted, with some difficulty. "I very much want to be clear about all this. You say your husband is there with you. Where? In the apartment in the Motzstrasse?"

"Yes! Where else?" she protested.

"Your first husband was dead by this time?"

"Yes, I think so. Yes, of course he was. What has that got to do with it?"

"But you were not yet married to Herr Heinkes?"

"No!" she said shortly. "No!"

"Please, about Bruno—?"

"It is not much of a life when once you have had rheumatic fever, is it?" she continued, fumbling around for the thread of her narrative. "And when you have had it twice"—she put her hand spasmodically to her heart—"like that, any day." She snapped her fingers.

Mr. Emmanuel was not *au fait* with the effects of rheumatic fever on the system. Frau Heinkes seemed well enough informed.

"It would not be a surprise," he murmured.

"Besides, there is another thing." A queer look came into her eyes, sly and furtive and afraid. "What sort of a life is it for those poor non-Aryan children? Who wants them any more? They have no father. They have no mother. They have no homeland. Poor little things!" Her eyes filled again with tears. Yet somehow, for the moment, she did not seem to be speaking with her own voice, if she had a voice of her own to speak with. He had a suspicion, which she at once confirmed, whose voice it was.

"People think my Karl is a bit stern, and God knows you've got to be able to look after yourself these days, with spies and Jews and grumblers at every street-corner. But really he's got a heart of gold. He always says it would be better for non-Aryan children, better than being a nuisance to themselves and other people in foreign countries, and spreading atrocity tales about our Leader—he says it would be better for them if they just died in their sleep!"

"Yes?" Mr. Emmanuel encouraged her.

"And so . . . and so . . ." She stopped. "Where was I?"

"Bruno was very ill. He was dying. He couldn't sign his name to his letters."

"Yes, the poor little mite!" The tears brimmed in her eyes again.

"So one day Karl comes in and sees a letter from England, from that school there, lying in the brass tray. You see, I always waited till he came in before reading the letters. Or rather, *he* would read them. I couldn't bear to open them myself. My heart is not too strong, you know, either. I suppose that's where poor little Bruno got it from."

"Yes, very likely."

"Any day I was expecting bad news, the worst. It was terrible, terrible! You must be a mother to understand how terrible such a waiting can be. So that day—I remember it like it was yesterday, it was a Tuesday—Karl comes in and picks up the letter. I do not even look at him, I am so frightened what sort of news it is going to be. He opens the envelope. The letter rustles in his hand. With all my nerves, with my whole heart I hear it. He says nothing. He is quiet. For a long time he is quiet. My heart begins to knock, knock, inside me. 'What is the matter, Karl?' I cry out to him. 'Why do you stand there, why do you say nothing?' And still he is quiet. I dare not talk, I dare not breathe. He goes up to the oven. He lifts the flap. He stands there one second, two seconds, three seconds. I cannot breathe. 'Karl!' I cry out. He lets the flap fall again. It is like the lid of a coffin.

"He comes up to me, and throws his arms round me. 'My darling!' he says to me. 'You must be brave!' But I do not let him say any more. I put my hand on his mouth. 'Do not tell me!' I shout. 'I know! I know! My little Bruno! My sweet one!' He takes me to his heart. He is whispering in my ear. 'Perhaps it is better like that!' I do not remember any more. I fall in a faint; it lasts I do not know how long, two hours, three hours. When I open my eyes again, Karl is there, and also a doctor. The doctor is very troubled. He is afraid of what will happen if I stay in that house. It is very dangerous, he says. I must leave at once, at once, the moment I am fit to travel."

"So you left quite soon, no?"

"Next day. Karl was being moved to Altona a month after. He asks leave, and next day he takes me to Hamburg. He stays a few days with me, then he leaves me with a woman looking after me, and comes back later. For two weeks I am like one that is neither dead nor living." A far reflection from vanished sunsets of grief shone waterily in her eyes.

"So I can believe it," murmured Mr. Emmanuel.

Yes, he could well believe it, though he would not have believed it an hour ago, half an hour ago. He could not, many years though he had lived, and witnessed some sorry spectacles as he passed—he could not till half an hour ago have permitted himself such doleful cynicism.

I am a child, he said to himself; who said an old man? I am ignorant like a young savage.

He could well believe certain things now which he could not have believed very lately. He could believe that for two whole weeks, and longer than that, she could act the part to perfection of the inconsolable mother, as she was acting it now, with herself as her most ravished spectator. She had before that, for fourteen years, acted the part of the adoring mother, the mother who blankets her child in such thick warm wrappings of mother-love that when they are stripped from him he is like a one-day nestling exposed to the March blasts. With just as complete a self-persuasion she had acted the part of the intellectual's wife, the gracious hostess, the singer of sweet songs to the piano in the rose-shaded lamplight, as now she was acting the part of the Nazi leader's wife, gold-haired Kriemhild, daughter and spouse and mother-to-be of Nordic heroes.

"Well, then, Frau Heinkes . . . please forgive me asking such questions, I am asking for your son Bruno, he has a right to know."

The point of view at once startled and reassured her.

"Yes, of course . . . I forgive. I still do not know your name."

"I was going to ask how it was that Bruno's letters never reached you. Because, of course, they cannot have reached you, or you would have known he was not dead."

"I swear," she exclaimed, clasping her breast with both hands, "I swear that never once did I hear from him! How was it possible? Would I not have flown to him on wings?"

"How did it happen, then?" he pressed softly.

She looked up quickly, then looked down again.

"You can understand. My husband wanted I should break away altogether from my old Jewish life. He said it was treachery to our race. He said how lucky I was to have a chance to be true again to my German blood. He did not like Bruno very much, you know," she confided. "He said that Bruno stood between us two. You see, perhaps, what he means?"

"I think I do. Did he know Bruno, then, before he went to England?"

"He had seen us together now and again."

"So you have known your husband for some time, then?"

"He fell in love with me," she admitted sullenly, "about a year before Norbert had to go off; we used to see each other from time to time."

"I see," he said with sympathy. He could guess with what style she would play that new role, the wife defending her honour against a dark primitive force that was at last to be too strong for it.

"As a matter of fact," she continued, in a sudden gush of confidence, "we are not married yet. It is getting a long time now, but he is so busy with party affairs, it is hard for him to get round to it. He has promised we shall be married on Midsummer Day, and it is going to be a wedding in the real modern style. *You* know. With fire, air, earth and water."

"I see. It will be beautiful. You have not been moving about all this time, since you first came to Altona?"

"No?" She opened her eyes wide.

"How was it, please, that none of Bruno's letters ever reached you? You see, I want to be able to explain to Bruno how the mistake happened."

"Well, that's simple." She seemed to derive some satisfaction from that. "As I told you, Karl said I must give up my Jew-life altogether. The name Rosenheim had nothing to do with me any more, he said. My husband was dead, my son was dead, I could start my life all over again, a German woman. As for my property in the apartment and my lease there, and our bungalow at Lübbenau . . . we had a very nice bungalow, you know, at Lübbenau." There was a far-away look in her eyes.

"Yes. I know."

"Really? Oh, little Bruno must have told you, I suppose?"

"Yes. Bruno told me."

"It was nice at Lübbenau. We had good times there." She sighed deeply. "Ah, well!" She shook her head as if to dislodge from it certain nostalgic memories. "Oh, I was saying, as for the apartment and all that, I gave Karl a power of attorney."

"And the letters?" Mr. Emmanuel asked again.

"I signed a form for all letters addressed to me to be forwarded here to Hamburg, care of Karl Heinkes, at his office address."

"So he has always kept back those letters which . . . which he thought would upset you . . . including your son's. Is that how it was?"

"I suppose so," she admitted heavily. "It must be like that."

"There is only one thing. Please forgive me." He clasped his hands. "I know how painful this must be for you." She brought up a sigh from the depths of her martyred motherhood. "I know how much you love Bruno . . . as much as Bruno loves you—and loves you still."

"Don't! Don't!" she begged him.

"If you only knew the way he talks about you——"

She pressed her lips together in a valiant effort to restrain her grief, but it broke through again. It was really very painful, that long low steady weeping, without pause, without end.

"I am sorry," he started, once and again. "I am sorry." At last he had her ear, though she did not lift her face from her hands. "Only one thing puzzles me . . . that letter that came from the English school. . . . You know, the letter Herr Heinkes threw into the oven. . . ."

She dropped her hands and looked up sharply.

"Well?"

"Oh, nothing, nothing." He did not like that expression in her eye. He could not bear to disintegrate the situation into its final elements, and he knew she would not permit him to. He had it all clear enough, he thought. The letter that Heinkes had picked up that day contained the first intimation that Bruno had turned the corner. Perhaps it had even included a word or two in Bruno's handwriting. Heinkes was evidently a man of resource and quick decision. If he let the moment slip, the old belly-aching would begin again and go on interminably. He cut the knot—how do they say it?—the Gordian knot. The letter went down into the flames.

It would be cutting her knot for her, too. He had put the whole thing across very nicely. She was nearly ninety-nine per cent convinced the boy was dead. Neither of them was going to let the one per cent trip them up.

Frau Heinkes waited a few moments for Mr. Emmanuel to continue, but he remained silent. There was an air of constraint during that time, herself waiting and Mr. Emmanuel remaining silent. Then she broke down again, which seemed the only sensible thing to do. In almost no time she was wallowing again in the sea of her tears like a pitching tug. She forgot Mr. Emmanuel. She forgot Herr Heinkes. She remembered only her baby, her precious, her treasure, her Bruno, so long withheld from her by the cruelest fortune that had ever beset a mother. What would Bruno think of her? Would the gentleman explain to Bruno how it had all happened? Would he get Bruno to write to her, to send her just one word of forgiveness?

(Forgiveness? What has he got to forgive you for? You were the victim of a cruel fortune, no?)

How is Bruno? Where is Bruno? He is still at that school, is he, where they let him get rheumatic fever?

(Hello! What's that? That is a key turning in a door. The door close by, just opposite. The door I came in by. Can she not hear it? No, she could not hear a house falling down, she is making such a babylam.)

He could not possibly live if he got rheumatic fever a third time. Are they looking after him properly now? My little Bruno, my *Liebling,* my *Schatz.* Do you think they are always careful about his underclothes?

(It is a man, he must be a great big man, with feet like those. No. She has not heard him. She would not hear even an elephant. I do not like it. He has stopped. He is listening just outside this door. I have been here a long time now, it is like years and years. If I could only just pick up my hat and go. . . . But he is standing there, between me and outside. That must be Heinkes. How quiet he is. God should help me, now in the last moment, when I have found out what I have come to find out. My rock and fortress. My rock and fortress.)

Tell him if he writes to me, I will write back at once. I will send him presents. When his birthday came round last August, tell him it was dreadful, I felt like throwing myself into the sea. It has been two Christmases now without him. We still have an old-fashioned Christmas tree. Perhaps during his holidays it might be possible to arrange a visit here; it is so nice, the sail-boats on the Alster, and the Hagenbeck Circus——

Her recital of the amenities of Hamburg went no further. The door was flung open so violently a heavy whatnot table behind it was sent flying. Framed in the doorway, and almost filling it, was a man in brown uniform, an officer in the S.A. The face was so enormous, under the completely bald pate, it looked less like a face than the pale underside of a fish. The illusion was heightened by the fact that the mouth, a great gash, was slightly out of the horizontal. It was crowded with small pointed teeth, in a quantity that seemed beyond nature.

The teeth parted. A great roar issued from the cavernous mouth slightly muffled by the thick pad of tongue.

"So you want your little Jew-bastard back, do you? You want your Bruno, your *Liebling*, your *Schatz*." He stepped forward into the room, and sent the door whistling back behind him. "You can have him! Take him off to Palestine, pig-Jewess, where you belong! You and your stinking brat! And you!"—he turned to Mr. Emmanuel —"Who are you? What in hell's blazes—!" But the woman, with astonishing agility, had launched herself from the chaise longue onto the floor below his knees. She was clawing at his breeches, kneading his thighs with her fingers, filling the whole room with her lamentations.

"My darling! My husband! My hero! How can you talk to me so? I am dying! I love you, *you*, only you in all the world! I want no one else, nothing else! You are my eyes, my soul!" He pushed the woman from him. Her hands slid down the polished surface of his leggings. She was shuddering, moaning, dying, within the hollow of her lovely hair.

The man had turned suddenly on Mr. Emmanuel, as if a stink had come up into his nostrils, the stink of a dead animal behind a cupboard door. The huge pale nostrils quivered.

"What? A Jew?" he yelled. It seemed he had a better nose for a Jew than his consort, the delicacy of whose sense of smell had been blunted by fifteen years of co-habitation with the defunct Rosenheim.

Mr. Emmanuel rose from his chair and tried to straighten out his shoulders, which both age and recent suffering had bowed. The other towered over him, yet somehow, mysteriously, as they stood face to face, he did not seem the bigger man.

"Well? What are you doing here?" the man shouted.

Mr. Emmanuel peered up into the brownshirt's eyes. It is strange, isn't it? he said to himself. I am not afraid of this man, I am not afraid of him at all, though in some ways he seems more of a brute than any of those men who have been ill-treating me all this time. Do me a favour, look at those fists, like things in a butcher's shop hanging from hooks. Perhaps within a minute or two he will bring his fist down on to my head, and I will fall at his feet like a lump of wood. But I am not frightened. They have done worse things to me. Whatever he does to me, whatever any of them do to me, I can never be frightened any more. It is a strange thing, and also a good thing. He wants to know who I am. Am I a Jew? He wants to know what I am doing here. I will tell him.

"I have come here with a message from this lady's son, Bruno Rosenheim. I have come from England. My name is Isaac Emmanuel. I am a Jew."

"What?" the man thundered, the volume of sound making the lustres tinkle in the chandelier. "Emmanuel the Jew? *This* Emmanuel?" He took out a copy of the evening paper from his pouch-like pocket. "Emmanuel the spy, the murderer?" He struck the paper with the back of his hand two or three times.

"No," said Mr. Emmanuel mildly. "Perhaps you have not read it. It is because I am not a spy or a murderer that they have had me released. I think you will find that is so."

"But . . . but . . ." the fellow spluttered. For half a minute he was quite speechless. It is not, after all, a very common occurrence, even in the life of a big regional boss, to come back to his own hearth and find it invested by an individual whose affairs have been filling columns of the national press for weeks and weeks. "But . . . but . . . what are you doing here with my wife?" That is a line of assault which is always useful till a man has found his bearings.

"I told you, Herr Heinkes. I am a friend of the small boy Bruno Rosenheim, now in England. I came to Germany a few months ago to see can I find out what has become of his mother. Well, I have found out. I was just going to say good-day to Frau Heinkes when you came in!" He moved three or four paces and lifted his hat from the chair where he had placed it. "I am sorry I have caused such a big trouble." He took two steps back again in the direction of the door.

"Stop!" bellowed Herr Heinkes. "Stay where you are!" The blood had suffused the whole of the great moon face and seemed to be seeping up into the bald pate. In his fury, the lips were pushing themselves out and being sucked in again like . . . like . . . (Isn't there a big fish that does that? Mr. Emmanuel wondered. Didn't I see it one time in a tank in Belle Vue?)

"You miserable stinking lump of poisoned Jew-muck! You think you can come to my house and pester my wife and snoop round asking questions and get away with it? You think you can come telling my wife lying tales of her bloody little squealing Jew-brat and get away with it?" His fist rose higher and higher as his voice rose in a crescendo of insane fury. "I'll show you whether you can or can't, you filthy turd! I'll show you what we do in Hamburg with lumps of yellow-squirt like you!" The fists were poised above Mr. Emmanuel's head, quivering for the impact. Mr. Emmanuel did not wince. He did not close his eyes.

A scream rose out of the shuddering mass at the storm-trooper's feet.

"Don't! Leave him!"

"He can do what he likes!" Mr. Emmanuel said indifferently. "It has all happened to me, and much worse. He cannot hurt me."

Herr Heinkes tore his legs free from the woman's encircling arms.

"I can shoot you down like a dog!" he proclaimed. He played with the butt-end of the pistol slung at his flank. "And bury your carcass by daylight in the front garden there!"

Mr. Emmanuel shrugged his shoulders.

"The authorities in Berlin have given me a day to clear out. If I do not, and it is my fault, something will happen to me. If I do not, and it is yours—" He left the rest unsaid.

"I'd very much like to risk it!" Herr Heinkes said through his teeth. He drew his slanting lips together till they were one long line.

"Much good would it do you!" Mr. Emmanuel observed. "Much good is it all doing you!" He spoke with great ease and matter-of-factness, as if he were not caged in the same room with a creature more dangerous than many beasts of the jungle. "Where do you think it is all taking you, where? You can beat me up. You can beat up a thousand other Jews. You can kill us. You can kill all the Jews in your country. Well? No, please, listen to me, and kill me after, if you like!" He had got into his stride. He had a tendency to treat a congregation of even two people at a time as a public meeting, and he had not been given much chance for oratory lately. "Well? Where will you be, then? Be quiet, please!" He was addressing Frau Heinkes, whose sobs and moans were coming in at the wrong places.

The woman quieted down. Herr Heinkes tried to say something, but could not. He was like a man with a scarf tightening round his throat. Great veins stood out on his forehead. His eyes goggled in their sockets.

"Where will you be, then, I ask you? You do not know!" exclaimed Mr. Emmanuel, in his best debating manner. "I will tell you. You will be, sooner or later, where all the enemies of Israel are now. You will be where Egypt is, where Moab is, where Rome is. And it will not be so long like you think, either. And we, where will we be? We will be where we always have been. Going to synagogue, bringing up families, writing a few books, making a little business, asking a few questions—that's where we'll be, Herr Heinkes." He walked over to the door and stood for a moment there, with his hand on the door-handle. He looked quizzically at Herr Heinkes. "It is a pity I should be such a trouble to you," he observed. "I also have had a bit of trouble to find my way here." He did not let his eyes fall to the heaving woman on the floor. He did not wish his eyes, his brain, his heart, to take any further note of her at all. He kept his head and eyes lifted.

"Good day, Herr Heinkes!" he said, and closed the door behind him. Even before he had shut the outer door to, hardly six seconds later, the storm was loosened again, the thunder ripped and roared among the swastikas.

Mr. Emmanuel managed somehow to get down the three front steps onto street-level. He managed to walk down the garden path, and to turn left several yards, so that he was no longer within eyeshot of the Heinkes sitting-room. Then his feet gave under him, his trunk slumped like a sack. He found himself sitting on the pavement, with his back arched against a low garden wall. There was a feeling in his mouth as if he had been chewing bitter wood. It was in his nostrils also, and the back of his throat. He leaned forward and tried to steady his knees. They seemed to run away like water from under his fingers.

"Hallo, sir, hallo!" a voice said. Someone was bending over him. Someone was dragging him to his feet. "You know, you'd already had a drop too much when you got here. Up now, up! An old gentleman of your age, sir! In there! That's right! Thought I might as well hang about a bit! Where can I take you, sir? Where? Station, did you say? All right, station! Cheer up, old cock!"

15

THE boat from Cuxhaven landed its passengers at Southampton rather earlier than had been expected, but it was quite a respectable time, just a minute or two to eight o'clock. Mr. Emmanuel showed his passport at the barrier. The official looked up swiftly, then looked down again, and reached his hand out for the next passport. He whispered a word or two in his colleague's ear. "No!" went that one's mouth. "Yes!" went the other's. The routine continued staidly.

"Anything to declare?"

Mr. Emmanuel had done no shopping to speak of in Germany. He had nothing to declare.

"Boat-train?" asked the porter.

"No, thank you. Luggage office, please. Where are the telephones?"

The porter showed him. "It's all right, sir," he added. "I'll bring your ticket over."

Mr. Emmanuel entered the telephone booth.

"Ringwood 42," he demanded.

Ringwood 42 answered.

"Is Mrs. Cooper there, please?"

"Who's that?"

"Mr. Emmanuel would like to speak to her."

There was a gasp at the other end of the telephone.

"Oh, Mr. Emmanuel, Mr. Emmanuel! God bless you! One moment, please! I'll fetch her!"

Another voice was at the telephone a minute later.

"Mr. Emmanuel! Mr. Emmanuel!" The voice was not at all distinct, being choked with joy and tears. "Are you all right? How are you? Oh, my dear, my dear!"

"I'm fine, Rose. Did you get my cable?"

"Yes, yes! I was just coming over to meet you! You're early! I'll come over for you now, at once! Is the refreshment room open?"

"Yes, Rose, it is! I will wait for you and have some breakfast. Rose, Rose, don't go away!"

"What is it, darling? I *can't* wait! I want to get over to you!"

"Please, I am not going straight back to Ringwood with you! *All right! At once!"* They were demanding more pennies, please.

"Why on earth not, Mr. Emmanuel? They'll all be here, everybody. John's just back, too. You *must* come back at once! You must rest up!"

"Rose! I want to go first to Bruno. I have sent him a cable, saying I have news. You understand, Rose?"

She was silent. Her voice quivered as she spoke again. It was hardly audible.

"Yes, Mr. Emmanuel, I understand. Is it good news, Mr. Emmanuel?"

"It is good and bad. I will tell you when I see you. After that, I go to Haslemere. The man said I could catch a connexion."

"Nonsense! I'll drive you over! It'll take no time at all!"

"Thank you, Rose, thank you! Just one more thing!"

"Yes?"

"Please. It is very bad of me. Will you come alone?"

"Of course I will, if you want me to! Go along and have your breakfast! I'll pick you up at the station in no time!"

She was so shocked when she saw him, he was so much less than half himself, that for a long time she just stood there and gaped. Then she recovered herself, flung herself upon his shoulder, and cried and cried. She was quite shameless about it. The women behind the counter took no particular notice. They were quite used to the sight of emotional females blubbering over men coming, or men going, as the case might be.

"You poor dear darling!" she sobbed. "You poor, poor, sweet thing!"

Mr. Emmanuel was himself not unaffected. A tear quivered in his eye.

"Please!" he called out to a waitress. "One more cup!"

A cup was brought. Rose tried her best to drink, but her tears kept on rolling into the tea.

"We'll soon get you right!" she wept. "We'll soon get you right! The swine!" she exclaimed. "The beastly, filthy swine! You should hear John on the subject!"

"Yes," he said gently. "I want to. It will give me a great pleasure. But there is someone we must think of first, before anything else!"

"Poor little chap!" she said. "Well? Won't you tell me now? Is she dead or alive, I must know."

"It is not easy to answer that question," he replied. "Come, I will tell you the whole tale in the car. It is like a sad, sad fairy-tale. How much, please, waitress? Thank you very much." They got up. "Now, Rose. I have two telegrams to send, one to Bruno's headmaster, one to Bruno. Shall we do it now, please?" That was duly done. Rose telephoned to Shipscar to tell them they must not expect to see Mr. Emmanuel and herself till later in the day. The porter got out the luggage and carried it over to the car. Mr. Emmanuel settled down in the seat beside Rose.

"It is nice to be with you, Rose," he said.

She seized his bony hand where it lay on his thigh and squeezed it hard.

"I can't believe it yet," she murmured. "It's like a bad dream over."

"It's not quite all over."

"No," she said shortly. "I hope he takes it well—whatever you're bringing to him."

"I think he will," declared Mr. Emmanuel. "It is a funny thing. Somehow, while I was . . . over there, I got to understand him more than I did all the time I was with him at Shipscar. Perhaps I got to understand everything a little better."

"You've had to pay for it, too!" she said bitterly. "You poor thing!"

"Well, who knows? Perhaps it will be worth while. I think it will. I will know later. Oi, Rose, I have such a lot to tell you!" They were out in the streets of the town now. "How *nice* the people look, Rose! They don't look frightened! You've no idea how frightened they look over there!"

She shuddered.

"How have you managed to get through it all? I can't understand."

He shrugged his shoulders.

"I had company," he said.

It was a cryptic and rather frightening remark. She did not pursue it further.

"Well, it's all over, my dear," she announced.

"Almost all over," he corrected her, under his breath.

"Damn!" she exclaimed. She had just missed the lights at a crossing.

"Let be!" he said. "We've waited long enough, no? We can wait half a minute longer." He turned his head, and let his eye rest on the window of the shop facing them across the pavement. It happened to be a pet-shop. An assortment of creatures was assembled in kennels, baskets, hutches, cages. He could not see with his body's eye at that distance through the intervening windows. But with his mind's eye he saw with sudden and magnificent clarity. He saw puppies, kittens, love-birds, budgerigars. He saw—bigger, more magnificent than any of these—he saw a white rabbit.

The lights were changing. Rose was getting into gear again.

"Please, Rose, please! Let me get out!" he cried.

"Why? What's the matter?" She looked very alarmed. "Wait a minute! I must cross the road!" She got to the other side of the road. "What's the matter? Aren't you well?"

"I am very well," he said with dignity. "Like a horse! I want to buy a present, there in that animal shop. Is it nice I should go on my holidays and not bring Bruno a present?" He had got out of the car by now.

"Shall I come with you, Mr. Emmanuel?"

"No, thank you. Please, I will buy it myself!"

"Very well." She smiled. He was certainly not less

funny in his own odd way than he had been before he went on his "holiday."

He crossed the road and stationed himself in front of the pet-shop window. It was almost exactly as he had envisioned it . . . puppies, kittens, love-birds, budgerigars. But it was not a big white rabbit he saw there. It was a small one, a nice little chap, one ear up and one ear down. He was washing himself at that moment, using his paw for a sponge, he was having a good time . . . like a cat! Like great Jo of Lübbenau, immortal Jo!

He went into the shop, his heart beating violently.

"Please, there is a little white rabbit in your window. Can I buy it, please?"

"Certainly. Or we have a nice young Angora here?"

"No, thank you. I want that one."

"Certainly. A very useful breed of rabbit it is, too!"

"It is not dangerous?" asked Mr. Emmanuel.

"I beg your pardon?" The assistant was quite sure he had not heard aright.

"I mean, when it grows up, will it be strong and brave, this breed? Will it run after cats and dogs?"

"Well, sir," the assistant said, wondering if he were really quite awake, or was it still last night, "it cannot be *guaranteed,* but I suppose they can be trained, you know."

"Ah, well, that will have to do," Mr. Emmanuel conceded.

"Where shall I send it, sir?"

"Could I take it with me, please? I have a car waiting over there."

"Oh, certainly, sir. We have a very smart line in hutches. I will get it bedded up for you nicely."

"Thank you."

"I'll get the boy to carry it for you."

"I will carry it myself," said Mr. Emmanuel sternly. "His name is Jo."

"Of course, sir," said the admirable assistant.

Mr. Emmanuel paid and went off with his prize.

"Is it all right, please, Rose? It will go in the back there, I think."

Her eyes started leaking again.

"Oh, dear!" she cried, and angrily brushed away her tears. "Yes, I think we can find room for him! Oh, what a darling! Come, I'll help you!"

"No! I want to do everything myself! Thank you! His name is Jo."

"Yes," breathed Rose. "I remember."

They were out in the country before long.

"How *green* it all is!" he murmured. "How *green!*"

"Are you going to tell me now?" she asked. "Don't you think I've been good? After all, I'm only a woman!"

"Yes, darling Rose. It is not because I want to make secrets. It is because it is not easy to talk of it."

They said nothing. They had over an hour's driving ahead of them, perhaps an hour and a half. There was no point in speeding. The fields, the leafy woods, haystack and cottage, passed by, as if those things were moving and they themselves were stationary. The hawthorn bloom had lost its freshness; the fallen petals lay in the ditches like spilt milk. In fields here and there and on the edge of ploughland poppies flickered.

It was in the height of winter he left, Rose mused. Half a year has gone by. It will be high summer soon. How has he managed to live through it all? He looks, if anyone just breathed on him— Quiet, Rose! He is talking! Listen!

He talked. He told his tale. They drove on in complete silence for a mile or two. Then she felt for his hand and lifted it to her mouth and kissed it.

"God bless you!" she breathed.

They drove on for another mile, still without talking. Then he spoke again.

"What is this place?" he asked.

"Petersfield," she told him.

"A nice place."

"Yes."

"I am glad to be in England."

"Yes."

"I am glad to be with you. I am glad I am going to Bruno. I am happy." He sighed deeply.

"Mr. Emmanuel!" she exclaimed. "There is one thing you have not told me."

"What is that, Rose?"

"Have you any idea how they came to let you go?"

"Yes, Rose. You would not believe me."

"Yes, I would. The whole country was seething with fury. John went over, you know, to stir them up."

"I know."

"You know? How on earth do you know? Who told you?"

"I don't know," he said, looking rather crestfallen. "How foolish I am! Once, I could have sworn I heard his voice——"

"Yes, of course, of course!" she soothed him. He must often have heard voices and seen visions. "Well, you said you have an idea who got you out?"

"Yes, Rose. You will think I am mad."

"Do you want to tell me?"

"I will tell you. It was Elsie Silver."

The car gave a sudden lurch towards the ditch.

"There you are!" he pointed out. "What did I tell you?"

"What are you talking about, Mr. Emmanuel?" She looked at him through the corner of her eye. "How on earth do you know that? It's ridiculous! That dreadful woman!"

"She rang me up," he said, "when they let me out. At that pension where I went to pick up my things."

"How did she announce herself? Frau Brockenburg?"

"Perhaps you do not understand how it is with her," he said mildly. "Perhaps nobody understands."

"I should think not."

"It says in the Bible——"

"How did she call herself? I'd really like to know that."

"She did not give her name!"

"She did not give her name? How did you know it was she?"

"I told you someone found out for me the address in Altona. No one else in Germany could have found out for me. Only Elsie Silver."

"Perhaps you're right," she said. She thought it would be unkind to argue further.

"How has he been, the boy?" he asked.

"He has been very good." The expression in her eyes softened. "I think you'd have been proud of him."

"Was he with you last holidays again?"

"Well, actually with Mary. They've become great friends. She's been awfully nice to him. So has he been to her for that matter. He's got a great gift for understanding people, that boy. He's growing up."

"Yes, he's growing up. Of course he is. But after today, it will be different again."

"How do you mean?"

"The thing that has been holding him bent, it will not be there any more. He will grow up straight and tall, I think, like a young tree. What is to happen to him, Rose?"

"I think, after today, his mind will straighten out too. There's an odd expression in his eyes, sometimes. It's been a great strain for him, of course—greater than for all the rest of us."

"Yes, of course. It is not enough for him, Rose."

"What is not enough?"

"He has no country, no father, no mother. We cannot make up for all that—an old man like me, an old maid like Mary . . . you forgive me, Rose? Not even you, and John, and your lovely children."

He was silent for quite a long time.

"What are you thinking of, Mr. Emmanuel?"

"I saw a cow."

"Yes, you poor dear. You saw no cows in those places you've been in."

"It did not make me think of those places. It made me think of Ain Charod."

"What?"

"Ain Charod, in Palestine. That is the colony where my son Moisheh is, and his wife and children, God bless them. They call him *Sar-Hachalav* over there, the big one from the milk. I will be there myself before long, Rose."

"Do you want to go, Mr. Emmanuel?"

"What else is there for me? I am an old man; I have finished my work."

"You are not too excited about going, are you?"

"I love Doomington, though it is not a picture, like Hollywood. I love Magnolia Street and all the people there. I love you, Rose."

"Well, darling, if you are not so excited about going, what's in your head? About Bruno, I mean? A young boy, with all his life ahead of him. He's a Christian, too. Are you remembering that?"

"In Palestine what does it matter, Jew, Christian? Christ also was a Christian! Are you remembering that?" He smiled wistfully. "No, Rose, no. You are wrong. Nothing is in my head for Bruno. Ideas come, ideas go, like in a fire, sparks. He must work out his life for himself. It should be something new, bright, that is all I think. Something different. Sunshine. Hard work. He should sweat. His muscles should be big and round, like stones. Perhaps, in that way, he will forget what he has lost . . . . the country that has pushed him out . . . the father and mother he hasn't got any more. What is this place, Rose? What? Haslemere already?"

"Yes, this is Haslemere. We've arrived. The school's a couple of miles further on, you know. I'll take you as far as the school gates, but I won't come in with you, of course."

"Perhaps I should see him alone, first," murmured Mr. Emmanuel. "Thank you, Rose."

They drove on for a couple of miles till they came to a wrought-iron gate set in a mellow red brick wall.

"Here you are!" said Rose. "Out you get! I'm going to go for a nice little walk. Don't worry about me! I'll be all right. I won't be far off."

"All right, Rose. You are a nice girl. Every day you get more like your mother."

She smiled, gratified. She still felt that her mother was

—and it was a great many years ago since her mother had died—the loveliest human creature she had ever set eyes on.

"Will you bring him out to say how d'you do to me? Perhaps old Forsyte will let us take him out to lunch, if you ask him nicely?"

"And Jo?" he asked. "He won't want lunch?"

She opened her eyes wide.

"Jo? Oh, yes, of course. Jo!"

Mr. Emmanuel had opened the rear door of the car and was bending down towards the hutch of the little white rabbit.

"No!" he decided. "He will not want lunch! He has had lunch already! He has eaten up nearly his whole house!"

The Reverend Andrew Forsyte, headmaster of Greystones, got up from his desk. He felt just a little embarrassed, as he would have felt if Mr. Steve Donoghue or Miss Greta Garbo had entered his study. For a time the name of Isaac Emmanuel had been hardly less celebrated than theirs. He was not easy in the presence of famous people, and had not had much experience of them.

"Good morning, Mr. Emmanuel, good morning! I am very happy to see you, very happy!"

"Pleased to meet you, sir!" said Mr. Emmanuel.

"I . . . I . . . won't you sit down, Mr. Emmanuel?" He pointed out a leather easy chair with its back to the light. "Ahem . . . er. You're looking very well, Mr. Emmanuel, very well indeed!" As a matter of fact, the old gentleman looked anything but well. He looked like a death's head. Mr. Forsyte could have bitten his tongue off.

"Thank you, I'm feeling quite all right. Are you feeling quite all right?" asked Mr. Emmanuel.

"Quite, thank you. Yes, yes—er . . . you want to see young Bruno, of course, Bruno Rosenheim?"

"Yes, please."

"You have some news for him, of course. Yes, yes, certainly. I'll have him sent in at once." Mr. Forsyte would dearly have liked to ask Mr. Emmanuel what news it was he brought. Mr. Forsyte had taken throughout a warm and kindly interest in the boy. But somehow it seemed quite impossible to ask Mr. Emmanuel questions. Those deep-sunk eyes, those lips twisted with pain, did not lend themselves to easy curiosity. Besides, of course, he would want to talk to the boy first. Of course. "I wonder—" he started off. "Perhaps you'd care to have . . . I wonder if you'd care to have a spot of lunch with us?"

"Thank you so much, Mr. Forsyte. It is so kind of you. But, as a matter of fact, I was going to ask you about lunch. You know that nice Mrs. Cooper from Ringwood, where Bruno goes for his holiday? That is where I met him, of course. Well, this morning she met me at Southampton and drove me over here."

"You and Mrs. Cooper would like to take the boy out to lunch, of course?"

"If it wouldn't be a trouble?"

"By all means. Very thoughtless of me. I don't think I ought to keep you from Bruno any more. I know he's expecting you. I myself have a class to take in a minute or two. I'll have him sent in at once. Perhaps, sometime, if we could have a little talk together . . . I'd like to find out from inside, so to speak—" He blushed awkwardly.

(Would you believe it? Mr. Emmanuel reflected. A

headmaster from Oxford College with a big gown, also a clergyman, with his collar the other way round . . . yet he is also a nice, shy schoolboy. . . . No wonder Bruno likes him so much.)

"Well, good-bye, Mr. Emmanuel. No, please sit down again! I can't begin to tell you how I feel about it all . . . all you've been through." He was hastening towards the door. "Monstrous! Infamous! As I was saying, perhaps, sometime——"

"One moment, please, Mr. Forsyte. You must forgive me. I have another favour to ask from you."

"Yes? By all means. What is it?"

"You know, Bruno had in Germany a wonderful white rabbit. His name was Jo. I think that Jo is dead now."

Mr. Forsyte looked very puzzled.

"In Southampton today I bought another white rabbit. His name also is Jo. He is not a big rabbit yet. But he will be some day. He is outside in the car now."

"Yes, Mr. Emmanuel?"

"Bruno once told me it is not encouraged for boys to keep animals here."

"Well, as a matter of fact, knowing what boys are——"

"But, please, if you would make an exception for Jo . . . do you think it is impossible?"

"My dear Mr. Emmanuel! The boy has been through so much, I don't think it would be criminal to make an exception in his case! And remembering what you've done for him—" He let the door-handle slip from his grasp, and, obeying a sudden impulse, strode back to where Mr. Emmanuel was standing, seized his hand, and tugged it so hard, he left it quite limp. "I feel I must say thank you, and God bless you! Lord, what a *sport* you've been!" And, colouring up to the eyebrows after this exhibition of hectic irreticence, he fled the room, the tails of his gown swinging copiously behind him.

Mr. Emmanuel sat down again in the leather easy chair; he had so little width and the chair so much, he seemed rather like an accident there than a tenant. He leaned forward, his elbows on his thighs, his head cupped in his hands. It is like it used to be in prison, he mused. How long was I sitting like this on the edge of the bed, sometimes saying Psalms, sometimes saying nothing! How many hours at a time, how many months was it? I knew that the day after, or the day after that, I would have to go into that room again, where the man was sitting on the platform, the one with the monkey-face; and the men were sitting against the wall, with the pieces of lead pipe under the form. Well, I was a bit frightened now and again. Why should I hide it any more? And sometimes I was a bit frightened in Moabit, too, waiting for that trial, wondering what lies they had got up for me, and how many people to swear false, and how many letters in my handwriting which I had not written.

Well, I was a bit frightened then, I admit it. But do you know, it is a strange thing, here, in the nice English school, in the headmaster's room waiting for Bruno—I am somehow just a little bit more frightened. What for? Did you ever hear from such a thing?

Well, God has helped me through all the other times. He will help me through this time also, I hope.

There was a sound of feet coming swiftly along the corridor. They stopped outside the door. There was a complete silence for ten seconds, twenty, as if the courage of the person standing there had failed. At length there was a knock at the door.

"Come in!" called Mr. Emmanuel. He rose, not without difficulty, from the low chair. (It is like a headmaster sitting here and saying: Come in. A pity I have not also got a black gown from Oxford College. So his heart always trifled when it was most desperately engaged.)

The door opened, and a youth entered, a youth so much taller than the boy he had known half a year ago, with eyes that seemed so much darker and more deeply set, that it hardly seemed the same boy.

"Bruno, my boy!" cried Mr. Emmanuel, and advanced, holding his hand out.

The boy advanced, his hand also outstretched. Then he stopped. The thing that had been merely a shape against the white light of the windows slowly assumed detail and lineament. He saw the old body bowed and gnarled with pain, the cavernous cheeks, the haunted compassionate eyes. The boy stopped. His hand fell to his side. He bowed his head, as a servant might, in the presence of a lord.

"Bruno!" cried Mr. Emmanuel. He came up to him and threw his arms round his shoulders and pressed his head against his chest. "You must not take it to heart, Bruno! It was nothing! I was proud and happy I was there! Did I not keep my word? Did you not keep yours?"

Blindly the boy sought for the old man's hand, and raised it to his lips, and let it fall again.

"Mr. Emmanuel!" he whispered. "I want to say first of all I am sorry! That, before everything else!"

"Come, come!" protested Mr. Emmanuel. "Sorry? What should you be sorry for? And perhaps we could sit down also! Does it cost any more?" He retreated towards the easy chair. "You bring over that stool, Bruno, and put it close by the chair! That's right! Sorry? You mustn't talk like that! Was anything your fault?" He patted the boy's cheek reprovingly.

"I want to know one thing," Bruno begged. "You were never thinking bad of me? You were never blaming me?"

"Tscha! Tscha! Such a nonsense! It is something more important to talk about!"

"Mr. Emmanuel, I got your cable. I know you have news for me. But before you tell me what it is, whether she's alive or dead, there's another thing I've got to say. Only this, Mr. Emmanuel. Thank you. Thank you. I won't say it again." (Rose was right. He's growing up. He talks like a young man. He talks better language too, not like he was a foreigner.) "Now I want the news you have brought me. Is she alive or dead?" (The moment has come now. Please, God, make it easy for both of us.) The boy turned his eyes away. His cheeks were very pale.

"It is not easy for me to tell you what I have to tell you, Bruno. It is not bad news; it is not good news, either."

The boy turned his eyes swiftly towards Mr. Emmanuel's, then as swiftly turned them away again.

"Tell me is she . . . very ill?" he whispered.

"Bruno, she is dead."

Every vestige of colour went out of the boy's cheeks. Even his lips were pale as tallow.

"How did she die, Mr. Emmanuel?"

"She was wonderful, Bruno. You can be very proud of her, your whole life long."

"Did she have pain?"

"It was not with pain. I will tell you how it was. Are you well, Bruno?"

"Yes, I am quite well. How was it please, Mr. Emmanuel?"

"It was like this. You know your father went away to Switzerland? You told me yourself."

"Yes."

"You know he was doing political work all that time? You understood that?"

"Yes."

"Your mother was keeping in touch with him all that time too. You did not know that. They worked together in the same organization."

"Yes?"

"You know there was a business on the border, don't you, at Schaffhausen, and your father was killed?"

The boy's lips tightened.

"I know that."

"I think, after that, your mother said to herself: 'I will give my whole life to the cause my man died for.' It seems like that, from what they told me. The apartment in the Motzstrasse became a centre from under the ground activities. You see, such a woman, an Aryan, with all that fair hair, people did not suspect."

"I see," whispered Bruno.

"But they always get to know everything, sooner or later—even when you have not done nothing, as well. They found out about her too. She got away just in time. One of the cars from her organization was waiting, and carried her from one place to another place, then at last she got to Hamburg. Bruno, are you all right? Shall we go out into the open air?"

"Please go on."

"She never went back to the Motzstrasse, of course. She

wasn't there to get your letters. You see, also, why they were never sent back to you by the post office. The Gestapo kept back all letters that were sent to her."

"But why, why, did she not write to me from Hamburg?" The boy's face had lost its lacklustre immobility. It was like an old man's, awry with pain.

Mr. Emmanuel's heart beat faster. He was coming to the most difficult part of his tale, the least credible, the nearest to story-book melodrama.

"You see, for some weeks she did not leave that house at all. The Gestapo was smelling rats. She wrote to you. Of course she wrote to you. But it was one of the other workers who posted the letters. You can see what happened?"

"It was a spy!" Bruno's lips projected uglily. "He kept the letters!"

Mr. Emmanuel breathed freely again.

"Yes!" he brought out. "It was like that!"

"Did they get hold of her?" Bruno asked, with a sudden gasp of alarm.

"No!" replied Mr. Emmanuel quickly. "She was too quick for them!"

"What do you mean, Mr. Emmanuel?" The voice was full of dismay.

"I mean," he said, "she died before any harm could come to her. Her heart was not strong; you would not know that. One night she went off, like this"—he snapped his fingers—"in her sleep."

The boy bowed his head, and stayed so for a long time. He lifted his head at length. A mist was on his eyes.

"Where is she?" he asked.

"She is buried in Altona, by Hamburg. That's why I came home that way. I saw her grave."

"I will never see," Bruno said, with an infinite sadness in his voice, "I will never see where she lies."

"It is perhaps better so," murmured Mr. Emmanuel.

"I will never go back to my country. I have no country."

"No, Bruno. It is a kind country here. It is kind people."

The boy did not seem to have heard.

"It is better so," he was saying. "Often I prayed for it, she should be dead." He raised his head suddenly and held it proudly. "She was a very fine woman, my mother. She was brave, and clever also. But, oh, how beautiful she was! In the evening, singing, when the lamp was shining on her hair. In Lübbenau, in the bungalow! You did not, of course, go to Lübbenau? Why should you!"

"No, I did not go to Lübbenau!"

"Mr. Emmanuel, please. How did you find out all this? Is it wrong that I should ask?"

"No, Bruno, no! It is your duty! I am going to swear you to a secret, Bruno. I can do that, yes? I know I can. There is living in Berlin at this moment a woman I knew in Doomington before the War. She is a daughter of my old friend Mr. Silver, who lives in Oleander Street, just at the back of my house. I think I have talked of him, yes?"

The boy nodded.

"Yes, I think I have. I cannot tell you more about her than this: she is in with a big man in Berlin, she is his friend. He is one of the biggest of them all. A girl from Doomington, eh? A Jewish girl? Well, it is like that. That woman helped me."

The boy did not seem surprised or puzzled. It was like that? That was enough for him. He fell into silence. His face looked peaked and wan. The silence continued. Mr. Emmanuel found it disturbing. He did not like the sombreness that had fallen upon the boy's eyes.

"Well, Bruno, what is it?" he demanded, with forced briskness. "You've lost a shilling, maybe, and found a threepenny bit?"

"Tell me, Mr. Emmanuel! Was it as bad as they say it is?"

"Was what as bad? In the prison, you mean? Well, in some ways it was not nice. It was bad for letters. I wrote and I wrote and I wrote—but did you get any letters? You did not, did you? Did Mrs. Cooper get any letters? She did not. So how could I get any letters from anybody? I could not. No!" he summed up sternly. "It was very wrong of them. I was angry."

The boy waited till he had finished. The expression in his eyes had not lightened at all.

"Did they beat you with sticks and lead pipes?" he asked.

"What should you ask such questions for?"

"Did they beat you with sticks and lead pipes?" he insisted.

"Well, once or twice, maybe, they forgot themselves a bit."

"Yes." The boy lowered his eyes. "It is a strange thing, Mr. Emmanuel, I wish to tell you."

"What, then?"

"I can forgive them, in a way, for killing my father. I can even forgive them for killing my mother. My father and mother were their enemies. They were working against them. But you? An old man like you? An old man who had done nothing? I cannot forgive them for that! I will never forgive them for that!"

"Oi, oi, Bruno! You *must* forget it! I have forgotten it a long time already!"

The boy rose. He looked darkly without flinching into Mr. Emmanuel's eyes.

"No!" he said slowly. "I will not forget! Never! Never! Never!"

Mr. Emmanuel rose.

"Please!" he begged. There was a good deal of pain in his voice. "You must not talk like that! It hurts me!"

"I am sorry!" the boy said. His voice was very cold. "I will not forget! I will not forgive! Some day I will have my revenge!"

"What?" The cry was like the yelp of a kicked animal. "What nonsense are you saying? You must not talk like that! I will not have it! Do you hear?"

But the boy did not seem to hear. He was, as it were, a long way away, in a bleak country where the erect grass has cutting edges like swords and the ice-logged fields are black as metal plates.

"Some day I will have revenge!" cried Bruno Rosenheim. As he spoke the lips drew back from the teeth. The eyes were like opaque glass. "I will buy a gun! I will hide in a dark door and wait till one of them comes!" The voice was toneless. He seemed like one speaking in a trance. "It will not matter who he is! I will shoot him dead, like a dog!"

"Bruno!" cried Mr. Emmanuel at the top of his voice. "Bruno! Bruno!" He summoned his last ounce of strength and slapped the boy's face; not as one strikes a person in anger or for punishment, but as one strikes a person who threatens to go off into a coma or a madness from which he will not emerge again. The colour flamed in Bruno's cheek, around the mark of the five fingers of

Mr. Emmanuel's hand. He blinked and shook his head violently several times. The mark of the five fingers slowly disappeared. Blood gradually suffused the face that had been so pale. Vision came back into the eyes that had seemed dead glass. His eyes saw. They saw the old man sitting back in the deep chair, sobbing, sobbing into his hands, the tears pouring steadily between them. They saw the whole frail body racked and twisted with utter grief.

Bruno threw himself down at the old man's knees, and pulled desperately at his wrists.

"Mr. Emmanuel! Mr. Emmanuel! What have I said? Tell me, what I have said? I was wicked! I know I was very wicked! If you do not forgive me, I will die! Please, please, Mr. Emmanuel——"

The sobs slowly subsided. The old man removed his hands from his face. He felt for his handkerchief and wiped his eyes; then, with a hollow casualness, he wiped the hanging pince-nez.

"What . . . are you . . . talking about . . . wicked?" he protested, with a sharp intaking of breath. "It was not you talking! It was someone else. A Bad Voice. These Bad Voices come sometimes to all of us; to me, to Mr. Forsyte, to everybody. Come, Bruno, get up! Sit on the stool again! There now, there's a good boy! I will tell you what the Bad Voice said, so that if ever he tries to talk to you again, you will not listen. You will shut your ears up." He halted a few moments, while his breathing steadied, then he went on. "He said, this Voice: 'Bruno, you must have revenge. Some day you will buy a gun. Then you will choose somewhere one of those people—you know who I mean, we will not say their name. You will hide in a dark doorway and shoot him. And that will be a revenge.' But Bruno, my boy, if anyone should do such a thing, it would not be that one that would suffer. It would not be *you,* Bruno. Like it was a few months ago in Switzerland. A young man from Yugoslavia shoots a leader in Davos. Well? They take poor Mr. Emmanuel, and they put him in prison, and, oi, oi, is it a cakewalk? It is not! And next time, Bruno, it would be much worse. It would not be that naughty one who would pay for it. Oh, no! What could they do to him? They could torture him and they could kill him! But that is happening every day, Bruno; it is nothing. It would be another Mr. Emmanuel. Perhaps a lot of Mr. Emmanuels, hundreds and hundreds of them maybe. Am I not right?

"Oh, no, Bruno, my little one. You see, you are in your religion a Christian, and it is not Christian, a thing like that. You have in you Jewish blood, and a thing like that is not Jewish, either. You must be true to them both, Bruno.

"So if ever such an idea like you said comes into your head again, you will ask God to forgive you, and your old Mr. Emmanuel, also, wherever I shall be, living or dead. And living or dead, I shall forgive you, and so will God, Bruno. And God bless you now, Bruno, and always. And"—he halted practically no time—"you promise, Bruno, don't you?" he said, exactly in the same tone as he had just been using, with practically no quality of interrogation in it, for the question was purely rhetorical. For he knew—that was the inference—that the promise had already been given deep down in Bruno's heart, before the question was so perfunctorily put to him with the tongue.

"I promise," Bruno whispered. But Mr. Emmanuel was off again before the brief words were out, launched into a subject as remote from the previous one as Heaven from Hell, still talking at the same speed and using the same tone of voice.

"For you see I have a present for you, I did not buy it in Germany, and perhaps it is better I should not buy anything in Germany, you should never remember that country again, you have finished with it, and so also have I. I bought it today in Southampton. It is an English present, like the lovely cigarette holder you bought me; for England is your country now, and it is a kinder country. I hope you will like it. I think you will like it. But will you? I am frightened. You are such a great big boy now."

There was no faltering for the fraction of a second in the subtlety and accuracy of the boy's response. The other thing was over. It had never been. The Voice would never speak. It had never spoken. He was a schoolboy visited at his school by his kind relative or guardian, or whatever Mr. Emmanuel was, and the visitor had brought him a present, and he was very properly grateful and excited.

"Oh, Mr. Emmanuel!" he cried. "A present! For me? Oh, how wonderful! What is it? Tell me at once!"

"Will you try and guess?"

"A fountain-pen?"

"No!" Mr. Emmanuel's voice was full of scorn.

"A camera?"

"You *have* a camera!"

"A set of tools? A pair of skates?" He was terribly afraid he might guess what it actually was. "A printing-press?"

"No! No! You will never guess, Bruno!"

"*Please* tell me!"

"Bruno!" He let the pince-nez slip from his nose, and

looked intensely into the boy's eyes. "It is a little white rabbit, Bruno. Its name is Jo. It shall take the place of another white rabbit you had once." Neither of them said one word more regarding Jo the First, old Jo of Lübbenau, Jo of the things that had been, the curly-haired painter-father, the gold-haired dream-mother with a tiny sweet voice that tinkled like a music-box. All that was over. There were new things to come now.

"You never saw such a rabbit!" proclaimed Mr. Emmanuel. "The man at the shop said some day he will grow up to be a very dangerous rabbit. He will chase away cats and dogs." He kept his eyes fixed on the boy's eyes. The boy did not flinch. "He will be terrible. You will have to look after him very carefully. He will chew up doors and fences!"

"But, Mr. Emmanuel!" the boy said suddenly.

"Yes?"

"We're not allowed to keep pets at Greystones! It's against school rules! Oh, dear! Oh, dear!" He looked quite desolate.

"That's all right!" stated Mr. Emmanuel airily. "I've arranged all that with Mr. Forsyte!"

"Have you?" He seized the old man's hand. "Oh, how *spiffing* you are!" Mr. Emmanuel grinned. It was a heartening word on the lips of Bruno. "Where is he?" the boy went on breathlessly. "Have you brought him with you? Can we go and see him at once?"

"He's outside!" Mr. Emmanuel stated. "He's in the car! Oh, God in Heaven!" he cried out guiltily. "What time is it? How long have I been here? Mrs. Cooper's outside there, as well as the white rabbit!"

"I suppose you're taking me out to lunch?" said Bruno placidly.

"Yes, of course we are! Come along now, quick! Did you ever hear from such a thing?"

"What are we going to have, Mr. Emmanuel?" The boy opened the door. The boy and man sped along the corridor.

"I don't know!" said Mr. Emmanuel. "What would you like to have, eh? A big nice steak?"

"I don't mind at all," said Bruno. "So long as I can have four meringues afterwards. And four éclairs, too, I think. Will that be all right?"

"We will ask Mrs. Cooper," said Mr. Emmanuel. "But perhaps it will be all right."

"Oh, one moment!" exclaimed Bruno, holding back at the head of the staircase. "What about poor old Jo's lunch?"

"You give me a headache with your Jo. We'll pick up some six-inch nails for him somewhere. Are you coming, Bruno?"

"I'm coming, Mr. Emmanuel! Oh, isn't it *swell!* And it's algebra next period, too!"

LONDON—PARIS—BOVINGDON
1938–1939